The Summer of
My Discontent

The Gay Youth Chronicles

The Summer of My Discontent

A Better Place II

Mark A. Roeder

iUniverse, Inc.
New York   Lincoln   Shanghai

The Summer of My Discontent
A Better Place II

iUniverse, Inc.

For information address:
iUniverse
2021 Pine Lake Road, Suite 100
Lincoln, NE 68512
www.iuniverse.com

ISBN: 0-595-29806-0 (Pbk)
ISBN: 0-595-66057-6 (Cloth)

Printed in the United States of America

This book is dedicated to Eric Egler,
who has added more to my life than I can express.

Acknowledgements

I'd like to thank Doug Kendrick for not only doing most of the proofing of this book, but also for coming up with a great title. I'd also like to thank Ken Clark for his insightful ideas and helpful criticisms, and Jim Hertwig and John Radez for their proofing of the manuscript. Finally, I'd like to thank the members of the Mark Roeder Yahoo Fan Club for all their input.

Chronology

This novel takes place immediately after *A Better Place*.

A Better Place II

Monday August 10, 1981
Dane

I squinted in the bright light, trying to make out the lettering of the road sign in the distance. Stinging sweat ran into my eyes, making them water. I pushed my bangs off my forehead and my hand came away dripping, as if I'd just plunged it into a pot of hot water. I wiped my fingers on my already sweat soaked t-shirt.

"Damn it!" I said out loud, then stripped off my shirt and wrung it. Droplets of perspiration fell onto the sticky, liquid asphalt. I could almost hear them steam.

My head swam from the pounding sunlight. I covered it with my shirt, now stinking of sweat and underarm odor. I needed to get out of the blistering sun before I started hallucinating or somethin'. I screwed my eyes half shut, looking toward the sign. It was closer now and I could make out some of the letters—V-E-R...damn it. I kept my feet going, one in front of the other, hot tar sticking to my heels, threatening to suck my shoes off. Closer. Closer. V-E-R...O-N-A. Verona. Civilization at last!

Several paces later I came to the sign itself. Just beyond it was nothing—absolutely nothing. Perhaps I was a bit hasty in proclaiming this civilization. There were only trees and bushes and plowed fields of pathetic corn withering in the sun. I forced my feet forward. They felt as if they'd spontaneously combust in my shoes. The heat of the sun reflecting off the asphalt seared my bare legs. Heat, heat, and more heat assailed me from both above and below. My throat was parched. I needed water—ice cold water and air conditioning. Yeah.

A few houses gradually came into view and then the spaces between each one and its neighbor lessened until the country became a town. Giant oaks sheltered me, but I still felt as if I were standing on the surface of the sun. Soon, my tired feet were treading on a sidewalk, passing block after block of decades-old homes surrounded by huge trees and delicious shade. Just when I thought my aching legs couldn't hold me up any longer, the business district came into view. Up ahead I could see a large park off to the left and a few businesses across the street. I saw what must have been an old movie theatre, judging from the marquee. Closer still were a couple of restaurants—one that looked a bit fancy, called *The Park's Edge* and one that was obviously some kind of burger joint, *Ofarim's*. I squeezed into my shirt and quickened my pace.

I pulled open the glass door of *Ofarim's* and was inundated by cool air and the scent of French fries and sizzling burgers. I walked up to the counter and ordered a double-cheeseburger, fries, and the biggest drink they had. While I waited on my food I took my cup over to the soda dispenser, filled it with ice and then water. I'd have some Coke with my burger, but for the moment I needed water. I could almost feel my body soaking it in, as if I were a dried out sponge. I gulped down two full extra-large cups before my lunch was ready.

I sat down at a booth that would've been at home in a 1950's diner. In fact, the whole place kind of had that look, with red checked tablecloths and matching curtains. There was a jukebox along one wall and a lot of old rock & roll and Marilyn Monroe photos and posters. But I was far more interested in my food and the cool air. I felt as if I'd narrowly escaped a nasty death in a desert and was now resting comfortably in an oasis.

When my burger arrived at last, I realized I was starving. I didn't rush my meal, however, as I was in no hurry to go back out into the blistering heat. Now that I'd arrived in a real town I had no place to go. This was my destination. Now I had only to find a place to sleep and then…and then I'd see what happened next.

I smiled. I was glad to get away from home. It was without doubt the most boring place in the entire world—no, make that the entire universe. I only wished I'd left sooner. I was a moron for not leaving at the beginning of the summer, instead of the very end. Each monotonous day had been filled with nothing except longing and unfulfilled need. It was a wonder I hadn't been driven mad. No matter, I was outta there at last.

After the last French fry had disappeared, I refilled my cup with Coke and ordered a large ice cream cone. I resisted the temptation to take it across the street to the park because I knew it was still sweltering outside. I was all comfortable and cool in *Ofarim's* and it gave me the illusion that deadly heat wasn't ready to pounce on me as soon as I stepped out the door. I sat back down in the booth, feeling the fizz in my mouth as I alternated between bites of ice cream and sips of Coke.

After I'd munched up the last of the cone, I just sat back and listened to the jukebox playing some old song I didn't recognize. I didn't stir until I got too bored to sit there any longer. I refilled my cup, making sure I loaded up on ice, and walked outside.

The heat was waiting on me like a fierce, sinewy dragon that blasted me with its flames as soon as I left the safety of *Ofarim's*, leaving my flesh scorched and stinging. I stepped quickly across the street to reach the shade under the trees. I gazed around at the park, sipping now and then on my Coke, sticking my nose nearly into the cup to feel the coolness of the ice. It was a large park, with plenty of benches upon which to sit and think, or watch passersby. The grass was even somewhat green under the trees, but it was dry and brown wherever the sun touched it. The flowers in the flowerbeds were puny and wilted. The drought that had lasted all summer was taking its toll.

"Mind if I have a sip?"

I jumped. I was lost enough in thought that I didn't know anyone was near. My attention was held by the sickly flowers and a group of shirtless boys on the distant basketball courts playing hoops. I jerked my head around and my eyes fell on an older boy of about nineteen. He was taking a drag on a cigarette and peering at me intently as if studying me. I felt almost naked under his gaze.

"Uh—yeah, sure," I said.

I looked him over as he drank much more than a sip. The first thing I noticed was his chest, which was bare, revealing hard muscle and smooth skin that made me breathe a little faster. He had a strong stomach, with abs that I could easily see. His shirt hung at his side and he was wearing worn jeans with a big hole ripped about mid-thigh on the right. His shoes were old Nikes, scuffed and worn.

"Ahh, that's what I needed," he said, handing me back my much lighter cup.

"You're welcome," I said.

He touched his upper lip with his tongue and gazed at me without smiling. "Well, I have places to be," he said and left without so much as waiting for a response. I watched his broad, sweaty back as he departed; realizing that I'd sprung a boner talking to him. I rearranged it and hoped he hadn't noticed. I doubted it. He seemed much more interested in my Coke than in me.

I hadn't asked his name. There hadn't been time. I wished I'd asked. His body and features were burned into my mind. He had a nice bod—that was for sure—all those muscles. Yum. He was all nice and bulging and tight, without being all gross like some guys who got too built. His face haunted me. He wasn't cute or even particularly good looking, but there was something about him…Those probing brown eyes—they made me feel like he knew things about me that even I didn't know. They were kind of scary, too—searching, as if looking for some sign of weakness to exploit. He had a hungry look to him, not like he was hungry for food, or even sex, but hungry for something life wasn't giving him. There was a violence in him, just under the surface. I'd only been near him for a few moments, but I was quite certain he was not someone to mess with. For some reason, that made him even more attractive.

I couldn't pry him out of my mind. Maybe it was because I was bored senseless with absolutely nothing to do, but most likely it was because he fed the hunger in me—the hunger I got when I looked at boys. Usually I went for the pretty-boy type or the jocks. This scruffy, frightening guy drew me to him, however. Maybe it was the danger I sensed, or maybe I was just plain horny and he walked along at the right time. I could just about get turned on by a tree if I was in the right mood.

The sun fell toward the western horizon and the shadows lengthened in the park. I considered exploring the town, but that could wait. Instead, I sat and watched boys playing basketball. I thought about joining in, but I wasn't here to make friends. I had something quite different on my mind.

Later, I walked along the well-tended paths and found myself a secluded bench surrounded almost entirely by shrubs. The park turned a bit eerie as the darkness deepened, but I wasn't afraid. I enjoyed the novelty of it. Anything was better than my exceedingly boring room back home.

As night fell, I lay down. Weariness from a long day's march in the sun put me out, even though the hour was early. I dreamed that night of deserts and shirtless boys in the sun.

Ethan

Uncle Jack was worried—I could tell. He didn't say anything to me or anyone else, but he was quieter than usual. I caught him more than once looking out over the dying fields—just staring. That wasn't like Jack. He was *always* working.

I wiped the sweat from my forehead with my shirt, then stuffed it back into my belt-loop and took up the hoe once more. Chopping weeds out of the soybeans seemed like a waste of time. I'd never seen such pathetic crops. The beans were puny, almost nonexistent, when they should've been lush and beautiful. The corn stalks were stunted in their growth and the ears were only miniature versions of what they should've been. The wheat was suffering, too. There'd been virtually no rain for far too long, and I feared the Selby Farm was looking at its worst harvest ever.

I needed a break and a few minutes out of the searing sun. I loved working shirtless in the sun, but even I had my limits. I turned my mind from the withering crops and headed for the barn. There was work to do there, too. There was always another task waiting on the farm.

Sure enough, the horses were nearly out of water. I uncoiled the hose and turned on the hydrant. Cool water spilled out of the hose, filling the horse trough. I turned it on myself for a few moments, shivering slightly in the sudden coolness as I doused my torso, and then returned to the task at hand.

Despite the drought, there was plenty to be happy about. I was surrounded by family and friends. Dave was busy feeding the chickens nearby and Nathan, Brendan, and Casper were elsewhere on the farm, performing their own chores. Uncle Jack was on the tractor, of course. Ardelene, Casper's grandma, was tending the garden that had quickly become her own, no doubt watering it furiously to keep the flowers and vegetables alive. I felt a sense of serenity, knowing that all was well and everyone was where they were meant to be.

It was hard to believe how much things had changed in just a few short months. A little more than a year ago, it was just Uncle Jack and me working the farm. Then, he'd hired Nathan and we slowly became friends and then, all of a sudden, boyfriends. Nathan and his little brother came to live with Jack and me not long after that and our family had doubled in size overnight. In the late spring, Brendan and Casper showed up answering an ad we'd placed in the *Verona Citizen* for farm-hands. Uncle Jack hired them and we soon became friends, and then family. The latest addition was Ardelene, who ended up marrying Jack, much to the surprise of all. So here we were, a family of seven where we'd once been two.

After I watered the horses, I headed out of the barn to take a look at the combine. I figured the hoeing could wait. It was early August and it wouldn't be all that long before the harvest would begin—if there was a harvest. Most of it was a few weeks off yet, but I knew how time could slip away. Jack said the combine was starting with difficulty. It was probably just the battery or plugs, but even if it was something simple, it needed to be taken care of. If the problem were more serious, then it was even more important that I get it fixed before it was time to harvest the vast fields of corn, soybeans, and wheat. We couldn't afford to lose a minute when harvest time was upon us.

The problem with the combine turned out to be simple: the plugs were fouled. It took only a few minutes to clean them with gasoline. I gave the rest of the combine the once over, just in case. I reminded myself that I needed to check out the baler soon, too. It'd been acting up a bit and it wouldn't be long at all before we were baling straw and hay once more.

As I worked, I thought about the upcoming wrestling season. It would be the first time since I'd come out that I'd be wresting on the team. All the guys had known about me for months, but what would it be like in the locker room and showers now that my secret was out? Attending classes with those guys was one thing, but being naked with them was another.

Zac would probably be back on the team. That was too bad. I couldn't look at him without wanting to pound him for all the shit he'd pulled. It was bad enough that he'd left anonymous, threatening notes in my locker for weeks, but trying to blackmail me into throwing the championship match was too much. Of course, things hadn't ended there with Zac, but the less said about that the better. If I thought too much about what he'd done, and what he'd tried to do, I'd have to hunt him down and kick his ass. If it hadn't been for Brandon and Jon…Well, enough of that.

I'd long feared being outed, but my fears hadn't been realized. When I came out to the team, all of them, except for Zac, were supportive. I thought they'd all turn on me, but they didn't. A few guys outside the team gave me some crap, but they knocked it off when I threatened to kick their asses. Being a wrestler had its advantages. I had friends and teammates who would back me up, too. One cool thing about coming out was that I found out who my real friends were.

I still got strange looks sometimes, especially when Nathan and I were together. Public displays of affection aren't allowed at our school, whether gay or straight, but I still gave Nathan a peck on the cheek now and then and sometimes kissed him full on the lips. That usually got a few looks, but no one said anything.

While some of the guys treated me differently, almost all of the girls did. That wasn't a bad thing, though. Girls used to hang around because they were interested in me, but now I had a lot more girls as friends. I think they liked the idea of a friendship with a guy without any sexual overtones. They knew I wasn't interested in their bodies or anything like that. I bet a lot of the straight boys wished they had girls around them like I did, but that wouldn't happen because the girls knew what the straight boys wanted.

I wasn't romantically interested in the girls, but I found that I'd enjoyed my new friendships with them. I still preferred the company of guys, but I enjoyed the best of both worlds. What was really funny is that guys would ask me to set them up with girls. I'd become a sort of go-between. My life was definitely interesting.

My thoughts floated back to Zac. I'd had serious second thoughts about the decision I made the night he jumped Nathan and me. After Brandon, Jon, and I kicked Zac, Devon, and their crew's asses, I let 'em go. I should've called the cops on them and had them locked up. At the time, I just didn't want to deal with it anymore. I'd had weeks of Zac's notes and too many things had happened. I wondered if maybe I'd sent the wrong message to those guys. Even though we threatened to beat them senseless if there was any more trouble, I think we let them off way too easy.

Brandon sure thought we should've done more. Brandon didn't like Zac, because of what he'd pulled, and he *hated* Devon with a vengeance. Brandon had just about killed him for all the crap he'd pulled and the way he had acted after Mark and Taylor's deaths, and he had threatened to kill him if he ever did anything like it again. Devon had kept his distance since then.

The baler checked out okay. There was still plenty of sunlight left, so I walked to the farmhouse, filled up a water-bottle, and then headed back to the fields. Sweat ran off my body in streams. I felt as if I had to drink constantly to keep dehydration at bay. I had cooling thoughts about skinny-dipping in the lake after work. I could almost feel the refreshing water engulf my body. Maybe Nathan would be able to join me.

Casper

I was exhausted as Brendan led me to our bedroom. I barely had the energy to pull off my clothes. Something about working in the intense heat just sucked the energy right out of me. I was too tired to even make love, and that's saying something!

Brendan lay on his back on top of the sheets. It was too hot for any covers. He slept naked and he was one beautiful sight. I still couldn't believe he loved me. I felt like I was in a Cinderella story. I'd definitely ended up with the prince, or, in my case, with the hunky football player with a heart of gold.

I hugged Brendan. He pulled me to him and cradled my head on his bare chest. He wrapped his arms around me, holding me tight and petting my hair. He made me feel safe. I could feel the powerful muscles of his chest against my cheek. Brendan was my boyfriend and my protector. When he held me, I felt secure—and loved.

"I wish I wasn't so tired," I said, sleepily.

"And why's that?" asked Brendan, as if he didn't know.

I giggled. "I'm sure you can figure it out."

"There's always tomorrow."

"Promise."

"First thing."

***

The next morning I awakened beside Brendan. He was awake and just laying there with his arm around me. I crawled up on him and kissed him.

Touching his hard body made my heart race. I wondered if he could feel my stiffness against his leg.

"Go take a quick shower," he said, "and then get back here."

I had my answer. I looked down at Brendan's waist as I slipped off the bed. His manhood was standing straight up. I grasped it for a moment and Brendan moaned.

"No fair—now hurry, I've already showered." I noticed then that his hair was damp.

My weariness of the night before was gone. I rushed through a quick shower, feeling like I might explode at any second. I didn't even bother to dress after I'd dried off. I just hurried down the hall nude and joined Brendan in our bed. He lay there naked. He was beautiful. I jumped on top of him and covered his face with kisses, then lay full length on top of him, feeling his hardness against my own. We started rubbing against each other and it was almost more pleasure than I could bear.

Sometimes, we made slow, unhurried love, but not that morning. We frantically went after each other, our hands and lips seemed to be everywhere at once. We writhed on the bed and I lost myself in Brendan's embrace. In less than ten minutes, we were both done.

I lay back in Brendan's arms panting, feeling his chest quickly rise and fall. He held me close. I smiled. I knew I was lucky to have such a kind, strong boyfriend who I loved so deeply. The fact that he was gorgeous and awesome in bed didn't hurt matters either.

We pulled on boxers and shorts and went downstairs. Jack, Ethan, and Nathan were gone, but Dave sat at the table munching on hot buttered toast and Grandma was bustling about the kitchen.

"Where are the guys?" asked Brendan.

"Working," answered Dave, with a mouthful of toast, "and Jack's gone into town for somethin.'" It figured that Ethan and Nathan were already working. Brendan and I were running a little late because of our love-making, quick as it had been.

"Want me to fix you boys some breakfast?" asked Grandma.

"No thanks," I said. "We'll do our own. I'm sure you have more than enough to do."

"That's for certain," said Grandma, as she filled the sink with water and prepared to do the dishes. I sure liked having Grandmother around. I didn't feel like I'd had any real family since my mom died.

I cut us thick slices of homemade bread, buttered them, and then stuck them in the toaster-oven while Brendan made some hot tea.

"So what are you up to today, Davy?" asked Brendan.

"Dunno. I'm gonna feed the chickens, then…whatever."

"Maybe we can all go fishing this evening after we're done with work," said Brendan. "I'm gonna catch one bigger than you this time!"

"Yeah, right!" said Dave. "Last time all you caught was that little bluegill—looked like a guppy." He giggled.

"Yeah, well, we'll see who gets the biggest this time."

Dave smiled. Brendan was good with him. I guess Dave was kinda like the little brother he never had. We all tried to take care of Dave. Jack was like a father to him, and Dave had taken up with my grandma like she was his own—almost as if she were his mother. I didn't mind. I knew Grandma loved me—I could share.

I smeared blackberry jam on my toast while I talked with Brendan and Dave. It was nice to have a family. Living with the Selbys wasn't anything like it'd been living back home in Kentucky. After my mom died, it was like I didn't have a dad anymore. He just kind of ignored me. And then there was Jason, my older brother. I wish he had ignored me. I thought of him for a moment, sitting in the *Cloverdale Center*—a "hospital" where they tried to turn gays straight. It was kind of ironic that my brother had ended up there. He was probably the biggest homophobe alive. But, after the horrible things he'd done to me…I didn't want to even think about it. All I knew was that I felt a lot safer with him locked up.

After we'd eaten, Brendan headed off to join Ethan, and Dave went to care for his chickens. I grabbed a hoe from the tool shed and walked to the garden. The neat rows of flowers and vegetables were almost free of weeds—partly because it was so dry even the weeds had trouble growing, but mostly because Grandma liked to keep the garden…she had a word for it that I couldn't quite remember. Imac…I'd looked it up in the dictionary. It was…immaculate. Yeah, that was it. I liked to help Grandma with the garden whenever I could. It was so peaceful. Whenever I had troubles, I spent some time in the garden, tending the peppers and sweet peas, and after a while my problems started to melt away.

I found a few small weeds that had dared to pop up from the tilled earth, but not many. I hoed them under, then went for the watering can. Watering the garden had become a full time job. The green beans, peas, tomatoes, peppers, and other vegetables were coming along nicely, but only because Grandma and I watered them daily. The flowers were beautiful, too— Zinnias, Marigolds, and a whole bunch of other kinds that I couldn't name. It was Grandma who'd added most of the flowers when she'd come to live on the farm. She said a garden should not only be productive; it should be beautiful, too.

I filled the old galvanized watering can at the hydrant by the tool shed and carried it to the closest row of peas. Even though it was morning, the weather was fine and hot with not a cloud in the sky. It must've been 80 already and the temperature would likely climb close to 100. The thirsty peas soaked up the water greedily. If only there was a way to let the good plants have the water and keep it from the weeds. I couldn't figure that one out, however.

I stopped and dug my hands into the earth. The dirt was dry on top and fell through my fingers like coarse sand. Farther down, it was darker, cooler, and retained a bit of moisture. I loved the aroma of the earth and plants that sur-rounded me. The scent of a tomato plant in the hot sun meant summer to me. Tomato plants might not smell as good as flowers, but when that scent came to me it brought with it images of sunshine and living, growing, green life. Grandma said it was a sign that I was a true gardener. I didn't doubt it one bit.

On my third trip to the peas, I thought of something—Grandma always did the watering in the late evening. I remember she said she did it then so the water wouldn't just evaporate in the sun. I smacked my head with my open palm. What was I thinking? Duh! I'd been so content working with the plants that what I was doing didn't cross my mind. After I emptied the watering can, I put it back up, having decided that I'd better follow Grandma's advice. She knew best.

Brendan

I'd little more than found Ethan and Nathan when Dave came running up to us. "Jack says to come to the house. We're having a family meeting."

Ethan and I looked at each other. I didn't know if I liked the sound of this—a family meeting in the morning? That kind of thing was usually after the day had ended. Ethan and Nathan dropped the axes they'd been using to clear some of the new land and we followed Dave back to the farmhouse.

When we arrived, Jack, Ardelene, and Casper were all sitting at the kitchen table. For some reason, I felt a knot of fear in my chest as I took my seat beside my boyfriend.

"We have a money problem," said Jack. "There are some debts and not enough money in the bank to pay them."

We all looked at each other.

"What happened?" asked Ethan. "I thought we were doing well."

"We were, but it's this drought…the loan officer doesn't want to extend our loan. He doesn't seem to think we can pull out any kind of harvest and I can't say I disagree with him. We're looking at a year's worth of expenses and no crops to show for it."

"Is it that bad?" asked Nathan.

"Even if we got a good rain right now, we'd be lucky to get 20% of the yield we did last year, even figuring in all the new acreage we put in production. I knew I shouldn't have tried to expand, but the price was just too good and it isn't often that land comes up for sale right next to the farm."

Jack looked angry. He was angry at himself.

"So we could lose all the new acreage?" asked Ethan.

"Worse than that. We could lose everything. The loan for the new land was secured by a mortgage on the farm."

Ethan looked ill. "But surely we can keep up the payments?"

"With what?" asked Jack, a little more angrily than he probably meant. "Our only income comes from the farm and it looks like there'll be no harvest this year. I've just used practically everything that's in the bank to keep our heads above water, but that'll only keep the bank off our backs for a few days."

"Could we sell some cattle?" asked Nathan.

"I've already sold as many as I dare. If I sell anymore, we'll be out of the cattle business. It may come to that. We may have to sell the cattle, the goats, the sheep, and the horses." Ethan looked like he was about ready to cry.

I'd noticed that quite a lot of cattle were being sold off, but I hadn't thought there was anything unusual in it.

"You won't sell the chickens, will you?" asked Dave, almost in a panic. I knew he was thinking of his little hen, Henrietta.

"No, Dave, we won't sell the chickens." Jack very nearly smiled at Dave, despite the gravity of the situation.

"You have some money, don't you, Grandma?" asked Casper.

"Not enough, Clint. Social Security is about all I've got." I knew things were serious. Casper was rarely called by his real name.

I wished I could get to my money, but my father had managed to tie most of it up in a trust fund that I couldn't touch until I was twenty-one. I wasn't sure how he'd managed it, since it was my money, but he was a powerful man. My guess was that he'd done it someway before I turned eighteen. I was willing to bet he'd tried to steal it from me, but couldn't manage it, so he'd tied it up for as long as he could. I did have some money, though. There was one savings account he either hadn't found out about, or hadn't been able to touch. I hadn't dared touch it before I turned eighteen either. My father would've known exactly where I was if I did and I'd have been sent back to the *Cloverdale Center*.

"How much do we need to keep the bank from foreclosing for now?" I asked.

"Ten thousand dollars," said Jack.

"Ten thousand!" said Ethan.

"I've got it—or nearly," I said. "My parents have cut me off from most of my money, but I had a lot put away. I have just about what we'll need—maybe not quite enough, but I know I had more than $9,000 in my savings and with the interest, it'll be close to $10,000."

"I can't let you do that," said Jack. "It's your money. I appreciate the offer, but…"

"Jack, Casper and I are living here. We're not paying rent. We're not paying for food. I've got the money and we need it right now. They way I see it, it's as simple as that."

"You don't pay rent and don't pay for food because you work here. What's more, you're family. I can't take your money. It's not right."

If the situation hadn't been so frightening I would've smiled. Jack called Casper and me family. I knew Jack was legally adopting Casper, but he'd never referred to us as family before.

"Okay, we're family—all the more reason for you to take the money."

"No," said Jack, "with that money, you could go somewhere else and make a new start. You'll need it for college. You'll…"

"I don't want to go somewhere else!" I said, far too loudly. "I want to stay right here! This is my home and if I can help to save it with a few dollars then I'm damn well gonna do it!"

I swallowed hard. I'd gotten outta control. No one talked to Jack like that. I looked at him fearfully. "Listen," I said more calmly, "you're the boss, but I'll be damned if I let some bank take the farm away when I can save it. You're taking the money and that's that."

Ethan smiled and looked at Jack, who remained silent. Jack rubbed his chin.

"We'll call it a loan," he said, finally. "I'll have my lawyer draw up legal papers. That way if we do go under, you'll be one of the farm's creditors and have a chance of getting it back."

I nodded. I knew there was little use in arguing with Jack. I'll already pressed my luck about as far as it could go.

"That still leaves us with day to day expenses," said Jack. "I've racked my brains, but I don't know how we'll keep this place going. Any ideas on how we handle that?"

Everyone sat and thought for several moments. There was no easy answer. "I'll get a job," said Ethan.

"I will, too," I added.

"There's a problem with that," said Jack. "We still have a farm to run."

"How about me?" said Casper. Everyone looked at him. "I'm not that much help on the farm. I'm not strong enough to handle a lot of it. I could get a job and bring in some money and still have time to tend the garden and help out some."

"Casper," said Ethan, "you're a lot of help. Don't sell yourself short."

"Well, maybe I do help, but I'm just sayin' I can't do a lot of the stuff that you guys do. You've gotta admit I'm small, and I'm kinda puny. I'm not puttin' myself down. I've even been getting stronger from farm work, but I'm the one we can do without most easily, so it just makes sense that I go out and bring in some money. I want to contribute and this way I can."

"I could get a job, too," said Nathan. "What you said goes for me, Casper. I'm not putting myself down either, but Ethan and Brendan are by far the strongest and most capable for the farm work. And Jack, well, this place can't run without you. Casper and I can bring in the bacon and the rest of you can grow the corn."

We talked it out for a very, very long time, but everyone agreed in the end. Casper and Nathan would each find a job and bring in cash to pay the bills and expenses, while the rest of us kept the farm running. I was so proud of Casper.

"Can we take the truck into town and start looking?" asked Casper.

"I can drive," said Nathan.

"Okay," said Jack. "And the rest of us can get to work."

Before we each went our separate ways, Jack pulled me to the side and shook my hand. "I can't tell you how much I appreciate this, son."

"It's no more than I owe you for taking us in," I said. I left before he had a chance to argue.

Dane

I awoke sometime before daybreak. I sat up with a stiff neck. The back of my head felt like it'd flattened out from pressing into the hard bench, but I knew it was only an illusion. I twisted my neck from side to side and was rewarded by a series of delicious pops. Ahhhh, that was better.

The bottoms of my feet ached as I stood. The first few steps were nearly painful, but then the pain lessened and went away. I'd walked much too far the day before. If only the ride I'd hitched had brought me all the way to Verona, my feet would've been in better condition. The lady I'd ridden with was kinda creepy, though. She smelled like cats and kept calling me Eric and asking me how baseball was going. I think she was a little crazy. She probably thought I was her son or something. Maybe she was having flashbacks. Anyway, I didn't mind too much when she let me off at the baseball field in the middle of nowhere, only it was a cornfield. I nearly pointed that out, but I thought it best not to. She might've gotten violent or something. I'd heard you weren't supposed to attack the delusions of crazy people. I was glad to get away from her.

The morning air was sweet and there was even a bit of dew on the grass, although where the moisture came from I didn't know. The birds were singing and chipmunks were scurrying among the roots of the trees. I stretched and yawned.

I walked back through the park the way I'd come the evening before. Across the street was *Ofarim's*, its windows dark. My stomach rumbled. Too bad they didn't serve breakfast. Maybe I could hold out until lunch if there wasn't someplace else to eat in town, although surely there was. I walked across the street to check out the hours and discovered I'd been wrong, *Ofarim's* did serve breakfast, but they opened at 7 a.m. I looked at my watch. It was just a bit past 6.

I ambled down the sidewalk, sightseeing and killing time until I could get something to eat. There was a space of grass and then a restaurant called *The Park's Edge*. It was the fancier place I'd noticed the day before. It didn't look too fancy, though, so I thought I might give it a try. Then again, maybe I wouldn't. My cash would only hold out so long.

Just beyond *The Park's Edge* was the old theatre I saw yesterday, called *The Paramount*. It had a big marquee with tons of light bulbs and even neon lights in it. I bet it'd look real pretty at night. I walked on, and for a few blocks there was nothing but houses. Then Main Street took a 90-degree turn to the left and continued on. I'd never seen a main street that turned like that. I thought they all just went straight.

After a couple blocks, I passed a gas station on the right and then a library and then a bank. There was a barber shop and some other small businesses across the street. I crossed into another block and walked past more businesses, including a restaurant across the street called, *The Iron Kettle* and one on my side called, *Café Moffatt*. There was also an antique store, a hardware store, and some other businesses.

Café Moffatt was open already, so I decided to have breakfast there instead of going back to *Ofarim's*. I pushed open the glass door and a little bell jingled. There were a few people having coffee or eating eggs or whatever, but no one took much notice of me. I took a seat in one of the booths that ran along the side of the café and looked at a menu. They had something called *Sinful French Toast*, made out of sweet rolls that I thought sounded good. When the waitress came, I ordered that, some bacon, and chocolate milk.

My eyes wandered as I waited on my food. *Café Moffatt* had a more run down look than *Ofarim's*—not that it didn't have its own charm; it just looked like it'd been there a long time with nothin' ever being changed. There were old Verona High School graduating class pictures from the 1940's and 50's on the walls and lots of other old high school stuff, too. There was a blue and white football jersey and a soccer uniform in the same colors. There were several trophies on a shelf and lots of pictures of old buildings on the walls that I guess were historic photos of Verona. It was kinda cool in there. I bet someone from fifty years before could've walked in and found things pretty much the same as when they left.

My Sinful French Toast arrived and damn, was it delicious! I put plenty of butter and syrup on it and just about licked the plate clean. The bacon and chocolate milk were good, too.

I spent the rest of the day wandering around aimlessly. I was mainly just spying things out. I decided I'd stay. Verona was as good a place as any and it was away from my folks. I was tired of all the crap they gave me, and living in the middle of nowhere had gotten boring. There was way more in Verona than where I'd come from—restaurants and a theatre and some cute boys, too. No one knew me here, so I was gonna be more open about things and get me a boy at last. I'd spent the whole school year drooling over Eric Michaels and never once worked up the courage to ask him out, even to just hang out like guys do. I wasn't gonna be like that here. I was gonna be a whole new Dane— interesting and outgoing and maybe even tragic. I was gonna live a life of freedom—at least for a while—and then I'd decide where to go from there.

I found myself back in the park and spent most of the rest of the day there—mainly because that's where the cute boys were hanging out. There were some not so cute ones too, but everyone couldn't be a hottie. I sure wasn't. I was good enough looking I guess, but I don't think anyone would think I was cute. I didn't have a hot bod either. I was slim and had abs that showed, but I didn't have any real muscle. I lacked the bulges in the arms, shoulders, and chest that most people—both guys and girls—found attractive. I was just glad I wasn't skinny.

I was more open about checking out boys than I'd ever been at home, but I didn't just stare or anything. No one knew me here, but I didn't want to get my ass kicked. A lot of guys had a real attitude about "fags" as they called them. I didn't think of myself as a fag—I just liked guys.

As I was sitting on a bench watching a three-on-three basketball game, I noticed the guy I'd met the evening before—the one with the nice chest who'd drank most of my Coke. He was leaning up against a lamppost looking toward the street. He had his shirt off and didn't seem to be interested in anything around him. He watched the cars go by and that was about it.

There was something cool about that guy. I think it was mainly his attitude—he was cocky and kinda dangerous. He was the "I don't give a fuck" type that probably got in a lot of fights. His face wasn't much to look at, but he did have some nice muscles. I felt a strange attraction to him. Maybe it was because I wanted to be more like him. Maybe it was because he tugged at something inside of me. I wanted him to pay attention to me, even if it was just to cuss me out or even hit me.

I tore my gaze away from him. The front of my shorts was bulged out and I felt a desperate need for relief. I was a little disturbed that my thoughts of that guy had done that to me. Why was I getting off on thinking about him being mean to me?

I watched the game some more and tried to forget about the guy leaning on the lamppost, but I couldn't keep from looking in his direction, over and over. Finally I just said, "Fuck it", got up, and walked toward him. I was still kind of hard, but it didn't show too much.

"Hey," I said, as I got close. "Want some more Coke?" I nervously laughed— he didn't.

"I'm Dane."

"Austin," he said, sparing me a glance.

"So, uh, you from around here?" I asked. Austin took a drag on his cigarette and blew the smoke out slowly. My eyes were on his chest. I liked the way his muscles were all taut beneath his tanned skin. His chest had those bulges in all the right places that turned me on.

He didn't answer for a while. I felt like I was a little kid, annoying an adult who didn't want to be bothered. It didn't make any sense because Austin wasn't much older, college age at most. I was sixteen.

"Yeah," he said, finally. "I'm from around here, but you're not."

"No, I ran away from home."

"Where's home?"

"Chicago," I lied.

"Yeah? I've thought about going to Chicago, or maybe New York or L.A., someplace far away from this little fucked up town."

"It's a big place," I said. "Lots of excitement."

"There's none of that here—absolutely none. You've heard people talk about the middle of nowhere, right? Well, this is it."

I didn't know what to say, but I wanted to keep him talking.

"I hitch-hiked all the way here—took me days."

"That's how I travel," said Austin.

"Any freaks pick you up?" I asked.

"Nah, a couple truckers didn't smell so good, but hey, they gave me a ride."

"The last one I rode with was an old lady. She smelled like cats and kept thinking I was her dead son or somethin'. She was a freak."

"She sounds interesting."

"Yeah? Well, the one before her was more of a freak," I said, warming to my story as I made it up. "He was a drug dealer."

"Drug dealers aren't freaks," said Austin.

"Well, uh, that wasn't the freaky part," I said, racking my brain. "He offered me some drugs and money to…you know…blow me."

"So did you let him?"

Should I say "yes" or "no", I thought.

"Nah."

"You should've let him," said Austin. I didn't quite know what to say about that, but his words intrigued me.

"I'm glad to be outta Chicago," I said, changing the subject. "My parents were bastards. My older brother was worse. He beat me up a lot and…well, I don't wanna talk about it."

"It's cool, dude."

Austin seemed to be taking a liking to me, but I wasn't sure. At least he was talking to me. Another car passed. Austin eyed it, then tossed his cigarette on the ground.

"I gotta go, man," he said, already walking away from me.

"I'll see ya later!" I yelled after him.

"Whatever."

I watched as he opened the passenger door of the car that had just pulled over several yards down the street. I felt abandoned as it pulled away. Austin was the only person I knew in Verona and he had his own friends. I wasn't going to give up on him, though. He had something I wanted and I intended to get it from him.

Ethan

I walked back toward the fields, the hot sun already sending trickles of sweat down my chest and back. The bombshell Jack had dropped on us was sure a shock. I had no idea we were in so much trouble. I knew farming was a tough business. More than one of the neighboring farms had gone bankrupt. Uncle Jack had even bought land from a neighbor to keep him from going under and now we were facing the same danger. I didn't know what I'd do if we lost the farm. It wasn't just my home—it was the only place I ever wanted to be.

One thing was for sure: if we were gonna go down, we'd go down fighting. I was proud of the way everyone jumped in to help—Nathan and Casper offered to get jobs and Brendan…wow. I just couldn't believe he was lending Jack all that money. I have no doubt he'd have just given it to him, but of course Uncle Jack wouldn't stand for that. The mere fact that he accepted the loan showed how bad off we were. I'd become good friends with Brendan and I respected him, but this…you really found out who your friends were when times got hard.

Even though Brendan's coming up with that money was a shock, the fact that he was doing all he could to help was not. He'd already made *so* many sacrifices in his life and mostly for Casper. Of course, Casper gave him a lot in return, but that didn't lessen the value of Brendan's selflessness. I'd seen just how much he was willing to give for others when we'd rushed Casper's brother, Jason, in the barn. We all knew he would shoot when we did it. We all knew that one of us would most likely die. But we did it anyway—Brendan, Nathan, and me.

I wondered how we'd be able to survive now. Even if Nathan and Casper found jobs, the money they earned might not be enough. There were lots of expenses. Jack took care of all the bills, but he usually had me sitting right there with him. He told me long ago, "You've got to learn how to handle this place all on your own. Someday I'll be gone, so I want you to know everything there is to know about the farm." There were all the obvious expenses like food, gas for the truck and tractor, feed for the animals, seed corn and so on. And then there were other expenses, like insurance, vet bills, parts for farm machinery, and more. Running a farm wasn't cheap.

My heart sank as I thought of wrestling. I'd been looking forward to my senior year on the team. I'd gone undefeated the last school year and had beaten Zac for the championship. I was just itching to get back on the mat, but now it probably wouldn't happen. I'd be needed on the farm, or perhaps I'd even have to get an after school job to bring in money. Either way, wrestling was out. It didn't bring in money and that's what we needed right now.

The thought of not being able to wrestle really depressed me, but that emotion made me feel selfish. We all had to make sacrifices. Nathan and Casper were taking jobs and Brendan had handed over every cent he had to his name. I sure couldn't wallow in self-pity. If I had to give up wrestling to save the farm, then so be it. Maybe, just maybe, there'd be a way I could still be on the team, but at this point I couldn't see it. I wasn't going to give up hope, however. Hope is something I needed badly—we all did.

Casper

The truck lurched slightly as we pulled out of the drive and headed for town.

"You sure you know how to drive this thing?" I snickered.

"Shut up," said Nathan, but he smiled.

I liked Nathan. In the very short time Brendan and I had been living on the farm, we'd become close friends. I like Ethan too, of course, but Nathan was a lot like me. We'd both had family problems—me with my older brother and him with his mom. It helped to have someone to talk to about stuff like that. It helped to heal old wounds.

"Think we'll be able to find anything?" I asked.

"I dunno," said Nathan. "Jobs aren't exactly plentiful in Verona, especially in the summer. I just hope we can turn up something."

"Yeah."

"I don't know about you, but I'm gonna take anything I can get," said Nathan. "I'll work in the freaking funeral home if it'll bring in some money."

"That could be boring. I hear things are really *dead* in there. Get it? Dead?"

"You are so lame," said Nathan, rolling his eyes.

"Oh, like that thing you yell sometimes when you're in the bathroom is so funny!"

"What thing?"

"You know—'*Corn, I didn't have corn!*'"

Nathan burst out laughing. I knew he would. For some reason, he thought that was the funniest thing ever. I couldn't help but laugh, too.

"Thanks, Casper."

"For what?"

"For making me laugh."

I just smiled at him. I knew what he meant. Things weren't really so funny just now. I felt like everything had just started going well and then, *Bam!*—disaster struck. Brendan and I at last had a home and now it looked like it might be taken from us. It sure wouldn't happen if I had anything to say about it. I felt very small and insignificant, though. Just how much of a difference could I make? I guess it didn't matter. I was gonna do what I could do.

Nathan parked the truck by *Café Moffatt* and we walked around looking to see if we could spot any "Help Wanted" signs. There were none.

"Let's check the paper," I suggested, remembering how Brendan and I had found our "jobs" on the Selby Farm. That had sure turned out well.

We didn't want to waste even a quarter, so instead of buying a paper, we went to the library and looked at one there.

"Anything?" I asked as Nathan scanned the classifieds.

"Not for us," he said gloomily, "unless you're secretly a registered nurse or an experienced mechanic."

We walked back to the truck and climbed in.

"Do you really think Jack might lose the farm?" I asked.

Nathan looked at me with fear in his eyes. "I hope not," he said.

He started the old Ford and we drove down by the park.

"Look at that!" I said, pointing to the old theatre. There prominently displayed in the window was a "Help Wanted" sign. "And that!" I said, pointing to *Ofarim's*, where a similar sign was on display.

"You worked in a diner, right?" asked Nathan.

"Yeah."

"Then you try for *Ofarim's* and I'll try at the theatre."

"Break a leg," I said.

"I think that's for actors, but thanks."

We headed across the street and then split up. I crossed my fingers as I entered *Ofarim's*.

Brendan

Even though it was too early in the day for it, I threw myself into stacking bales of hay and straw in the barn loft. That kind of thing was usually reserved for the evening hours when it was cooler, but I needed to exert myself and sweat.

I was pissed at my parents and particularly my father. If he hadn't tied up my money in a trust fund, I could've loaned it all to Jack. I wasn't rich, but I did have several thousand bucks put away. Back in the days before my parents found out I was gay, they were generous with my allowance. On top of that, I'd always had some kind of job for as long as I could remember and most of my money went into the bank. It was almost like I secretly knew I'd need it someday. I needed it now, but I couldn't get at it. It was frustrating. I wondered if I shouldn't get a lawyer and see what could be done, but my dad had the best lawyers around. I had no doubt he'd tied up things good.

Sweat ran into my eyes, making them sting. My eyes watered and I wasn't sure if it was all from the sweat. I didn't think about my parents very often. It was hard to think about them after they'd turned on me. I'd never forgive them for what they'd done to me, not if I lived forever. The night they called the cops and had me taken to the *Cloverdale Center* because I was gay was the night they ceased to be my parents. I'd never get over the horrible memories of that evil place and I'd never forgive them for putting me there. If it hadn't been for Chad and my best friend Brad, I'd probably still be there, being tormented, mind and body, in a deluded attempt to turn me straight. Well, maybe not deluded. I had more than a sneaking suspicion that all the crackpot doctors in that place knew that what they were doing was bullshit. They were just in it for the money, ripping off parents who couldn't accept their kids as they were, but were desperate to try and change them—even if it meant putting them through hell, and all for nothing.

I grabbed another bale of hay, feeling my biceps tense. Even though the door was open, the loft was still like an oven. Sweat poured off my bare chest and little bits of straw adhered to my moist skin. I thought that Ethan must be rubbing off on me, because I'd actually come to enjoy working. Ethan seemed happiest when he was hard at it and sweating up a storm. I felt just like him. That was likely a good thing, for there was plenty of work to do on the farm. With Casper and Nathan not helping anymore, there'd be even more to do. Casper might think he didn't contribute much, but I knew Jack, Ethan, and I were all going to have to work harder to make up for his absence—and the same was true of Nathan.

I thought about Ethan. In another life we could've been more than friends—much more. If I didn't have Casper, I could see myself falling for him. He was handsome and strong and just one hell of a nice guy. He was funny and sexy and had more going for him than most guys I'd met. Sometimes I wondered…but no; there was no use in thinking about that. I felt guilty for the thought even crossing my mind. I had Casper and he's all I really needed. Still, a little part of me was drawn to Ethan. How could I not be attracted to him? Was that so bad? I'd never do anything about it, of course. There was that one time, when we'd almost kissed, but we didn't. We'd both remained faithful to our boyfriends. I was kind of glad it happened, even though it made me feel guilty. At least I knew how Ethan felt and we'd both passed the test. I'd never cheat on Casper. And, even if I wanted to, I was sure Ethan would never cheat on Nathan. Yeah, we could've been boyfriends in another life, but instead we were friends and that was fine. I had Casper and I was content. Sometimes looking at Ethan got to me, but I could handle that because I knew that Casper had my heart.

I wondered how Casper was faring in his search for a job. I loved that little guy with all my heart. I felt so lucky to have him in my life that even our present troubles couldn't get me completely down. Besides, Casper and I had been through much worse.

I inhaled, drawing in the scent of the hay. Who would've thought that I'd turn into a farm boy? I laughed, then sneezed. Maybe I'd inhaled a little too deeply. No matter, I loved the aroma of the hayloft—that scent meant home.

Dane

I was sitting in *Ofarim's*, chowing down on a juicy burger, when a cute blond boy walked in. He didn't order. He just asked about the "Help Wanted" sign displayed in the window. It was mid-afternoon and the place was deserted, except for the boy, the waitress, and me. The waitress, who turned out to also be the owner, came from behind the counter and sat down a couple of booths away with the kid. I eavesdropped out of boredom. The owner asked the boy if he'd worked in a restaurant before, if he knew how to work an ice cream machine, and so on.

I didn't much care about what they were saying, but I liked the boy's voice. I was surprised when he said he was sixteen. I'd have thought he was fifteen, tops, and more likely fourteen. He was kinda short and thin. I was thinkin' he might be a good target. I didn't know if he was queer or not, but since he was small he probably couldn't hurt me too much if he freaked out on me or somethin'. It'd sure be a lot safer putting the moves on him than it would be some real built dude. I'd waited sixteen years for somethin' to happen and that was long enough. Maybe it was time I *made* it happen.

At least I knew where to find the kid—Casper, that was the name I'd overheard. The lady had hired him before I'd finished my fries. She must've been desperate for help or maybe it was the fact that he said he'd worked in a diner before. Anyway, I knew I'd be seeing more of Casper. *Ofarim's* was my hangout, and now he was going to be working there.

I lingered a bit longer, and then went in search of Austin. There was no reason not to continue pursuing him, even though I'd just acquired a new target. This summer was about having fun—about being bold and going for what I wanted, instead of sitting on the sideline of life. I'd been too much of a little coward to satisfy my desires at home, but here no one knew me. I was determined to be assertive and aggressive. I knew I could learn a lot from Austin. He was tough. He knew things. Even if I couldn't get what I really wanted from him, he was still a means to an end. Who knew? Maybe he'd even become my boyfriend.

It didn't take any time at all to track Austin down. If I'd been facing the entrance to *Ofarim's* instead of the counter and grill, I'd have seen him standing where he'd last left me: at the edge of the park, near the street. He wasn't alone this time though; he was talking to some guy.

"Hey, Austin," I said as I walked up.

"Hey, man," he said. He turned to his companion and introduced me. "This is Dane."

"Boothe," said the other guy.

They talked about what they might do that night without paying me any attention. I felt a little awkward, like an unwanted third-wheel. As I shifted my weight from one foot to the other, I surveyed Boothe. He looked to be about seventeen. He had pitch-black hair, black eyes, and tanned skin. Boothe was tall and slim and looked like he might have a decent build, although he was sure no muscle boy. His features were ordinary, but sort of good looking in a way. He was dressed in a black t-shirt and black jeans, giving him a mysterious and somewhat intimidating look. His hair was kinda long and shaggy. He wore an expensive looking gold chain around his neck and a big gold ring on his finger that looked like it cost a fortune. The chain and ring seemed out of place with the clothes he was wearing, as did his obviously new and costly Nikes.

I wiped the sweat from my brow. I wondered how Boothe could stand being dressed in all black. His shirt and pants must've just sucked the heat in.

"You wanna come?" Austin asked me.

I stood dazed for a second, while my memory of their conversation caught up to me. I hadn't been paying much attention. Austin had said something about beer, however.

"Yeah, sure," I answered.

Boothe eyed me. I had the feeling he didn't like me too much, but I wasn't sure. Maybe he thought I was horning in on his friendship with Austin. They seemed to know each other well enough.

Boothe led us to a Ford pickup that looked like it was brand new. When I climbed in and sat between him and Austin, I could even detect that "new" smell. I guessed he had rich parents. Boothe drove us to a liquor store and went in while we waited. He came back soon with a couple six packs. I wondered how he bought them as I was sure he wasn't twenty-one.

A few minutes later we were parked by the graveyard, standing beside the truck, each with a beer in hand. Austin and Boothe both finished off their first can fast, but I went slower. The truth was, I'd never tasted beer before because I'd never had the chance. Now I was thinking that hadn't been such a bad thing since it tasted absolutely awful. I kept that to myself, however, and forced down one swallow after another, trying to keep the "nasty taste" look off my face. Boothe looked sidelong at me and grinned, like he knew I couldn't stand it. He pushed a second beer into my hands as soon as I'd finished the first. I hoped I wouldn't get sick.

Austin and Boothe were sucking down beers like they'd just walked out of a desert or something. I hadn't even finished two before they'd polished off the remainder of both six packs. Boothe pulled out a bottle of something that I guess was whiskey and they started in on that. Boothe got me to try it and it tasted like liquid fire. He laughed his half-drunken ass off as I gasped and sputtered.

An hour later, I had a buzz, but Austin was out cold, leaning up against the right front tire. Boothe was sitting near him, also leaned up against the truck, looking like he was in some kind of daze. I was on the other side of Austin and was the most conscious of all, since I'd never quite finished my second beer. Austin looked fucking hot sitting there with no shirt. My eyes devoured the muscles of his chest and his tight, six-pack abs. Just looking at him made me spring a massive boner. Austin's worn jeans with the tear on the thigh got to me too, especially when I looked at his bulge. I wanted to just reach over and grope him in his sleep, but I was afraid Boothe might notice.

I'd about fallen asleep myself when the distant barking of a dog awakened me. I opened my eyes. Austin hadn't moved, but Boothe was now leaned back with his eyes closed. It was an opportunity to look Austin over that I wasn't about to pass up. I sat up ever so slowly and drank in the sight of his body. I looked first at his face. He really wasn't good looking when I focused just on his facial features. There was no beauty to his face and his brown eyes were ordinary, not that I could see his eyes at the moment. His brown hair didn't add much to the package—most guys had brown hair. When I allowed my gaze to widen and take in the rest of his body, he became attractive, even his plain, ordinary face looked better somehow. Maybe it was because I was turned on by his muscular chest and sexy stomach. Guys like that had always gotten to me. I had a little bit of muscle myself, but *very* little. I was slim and in danger of being skinny. Yuck. Austin had those nice bulges, though; the chest, arm, and shoulder bulges that made him look strong.

I reached out to Austin with my hand, drawing my fingers closer and closer to his hard pecs. I felt like it took me ten minutes to actually touch him, but it was probably only seconds. My fingers grazed his right pec and I spread them out over it, feeling the smooth skin over hard muscle. I allowed my hand to creep down over his nipple and onto his washboard abs. I was trembling. It was the sexiest thing I'd ever done in my entire life. Touching Austin's naked skin seemed more sexual to me than all the times I'd jerked off. Getting myself off was just me, but this was something with another guy—a guy who could jump up and kick my ass. It was dangerous and forbidden; it was exciting.

My fingers inched nearer to the bulge in Austin's jeans. I wondered what he looked like down there. Was he big? I'd snatched looks at other guys in the showers at school and figured I was about average, but I wasn't sure. I was acutely curious about what Austin had between his legs. I was just about to run my hand over his bulge when Boothe opened his eyes and caught me with my hand on Austin's belly, crossing over the forbidden line onto his jeans. I pulled my hand back and Boothe smiled at me ever so slightly and exhaled quickly. It wasn't a smile of kindness; it was a smile of knowing. It was a smile that said, "I know you're a fag."

I pulled my hand back and leaned against the truck, acting as if I hadn't been doing anything wrong. I was a good actor. I was trembling on the inside, but the attitude I showed Boothe was one of indifference. He didn't give me any shit about it, nor did he say anything later when Austin finally woke up and we all rode back to the park in Boothe's truck.

***

"You have a place to stay tonight?" asked Austin, as Boothe drove away.

"Just the park."

"Come with me."

I followed Austin as the evening shadows deepened and the air began to cool the perspiration on my bare chest. There was a distant rumble of thunder, promising rain. The wind got up and lightning rent the sky. The wind whipped dry leaves around us, and they scraped my bare legs. We passed several blocks of houses and I was wondering where Austin lived when he stopped before an enormous iron gate. By then it was dark enough it was difficult to see, but I could make out a vast, ancient house before us. Even in the dim light it was obviously abandoned. I trembled as Austin led me through the gate and toward the old monstrosity.

The old Victorian house was impossibly huge and terrifying to behold. The hair on the back of my neck stood on end and I felt a shiver pass down my spine. Even though it was warm, I felt chilly, as if I'd just walked into a room with the air conditioning turned on full blast. I suddenly decided that sleeping outside in the park wasn't such a bad thing after all. It would be far better than setting foot in the obviously haunted house that stood before me.

My relief was great when Austin pulled me around the side of the house and led me around back to a much smaller structure. It must've been a summer kitchen or something at one time. Austin opened the door and we stepped into darkness. Moments later, I heard the flick of a lighter and then Austin's face appeared in the golden glow of an oil lamp. We were in a large room, which was empty for the most part, but along one wall was a table and two old chairs; in a corner lay a mattress and some twisted sheets. There was a doorway to another room, but I couldn't see inside.

"This is home," said Austin.

"This is yours?" I asked, trying to keep the shock out of my voice.

"No, I don't know who owns it, but no one ever comes here because of *that*," he said, pointing in the direction of the huge house. "Well, almost no one. Just about everyone is too terrified of it to come near, so I'm left alone. It's haunted." Austin lit up a cigarette and sat in one of the chairs.

I had no doubt that he was speaking the truth. I didn't even like looking at the big house out the window.

"You ever been inside?"

"Nah, no reason to go in," said Austin. "This here suits me just fine."

I didn't know if that was true, or if it was just a cover for fear. I doubted very much if Austin was afraid, however; he didn't seem to fear anything. I, on the other hand, was definitely afraid of the house. I don't know what I'd have done if he'd lead me in there.

"You hungry?"

"Yeah, kinda."

Austin led me into the other room. There was a portable butane stove sitting on an old kitchen counter, along with canned goods, a can opener, a partial loaf of bread, and open boxes of cereal. A couple of pots and a skillet hung on the wall. There was another old table in the center of the room, surrounded by four matching chairs with leaves carved into the backs. They looked like they'd sat there forever.

"So, Dane, what's your story?"

"My story?"

"Yeah, why are you in this little fucked up town?"

"I ran away from home. My dad's an alcoholic and he beats on me whenever he's drunk, which was practically every night. Mom, well, she's a real bitch—she's always on my ass about something. And my older brother, well, the less said about him the better."

"Sounds tough," said Austin.

"Worse than you know," I mumbled.

"What do you mean?"

"Some fucked up shit went on at my house," I said quietly. I was pleased by the look of interest on Austin's face.

"Like what?"

"It has to do with my dad and my brother. You don't wanna hear about it, man, believe me."

"Yeah, I do," said Austin as he cranked open a can of pork and beans and dumped them in a pot.

"It's sick shit, man."

"Go on," said Austin. His eyes didn't leave me as he lit the little stove and placed the pan on top. He nearly dumped all the beans, but managed to catch the handle of the pot before it slipped off the side.

"They...well..." I stammered. I was pleased with my performance. I had Austin hanging on every word. It was all bullshit, except the part about me running away, but the real story was boring.

"You can tell me man. I came from a screwed up home, too. My dad used to kick the shit out of me all the time."

"I wish that's all my dad had done."

"What do ya mean?"

"Wanna take a guess?"

"Dude. He molested you?"

"That's putting it lightly," I said. "Dad and Stephen, that's my brother, they used to rape me."

"Together?"

"Yeah, sometimes. A lot of the time it was just one or the other, but sometimes it was both."

I bowed my head and summoned tears—I thought about dead pets.

"Hey, man, you're okay now. They can't hurt you here. Did your mom know?"

"She liked to watch."

"Oh, man, that is gross. Sorry…I mean…"

"It's okay. You see why I had to run."

"You should've offed 'em and then run away."

"I beat up my brother the night I left."

"Yeah?"

"The house was empty. I was packing and he came in. He was gonna rape me, but I'd swore I wouldn't let it happen again. When he got close, I kicked him in the nuts as hard as I could. He doubled over and I kicked him again, and then I just fucked him up. He's a lot stronger than me, but he didn't know what was coming. I left him on the floor moaning and ran for it."

"Good for you, dude. I thought you were tough, but you're a bad ass, aren't you?"

"Yeah," I said, grinning. I laughed to myself. Maybe my fictional life would get Austin interested in me. I could only hope.

Ethan

I pulled the truck up to *Wahlberg's Farm Store* and Brendan and I got out. We went in and I wasn't pleased to see Clark Isaac behind the counter. He'd given me a lot of shit last year in school and ever since. Most guys were pretty cool with me being gay, but Clark was always there with his little snide remarks and coughs that sounded like "faggot" and "fudge-packer." He'd never gone far enough for me to kick his ass, but he was always hovering just on the line.

He looked Brendan and I over as we came in, like he was sizing us up and thinking of some smart-ass comment to make. I gave him my stern look and walked right up to him.

"We need six 100 pound bags of horse feed, eight salt blocks, and a couple of cans of bag balm."

"Your nuts been givin' you trouble there, Ethan?" asked Clark.

"No, smart-ass. If you knew anything about farming, you'd know bag balm is for cow udders." I thought that might get him. His daddy owned one of the biggest farms in the county, but Clark was too inept to work it.

Clark scowled.

"How will you be paying for this?"

"As always, put it on our account."

"Your account? I don't think I can do *that*. How do we know you'll pay?"

My eyes narrowed and I could feel myself tense. This wasn't about money. This was about the same bullshit that all minorities had to put up with. It was thinly disguised prejudice.

"We'll pay after harvest, like always."

"And if you don't have the money then? If this drought continues, there may not be much of a harvest. How do we know you won't go bankrupt or something?"

His use of *we* ticked me off. You'd have thought he owned the farm store instead of Mr. Wahlberg. Clark was just an employee.

"We won't," I said.

"We? Oh, yeah," he said, looking Brendan over. "I forgot, you've got extra help now, don't you?" Clark coughed just then, thinly disguising the word "faggots" within it. I'd had more than enough. I grabbed Clark by the front of the shirt and jerked him right over the counter, sending papers flying. Clark cowered, his eyes full of fear. I was just cocking my arm to punch him in the face when Mr. Wahlberg came out of the back and yelled, "Clark!"

I released Clark. Mr. Wahlberg stomped up to his employee and gave him a withering glance. "What *are* you doing?"

"It wasn't me, sir. They were…"

Mr. Wahlberg held up his hand, warding off the explanation.

"The Selbys have traded with us for generations and there's never been any trouble. I find it hard to believe that Ethan would…"

"But, he jerked me across the counter!"

"Why?" asked Mr. Wahlberg. The question was directed at Clark, not at me.

"I was…I was just asking how he thought he'd manage to pay for his order if the crops didn't come in."

"First of all, son, the Selbys always pay their bills. Secondly, their word is as good as gold. Don't let me catch you insulting my customers like this again or you're finished. Understood?"

"Yes, sir!"

"Now, you get to filling their order, on the double."

"Yes, sir!"

Clark was shaken. I must admit I derived some satisfaction from watching him grovel. He should've been thankful Mr. Wahlberg came out or I'd have given him a pounding. He'd been asking for it long enough.

Mr. Wahlberg turned to Brendan and I as Clark disappeared into the back.

"I'm very sorry about that, Ethan. It's hard to find decent help nowadays. Your credit is always good here, you know that. And I admire you for how hard you're willing to work with Jack on the farm."

"Thank you, sir." I appreciated his words and the implied acceptance in them. Mr. Wahlberg was a shrewd old man and I had no doubt he knew what lay beneath Clark's hostility. Everyone in town knew I had a boyfriend. When Mr. Wahlberg respected me, he respected *everything* about me.

"Let me go make sure he's getting the order right," he said. "We'll have it ready for you in a jiffy. I'll have Clark load your truck for you."

Brendan and I looked around while we waited. *Wahlberg's Farm Store* was a long, old-fashioned structure cram packed with all kinds of farm supplies and hardware. One could get anything from seed corn to tractor tires there. I pointed out some boxes on a shelf to Brendan. They were parts for a cream separator. No one had used a cream separator for decades. There was a lot of stuff like that in the old store.

The floor was wooden and well worn, hinting at the decades of tromping feet that had trod them. Painted on one of the front windows in red letters was *Established 1902.* The store had been opened by Mr. Wahlberg's grandfather and had been in continuous operation since then. I loved the feel of the place and its "farmy" smell. It's hard to explain, but Wahlberg's smelled like a pleasant mixture of corn, lumber, and burlap feed sacks. It was wonderful.

I tossed Brendan a piece of taffy from the candy jar that'd sat on the counter since the beginning of time. We both turned and watched Clark stagger under the weight of a 100 pound bag of feed. Usually, we loaded the truck ourselves, but Mr. Wahlberg had obviously decided it was a good punishment for Clark and I didn't intend to interfere. There was a certain poetic justice to it that I relished.

A few minutes later, we were back in the truck. We had the windows rolled down to cool ourselves a bit and the wind rushed through our hair. We were both shirtless. With the daytime temperatures approaching 100 and often topping it, we never wore a shirt unless we went into a store or something and that was rare. Even the evening hours were far too warm. I'd never witnessed a summer like this one before. I doubted even Jack had seen one as hot as this.

"Let's stop and check on Mrs. Pearson before we go back," I said.

Brendan nodded. Mrs. Pearson was an elderly lady who Jack had long looked after. I don't know how it got started, but he was "off to check on Mrs. Pearson" at least once a week and more often twice. Jack was doubly busy with the farm now, so the rest of us were going to share the job of looking after her, not that we really considered it a chore. Mrs. Pearson was a sweet old lady. I felt sorry for her. She lived all alone in a rickety house with no one for company except a couple of cats. She seemed happy enough, but I kind of worried about her. I knew Jack had helped her with her heating bills and stuff once in awhile, and I wondered how we'd be able to manage that since we didn't have enough money to pay our own bills. We sure weren't going to let her go hungry, though. We wouldn't have to worry about heating bills for months. If things got bad when the time came, maybe we'd just have her come and live with us for the winter.

Brendan and I pulled on our shirts once more as we pulled up in front of Mrs. Pearson's one-story home. It was one of those built sometime between the 1930's and 50's, with the heavy, concrete-block front porch. It had a depressing, rundown look to it on the outside, but she kept it all neat and tidy on the inside.

We knocked on the front door and waited for about three minutes before she answered. Mrs. Pearson's hearing was as sharp as mine, but she didn't move very fast. She grinned as she opened the door.

"How's my boy?" she asked. I'd become her "boy" on a previous visit with Jack.

"I'm just fine, Mrs. Pearson, this is my friend, Brendan."

"Come in. Come in."

"We can't stay long because we've got to get back to the farm, but we were wondering if you needed anything. We thought we'd stop by since we were in town."

"I'm just fine, Ethan, but if you could, I'd love to go to the library next week. I've about read through all the books I got last time."

"You just give us a call when you want to go and we'll get you there. You need any groceries or anything else?"

"No, I'm fine, but thanks for asking. You're such a good boy."

I smiled. We talked with her for just a while. She asked Brendan a few questions while he sat and petted one of her cats.

Bright sunlight streamed in the windows, illuminating a scene that could've been the same in the 1950's. All the furniture was from that time, but spotlessly clean. There wasn't a speck of dust anywhere. Maybe Mrs. Pearson spent a lot of time cleaning because she didn't have much else to do.

Mrs. Pearson asked after Uncle Jack and Ardelene. She seemed interested in every little event, no matter how minor. I liked her. She had the feel of an elderly aunt.

A few minutes later, we got up to leave. "You give us a call if you need anything," I said, "or if you just want someone to talk to. You may have to try several times to catch us inside, but we'll be around. Nights are best if you need us quick."

We all said our goodbyes and then Brendan and I hopped back in the truck and headed for the farm.

"She kind of reminds me of my grandma," said Brendan.

"She's a nice old lady."

"Yeah. So after we get this unloaded, what's next?" asked Brendan.

"What isn't?" I laughed.

Our work was never done. Both Nathan and Casper were working off the farm now and it left us with two less people and just as much work. They both still helped out when they weren't working at their paying jobs, but there were nearly more tasks than we could handle. Brendan and I started early and worked until late, often until ten, eleven, or even twelve o'clock at night. Dave was pitching in and he was a lot of help, for a ten-year-old. He took care of all the small tasks that required a lot of time, but not too much muscle. And I was sure glad Brendan was there to help us. He was strong and tireless. Without him, I don't think Jack and I could've kept things going.

"So how's Nathan doing at *The Paramount*?" asked Brendan.

"He likes it, but he'd be happier if the hours were different. I told him it shouldn't matter too much, since we were all so busy it wasn't like he was missing out on anything."

"Ain't that the truth?"

Nathan had found himself a job at the old theatre in town. It was open every night, but only had one show. Nathan worked from 5:30 p.m. to around 10:30 p.m. on weekdays and from 1 p.m. to about 10:30 p.m. on weekends.

"Nathan said he could get us all free tickets anytime we want them."

"If only we had the time to go," said Brendan.

"Yeah, we'll just have to make the time some evening, when something good is playing."

"Wow. You mean, like, leave the farm to go someplace besides the farm store or the grocery?" laughed Brendan.

"I do feel like all I ever see is fields," I said.

I didn't really mind not getting away much, I was fairly content on the farm. It's where I wanted to be. Living there with Jack, Ardelene, Nathan, Dave, Brendan, and Casper just felt right.

My main worry was keeping the farm going. I wasn't sure we'd be able to manage it. If we failed, it sure wouldn't be because we hadn't tried. I didn't know what we'd do if we couldn't make a go of it. I couldn't bear the thought of Jack selling. That farm was my home and I wanted to live out my days there until I died.

I kept my worries about the farm to myself. I knew I had to be strong for everyone else. If the guys saw me with a long face it would just make it harder on them. We had enough troubles without that. Besides, there was still a lot of good in life, even in the worst of times.

I backed the truck up to the barn and Brendan and I unloaded the feed and other supplies. We were soon done.

"I'm heading off for the south field, right after I do a little repair on the tractor," I said.

"I better take care of that fence behind the barn before the cattle tromp it down and we have to go looking for them," said Brendan. He grabbed a pair of wire cutters, a spool of heavy wire, and some gloves, and then took off for the pasture.

I stayed in the barn a while, replacing a gasket on the tractor that had cracked and started leaking. It took longer than I would've liked, but that was the way of farm work. Few things were simple. As I drove the tractor out of the barn, I waved at Nathan. He was doing some work in the garden before heading out to *The Paramount*. I stopped the tractor for a moment and hopped off. Nathan ran to me and we hugged and kissed.

"It seems like it's been a long time since we've been able to do more than kiss," he said.

"Three days," I said.

"Yeah, forever."

"I'll save a little energy for tonight, if you'll do the same," I said.

"Sure thing, babe, but maybe you'd better save a lot of energy." Nathan's hand wandered down over my butt as he hugged me.

"We'd better knock this off or neither of us will be able to get any work done."

Nathan giggled and we kissed deeply once more, our tongues entwining as we held each other close.

I hopped back on the tractor and chugged along toward the south field. Despite my worries, I was happy. How could I not be with such a wonderful boyfriend?

Casper

I wiped off the counter, then moved to the first booth that needed cleaning up. Working in *Ofarim's* reminded me of last winter when Brendan and I lived in a cheap motel and worked in a diner in Purity, but things weren't so bad now. Brendan and I were safe and had a good home. Not all my memories of Purity were bad, however. We'd been pretty happy in our little motel room. It was sure a lot better than sleeping outside as we'd done for weeks before that. Brendan and I had our first Christmas there together too, and I knew I'd always remember it with fondness.

Ofarim's was empty at the moment. The lunch crowd was gone and I was at last able to catch up on the cleaning. It was no wonder Agnes needed help so badly. She'd been running the whole place on her own since her last employee left. *Ofarim's* wasn't exactly a booming business, but there were plenty of customers. Lunch was the real rush. On most days, Agnes had me come in about eleven and then I stayed on until six or seven and sometimes as late as ten, which was an hour after closing time. I was glad to get the hours, because we needed the money. Jack, Ethan, and Brendan were breaking their backs to keep the farm running and I wanted to do all I could to bring in some cash. I was already looking forward to my first paycheck. I'd only been working for three days and I'd made $19.00 in tips. It wasn't a lot, but it was on top of my salary, which wasn't bad considering where I worked. Most restaurants paid under minimum wage, but not *Ofarim's*. Agnes gave me fifty cents an hour above minimum and all the food I could eat. We grew most of our own food on the farm, but as much of it wasn't ready yet, I made sure to take advantage of free meals at *Ofarim's*. I figured the more often I could eat there, the more money it would save.

I looked up when the bells on the door rang. The boy I'd seen every day since I'd started entered and took his usual booth. He was an okay looking guy with dark blond hair. What I really noticed about him, however, was his ice-blue eyes. When he looked at me, I felt like he could see inside me. He looked at me a lot. Sometimes, I was a little uncomfortable because I could feel his eyes on me while I was working. Whenever I looked up, he was either gazing at me, or shifting his eyes so that it looked like he wasn't. Most of the time he just openly stared.

I wiped off my hands on my apron and walked over to his table.

"Know what you want?" I asked.

He just gazed at me a moment before answering. Finally, he said, "Yeah, I think I'll try a cheeseburger, fries, and a large Coke."

"Try, huh?" I said. It was exactly the same thing he'd ordered every single time he'd been in, except for once when he came in late for a chocolate milk-shake. He grinned.

"Hey, I'm Dane, by the way."

"Casper."

"Yeah, I know."

"How?"

"Oh, I know lots of things," he said, trying to sound mysterious. I wasn't buying it.

I turned and walked to the grill. I started to work on his cheeseburger while Agnes put in some fries and got his drink.

When I returned to the table with his order, Dane was looking me over, as always.

"Can I get you anything else?"

"What time you get off?"

"About seven this evening, unless we get busy."

"You want to go out and...do something?"

"I can't. I have to get back home."

"Parents?"

"Nah, I live on a farm and we have tons of work to do."

"Maybe some other time then," said Dane, not at all happy.

"Yeah, maybe."

I went back to work wiping down tables. I felt like I'd just been asked out— on a date. I wondered if maybe I should've told Dane I have a boyfriend. Maybe I was just jumping to conclusions, though. Why would anyone be interested in me? Then again, Brendan was sure interested and he was a hundred times hotter than Dane, so who knew?

A group of four kids I knew from school came in just then and I got way too busy to think about it. I'd only attended school in Verona for a couple weeks before summer vacation, but it was time enough to sort of get to know a few people.

I was friends with the guys who had just entered—Brandon and Jon. Ethan had introduced us shortly after Brendan and I arrived in Verona and we'd hit it off pretty well. I wasn't as familiar with the girls they were with. One of them was named Jennifer and I couldn't remember the other's name.

"Hey, you working here now?" asked Brandon.

"How'd you guess, man?" I said, laughing.

"Does this mean we get to order you around?" asked Jon.

"Only if you leave a *very* big tip," I said. "A twenty will be fine. Otherwise, I'll have to sick Brendan on you."

"Not that!" said Jon, holding up his hands. "I'm not messing with Brendan." He grinned. Everyone knew Brendan could kick butt, just by looking at him. Brandon and Jon knew he was my boyfriend, although they were about the only ones—except for everyone on the farm, of course.

I jotted down their orders, and then headed back to help Agnes get everything ready. We worked well together, and the experience I had from working at the diner in Purity came in handy. Agnes said I was the best helper she'd ever hired and she'd run the diner for over thirty years.

I liked my job. It got a little boring sometimes, but there were lots of interesting people going in and out and there was always Agnes to talk to. She wasn't married and seemed kind of lonely sometimes. I think running the restaurant was as much about having something to do for her as it was about making money. Everybody really liked her—even teenagers who didn't seem to like any other adult got on well with Agnes. She was kind of everybody's Mom. Her place was popular with kids my age and maybe that was why.

Dane kept stealing glances at me, although I noticed he was dividing his attention between Brandon, Jon, and me. He seemed to have an eye for guys. There was something in his eyes as he looked at them too—a look of hunger. I would've probably had that look myself at times if I didn't have Brendan.

It was hot by the grill, but even back there air conditioned air wafted across my face like a cool breeze. I looked across the tables and through the windows at the bright afternoon sun. It was a scorcher outside. I felt a little guilty luxuriating in the cool interior of *Ofarim's* when I knew my boyfriend was toiling in the hot sun, sweat trickling down his bare, muscular chest and...I had to stop myself before I got all worked up. Yeah, I knew what lay behind the look of hunger in Dane's eyes.

"See ya later, Casper," called Dane as he got up from his table and opened the door.

"See ya," I called back.

I went to clean up his table and saw that he'd left me a dollar tip. That was about twice what most people left, if they left anything. Dane was just a bit odd, but he was likable enough. I stuck the dollar in my pocket.

"Order's up!" said Agnes.

I went back and picked up a tray piled high with burgers, hot dogs, and fries and brought it out to Brandon, Jon, and the girls.

The place was deserted except for Brandon & Company, and I was all caught up on cleaning, so I grabbed a Coke, pulled up a chair, and talked to them a bit. Agnes didn't mind if I did that when there was no work to be done. It was great being around Brandon and Jon. They were cool guys.

"How's life on the farm?" asked Jon, with his mouth half stuffed with French fries.

I hesitated. I wasn't sure I wanted to tell the truth. Jon leveled his gaze.

"Things are...okay, kinda, but not the best."

"What's wrong?" asked Jon.

"We're havin' some problems. There are lots of bills and stuff and Jack, Brendan, and Ethan are trying to do all the farm work by themselves."

"Yeah, I bet it's tough," said Brandon.

"Nathan and I started working to help out. He's got a job at the *Paramount*."

"That sounds like a sweet job," said Jon.

"He likes it. Mr. Barr is cool and Nathan has the run of the concession stand—anything he wants for free."

"I wouldn't mind that," said Brandon, "but I like my nights off." He put his arm around Jennifer and drew her closer. They kissed.

I sat there and talked until an elderly couple entered a few minutes later, and it was back to work.

Brendan

Football. I'd been itching to get back into it. One of the things I sorely missed from my life in Kentucky was playing football. Right before everything had gone wrong, I was the first string quarterback and the team captain. The team even stuck by me when they found out I was gay. Some player's mom made a big fuss over it, but the guys actually threatened to walk if I was removed as captain. That had floored me. The coach was very supportive as well. No one on the team even seemed to care I was gay. They were way more interested in my skill on the football field and my personality. I'd been all worried over them finding out. I'd even come pretty close to killing myself when I thought it was about to happen. What a huge mistake that would've been. I missed those guys, especially my best friend Brad. If I'd had some warning about what my parents were going to do, I'm sure the guys would've helped me get away. Brad did help me escape from the *Cloverdale Center,* and for that I'd be eternally grateful.

I'd been looking forward to joining the Verona High School team, but it looked like that wasn't gonna happen now. I'd have been thrilled to play any position. I didn't have to be the quarterback like I was at my old school. Just getting to be out on that field would've been enough. I loved playing. I loved how it made me feel. I even loved the smell of football—the turf, the locker room, all of it.

I knew I had a pretty good shot at getting a good position. More than one person had told me that the guys tried hard, but V.H.S. didn't do so well in football. I gotta admit, I had thought of being the quarterback. There's nothing like it. I didn't know what I was going to do with my life, but I hoped football would be a part of it. I knew I'd never have a career in the pros, at least that was pretty unlikely, but I wanted to do something connected with football—

coach or cover it as a sportswriter or whatever; it didn't matter, so long as I was part of the game.

But with all the demands of the farm, the luxury of football didn't seem very possible. I guess not getting to play wouldn't kill me, although I kinda felt like it just might. Maybe I could at least *watch* some games, if there was time. Missing out on football my senior year would kinda screw up my chances for football in college. Oh, I might still be able to make the team, but I'd have a poor chance of being more than a lineman. That wasn't so bad, however; football was football.

When you put it in perspective, having to give up the game wasn't the worst thing in the world. I could've still been stuck back in the *Cloverdale Center*, Casper could've been killed when Jason attacked him, or I could've been killed myself. There was a stack of stuff that was worse than losing football. I just had to suck it up and go on. There was still plenty to enjoy in life. For one thing, I had Casper, and that alone made me a lucky guy.

Dane

I wasn't too happy that Casper turned me down. I really wanted to get him alone and talk to him. I wanted to feel him out—and up, if possible. I'd overhead the guys that came in after me talking to him. I wondered who the Brendan was they mentioned. He was obviously connected with Casper in some way—probably his older brother or something. I probably should've stayed longer to see if I could overhear anything useful, but I wanted to hang around with Austin for a while. I'd see him that night at his place, since I was staying with him for a while, but I was trying to spend a lot of time with him. He kept disappearing on me. He was a damned busy guy for someone who didn't have a job.

I walked up the street past the theatre. A couple of blocks farther on, I noticed a car, going in the opposite direction. There was a middle-aged lady driving, but Austin was in the passenger seat. That's why I noticed it. I thought for a moment that Austin was with his mother, but that wasn't right. It couldn't be. I thought I might ask him about it when I saw him that night, but I wasn't sure. I didn't want to appear too nosy or do anything to get on his nerves. He seemed kind of tense and angry sometimes, pacing back and forth as if he were a caged animal. He was frightening then, as if he'd lash out without reason.

I'd been in Verona only a few days, but it seemed longer. It's not that I was bored; I was just impatient. I'd fed Austin a lot of lies about why I left home, but the real reason is that I wanted freedom—to have no limits on what I could do—to be the Dane I wanted to be, instead of the Dane my parents and friends expected me to be.

The main reason I'd run away was quite simple—sex. I wanted sex. I needed sex. And I sure wasn't going to get any where I'd lived before. I'd been trying for two years. I'd been looking and watching and hoping, but nothing ever happened. That was mainly my fault. I was too uptight. I was too afraid my parents would find out about me. I desperately wanted to flirt my way into another boy's pants, but I lived in fear of rejection and retaliation. I had a good idea what could happen if I came on to the wrong guy. Not only would I get my ass kicked, but word would be spread all over school and would soon get back to my parents. I was too big of a coward to take a chance.

I wanted a boyfriend, someone to love who would love me back. I wanted to be held and kissed. Somehow I just knew Austin would make a good boyfriend. He was kinda rough on the outside, but I bet he was sweet on the inside. I just had to crack him open somehow. If I could get into his pants then I could make him mine. I was getting impatient. I wanted it to happen—now.

In Verona, things were different. No one knew me here. I could make a new start. Sure, I could still get pounded if I approached the wrong guy, but my friends wouldn't know and neither would my parents. I wasn't that afraid of getting hit in the face or something. At home I was afraid of people I knew finding out I was queer. Here, I didn't have to worry about that. If I tried and failed the failure wouldn't be so bad. I was kinda growing afraid about Austin. I felt for him. What if I tried for him and he didn't want me?

Almost three days and no action; I wanted some and I wanted it now. I yearned to try something with Austin, but something inside me warned me it was a bad idea. He was probably the one person I shouldn't take a chance on, at least not until I was more sure of things. He was letting me stay with him. I didn't want to risk losing that. It was nice out most nights, but I sure didn't want to sleep on a park bench if it stormed or something. Someone might mug me or something, too. And then, there was the way I felt about him. I guess you'd kinda call it a crush, but it felt like more. I was kinda afraid to try anything because I didn't know what I'd do if I failed.

If Austin put the moves on *me*, I'd be all over him in a flash, but I wasn't going to do more than give him the barest of hints that I was hot for him. It was too risky. Where Austin was concerned, I still had to be cautious, but otherwise I intended to grab life by the balls and aggressively pursue whatever I wanted—or I should say, *whomever* I wanted.

My eyes roved as I walked. I was always looking around for hot guys at home, but here I was far more obvious about it. Whenever I saw a cute boy, I looked him over good. I didn't exactly stare, but I didn't steal quick glances in hopes that he wouldn't notice. I wanted guys to notice I was looking, so that hopefully one of them would be interested and maybe even make a move on me. I was ready to make my own moves, but so far, I hadn't picked up on even a glimmer of interest. There was no green light to give me the go ahead—not yet.

Truth be told, I wasn't sure how to make a move, but when the time came I was sure as hell going to try *something*. Maybe I'd even make some moves without the green light. I thought of the boy in *Ofarim's*, Casper. I could see myself putting the moves on him. He was small and about as intimidating as a bunny. He'd be a good place to start. Maybe he'd be up for some fun, or maybe I could bully him into it. I wouldn't actually force him or anything—not like rape. That wasn't cool, but I was willing to push him into something or scare him into it. I'd waited sixteen years for sex and I'd waited long enough. Something had to give or I was gonna go crazy!

I walked to the edge of town and into the graveyard. It was a good place to think. The sun was shining bright, but the cemetery was still foreboding. I think it was the stillness that made it so. I felt as if the silence didn't want to be disturbed. I felt this odd ache in my throat, as if I had to make a sound just to see if I could. I almost felt like I didn't have the ability to speak anymore. I cleared my throat, then hoarsely said, "Hello", feeling instantly foolish. No one answered back. Now, *that* would've been freaky!

I thought more about my tortured virginity and how I might rid myself of it. I wasn't making much progress. I just kept going over and over the same thoughts in my head. Maybe I didn't need to think about it so much. Perhaps I just had to wait for my chance and then act.

I strolled around the weathered stones, thinking how the cemetery was kind of like a park—big trees, benches, flowers. Parks didn't have tombstones and mausoleums, though.

I was almost upon Boothe before I saw him. I'd have avoided him if I could, but it was already too late. He was standing near a recent burial, apparently lost in thought, when he jerked his head up at my approach. A smirk curled the edges of his mouth and he snorted, as if to say, "Oh, it's *you*." I didn't much care for Boothe. I knew he looked down on me, as if I was nothing more than an immature kid. He treated me like I was eight and I *hated* it. He was Austin's friend, though, so I had to play it cool.

"Someone you knew?" I asked, indicating the grave.

"Yeah, a great aunt. I didn't know her well." He peered into my eyes. "So what you are doing out here?"

"Just walking and thinking."

"Not hanging out with Austin?" he asked. His tone almost seemed jealous. "Or is he busy working?"

"Working? He doesn't have a job."

"Oh, Austin's a working boy, believe me."

I just looked at Boothe confused. His expression clearly showed he thought I was the stupidest little freak who had ever walked the face of the earth. I wanted to punch him in the stomach.

"You don't get it, do you?"

"Get what?" I asked, feeling genuinely ignorant. It pissed me off that Boothe could make me feel like that.

"Damn, you are a dense little fucker, aren't you?"

I bristled, but Boothe was quite a bit bigger than me, so I didn't fly into him like I wanted.

"Just tell me, all right?" I shouted.

"He's a *working* boy—a rent boy—a whore."

"Huh?"

"You stupid little fuck, he has sex for money. Can you get that? He gets paid for having sex."

"You're a liar!"

"Where does he always hang out, huh? At the park. He stands near the street, leaning on a light pole with his shirt off. You think he just does that for fun? He's advertising, dude."

"You're messed up," I said. "Austin wouldn't do that."

"And just how would you know? You've known him for what, two days? I've known him since we were little kids. He's been doing it since he was fifteen, ever since his folks kicked him out. He's nineteen now, so he's been going at it for a good long time. He's probably loaded up with diseases."

"You're lyin' about him doin' *that*," I said.

"Damn, little kid, you can't even say it, can you? He's a whore."

"I'm not a little kid!"

"Sure you're not," said Boothe, as condescending as hell.

"Why are you sayin' shit like this about Austin? I thought you guys were friends."

"I don't have friends. Friends drag you down. They try to control you. Fuck friends. Austin and I are acquaintances. We talk. We hang out sometimes. We get wasted together. We don't fuck with each other's shit. We mind our own business and don't ask questions."

"So how do you know about him then, huh?"

"Guys have told me they've had him. And, I've *seen*."

"Guys?"

"Guys, women, anyone who'll pay. He's a whore, that's what whores do."

Boothe was blowing my mind, even though I was 90% sure he was full of shit. "What do you mean you've seen?"

Boothe sighed loudly and looked at me disgusted.

"I saw Austin with Mr. Everson in the woods near the park. I saw Mr. Everson on his knees. When he got up, I saw Austin stuff his dick back into his pants and Mr. Everson hand him a twenty. That good enough for you, kid?"

"You're a liar!"

"Why are you so upset? You in love with him or somethin'? Huh?"

"Shut up."

"If you don't believe me, just ask him. He'll tell you. Now go away and stop wasting my time."

I wanted to say something really nasty to Boothe, but I couldn't think of anything suitable and he'd likely pop me a good one if I did. I turned and walked away, trembling with fury. Boothe was such an asshole.

Ethan

I ran a soapy washcloth over my chest as hot water pounded down on my tired muscles. It was after 11:00 PM, and Brendan and I had just come in from the fields. I was so tired I just wanted to sink into bed and fall instantly asleep. My shoulders and back were tight from lifting heavy sections of an oak tree Brendan and I had cut up. It'd fallen right across the grassy road that led between two fields, blocking the route of the tractor. It had taken a good hour for us to saw it up and move it to the side with only moonlight and the lights on the tractor for illumination. Tomorrow, I'd take a wagon down and gather up the logs. After it had been split, it would make good firewood for this winter or the next.

The hot water eased my muscles, but they were still knotted and tense. The shower sure felt good, though. There was little better than a good hot shower after a long day's work. I'd thought about a cool shower, since I'd come in all sweaty, but my muscles demanded a hot one and I gave in to them.

I began to cool off as I stepped out of the shower and the air hit my wet body. I dried off and wrapped the towel around my waist. I walked barefoot back to the bedroom, passing Brendan heading for his own shower. As I stepped into the room, the light was on. Nathan was home from work and waiting for me, lying on top of the covers wearing only his boxers. As I gazed at him, weariness fled from my body. He stood, came to me, and wrapped his arms around my torso. He gave me a long, passionate kiss.

"Hey sexy, I saved some energy like you told me," he said.

"Mmmm."

"Your shoulders are so tight," said Nathan, as he rubbed them. "Lay down on the bed and I'll give you a massage."

I crawled onto the old double-bed and lay face down, pulling a pillow under my chest for support. My towel came loose and Nathan pulled it away. He straddled my bare buttocks and grasped my shoulders in his hands. He began to knead and rub the knotted muscles in my shoulders and neck. I released a loud *mmmmmm*.

"How was your day?" asked Nathan.

"Long, but good. That creep from school gave us some trouble at the farm store, but I jerked him over the counter."

Nathan giggled. "Which creep from school?"

"Clark Isaac."

"Oh, that one."

"Yeah, Mr. Wahlberg jumped down his throat for it. We dropped in to check on Mrs. Pearson, too. How'd things go at work?"

"It was a slow night. There were only about twenty people. I saw Devon there."

Devon—I hated the very name. I didn't believe in hate, but I hated him. He'd pulled some nasty shit on Nathan and me, and did worse to a couple of our friends. He was a walking menace. Brandon, Jon, and I had straightened him out, though.

"What did he do?"

"Nothin'. When he saw me he looked away, and then avoided me. He didn't even look me in the eyes when I took his ticket."

"I guess he's still running scared. That's good."

"Yeah."

Nathan massaged my shoulders and upper back in silence for a while. I relaxed under the expert care of his hands. Nathan and I gave each other back rubs now and then. His touch just about made me melt.

"How do you think we're doing on money?" he asked at last.

"Well, it's going to depend on the crops, but with you and Casper working, we should be all right for the time being. Of course, if the tractor breaks down or one of us gets sick or whatever…I dunno what we'll do."

"Let's not worry about all the bad stuff that *could* happen," said Nathan.

"You're right. We're in pretty good shape now. If we get a decent harvest, we could even make some headway on the loans. I've been talking about it with Jack. If we don't, we'll just have to talk to the bank and see what can be done. We'll be okay. I'm just sorry everyone has to work so hard."

"Don't be sorry. No one minds. I like working at the theatre. I've already got to see the last 30 minutes of *Dragonslayer* twice already," laughed Nathan. "Casper seems to enjoy working at *Ofarim's* and I know you love farm work, even if it is hard. I think Brendan likes it, too."

"Yeah, he does. He's a whole lot like me, actually. He likes working with his hands and using his muscles."

"So don't be sorry. Everything is working out just fine."

I loved Nathan's easygoing attitude. It helped me to relax as much as his hands massaging my muscles. I hadn't been completely truthful with him about our financial situation. Things were a little tighter than I let on. Deep down, I figured we'd make it, though, and we were already doing all we could to make a go of the farm, so there was no use worrying anyone about it. Only Jack and I knew how bad things really were.

Nathan worked down my lower back and scooted himself down onto my calves. His hands wandered onto my buttocks and I moaned with pleasure.

"You're making me hard," I said.

"I know." His voice was so sexy.

I turned and lay on my back, pulling Nathan down on top of me. I held him in my arms and kissed him on the lips. He opened his mouth and our tongues entwined. I lowered my hands and pushed down his boxers. Nathan kicked them off and we rubbed our naked bodies together as we made out.

"I'm not the only one who's hard," I said, smiling.

"Well, I guess you're just going to have to do something about that."

Nathan sat and straddled me, moving his cute little butt up onto my chest. I lifted my head, engulfed him, and made him moan.

We went at it hard for several minutes, indulging our sexual needs and desires. Nathan was a wild boy in bed and left me wanting for nothing. When we'd finished, I lay back and Nathan rested his head on my chest. I wrapped my arms around him and we quickly drifted off to sleep.

***

The next afternoon, the tractor clunked to a halt just as I reached the south field. I feared the worst, but was relieved to discover it was only a busted fuel line. It was a minor problem, but the tractor wasn't going anywhere without gas. I plugged the ruptured line with a wad of chewing gum and walked back toward the farmhouse.

Jack and Ardelene were sitting at the kitchen table. Jack was having a quick bite to eat. I wondered how Ardelene liked having Jack as a husband. He was always busy, always out on the farm somewhere. Being married to him was probably a lot like being married to a doctor.

"The fuel line on the tractor busted," I announced. "I'm going into town to get a new one. You need anything?"

Jack thought for a moment, then said, "Nope."

Ardelene offered to make me a sandwich, but I wasn't hungry. It hadn't been all that long since I'd had lunch.

I considered looking for Brendan and Nathan to tell them where I was going, but I wasn't sure where they were. The farm was vast and the work we did on it could take us to any part of it at any time. It didn't matter. Ardelene would tell them where I'd gone if they showed up to ask. She usually stuck pretty close to the house. She worked hard taking care of most of the laundry and cooking while us guys worked in the fields. Things had been shared a lot more equitably before our money problems, but, like the rest of us, Ardelene was doing her part and making sacrifices. When things returned to normal, if they did, then we'd all take our turns at the laundry, dishes, and etc. once more. I intended to do some of that before things got back to normal, but so far there hadn't been time.

The truck was like an oven when I climbed in. Sweat immediately began running down my bare torso. I rolled down the windows, and then drove slowly down the long, winding, gravel drive to keep from stirring up any more dust than was necessary. If I whipped up the dust, it would fly right into the cab and coat my sweaty face and body. I wasn't able to go above 15 M.P.H. until I'd reached the paved road that led into town.

I begrudged the time lost to making a trip into Verona, but it couldn't be helped. That was part of farm life—something unexpected was always happening. It wouldn't take long to get a new fuel line anyway, and I could install it in less than ten minutes. I was just relieved it wasn't a major mechanical problem.

When I pulled the truck up to *Wahlberg's Farm Store*, there was a kid sitting out front I'd never seen before. I noticed him for a couple of reasons. First, as I said, I didn't recognize him. That was a little odd because he looked a couple of years younger than me and I'd have surely seen him at school. Second, his eyes were glued to my chest the moment I stepped out of the truck. I had a good build and was used to people looking me over, but this boy was staring *hard*. He was practically drooling. I smiled to myself as I stepped through the doorway because I could just about read his mind—he was a gay kid trapped in a small town with no outlet for his sexual desires. He probably drooled over every boy that passed, especially those not wearing shirts. I knew how that was—I was much like that myself before I met Nathan. I was sure as hell a lot more careful about checking guys out, however, and even I hadn't been careful enough. I almost felt like taking the boy aside and telling him he needed to watch it. He could get his ass kicked if he checked out the wrong guy.

Clark didn't give me any lip when I asked for a replacement gas line. I think the combination of me jerking him across the counter and Mr. Wahlberg reaming him out had taken the wind out of his sails. It was a good thing for him that he was civil. I was in a rush and not in the mood for any of his crap.

When I exited the store, the boy was still sitting there. I felt kind of sorry for him, so I said, "Hi!" in as friendly a tone as I could manage.

"Hey," he said. "Sure is hot, isn't it?"

I kept myself from laughing. I'd always found it funny when someone commented on the obvious. It was over ninety degrees.

"Yeah," I said, wiping the sweat from my forehead with my hand. I opened the truck door, and the boy got up and stepped toward me.

"You from around here?" he asked.

"Yeah, I live just out of town." I noticed that the boy's eyes were devouring me again. "I'm Ethan."

"Dane."

"Nice to meet you, Dane."

"You, too," he said.

"Listen, I'm in a rush, but maybe I'll see you around."

"Yeah, okay," said Dane, looking none too happy. I felt a little bad for not talking to him longer, but the look in his eyes made me doubt the wisdom of getting to know him better. I knew desire when I saw it.

"Bye."

"Bye, Ethan."

As I drove away, I wondered if maybe I shouldn't have had a talk with Dane—gay boy to gay boy. Maybe I could've kept him from getting himself in trouble or helped him out someway. I smiled for a moment. I knew what Dane really wanted, but he wasn't going to get that from me. I was devoted to

Nathan. Dane probably thought he'd never find anyone. It's like that for gay boys at first. I was sure he would, though—he wasn't half bad looking. His dirty blond hair was kinda cool and he had real pretty light blue eyes—kinda like ice. I just hoped he wouldn't get with the wrong kind of guy, or worse, get himself beat up.

I pushed Dane out of my mind. I had work to do and I couldn't take care of the whole world.

***

When I pulled up the drive, I saw Brandon's car sitting near the farmhouse. He and Jon were leaning up against it with arms folded.

"Hey, guys," I said, as I hopped out of the truck.

"You are in trouble," said Jon. He had a scowl on his face that appeared sincere.

"What did I do?"

"You didn't tell us you needed help."

"Oh, that."

"Casper said things weren't going so well."

"No. We're havin' some pretty serious money problems." I explained the situation to them, including the reason Nathan and Casper were working.

"Well, we're here to help," said Brandon. "We're the new farm hands."

"You guys don't have to do that," I said.

"Hey, it's summer. What else have we got to do?" said Brandon. "Well, besides our jobs, but we can spare you a few hours here and there. Besides, I hear this farm work is as good as belonging to a gym and from the looks of you, I'd say it's true."

"Guys…thanks," I said, almost getting teary-eyed.

I put the guys to work, then left to put the new gas line on the tractor. As I departed, I looked back to see Jon and Brandon working away, talking and laughing. I knew I was lucky to have friends like them. Someday, I'd have to find a way to repay them.

Casper

I was just getting ready to take my tray to a table and have a late supper when a customer entered *Ofarim's*. It was Dane.

"I'll take care of this one. You go eat before your food gets cold," said Agnes. She was such a nice old lady. She reminded me of my grandma in a lot of ways. I wondered if I shouldn't introduce them. They might even become friends.

Dane walked up to the counter to order. I sat down at a booth and took a sip of Coke. It sure felt good to sit down. My feet were aching. I took a bite of my double bacon cheeseburger and chewed slowly. The food in *Ofarim's* was really good, way better than most burger places. Of course, *Ofarim's* was more than just a burger place. The menu included breakfast stuff and we also had the best ice cream around. In fact, most people thought of *Ofarim's* as an ice cream shop. I guess that's because we had so many different kinds—over two dozen!

"Mind if I sit here?"

I looked up. It was Dane. Who else could it be? Except for Agnes, we were the only people in the restaurant. I motioned to the seat across from me with my head. I couldn't talk just then because my mouth was stuffed with burger and it would've been pretty gross if I'd opened it.

"So where ya live?" asked Dane.

"On a farm, just out of town. You?"

"Oh, I'm stayin' in town with someone for a while."

"So you're not from here?"

"Nah."

"I didn't think so. I've never seen you around before. I haven't seen you at school either, although I'm sure I haven't seen everyone there is to see."

"Big place, huh?"

"Not really, but it's hard to get to know everyone."

"You like workin' here?"

"Yeah. It's actually fun most of the time and I don't mind when it's not. Agnes is really cool, a lot of my friends come in, and the pay's pretty good too."

Agnes brought Dane's food out in near record time. Dane picked up a French fry, dipped it in catsup and slowly ate it. I noticed he'd switched from his usual meal. He had a foot-long hot dog instead.

"Get tired of the cheeseburgers?" I asked.

"Huh? Oh, no, I was just wanting somethin' long and hard." He raised an eyebrow at me.

I laughed. I was surprised he said something like that since he didn't really know me. I could see Brendan, Ethan, or Nathan saying it, but not someone I barely knew. Dane smiled.

I noticed as we ate and talked that Dane was always looking at me. I don't mean the way people usually look at someone else when they're talking to them, but something different. His gazes were just a little too long and sometimes he stared at my arms or chest. I thought that was a bit odd. There was sure nothing to look at there. I was no Brendan or Ethan. I could understand someone staring at their chests—*they* were built. I was just a skinny kid. Dane was probably just lost in thought at those times, though. It was most likely nothing.

I really began to wonder about Dane while he was eating his hot dog. He didn't just bite into it; he used his teeth to bite off the bun around the hot dog, leaving it bare. Then, he sucked the hot dog into his mouth, sometimes moving back and forth a few times, before taking a bite. I'd have thought it was another joke, but when he did it, Dane kinda gazed into my eyes as if speaking to me without words. It made me uncomfortable.

We talked more as we finished our meals, mostly about nothing in particular, but Dane asked a lot of questions.

"I think it's going to be a dead night," said Agnes from behind the counter, "so why don't you go ahead and take off, honey."

I looked back over my shoulder. "Okay, Agnes. Thanks."

I was just finishing up and so was Dane.

"Hey, you wanna go do somethin'? Just hang out in the park or walk around or somethin'?"

"Um…well, okay," I said. The truth was, I didn't really want to, but I'd already turned Dane down once and I didn't have much of an excuse. I would rather have gone back to the farm to help out, but an hour or so wouldn't hurt. Dane seemed kind of lonely, too. I knew what that was like. Before I met Brendan, I felt like I was the loneliest boy in the world. It wouldn't kill me to spend a little time with him. I didn't know much about him, but at least he was a good tipper.

Dane and I dumped our trays, and then walked outside. We crossed to the park and sat on a bench.

"So, you have a girlfriend?" asked Dane as he fidgeted.

"No. You?"

"Nah, not me. I'm not all that interested in girls, you know?"

Dane pulled out a pack of cigarettes.

"Want one?"

"No thanks."

He lit a cigarette and took a drag on it. I tried to avoid the smoke.

"So…" he said slowly, taking another drag. His voice quavered slightly.

"How long you going to be in town?" I asked, trying to keep the conversation going.

"I'm here for the rest of the summer, maybe longer. I'm not sure."

"You said you're staying with someone?"

"Yeah, with a friend of mine."

"Cool."

Our conversation was halting and awkward, skipping from one topic to the next. I wasn't all that interested and Dane…well, I didn't know what was up with him. He seemed kind of nervous.

"Did you know those boys?" he asked. "The ones that killed themselves last fall? My friend was telling me about it."

"No. I wasn't here then. They were friends of my friends, though. Most of them are still pretty torn up about it."

"Friends of your friends, huh?" asked Dane, as if it were significant.

"Yeah."

Dane kept glancing at me as he smoked. He was making me a little uncomfortable.

"How do you get your hair to lay like that?" he asked.

"I just…comb it," I said.

"I like the way it kind of feathers back."

"Thanks."

"It looks real good." Dane threw the butt of his cigarette down and ground it out with his heel. He took a roll of Certs out of his pocket and popped one into his mouth. He silently offered me one, but I passed.

"Let's walk," he said.

I followed Dane across the park. It was growing dark fast, but the light of a nearly full moon gave the air a kind of silvery look. It was pretty. We walked onto the trail at the edge on the park. It was darker under the trees where the moonlight didn't penetrate. It was still light enough to walk along the path, however, and the darkness made everything seem mysterious.

"So you don't have a girlfriend?" said Dane.

"No."

We were walking very slowly. Dane stopped and turned to me. He leaned in. Before I knew what he was doing, he'd pressed his lips to mine and kissed me. I pushed against his chest and turned my head.

"Dude, no," I said.

"Come on, man. I am right, aren't I?"

"What?"

"You know what I mean. You don't have a girlfriend, so…"

"Lots of guys don't have girlfriends," I said. "It doesn't mean anything."

"Do you want one?"

I didn't want to answer. It's not that I was ashamed of being gay or of having a boyfriend, but Dane was being too pushy and too nosy. I had a pretty good idea of what he wanted and he couldn't have it. I didn't want to encourage him in the least. I didn't want him thinking it was okay.

"That's not really your business."

"So that means *no*," said Dane. "I am right. Come on, man."

He grabbed me and pulled me to him. He kissed me on the lips again before I could push him away. Dane wasn't muscular, but he was still stronger than me. It was hard to wiggle out of his grasp.

"Don't do that!" I said loudly. "I don't want to kiss you!"

"Why not?"

"Because I have a boyfriend!"

"Ah!" he said, his face lighting up. I could see his expression change even in the dim light. "You are queer, aren't you?"

"Yeah I'm gay, but that doesn't mean I wanna kiss you."

"Ah, come on Casper, you know you like it."

With that, he grabbed me again. He kissed me on the mouth as I twisted and turned my head in an effort to keep him from doing so. He held both sides of my face and forced his tongue into my mouth as I struggled to push him away with my hands. He shifted his grip, encircling my back with one arm, while he ran the other down my chest. I fought against him, but he managed to hold me. He ran his hand down over my stomach, and then he groped me.

"Get off me!"

We toppled over as we struggled and Dane fell on me, nearly knocking the wind out of me. He pressed down against me. His hands were all over me and he kept kissing me on the mouth. I turned my head from side to side and struggled, but he was too strong for me.

"Come on, Casper. We can do this the easy way, or the hard way. You know you want it."

Something inside of me snapped and I went nuts. Memories of what my brother had done to me flooded my mind and I wasn't going to let it happen again. Dane had my arms pinned to my body pretty well, but I broke loose as he was groping me. I punched him in the face and then the chest. I just kept lashing out, hitting him wherever I could. He rolled away after I got him in the face again.

I jumped to my feet, holding my fists up. Dane was bigger than me, but he wasn't going to get me easy.

"I love it when you struggle," said Dane in a tone that frightened me.

He came toward me again. He grabbed for me. I saw my chance and brought my knee up as hard and fast as I could, smashing it right into Dane's nuts. He crumpled to the ground in pain, moaning and clutching himself.

"What did you do that for?" he asked between moans.

"I told you *no*," I said. "Do you understand what *no* means?"

"I'm sorry, man. I just thought…then, I…I'm sorry."

"Bull-shit!" I said, my voice trembling. I was angry and frightened.

"Dude, chill. I just thought you'd be into it. I got carried away. I didn't really do anything. You didn't have to kick me in the balls." Dane was still doubled over on the ground, but I kept my distance.

"You kissed me when I didn't want to be kissed," I shot back at him. "You forced your tongue into my mouth. You groped me. I'd call that doing something, especially when I was telling you to stop! You're a rapist!"

I was just about in tears.

"Dude, I…" Dane painfully stood, then took a step forward. I backed away.

"Stay away from me!" I yelled. I didn't care who heard. If he tried to lay his hands on me again, I was going to scream loud enough to bring the whole town running.

I backed away and then bolted toward the park. I didn't hear Dane follow. I was crying and trembling with fear. He hadn't really hurt me physically, but what he'd done was worse than that. I'd almost rather have been jumped and beaten. I forced myself to calm down and walk as I made it to the street lights. Dane didn't try to follow me. My fear began to ebb, although I was still shaking.

I sat on a park bench for a few moments, allowing my breath to slow. I'd had a narrow escape, but it was over. Even though I was still afraid, a small smile crept onto my lips. I was pleased with myself for fighting off Dane. I was proud of the way I'd handled the situation. Looking back, I knew I wasn't too bright for going into the woods with him, but at least I'd had the guts to fight him. He was bigger than me, but I stood up for myself anyway.

Once I had myself under control, I walked to the theatre. I'd stay with Nathan until quitting time and then we'd call and get a ride home. If Dane was waiting to jump me again, he'd have a hard time of it when Brendan or Ethan came to pick us up. I'd feel safer just being with Nathan. He'd help me if there was trouble. It was good to have friends.

Brendan

"I'm gonna rip him apart! What does he look like? What's his name? Where is he?"

"Brendan, calm down," said Casper.

I'd just come in from the fields a few minutes before to find Casper having a snack in the kitchen. Ethan had picked him and Nathan up from work while Jack and I finished up in the fields. Casper didn't tell me anything, until I'd returned to our room after a quick shower. He was sitting on the bed and I could tell something was up. He looked uncomfortable. When he'd started speaking, his words both frightened and angered me. I didn't like anyone messing with my boyfriend.

"Are you okay?" I asked as I pulled the towel from my waist and dried my hair some more.

Casper told me about the boy who'd tried to take advantage of him. I thought that kind of thing was in our past. I was furious.

"I handled it," said Casper. "I punched him in the face and then, when he came back at me, I nailed him in the nuts."

I couldn't help but smile. "Good for you."

I noticed then that Casper didn't seem so much scared as pleased with himself.

"I'm proud of you for standing up for yourself like that," I told him, allowing my anger to calm down a bit. "You did just the right thing, except for going into the woods with him. That was definitely a mistake."

"I know, I know. It was stupid. I've already jumped my own case for it. I didn't know he was gonna do something like that, but it was still dumb. I'll be more careful from now on."

"Good," I said. "You're too trusting sometimes, Casper. You've got to remember that not everyone is nice. There are guys like this, what was his name?"

"Dane."

"There are guys like this Dane and then there are others. People are going to find out you and I are gay before long and when they do, there could be trouble. Ethan said everyone at school is pretty cool with him and Nathan being gay, but there's always a few, you know? Someone might try to get you alone just to beat you up or something, so don't take chances."

"I won't, Brendan. I'm sorry."

"I'm sorry to lecture you, but I don't want you hurt. I couldn't stand that."

Casper hugged me around the middle. I hugged him back and mussed his hair.

"So you kicked his ass, huh?" I asked.

Casper giggled. "I wouldn't exactly say that, but he might be walking funny for a few days."

"Listen, Casper, I think you handled the situation well, but I'm still gonna track that punk down and let him know he can't try crap like that with my boyfriend."

Casper didn't say anything. He just hugged me harder. I was proud of Casper and pissed at Dane. I'd track that little bastard down as soon as I could and he wasn't gonna like it when I found him.

Dane

I quietly made my way back to Austin's place. I didn't see Casper anywhere. That didn't shock me, especially after the way he'd torn away from me. I'd really messed that up. He wasn't as easy a mark as I thought. I'd gotten carried away too, and it kind of frightened me. For the moment, I just didn't want to think about it. I had plenty of other stuff on my mind. I thought about what Boothe had told me about Austin. Should I ask him? I just couldn't believe it. Did Austin really do that? It fit with what I'd seen, but…ewwww.

I wondered if Austin would get pissed if I asked. I was intensely curious about it, however. I wanted to know anything and everything about Austin. He intrigued me. If what Boothe had said was true, maybe I could score with Austin. If he did it for money, maybe he'd be willing to do it with me. My virginity had to go, and soon. I'd failed with Casper so far, but I wasn't about to stop trying. Before the summer ended, I was going to get laid.

Damn! It was dark and it was *still* hot! I wondered what was up with the weather. I guess too hot was better than too cold. August in northern Indiana was rarely cold, but the nights could be downright chilly. I was kind of glad they weren't, even though I was getting tired of being sweaty practically twenty-four hours a day.

Austin wasn't there when I arrived—that was no surprise. He was gone more often than not. He seemed to follow no pattern or schedule. He slept at odd hours and I never knew where he was unless I was with him.

I lit the oil lamp and waited. I gazed through the window at the frightening house that was way too close for comfort. I swore I'd once heard screams coming from inside. I didn't dare investigate. My curiosity ended where my fear began. I'd rather not have been so near that old monstrosity, but what I had was better than nothing—way better, actually, because of Austin. Being near him was a thrill. One good thing about the heat was that he went shirtless all the time. I loved checking out his chest. Those muscles of his made me drool. When I looked at him, I just wanted to lick him.

I peeled off my shirt and looked at my own chest in a broken mirror. It wasn't easy to see myself by the light of the old lamp, but what I saw didn't please me. I didn't have any cool bulges in my pecs, shoulders, or arms the way the hot, built guys did—not like Austin and certainly not like the guy I'd seen in town, Ethan. He was ripped! I was pathetic beside him. I was a loser in the build department when compared with most guys. I wished I had a weight set or something. I couldn't stand not being built.

I dropped to the floor and did a few pushups. I collapsed on eight. I definitely needed to work out. At least I wasn't all pudgy and I was kinda cute. If I could only get my bod in shape, then I'd be able to score for sure. That would take time, however, and that's one thing that was short. Every second I went without sex was a hundred years. I needed it and I needed it now!

I sat in a rickety chair and waited while the minutes crawled by. Austin showed up a couple hours later. I'd dozed off waiting for him, even though it was not yet midnight. He pulled a wad of bills out of his jeans and tossed them on the table. It made me wonder. Where did he get his cash?

We engaged in idle chit-chat for a bit and then I steered toward more interesting topics.

"Austin…I was talking to Boothe today…"

"How is old Boothe?" asked Austin.

"Same as always."

"Horse's ass, huh?" laughed Austin.

"Yeah."

"He's sure a lot of fun, though."

"He told me something and I was wondering…"

Austin looked at me, his eyes shining in the dim light.

"Yeah?"

I looked at the cash on the table.

"Boothe said you sell your body." I waited for Austin's reaction, fearing anger. There was none.

"Yeah."

"Yeah? That's it?"

"I answered your question. What else is there?"

"But dude! That's…"

"It's what?"

"Nothin'."

"Damn straight, nothin'. What I do is my business."

"Why do you do it?" I asked quietly.

"I'd think that's obvious. Look, there ain't shit around here. I could work in some factory maybe or some fast food joint for minimum wage, but I don't want that life. I saw my dad waste his freakin' life workin' for someone else and gettin' paid nothin' for it. My life's not gonna be like that. I can turn a trick every few days and get by. It's fast, it's easy, and sometimes I even like it."

"Is that what you're going to do with your life?" I asked.

"Fuck, no! As soon as I can afford it, I'm outta this shitty little town. I'm going to Chicago, or New York, or maybe Los Angeles. That's where the real money's made. Instead of $50 an hour, I can get $250 or more. I was thinking about getting into porn movies. I hear that pays *big*."

I didn't want to hear what he was saying. I wanted Austin to be something more than that. I liked him. I'd been thinking dreamy thoughts about him maybe being my boyfriend, but what kind of boyfriend would he make when he sold his body all the time?

"Don't you feel kinda…gross, letting women you don't even know touch you?"

Austin rolled his eyes.

"Most of them aren't women."

"You mean…guys?"

"Duh! Yeah! Not many women are willing to pay. Too many boys will give it up for free—horny little bastards. Guys'll pay, though. They can't get a guy like me easy, so they'll fork over the cash."

Boothe had told me Austin sold himself to men, but I hadn't believed him. Now I guess I had to acknowledge it was true. But I was torn. On the one hand, I didn't like Austin selling his body. On the other, the fact that he sold himself to guys gave me hope that I could get into his pants. I'd been hoping for that before, but my chances seemed improved.

"There are a few women who pay. Like Mrs. Wheeler. She's divorced and needs a man now and then, but doesn't want one around too often. Then there's Mrs. Keller. Her husband can't get it up and she loves younger men, so I take care of her and she pays me in cash. Nice arrangement, huh? Most are guys, though. I could tell you some stories."

"That's okay," I said. Part of me wanted to hear, but part of me had already heard too much.

"You oughtta give it a try."

"Huh?"

"You're not half-bad lookin'. I know some guys that'd pay. I've got a regular in town who's always asking if I can find another guy and he likes 'em young. We might pry more than the usual $50 out of him. I bet we could get $75, maybe $100 each."

"No thanks, dude."

"It's up to you. If you change your mind, just lemme know. I imagine you'll be getting short of money soon."

That was certainly true. I'd brought over a hundred bucks with me, but it was about gone. I had no idea I'd spend it so fast. I wasn't going to sell my body, though. No way!

***

Oh Fuck, I thought to myself as a tall, muscular guy, maybe a year or two older than me, came stomping straight toward me. He was handsome, but obviously pissed off about something. I was sitting on a bench in the park when I looked up and saw him making for me, like an angry bull seconds from charging. I sat there frozen, unable to move. I wanted to run for my life, but I couldn't get my body to function. In seconds, he was standing in front me, a broad-shouldered, shirtless jock. His muscles rippled as his fists clenched and unclenched. I knew I was gonna get my ass kicked, although I wasn't quite sure why.

"I'm Casper's boyfriend."

Uh oh! Who would've guessed that little shit would have a boyfriend who was a mass of flexing muscle? I swallowed. "Hey, man, listen…"

He grabbed me by the front of the shirt and jerked me off the bench. He held me up with one arm. My legs dangled in the air.

"You keep your hands off Casper! You don't touch him! You don't even look at him like you'd like to touch him! He's been through enough shit already without some dumb-ass punk like you trying to take advantage of him! You understand me?"

"Yes, sir," I stammered. Casper's infuriated boyfriend wasn't much older than me, but he was way bigger and stronger. I knew he could do anything to me he wanted and I was scared shitless.

"If you *ever* give him any trouble again, I'll kick your ass! Is that clear?"

"Yes, sir."

He dropped me back onto the bench, still looking as if he'd like to beat me senseless. He was steaming. I had the feeling he was using every ounce of control he had not to pound me. I wasn't quite sure why he was holding back, but I was sure glad he was.

"Listen, dude," I said. "I'm sorry about Casper. I really am. I didn't mean to…well, things just got out of hand. I wouldn't have…well, I'm just sorry."

He took a deep breath, calming just a fraction.

"I love Casper very much. If you don't cause him any trouble, you'll have no reason to fear me, but if you touch him…"

"I understand."

"Okay, we're through here then."

He turned on his heel and walked off the way he'd come. Only then did I look down and realize I'd pissed my shorts. *Shit.* I got up and quickly made my way to the trail that goes into the woods. I didn't want to meet anyone until the evidence had dried. I was embarrassed. I felt like a little kid. I took a few deep breaths to try and calm myself. I was still trembling.

I thought about what had happened with Casper. I wasn't lying; I didn't intend for things to go quite so far. Well, maybe I did, but I wouldn't have taken them much further. I hadn't expected Casper to fight like that. I figured he'd submit. I figured that once I got him going, he'd be into it. Or, he'd at least let me do what I wanted out of fear. I wouldn't have actually forced him. *Fuck.* I never dreamed he had a boyfriend like that. Whoa. Casper's boyfriend was the kind of guy I dreamed about. I must admit that even though I was scared shitless, I kinda got off on him threatening me. I'd always had this fantasy…no, that was just a little too fucked up to think about.

You're okay, Dane. You're safe. It's over, I thought to myself. That was sure one narrow escape. I needed to be real careful to make sure nothing like that happened again. I sure didn't want to get my ass kicked. I definitely needed to mark Casper off my list of potential candidates for sex. He was just too risky.

Ethan

I rubbed my hands on my jeans, wiping off the sweat that made them nearly too slick to hold the handle of the shovel. I took a breather. I loved hot weather, but when the temperature topped 100, even I withered. My hair was dripping with sweat and perspiration ran down my torso in little streams. My breath came faster than it should've. It was that kind of day when it was wise to take it slow. Even young guys could have a heat stroke.

I watched Brendan as he dug away at the hard earth. His naked torso glistened in the sun. His powerful muscles tensed and flexed. I'd always thought of the male body as a work of art, and Brendan was truly beautiful. His chest, abs, arms, back, and shoulders looked as if they could've been sculpted by Michelangelo himself.

I looked away guiltily. I thought I'd overcome this on that day weeks ago, when Brendan and I had stood by the barn, nearly touching our lips together. I felt a raging fire within myself then. I had *wanted* Brendan. I'd been consumed with lust for his hard, tight body. I was drawn to him as if by some unknown, but virtually irresistible force. I'd resisted it, though. Just when I was about to kiss Brendan and launch myself at him, I thought of Nathan and how very much I loved him. Brendan's mind had turned to his boyfriend at that moment, too. He told me so moments after we'd *almost* kissed. We'd come perilously close to cheating on those we loved, but at the last moment, that love saved us. Why was I tempted again now?

I thought of Casper. He'd seen us from the loft on that day long ago. He wasn't spying, but he'd heard our voices and looked out a crack just when Brendan and I nearly succumbed to temptation. If we'd failed, Casper would've known. There would've been no hiding it from him or Nathan. What damage would that have caused?

I knew Casper saw us because Brendan told me as much later. He'd confessed to him not knowing Casper had seen. Casper forgave him. I confessed to Nathan, too. It was something I just couldn't hide from him. Nathan went so far as to tell me there was nothing to forgive. We were all glad that our love had seen us through the temptation. The love we each felt for the other was now much stronger for having weathered that test of our faithfulness.

Damn it! Why was I gazing at Brendan with lust filled eyes? Was Nathan not enough for me? Did I need someone bigger and stronger? Nathan met all my emotional needs, but was there some untamed part of me that had physical desires that were not met?

I rubbed my temple as if I had a headache. If only I could just squeeze my lust-filled thoughts of Brendan out of my head. It wasn't supposed to be this way. I loved Nathan—I truly did. I wasn't supposed to be thinking about other guys. What was wrong with me? Was I such a sex-crazed maniac that I couldn't get enough from my boyfriend? Is that what made my eyes rove? My lust both sickened and excited me. I wanted everything to be perfect, but I felt myself drawn toward destruction.

"Are you okay?" asked Brendan.

I was so lost in thought I'd nearly forgotten he was standing near.

"I was just…thinking. I was just worrying about whether or not we're going to make it," I lied.

"We'll be okay, Ethan. Just you wait and see."

"Yeah, I'm sure you're right. Why don't you take a break and let me dig. We shouldn't go at it too hard in this heat. In fact, would you mind going up to the house and bringing us back a gallon of cold water? I feel like I've sweat out ten pounds."

Brendan smiled. He made me want to…no, I wouldn't think it.

"I'll be right back," he said.

"Don't hurry. Take your time. I'm going to take it easy myself. It won't help matters if one of us keels over with a heat stroke."

Brendan walked slowly toward the farmhouse. I was glad to be alone for a while. I needed some time to think without the distraction of Brendan's body. I wondered what I should do about the yearning lust I had for him. Should I bottle it up and keep it hidden? Should I reveal it to Brendan so he could help me deal with it? Or, should I discuss it with Nathan?

Each possibility seemed fraught with danger. If I kept my lustful thoughts to myself, they might gain control of me. I might try something with Brendan in a moment of weakness and who knew if he'd be able to resist? If I talked to Brendan about it, I might discover that he wanted me just as badly. What would we do then? What might that lead to? And, if I discussed it with Nathan, what would be the outcome? Would he be angry? Hurt? Maybe he'd be able to help me, but maybe not. I didn't want to risk hurting him and yet it seemed that would happen no matter what course I chose to tread.

Damn it! Why did such a small part of me control so much? Sometimes I felt like my dick did all my thinking for me. It made me feel weak and pathetic, yet powerful and strong.

I wondered how long it would take Brendan to make it back. I looked down at the bulge in my jeans. I was so aroused I felt like my manhood was going to rip right through the worn material. I felt the need to release some tension, but I was out in the open and Brendan might return far too soon. I decided against the idea. I'd just have to suffer. It was my penance for thinking thoughts I shouldn't be thinking.

Casper

Dane didn't show up at *Ofarim's* the day after he'd attacked me. If he did, I'd planned to be professional and polite—nothing more or less. He was a customer after all. Outside of *Ofarim's* was a different matter, but inside I worked for Agnes and wasn't going to allow my personal life to affect her business.

Brendan was going to pay Dane a little visit. It was mid-afternoon now, so I assumed he'd already done so. He was furious when I told him what Dane had tried with me. He was proud of the way I'd stood up for myself. I was rather pleased with myself about that, as well. Dane was bigger than me, but I hadn't been a victim. I'd fought back. He could've likely overpowered me if he wanted, but I'd put up a fight and he'd eventually backed off. Maybe I could've even beaten him in a fight if he just kept coming back at me. Who knows? I was pretty sure he wouldn't try anything like that again, especially after Brendan got done with him. I hoped Brendan didn't do anything that would get him in trouble. To be honest, I wouldn't mind him beating up Dane—he deserved it. I didn't want Brendan getting in hot water over it, though. I was a little worried about Brendan. He was a bit of a hothead when he got upset and he was pissed when I told him about Dane. Hopefully, he'd had time to cool off.

Dane made me think of my brother, Jason. They were kind of alike. Dane had tried to take what he wanted from me. He'd tried to make me submit my body to him. Jason had done it. I shuddered at the memory. Things like that didn't go away. Sometimes, I would awaken during the night quaking with fear, as if I were back home in Kentucky, ears straining for any sign that my brother might be coming to get me. That's when I clung to Brendan and he wrapped his arms around me tightly even in his sleep. Sometimes, I woke up crying and then Brendan would awaken and hold me and kiss me until I felt safe again.

Jason was locked up in the *Cloverdale Center* receiving treatment. It was worse than prison, which is what awaited him if his treatment ever ended. After what Brendan had told me about the place, I doubted it ever would. They'd just keep him there, tormenting him and messing him up further with drugs, until the years of his sentence were over. I pitied him in a way, even though he'd done unspeakable things to me and had tried to do worse. On the other hand, he deserved the treatment he was getting. He'd done it to himself. At least I was safe from him, but there were others like him—guys like Dane. I wondered what he'd have done to me if I hadn't fought back.

The day was fine and hot, and I pushed all dark thoughts from my mind. I was safe. I had a boyfriend who loved me and protected me. He was strong enough to do a good job of it, too. We weren't alone, either. Ethan and Nathan would come running if we needed them, just as we'd be there for them. I was safer than I'd been in my entire life. Instead of being alone, afraid, and in con-stant danger of being on the receiving end of a beating, I had friends who looked out for me and the best boyfriend in all the world. I also had a great place to live and a job I enjoyed. Who could ask for more?

The bells on the door rang and I looked up to see Casey Hendricks enter. I smiled. She was one of the few girls I knew at school and was probably the friendliest I'd ever met in my life. She reminded me a little of my friend, Stacey, from Kentucky.

"Casper!" she said. "I didn't know you worked here!"

"I haven't for very long."

"I bet Agnes hired you because you're such a cutie. I bet all the girls will be coming in once they find out you're here. Agnes is a marketing genius."

"She hired me for my *talent*," I said, with mock seriousness. "I'm more than just a pretty face."

Casey laughed. "Well, you sure are pretty, Casper. I mean handsome."

I smiled and shook my head. I'd missed Casey since school let out. She was the first friend I'd made all on my own in Verona. All the others before her were "hand-me-downs" from Ethan and Nathan, for lack of a better way to put it. I liked their friends to be sure, but it made me feel good to make my own.

I brought Casey a glass of ice-water. "You ready to order?"

"No, I'm waiting for Shawn Myer."

"He's the tall jock that always wears the letter jacket?"

"Yeah, he plays football."

"This mean you aren't with Devon anymore?"

"Oh please, that lasted two days! I must've been out of my freaking mind." Casey looked to the back of the restaurant, then yelled, "Hey, Agnes! You mind if I borrow your boy for a minute?"

"Nah, he's all yours Casey."

Casey grabbed my arm and pulled me into the seat across from her.

"Let me tell you about Devon," she said. "You were right when you warned me about him. He was a jerk. You know what he did?"

"No."

"He took me out parking. We were just talking and then without so much as a hug or a kiss beforehand, he pulled out his, um...you know and said, '*Suck it, baby!*' Talk about lack of foreplay." Casey giggled. My eyes grew wide.

"What did you do?"

"I told him I'd suck it when he got a real one. I swear, Casper, he was hard and it wasn't even four inches long."

"It couldn't have happened to a more deserving guy," I said, loving the idea that Devon was stuck with a tiny pecker. We both giggled.

"That pissed him off and he acted like he was going to hit me, but I slapped his face and got out of the car. That was the end of him."

"I'm glad," I said. "I mean, I'm glad you dumped him. He's bad news."

"Yeah, I should have my head examined for even *thinking* of going out with him. I'd heard rumors about some crap he'd pulled, but I thought there was nothing to it. Now, I'm not so sure."

"The rumors are true," I said quietly. Ethan and Nathan had told Brendan and me all about what Devon had done to them and what he'd done to their friends, Mark and Taylor. Devon was one sick, twisted dude.

"Then, I *really* should've avoided him," said Casey.

"But you've got...um...Shawn now."

"Yeah and he's sweet and kind—nothing like Devon."

"How long you two been going out?"

"Just a few days and he hasn't once tried anything with me."

"Hasn't whipped it out and asked you to suck it, huh?" I laughed.

"Not once," giggled Casey. "So," she said, changing the topic, "how are all those gorgeous guys you live with out on the farm?"

"Working hard," I said.

"That Ethan has a fine bod—so does your buddy, Brendan." Casey winked at me just then. Did she know more than I thought or did she just guess? Ethan and Nathan were out at school. Brendan and I weren't, but we didn't really try to keep things a secret either.

"Of course," continued Casey, "you and Nathan are little blond cuties. The girls would be all over Nathan I bet, if he liked girls."

"Yeah, they probably would."

Casey stopped short of asking me anything personal, although I could tell it was on her mind. I was glad, but I wouldn't have minded telling her about Brendan and me. It might even be cool to have someone to talk to about us, besides Ethan and Nathan. Shawn came in just then and I gave him my seat. He was very polite to me. I liked that. He was a jock, but he didn't act like a jerk the way some jocks did. Of course, Brendan and Ethan were jocks too and so were most of Ethan's friends and most of Brendan's back in Kentucky. Most every jock I knew was cool. Maybe the stereotype about them being jerks was wrong. I didn't know about that, though—I'd run across some of the jerks, too. I guess just like people in general, some of them were cool, while others were assholes.

I took their orders then went back to help Agnes get everything ready. I was glad Casey was with Shawn. He seemed like a nice guy. I could see why she'd be attracted to him. He was tall, dark, and handsome. He wasn't as hot as my boyfriend, but he was good enough looking. Besides, there was more to a relationship than looks. Thank God for that, otherwise Brendan might not be interested in me. I knew I had a decent face, but I sure didn't have a good body. I hadn't been called *Casper The Friendly Runt* back at my old school for nothing. I hoped that nickname didn't get started up in Verona. So far, I'd lucked out, but you never knew when something like that might happen.

Brendan

Ethan and I stepped through the back door into the kitchen. It was nearly two and we still hadn't had lunch. Sometimes we got going on something and just couldn't, or wouldn't stop. Jack was already sitting at the table, eating cold chicken and potato salad. We washed up at the kitchen sink, grabbed plates from the cabinet, and sat down near him.

"I'm glad you boys came in. There's something I wanted to talk to you about," said Jack.

"Yeah, Uncle Jack?" said Ethan, as both of us helped ourselves to chicken and potato salad.

"Would you boys like some iced tea with that?" asked Ardelene.

"I sure would," I said, "but I can get it."

"Me too," said Ethan.

"Nonsense, you sit down and eat. I'll get it."

"Thanks, Ardelene."

I loved Ardelene. She was Casper's grandma, but I felt like she was my own.

"School will be starting up again next week and I wanted to talk to you two about your sports."

Here it comes, I thought. There was no way either Ethan or I could participate in sports. There was too much work to do on the farm. I'd already resigned myself to it. School was sure coming up fast. I'd almost forgotten about it.

"It's okay, Jack," said Ethan. "You don't have to talk to us about it. We both know we won't be able to be on teams this year. I had a great wrestling season last year and I'll just be happy with that."

"But, I think you should wrestle again this year," said Jack. "And, Brendan, I'm sure you want to get out on that football field again."

Ethan looked much as I felt—shocked, happy, sad, and bewildered all at once.

"But, Jack, the farm…" said Ethan. "We're already going to be in school *all* day. There's no way we can get everything done if…"

"Listen, I've been doing a lot of thinking on this," said Jack. "With this drought, there isn't going to be as much work to do. I wish the fields were loaded up with crops to be harvested, but that just isn't the way it is. You two are gonna have to put in some late hours and work most of the weekends, but I think we can do this."

I didn't know what to say. Neither did Ethan. He'd told me how he'd had to talk his uncle into letting him be on the wrestling team each and every year and now here was Jack, convincing him to join wrestling, and me football.

"You know I want to wrestle this year so bad I can taste it," said Ethan, "but, I just don't know…the farm's gotta come first."

I reluctantly agreed with him, and I felt like crying. It was cruel to have football dangled out in front of me when I couldn't have it. It was doubly hard to want football so much and to have Jack insist I play. But I knew it just wasn't practical. Life was just cruel sometimes, I guess.

"Boys, listen," said Jack, "you've got to live life as you go along. You've got to squeeze every bit of enjoyment you can out of it. If you don't, then it's not worth living anyway. Now, you're both big boys—men, but I'm putting my foot down." He looked Ethan straight in the eyes. "You are going to wrestle this year. And you," he said, turning to me, "are going to play football. That's all there is to it—end of discussion."

Ardelene was smiling as she leaned against the kitchen counter. Jack himself gave no hint of his emotions, but then that didn't mean a thing. I had little doubt he was smiling on the inside. Ethan grinned. He looked so happy he was about to cry. I felt much the same myself. I couldn't believe it. I was gonna play football!

Dane

"Who's that?" I asked Austin, as the guy I'd seen at the farm store drove by in a pickup.

"That," said Austin, "is Ethan, one of the town queers. He's also a bad-ass wrestler and one of the toughest guys around, so no one fucks with him."

"He's a queer?" It didn't seem at all likely. I'd never seen a boy built that well before. I thought queers were supposed to be weak.

"Oh yeah, he has a little boyfriend and everything. You should see them together."

"Boyfriend, huh?" A wicked thought popped into my head. "So is his boyfriend his bitch or what?"

"Nah, it's not like that. They're ape-shit over each other. It's kind of mushy, really."

I smiled. I felt a stirring in my shorts. Maybe I could not only end my virginity, but get it on with one of the hottest guys around. I had to think on it, though. What I had in mind could be dangerous. If it went wrong I could get my ass kicked. *It just might be worth the risk*, I thought to myself. If I could get my hands on Ethan, I'd be willing to chance a beating. My mind raced with possibilities, plans, and dangers.

We stood for several moments without speaking. Finally, my stomach rumbled and broke the silence.

"You want to go get something to eat?" asked Austin.

"I can't," I said. "I'm just about broke."

"I'll spot you this time," said Austin, "but you're gonna have to do something to make some money soon." He leveled his gaze at me and I felt uncomfortable.

We crossed the street to *Ofarim's*, increasing my discomfort. Casper looked up as we entered. His eyes were wary, but unafraid. *Yeah*, I thought, *you know your big, bad-ass boyfriend threatened to kick my head in if I touched you again. If it wasn't for him…*

We sat at a booth far away from the counter. Casper looked me in the eyes as I ordered, but he didn't say anything. I didn't either. I didn't want to give his boyfriend any excuse to come after me. When he came back with our drinks, I didn't even look at him.

"You given any thought to what I suggested?" asked Austin. "You're gonna need some cash soon and I could set you up with one of my nicer clients. I know a guy who…"

"I don't wanna do that," I said.

"I know you don't. The question is—will you?"

I was silent for a moment before I said, "No."

"Then I don't know what you're gonna do, buddy. I'm not payin' your way. I don't know of anything…unless…"

"What?"

"Maybe you could help out Boothe for some cash."

"Boothe? Yeah, right!" I didn't mean for my dislike of him to come out into the open that way. I adjusted my attitude before I pissed off Austin. "So what's he do, anyway?"

"What do you think he does?"

"My guess would be he's a drug dealer."

"No. Well, not anymore," said Austin. "He's found a more lucrative business."

"What?"

"Grave robbing."

"Grave robbing?" I nearly choked on my Coke. "You're shitting me, right?"

"Nope."

"You mean he…like…digs up dead people and…"

"Robs them blind, so to speak."

"That's sick."

"Hey, I'm not sayin' whether it's good or bad. I'm just tellin' you about an opportunity. He's asked me to help out in the past, but I have easier ways to make cash."

"So, um, not that I'm interested, but what would I have to do?"

"You'll have to ask Booth about the particulars, but mainly you'd be digging. They bury people deep, you know and it takes a while to get to 'em." I wrinkled my nose. "Hey, if you don't wanna do that, you can always join me, or maybe you can get a nice minimum wage job somewhere."

"Fuck that."

"Then maybe you ought to go check and see if Boothe will take you on. He offered me $50 per grave."

We hushed up as Casper came with our burgers and fries. My stomach rumbled again and I dug in. I wasn't in the least thrilled with robbing graves or working for Boothe, but I didn't like the idea of going hungry either. I had to make some cash somehow and working for Boothe seemed like the easiest way to do it without selling my body.

"Where can I find him?" I asked when we were half finished with our meal.

"You're in luck. Tonight I think he's digging at the old cemetery just to the north of town."

"You're not just screwing with me, are you?" I asked. "This isn't some trick to get me into a graveyard and then scare the crap outta me, is it?"

"If I wanted to scare you, I have a lot easier ways than *that* to do it," said Austin. His tone frightened me. "So, you want to check it out?"

"Yeah," I said finally. "I gotta eat somehow."

***

"Graveyards give me the creeps," I said, as we waded through tall grass toward a clump of trees.

"There ain't nothin' to fear, man. They're already dead. It's the living that'll get you," said Austin. I was sure there was truth in that, but it didn't calm my fears. My heart pounded in my chest like I'd been running.

"Are we there yet?" I asked.

"If we were, we wouldn't still be walking, now would we? '*Are we there yet?*' You sound like a little kid on a family vacation."

Sometimes, I just wanted to spit on Austin, but mostly, I wanted to lick him. I giggled.

"What's so funny?"

"Nothin'."

As we neared the clump of trees, I could just make out a dim light. We took a few steps more and Austin called out, "Boothe, it's me, Austin." There was silence for a few moments.

"I'm over here, man."

We followed the sound of the voice into an old, old cemetery. There were only about two dozen or so tombstones, from what I could make out in the dim light. There was no fence or gate and the whole place was overgrown and forgotten. Likely as not, no one had been buried there in a hundred years.

"I brought a possible employee for you," said Austin, when Boothe's features became visible in the light of a Coleman lamp.

"Him?" he asked, indicating me, as if the thought were ridiculous.

"Yeah, you're always saying you need help and it's not like you can place a 'help wanted' ad."

"Neither can you, buddy," said Booth. They both laughed.

"You squeamish?" asked Boothe, turning to me.

"No." I wasn't sure if that was the truth or not.

"You're kind of puny. Think you can do some serious digging?"

"I'm not puny and yes."

I looked over at a large mound of fresh earth. It sure did take a lot of digging to get down to a coffin. Boothe looked me over, as if sizing up a piece of beef.

"I'll pay you $40 per casket we open up."

"Forty? You offered Austin fifty!"

"Yeah, well, Austin's got some biceps, man. He can do some serious digging. You…well, we'll just see what you can do."

"Okay," I said, none too happy. I didn't care for Boothe and I didn't like hanging out in a graveyard at night or doing physical labor. There wasn't much of an alternative, though.

"I'm such a nice guy I'll even pay you for tonight, even though I've already done a lot of the digging."

He handed me the shovel. "Now, get in there and dig, boy."

I wanted to smack the shit out of him. He never passed up a chance to put me down. As I took the shovel and dropped down into the hole, I indulged myself with the vision of Boothe tied to a tree, begging me to let him go, while I punched him in the gut.

It was a little freaky in the hole, knowing I was inside an actual grave. The shovel bit into the earth and I tossed the dirt up and out. The lantern cast a shaft of light over half of the hole, illuminating the worms wiggling out of the dark earth. I was sweaty in no time at all, even though it was the middle of the night. I wasn't used to digging and it made my muscles ache, but I wasn't about to complain. I wouldn't give Boothe the satisfaction. Damn, it smelled funny in the hole. I tried not to think about what I might be smelling.

Austin departed and Boothe stood over the grave. "Put your back into it, boy. We don't have all night."

The more I spent time with Boothe, the less I liked him. I'd already worked my way up to loathing him. When we had arrived, he'd climbed out of the hole, shirtless and sweaty. The sight of a shirtless guy was usually enough to make my nads ache with desire, but I didn't feel that with Boothe. He had a nice chest. He wasn't real built, but he had some hard muscle. If it'd been any other boy, I'd have been drooling, but it was different with Boothe. He was probably the one young guy I didn't want to get it on with. The only way I'd do it with him was if he was tied up and at my mercy. Then I'd have some fun. I laughed.

"You are a weird little boy," said Boothe, from above.

"That means a lot coming from someone who plays with dead bodies," I shot back.

"I don't play with them, you sick little fuck, I rob 'em. I ain't no necro...necro...damn it. I'm not one of those people who do stuff with dead people."

I grinned. Boothe was definitely not the sharpest tool in the shed. "*Necrophiliac* is the word," I said out loud, then "You dumb fuck," under my breath.

"It figures you'd know." Boothe laughed so hard I thought he might fall in on top of me. "That's probably the only way you can get laid."

"Shut up!" I shouted.

"Not so loud, boy. We don't want anyone coming up here. This isn't strictly legal, you know."

"It's not legal at all."

"Well, you're involved, so keep your trap shut. You'll be in as much shit as me if we get caught."

I kept digging for what seemed like hours, but was probably much less. Finally, I heard the shovel hit something solid and hollow sounding. My instinct was to bolt right out of the hole, but it was now so deep I could just barely grip the edge.

"Come on up outta there," said Boothe. "I'll finish."

I accepted a hand up, even though I didn't like him touching me. Boothe hopped down in the hole. I wondered if he'd be able to get back out if I started pushing dirt in on top of him as fast as I could. It was a nice little fantasy anyway.

"We're lucky tonight. A lot of 'em are buried deeper. Some of these real old graves are kinda shallow, though. The old ones are good because they aren't in big cement crypts either, although there's ways to get into those without too much trouble."

I could hear him digging and scraping around. Suddenly, I heard the eerie and unmistakable sound of a coffin lid being opened. I couldn't resist the urge to pick up a flashlight and peer down into the grave to get a good look.

My heart jumped in my chest, even though the sight below wasn't nearly as frightening as I'd expected. Instead of a rotting corpse, there was only a skeleton in a plain wooden coffin. As I peered closer, I saw traces of hair fallen from the skull, but whether the deceased was male or female, I couldn't tell.

"Jackpot," said Boothe as he held up a gold ring. He reached down into the coffin again and I heard him rummaging around. Moments later he stood, a gold locket on a chain in his hand. The skeleton's head had rolled to the side.

I gave Boothe a hand up. He seemed pleased. He was almost nice to me.

"Sometimes, all the digging is for nothin'. That totally blows. But this stuff," he said, waving his handful of gold, "will bring in a pretty penny."

"Where d'you sell it?"

"Antique shops, usually. There's one here in town and more not far off. I give 'em some story about my great aunt or someone biting it and leaving me stuff. Now, help me push the dirt back in."

Refilling the grave was a lot easier than digging it out. Boothe used the shovel while I pushed in dirt with my hands. It only took a few minutes to fill the grave. We weren't quite done, however. Boothe bent over and grabbed a wad of grass from a small mound I hadn't noticed before and carefully placed it over the grave. I helped him put the irregular chunks of grass covered dirt in place while he explained.

"I'm real careful removing the grass on top so I can put it back in place. This way, it's hard to tell the grave has been disturbed. After a rain, it'll be impossible to tell. If people catch on to the fact that graves are bein' robbed, my job will be much harder. As it is, no one even suspects."

We finished and Boothe reached into his pocket and pulled out two twenties. "Here ya go, boy. I'll let you know when I need you again."

With that he turned and walked away as if he had no further interest in me. I followed quickly, because I didn't want to hang around that old cemetery alone, especially since we'd just violated a grave. I wasn't all that superstitious, but there was no reason to take chances.

I wondered how much Boothe would get for the ring and locket—probably a shit-load, while I only got $40. It sure as hell beat selling myself to some disgusting old guy like Austin did, though. If I was careful, my pay for the night could last quite a while.

I wearily made my way back to Austin's place. He wasn't there. I didn't care. I was past caring, too tired to even undress before I threw myself down and went fast asleep.

Ethan

Brendan and I struggled to get the kitchen table through the back door. Once we'd managed it, the rest was easy. We carried it off the small, concrete porch and set it down under the shade of a massive maple. Nathan was filling coolers full of ice, while Casper and Dave were setting out stacks of paper cups and plates. A large grill sat at the ready, filled with charcoal waiting to be lit. It was August 21st, Mark and Taylor's birthday, and we were waiting for the guests to arrive.

Mark and Taylor were my friends. They were gay boys just like me. Only a few months before, on November 3, 1980, they both died. At Christmas, I unwrapped a gift Mark had sent me just before his death. Inside, among other things, was an envelope stuffed with cash. Mark instructed me to use at least some of it for something fun, so one of the things I'd decided to do was have a big party on Mark and Tay's birthday, which just happened to be exactly the same day. The party was really Nathan's idea and it was a good one. I was sure Mark and Taylor would've approved.

I went back in the kitchen where Ardelene was putting the finishing touches on a giant round cake. It was chocolate, Mark's favorite, with white icing and purple sprinkles. Ardelene was writing *Happy Birthday Mark and Taylor* on top.

"Thanks, Ardelene," I said, giving her a hug. She was so sweet to make a cake for the party. She hadn't even known Mark and Tay, although I'd told her their story and it brought tears to her eyes.

Ardelene just smiled and nodded and hugged me back. I was so glad she'd married Uncle Jack. I was happy for him to have someone at last, but I was happy for selfish reasons, too. Ardelene was now my aunt by marriage, but she was even more than that. She felt like a favorite aunt, or a grandma. She added a special touch to the farmhouse, too—mainly little things, like sweet peas in a vase decorating the table or new curtains in the kitchen windows. And then there was her baking. Ardelene was forever making a blackberry pie, a peach cobbler, yeast rolls, or a chocolate cake like today. It was a little bit like having my mom back.

Brandon stepped through the back door and into the kitchen. He nodded at me, and then crossed the small space between us and hugged me tight. When he stepped back, his eyes were watery. Brandon had been Mark's best friend and the loss hit him hard. Sometimes, Brandon came and we talked about it, sharing our pain. Oddly enough, it was Mark's death that'd brought us closer together. I was friends with Brandon before, but our shared grief cemented us together forever.

Brandon smiled at me. He knew this wasn't a day of grief. Mark and Tay's friends were here to have fun. That's what they would've wanted, so that's the way it was gonna be.

"Anything I can help with?" asked Brandon.

"Yeah, you can help me carry out the drinks."

We grabbed cases of Cokes, A&W Root Beer, 7-UP, and Orange Crush and carried them outside. Brandon and Nathan started dumping them in the coolers, while I went to fire up the grill.

People started coming in and the crowd slowly grew. I'd invited all of Mark and Taylor's friends. Jon was there, of course, as well as a lot of guys from the soccer team. Steve came with his girl and Jennifer, Brandon's girlfriend, came in with Andrea, a girl who'd been after both Mark and Tay before she found out they were gay. There were lots of others—I'd say some forty people or more.

Brandon brought an older lady over to me as I was setting out more bags of chips. "Ethan, I'd like you to meet someone. This is Mark's aunt, Anne Hertwig."

I smiled and reached out to shake her hand, but she hugged me instead.

"Thanks for inviting me," she said.

"I thought you should be here." Brandon had told me how supportive she was of Mark, Taylor, and their relationship.

Just about everyone at the party was in their teens, but of course Jack and Ardelene were there, so Anne had people to talk to. She got on especially well with Ardelene.

The party was a blast. Everyone mostly stood around talking and eating, but there was dancing, too. A boom box supplied us with music in the front yard and the grass under the giant maple trees became a dance floor. There were also *Monopoly*, *Life*, and card games going on and it was all a lot of fun.

Casper introduced me to his friend, Casey. I sort of knew her from school, but not very well. He also introduced Agnes, his boss and the owner of *Ofarim's*. I knew her pretty well from all the times I'd eaten there over the years. Agnes had actually closed down *Ofarim's* for the afternoon and evening so she and Casper could be at the party.

Ardelene brought out the cake with seventeen candles on it. Both Mark and Taylor would've been seventeen today. I tried not to cry while everyone was singing, *Happy Birthday*, but it was hard. I noticed a lot of people had watery eyes. Some of the girls were sobbing.

After the cake and ice cream, we got up a soccer game. It seemed appropriate since both Mark and Taylor had been soccer players. As we played, I couldn't help but think about my friends; Mark who was a terror on the field when he lived and Taylor with his flowing blond hair. God, he was beautiful. It just wasn't right that they'd died. Tears welled up in my eyes until I couldn't see to play. I just couldn't help it. Brandon and I ended up standing by our makeshift soccer goal, leaning on each other and bawling our eyes out. No one made fun of us. They knew why we cried.

Mostly, it was a fun day. The party was a blast. It didn't break up until late that night. We didn't get any work done, of course, but that didn't matter. This day was important.

***

I was driving into town in the old pickup, heading for the farm store yet again, when the boy I'd met a couple days or so before flagged me down.

"Can I get a ride?" he asked, as he stuck his head in the open window.

"Sure, but I'm just going to *Wahlberg's*. It won't be much of a ride."

"That's okay," he said, hopping in and slamming the door. "I really just wanted to talk to you anyway."

"Oh? Um…I'm sorry, but I've forgotten your name."

"Dane."

"Yeah, that's right. Don't be offended, I'm terrible with names."

"That's okay, Ethan."

Dane was looking me over. His eyes seemed glued to my bare chest. It'd been so hot lately I hadn't worn a shirt in days. I looked at Dane. He knew I'd caught him checking me out, but he didn't look away. Instead, he gazed at me evenly and smiled. I was suddenly a little uncomfortable.

"So, what are you up to today?" I asked, trying to make small talk.

"Just seein' what trouble I can get into," said Dane. For some reason, I didn't doubt that.

"I hear you're a queer," he blurted out, taking me by surprise.

"I'm gay," I said. "It isn't a secret."

Dane just nodded. His eyes roved over my chest, my biceps, my abdomen, and my crotch. *Oh boy*, I thought to myself, *now I have to deal with a horny little teenager.* I laughed to myself. I was just eighteen and Dane couldn't be more than a couple years or so younger than me, and yet, he seemed like a kid.

"What's funny?"

"Nothing. How old are you, Dane?"

"Sixteen. How old are you?"

"Eighteen."

"You're sure strong," he said, once more staring at my muscles.

"I work out and I've wrestled for years. I do farm work all the time, too. It's hard not to put on some muscle doing all that."

"You look *real* good."

"Thanks," I said. I felt uncomfortable. A trickle of sweat ran down my chest.

"Thank *you*," said Dane with great exaggeration.

I pulled the truck up to *Wahlberg's* and got out. Dane stayed in the truck. I went in to see if they had the tire I needed. One of the front tires on the tractor had finally given out and I needed a new one pronto. I was in luck. That's what I liked about *Wahlberg's*. The old man usually had just about anything a farmer might need. He kept track of details like who owned what model tractor so he could keep parts on hand for it. Things weren't like that in the big towns.

Clark was there, of course, but he didn't give me any crap. Maybe he'd learned his lesson, though I wasn't sure about that. I wasn't sure Clark was sharp enough to learn so quickly. He struck me as being kind of like a dog that had to be whacked on the butt with a paper quite a few times before he learned not to chase the chickens.

I carried the tire out to the pickup and put it in back. Dane was sitting in the cab, waiting on me. He was so sweaty his bare chest gleamed in the sunlight.

"Can we go somewhere and talk?" he asked, as I started up the old Ford.

"I'm pretty busy," I said.

"It won't take long. I just have some stuff I wanna discuss with you."

"Okay, I guess, if it won't take long. What kind of stuff?"

Dane grinned and something about him looked sinister. I wasn't frightened. He was just a boy.

"About us. About what I want."

"Us?" I asked. "I don't understand."

I drove through the streets of Verona, while we talked.

"I want to blow you," said Dane.

"What?" I nearly slammed on the brakes, but I kept going.

"I want you, Ethan. You're fuckin' hot. I wanna blow you and I want you to blow me. I wanna run my hands all over your chest. I wanna lick you and…"

"Just stop right there," I said. "I'm flattered—I think—but I have a boyfriend."

"I know you do. I don't care."

"Well, I do."

"Come on, man. He doesn't have to find out. He'll never know."

"I'd know. I don't cheat on him."

Dane's features became angry. It made him ugly, as did his words.

"Come on! It's just a blow!"

"Maybe to you," I said. "To me, it's cheating on someone I love. I won't do that."

"Yeah, right. I bet you've done it before."

Now I was growing angry. "You don't know me," I said. "I've never cheated on Nathan. I never will. He's all I need and, even if he wasn't, I still wouldn't betray him like that."

Dane rolled his eyes. "Yeah, sure. Whatever."

"Listen, Dane. I don't know what kind of people you're used to dealing with, but I don't have sex behind my boyfriend's back. Even if I didn't have a boyfriend, I wouldn't have sex with just anyone."

"So, you're saying I'm too ugly for you? Is that it?"

"No. I didn't say that. I'm saying I don't know you. I wouldn't have sex with you because of that, even if I was single, which I'm not!"

Dane crossed his arms and smoldered.

"I'll tell him."

"What?"

"If you don't do what I want, I'll tell your boyfriend."

"Huh? There's nothing to tell. You going to tell him I didn't have sex with you?"

"I'll tell him you did."

Silence reined in the cab for a few moments. I pulled over to the curb in a residential area and shut off the truck.

"Don't try and pull that shit on me," I said.

"You think he'd like that? Huh? You think he'd like to find out his boyfriend cheated on him?"

"Get out," I said.

"You'll do what I want or I'll ruin you," said Dane. He moved closer and attempted to grope my crotch. I shoved him away, using more force than I should've. His back slammed against the door of the truck and he cried out in pain.

"You'll pay for that, fucker!" he yelled.

I was a little frightened. The boy was some kind of psycho.

"Get out," I said evenly.

"Yeah, I'll get out. I'll give you some time to think about it. Just picture your little boyfriend crying his eyes out after I've told him you and me fucked all night!"

I wanted to grab Dane and punch him in the face as hard as I could manage. I controlled my temper. He got out of the truck and slammed the door.

"You better be thinkin' about it, Ethan. All I want is to have a little fun with you. Do it with me and we're cool. Don't, and I'll make sure you don't have a boyfriend anymore."

I didn't say anything. I just started up the truck and drove away.

I was smoldering. How dare that little creep threaten me like that! It infuriated me and frightened me just a little bit, too. Nathan and I trusted each other, but I didn't need some boy telling him I'd cheated on him. What if it created some doubt in Nathan's mind?

I was pretty sure that the next time I saw Dane I was going to tell him he could go screw himself, but I wasn't certain. I had to think on it a bit first. I definitely didn't want to cheat on Nathan. There's no way I'd do that. It wasn't an option. Still, I had to take Dane's threat seriously. Why did life have to be so full of problems?

I parked near the farmhouse and hauled the tire out of the bed of the truck. I could make out three figures far down the hill. Jon and Brandon were helping out again. At the moment, they were assisting Brendan in repairing the wooden bridge that went over the creek. The little stream was barely a trickle now, but we still needed the bridge to get the tractor over the gully. I'd heard a disturbing crack as I drove over it earlier in the day and felt the tractor shift beneath me. I checked and, sure enough, one of the main support beams was giving way. I was just glad the bridge hadn't collapsed. It was only a three foot fall, but it wouldn't have been fun and might've damaged the tractor, or me.

I grabbed a jack and headed for the tractor, which was about halfway down the hill; that's where the tire had ruptured on me. After I dumped off the new tire and the jack, I walked to the barn to gather the tools necessary for replacing the tire. I was sweating freely as I walked back down the hill.

I grunted as I tried to loosen the lug-nuts. I had to use all my might on each one before they finally busted loose. I wondered how Jack had got them on so tight. The rest was easy. In a few minutes' time, I had the front jacked up, with a concrete block behind a rear tire to keep the tractor from rolling away.

Dave walked up with Jack as I was putting the new tire in place. They helped me finish up, and then Jack drove off to plow under some of the crops that were dead, while Dave stood beside him on the tractor. Dave loved Uncle Jack and spent a lot of time with him. I could tell Jack thought a lot of little Dave, too. He was kind of like a grandson to him.

After I put up my tools, I hopped in the truck and drove down the hill to join Brendan, Jon, and Brandon in their repair efforts. They'd ripped up the surface of the bridge and put in a new support beam. They'd also replaced another that was weakening. Brendan and Brandon were busily hammering in a board when I walked up and Jon was selecting another board from the large pile that sat to the side.

"Need any more lumber from the barn?" I asked.

"No, I think we're fine," said Brendan.

"How about some help, then?" I asked.

"Oh, yeah!" said Jon.

I teamed up with Jon to nail the surface back in place, while Brendan and Brandon worked from the other end. With an additional pair of hands, it only took an hour and a half to get the whole thing done.

It was sure pretty out. The sky was perfectly clear and the day bright and beautiful. We would've been better off with clouds and rain, but that didn't mean I couldn't enjoy what life threw at me. Sometimes, I thought life was a gift from God and I found pleasure in whatever I could—the beautiful little yellow flowers that grew by the stream, the fawns that sometimes ambled out of the woods just after dawn, the smell of hay, the sound of water rushing in the stream, and so much more.

Sometimes, it seemed as if life was just something to be endured. That was when enjoying all those little things became that much more important, for if life was mostly unpleasant; it just made sense to find whatever little bits of happiness I could.

It was Nathan that had drawn my attention to the little things, like the scent of tomato plants on a hot day or the beautiful sound of baby chicks as they called for their mama. He'd never had much, so he'd been given the gift of finding pleasure in things most people ignored. In turn, he'd given that gift to me.

I stood, sweat streaming off my body. It was simply unbelievable that it was so very hot and had been for so long. All of us were slick with sweat and covered with grime. I felt absolutely disgusting.

"Who's up for a dip in the lake?" I asked. "I think we've earned a break."

"I'm in!" yelled Brandon.

Brendan hopped in the truck and started it up. Brandon jumped into the cab beside him and Jon and I got in the back. We stopped and picked up Dave as we were driving past where Jack was working in the fields. Brendan drove us to the edge of the woods and parked the truck. From there we walked because the path was too narrow for the old Ford.

Sweat stung my eyes as we walked under the trees. It felt good to be out of the sun, but I couldn't help but feel like I was walking around inside an oven.

"Someone poke me with a fork and see if I'm done," I said. The guys laughed.

The leaves of the trees were dark green in the shade and the humidity trapped by the overhead canopy gave things in the distance a misty, mysterious look. The forest seemed unthinkably old. It held many secrets, only some of which I'd discovered.

I smiled as we passed the old cabin, remembering the night I'd taken Nathan there. It was our first time together. I'd filled the cabin with candles and we made love for hours in their warm golden glow. I loved Nathan so much that it hurt sometimes. I wished he was with us, but he'd already gone to work.

The lake was just beyond the cabin and we were there in just a few minutes. Clothes flew everywhere in our rush to get to the water. We were half-naked already, so it didn't take long to strip down and jump in the cool, clear water. It felt better than just about anything.

It wasn't long at all before we were wrestling around in the water in a big match that pitted everyone against everyone else. Jon and Dave teamed up on me or one of the others now and then, but mainly it was every man for himself. Dave giggled; he thought it was great fun.

Most people would think that a bunch of naked boys wrestling around in a lake would've meant something sexual was going on, especially when two of those boys were gay, but that wasn't the case at all. True, Brendan, Jon, and Brandon did look fine and I didn't mind seeing what they had, but thoughts of sex were far from my mind. I was glad that Jon and Brandon could wrestle around with a couple of gay boys like Brendan and me and not be uptight about it. They were true friends and their trust meant a lot. Dave, of course, didn't think a thing about it. He thought of Brendan and me as older brothers, and there was nothing but trust between us.

All of us, and especially Brendan and I, had been tanned a golden brown by the sun. It was a fact made apparent by the contrast between the tanned areas of our bodies and those parts that didn't regularly see the light of day. Brendan's butt was lily white in comparison to his torso and legs. Damn, was that boy beautiful; Brandon and Jon weren't hard on the eyes either.

The water was much warmer than usual, but still pleasant and refreshing. I luxuriated in its coolness, diving under and then standing to let the water run in streams over my naked skin. This was one of those little things I took the time to enjoy.

Cardinals, blue jays, and other birds I couldn't name sat on the branches of the trees that surrounded the little lake on three sides. One of the cardinals, a bright red male, cocked his head and watched us swim and wrestle in the lake. He looked almost as if he wished he was a boy so he could join us.

We played around for a good half-hour and then it was back to work. I, for one, felt much refreshed. Our little break was well worth the time it took away from the farm work.

Casper

I sat on the counter in *The Paramount*, kicking my heels while Nathan popped more popcorn. I loved the smell of the old theatre. It smelled like...well, buttered popcorn. I guess that should've come as no surprise. I was telling Nathan the story Casey had told me about Devon.

"Four inches?" laughed Nathan. "Oh my God, wait until I tell Ethan!"

We both giggled.

"When school starts back up," said Nathan, "you've got to spread that around the whole school. Although, it would probably be best if Casey did it."

"I bet she will."

"If it was anyone else, I wouldn't make fun of them, but Devon...that creep deserves whatever comes to him."

"Yeah, that's for sure."

"You say Casey was with Shawn Myer?"

"Yeah."

Nathan looked very thoughtful.

"What?" I asked.

"Well," he said, "that's just a bit...queer."

I raised my eyebrow. "Why? He's hot."

"Well, yeah, but...you can keep a secret, right?"

"Of course I can!"

"Ethan and I saw Casey last fall—in a car out by the graveyard—making out with Erica Reynolds."

"With a girl?"

"How many guys do you know named Erica? Yeah, with a girl."

Just then, a little red-headed boy came into the lobby and bought a Milky Way and a Coke. I used the time to think about what Nathan had said. Why would Casey be dating guys if she liked girls? The boy went back in to watch the rest of the movie.

"You think she's bi?" I asked.

"Maybe, or maybe Shawn's just a cover."

"Yeah, but that wouldn't be much fun for him."

"I dunno, maybe she sleeps with him anyway or somethin'. Or maybe she's not dating him. Perhaps they're just friends and they look like they're dating. Who knows?"

"She sure acted like they were dating yesterday."

"Another great mystery is afoot in Verona," said Nathan dramatically in his fake British accent.

"You mean, like the mystery of the green cheese in our refrigerator?"

"Exactly, Watson. What could cause ordinary cheese to turn green like that?"

"Um, maybe being left in the fridge for eight months?"

"Watson! You're a genius, old boy!"

"And you're nuts, Nathan."

"Nathan! Who is Nathan? I am the famous Sherlock Holmes and you..." Nathan peered at me closely over the counter. "You are not Watson! You are Professor Moriarty and I must tickle you into submission."

Nathan jumped over the counter and grabbed me before I knew what was up. I was down on the floor giggling and gasping for breath in no time at all.

"I give! I give!" I said, still laughing.

Nathan helped me up.

"You're crazy, Nathan, and fun." He smiled.

"I think Casey guesses about Brendan and me," I said, getting back to the topic. "She hinted at it the other day. Well, she just winked at me when she said Brendan was hot, but I felt like she knew."

"I guess it won't hurt if she finds out, especially since she's one of us, or at least bi."

"Yeah, I'm not scared or anything."

"Maybe I should just ask her about Erica and Shawn. She knows I'm gay and that I won't tell anyone," said Nathan.

"Yeah, maybe."

We were silent for a few moments. I thought about Casey. It wasn't really any of my business if she was gay, straight, or whatever, but I was curious about the whole situation now. On top of that, it would be cool to talk to her about gay stuff if she was one of us. A girl's point of view would be interesting.

"That guy give you any more trouble?"

"Huh? Oh. No. He came into *Ofarim's* with some other guy, but he wouldn't even look at me most of the time. I think he's scared."

"Yeah, you're a pretty scary guy, Casper."

"Yeah, right! He's scared Brendan will kick his butt."

"Well, he should get his butt kicked if he's going to pull something like that. What a jerk."

"That's putting it lightly."

"I'm glad you kicked him where it counts."

"Actually, I used my knee."

"Same difference. Has anyone ever got you in the balls?"

"Oh yeah, it hurts like hell."

"Yeah, it's happened to me; nothin' feels as painful as that."

We stood there in silence for several minutes. Nathan cleaned off the counter and busied himself with restocking the candy selection. I let my eyes wander over the interior of the old theatre. It wasn't a real big place, it had only one screen, but it was ornate and old. It'd seen better days to be sure, but the wear and tear of decades had given it character. I loved the red, velvety wallpaper with its intricate designs and the golden fixtures for the lights that hung on the walls. In the lobby where we were standing, there was even a big chandelier with lots of glass icicles hanging from it. It was all sparkly.

The floor by the concession stand was covered with a deep red carpet that extended down the aisles in the theatre. The front two-thirds of the lobby had a red and white marble floor, laid out kind of like a checkerboard, only with diamond shaped pieces instead of squares. It was worn and a bit dulled, but still beautiful.

"When was this place built?" I asked.

"In the 1920's I think," said Nathan. "They used to have both plays and movies here. At least I guess they had plays—there's part of some old sets backstage behind the screen. The stage is sure big enough for a play, too. I don't think they would've built it that wide just for movies."

"I wonder if Uncle Jack came here as a kid," I said.

"I don't know. I never thought to ask him, but I bet he did."

The movie ended and the crowd streamed into the lobby and out into the street. A few hit the restrooms and some bought candy or got refills on drinks or popcorn. In ten minutes, the place had cleared out.

"Wanna help me clean up?" asked Nathan. "It's big fun!"

"Isn't that what Tom Sawyer said when he was painting that fence?"

"Something like that."

"I'll help," I said.

Nathan handed me a trash bag and we walked down the aisles and through the seats, picking up cups, popcorn tubs, and candy wrappers that people had left behind. There wasn't too much trash, but it still took a lot of time walking between all those seats.

Mr. Barr, the owner of the *Paramount*, rewound the reels and shut down the projector while we were working. He said he'd lock the doors and we could kill the lights as we left. I liked Mr. Barr. He was the reason the *Paramount* was still in operation. Nathan had told me they were going to tear down the theatre a few years before, but Mr. Barr bought it and fixed it up a little and ran it with very little help. I don't know if he made much money on the place, but I had the feeling he didn't care. Everyone knew he loved movies. Even I knew it and I'd only lived in Verona for a little while.

"You know this place is haunted," said Nathan, as he killed the lights in the auditorium.

It was eerie in there with only the "Exit" signs throwing a pale, red light. I made my way toward the doors as quickly as I could manage in the darkness. Nathan was right behind me, speaking as we walked.

"There was this old projectionist, Willie. He worked here for decades. He started as an usher when he was just a kid, back in the 20's when they opened this place. Later, he sold tickets and worked the concession stand. Finally, he became the projectionist and he did that until his dying day."

We were out in the lobby now. It was lit only by the small golden lamps on the walls. The chandelier had been turned off. Nathan kept telling me about the ghost, although I'd just as soon not have heard about it.

"He died right in the projection booth, near the end of *Cleopatra* with Elizabeth Taylor."

"Who?"

"She was a real big movie star. I saw her in something recently. Um…I can't remember. But she's cool. Anyway, they found him slumped over on the projector table with the reel going round and round, even though the film had run out.

"They say he's still in the theatre. People have seen him sitting and watching the show. Others have seen him up by the projection booth and in the restroom."

Why did he have to say that? I had to go, but now I thought I'd wait until I got home. I hoped I wouldn't pee my pants.

"Have you ever seen him?"

"Not yet. Mr. Barr says he's seen him several times, but I never have. Lots of people are supposed to have seen him, but no one's afraid of him. He's a friendly ghost."

I jerked my head quickly toward Nathan, thinking that perhaps he was making fun of me. I'd been called "The Friendly Ghost" plenty at my old school, even more often than I was called "The Friendly Runt." I guess it wasn't surprising because of my name. I had always been kind of pale, too, although that was no longer true. Working outside on the farm had given me a tan.

Nathan showed no sign that he was taunting me. He didn't even know about the nickname. I don't think he'd have called me that even if he did. And if he did use the nickname, it would have been in fun. I needed to loosen up and remember I wasn't back in Kentucky. I was in a better place.

"Hey you wanna look in the basement at some of the old movie posters and props? I haven't gotten the chance to do more than just glance at what's down there. There are a few things backstage, but Mr. Barr said the basement is full of stuff."

"Um…maybe some other time," I said. Willie might be a friendly ghost, but I was still kind of spooked.

"Okay. Hold on while I get the lights."

I waited by the doors as Nathan shut off all the interior lights. The marquee had already been shut down for the night.

"Good night, Willie," said Nathan as he opened one of the doors. We stepped out into the night and the door closed and locked behind us. I had the strangest feeling that someone was watching us, from the inside.

Brendan

It was the first day of school. I'd been eagerly anticipating it and dreading it. The doors of Verona High School loomed before me like some portal to another world. True, I'd attended V.H.S. for a handful of days at the end of the previous school year, but that was more like a visit. Now, I was moving in.

I felt like hugging Casper as we parted by the lockers, but so far none but Ethan and Nathan knew he was my boyfriend. I had no intention of going to great pains to keep that a secret, but it wasn't exactly the kind of thing I wanted to announce on the first day of school.

I found my own locker easily enough and dumped my books into it. I glanced at my schedule, *first period, Government;* what a way to start the day. I slammed the locker door and headed off in search of my first class, pressing through a sea of unfamiliar faces. Somewhere in the school were Casper, Ethan, and Nathan, but I had no idea where. I'd met very few people during my short days at V.H.S. the previous school year and could remember none of them, other than Brandon and Jon, who'd visited the farm regularly. I was sure I'd make new friends soon enough. I'd never had a problem with that.

I passed plenty of guys wearing letter jackets. My own was in my closet at my parent's home, if they hadn't tossed it out, which I thought likely. A year ago, I'd never have guessed that the beginning of my senior year would find me in a new school, a new state even, living far away from my former home, on a farm of all places. I wasn't sorry, though. I'd do it all just the same again, except that I'd run away before my parents had a chance to put me in that horrible *Cloverdale Center.* I pushed that thought out of my mind fast. I had plenty of other things to think on. I was eighteen and my parents couldn't touch me now.

I hoped Casper was okay. I had to remind myself that we weren't in Kentucky anymore. There was no terrible trio or older brother to torment him. Like me, Casper had a clean slate and a chance to start over. Still, I worried about him a little. He was so small he was an easy target for any bully or punk. I'd protect him, though, and so would Ethan. I doubted that too many guys would mess with either of us. Ethan was a wrestler, one of the best, and I was no slouch either, although my sport was football. Brandon and Jon would no doubt look out for Casper too.

Football—I thought about it all day. I was just itching to try out for the team. The one thing I'd really regretted about leaving Kentucky behind was missing out on football. It figured that all hell would break loose just after I'd been made team captain. Quarterback and captain—that was my dream. At least I'd been able to live that dream for a little while before all was lost.

Now, I had to start over. No one knew me here. I'd talked to some of the players last year, but hadn't set foot on the field. I'd have to prove myself all over again. I was kind of looking forward to that, however. It was kind of like getting to live part of my life all over again. It's too bad everything couldn't have worked out back in Kentucky. I could've started out the year as the quarterback and team captain of the varsity squad. That was all gone, though, and there was no use crying about it. Besides, I had to get Casper out of that place. He was worth any sacrifice.

My day passed in a blur until lunch. I met up with Ethan as I entered the cafeteria and soon we were sitting at a table with Casper, Nathan, Brandon, and Jon. Casper seemed a bit edgy, but happy for the most part. I knew he was a bit apprehensive about fitting in. Like me, he'd only attended V.H.S. for a few days at the end of the last school year. Casper was the quiet and withdrawn type. Where I generally made friends easily, it took him a while. I patted his knee as he sat beside me and he smiled.

Just as I was eager to hit the football field, Ethan was impatiently waiting for the day to end so he could get to wrestling tryouts. Brandon and Jon were equally excited about soccer. Only Nathan and Casper weren't much interested in sports. That was a good thing, as both of them were keeping their jobs to keep some money coming in. I knew things were gonna be tough. It would be tiring to do farm work after attending school all day and then going through football practice. But I doubted that it would be any worse than working all day long on the farm.

After lunch, we all went our separate ways. I liked my classes okay, but I thought the end of the day was never going to come. When it finally did, I dumped my books in my locker and then walked toward the football field.

There were a lot of guys I recognized from classes sitting on the bottom row of bleachers by the field. There were even more guys I didn't recognize at all. There was quite a large group, but then everyone trying out for the varsity and junior-varsity teams was there, so the number wasn't that great. I took my seat among the others and waited for the coach to arrive and begin his talk. In the distance, a custodian was trimming the football field with a riding lawn-mower, while a sprinkler system was watering another section. The scent of newly mown grass came to me and I breathed it in. Yeah—football season was upon us.

I recognized Coach Jordan from our brief meeting in late May. I'd told him about my interest in football and my hopes for being on the team. I think he remembered me. His eyes locked on mine for a moment when he spotted me sitting in the bleachers. He gave me a little smile.

I tried my best to listen as the coach began his talk, but it was much the same sort of thing I'd heard before—not everyone would make the team, those who did would be split into varsity and junior-varsity, practice times, commitment to the team, etc. I perked up when he said we were heading out onto the field so he could begin to size us up. It'd been a long time since I'd been on a football field and I was just itching to get my hands on a ball.

Coach called me to the side as the guys were getting off the bleachers. "Brewer, I contacted Coach Howell from your old school over the summer. I don't think you were entirely truthful with me when we talked."

"Sir?" *Uh oh,* I thought, *in trouble from the start.*

"You said you were the quarterback and that you were good. Coach Howell said you were the best damned quarterback that ever played for him."

I smiled and released the breath I hadn't realized I was holding.

"Now, I'm not promising anything, but our varsity quarterback graduated last year. There are a couple of other guys I have my eye on for the spot, but you're definitely in the running, so show me what you've got out there."

My grin widened. "I will, Coach!"

The hot asphalt on the track around the field was steaming where the sprinklers were wetting it. The oily, moist scent brought back memories of more football practices than I could count. I began to feel more alive than I had in a long time—not that things had been bad lately, but I felt like my life was finally getting back on track.

Coach Jordan was different from Coach Howell. He started right in by dividing us up into two teams. He assigned me a position as a receiver first, with some boy named Tom as quarterback for our side. Tom seemed to know what he was doing—at least he knew how to set up a play. He looked like a quarterback—strong, but not overbuilt or heavy. I eyed him closely, knowing he was my competition, as well as Shawn, who was quarterbacking for the other side. I discovered a short time later they were brothers.

We broke our huddle and the guys took their positions. Some of them had obviously never played before, but Coach got 'em lined up fast enough. Tom nabbed the ball after it was hiked, while I went long, along with some guy whose name I didn't know. I broke in the clear and Tom passed to me. His pass was a little long, but I sprinted and snatched it out of the air. After that, it was child's play. Only a couple of the defensive linemen gave me any kind of trouble and I out-maneuvered and out-ran them with comparative ease. Of course, like I said, some of these guys had never played before.

We tried a couple more plays, and then Coach gave the ball to the other side so he could see what they had. Shawn wasn't bad, but I didn't think he'd cut it as quarterback. I didn't get to observe much, but he was a bit timid. He had a tendency to get rid of the ball as fast as he could; as if afraid he was in imminent danger of being sacked. Sometimes as quarterback, it's necessary to hold onto the ball, even though you're about to get clobbered by linemen who weigh more than two-fifty. Shawn didn't look as if he had the nerve for it.

Before long, it was our turn again and Coach put me in as quarterback. Tom shot me a contemptuous look as I set up the play. I just glared right back at him. I was pleased with my performance during the "game." I called three plays and we scored a touchdown on the last. I just about got sacked on the last play, but I held the ball until my receiver was in the clear—just like Shawn should've done on one of his plays, but didn't.

Coach had us passing and receiving after that, which was more like a normal practice. The ball felt good in my hands. Even though some of the passes were pretty wild, I caught 'em all. Tom passed to me once and I knew he deliberately threw off, but I got it anyway. I was starting to dislike him.

Coach ran us through some drills, taking notes, and then sent us off, saying he'd have a list posted first thing the next morning of who made the team.

There'd be a few assignments to varsity now, with the rest of the varsity team being decided after a few practices.

I was dirty and sweaty as we walked off the field, but I hadn't felt so pumped in a long time. I was playing football once again and even had a shot at varsity quarterback. I wanted it bad. I told myself I'd be happy with whatever position came my way, and it was true, but I'd be happiest as quarterback. I guessed that I'd just have to wait and see.

Dane

The darkness was deepening, finally. The day had been much too long. I was frustrated. I felt thwarted at every turn. Casper wasn't the easy mark I'd taken him for and Ethan wasn't willing to give it up, either. I couldn't believe I had the balls to threaten blackmail. I'd thought about doing that to some guy, but the words just started coming out of my mouth when Ethan rejected me. I'd been thinking on it, ever since I found out he had a boyfriend, but I hadn't known until the words were out of my mouth that I was going to do it for sure. Once I started, I just kept going with it. He obviously wasn't going to do it with me otherwise, so there was little to lose.

I entered *The Park's Edge*. It was a nice restaurant between *Ofarim's* and the theatre. I could afford it. I had nearly $30 in my pocket and I was helping Boothe out again the very next night. I'd had breakfast and lunch at *Café Moffatt*. They had a $2.99 breakfast special that included a couple of pancakes, two slices of bacon, two sausage patties, two eggs, and toast. I had that and iced tea for breakfast and then the lunch special of a fish sandwich and fries at noon. I was kind of avoiding *Ofarim's*. I was afraid of Casper's boyfriend, but the little blond was still tempting. I wanted to make sure I didn't do anything stupid. Of course, he wasn't there during the day, now that school had started.

The start of the school year posed a problem for me. I wasn't going to school in Verona, of course, but I was afraid someone would notice me running around during the day and turn me in or something. I'd already been hiding out some during the day. My parents were no doubt looking for me, so if I got picked up by the police or something, it wouldn't take them long to find out just where I belonged. I was getting a little edgy about skipping out on school, too. I was beginning to wonder if I shouldn't just go back home. Things weren't working out here like I'd planned. Of course, I still had some things going—like with Ethan. If I could get him to crack, it would be worth any trouble I might get into.

The waiter led me to a nice table. It had a linen tablecloth, a candle, and cloth napkins. He handed me a menu and left me to myself for a bit. The prices weren't nearly as high as I'd expected. When the waiter returned, I ordered Chicken Alfredo and a Coke.

The waiter was kinda cute. He was college-aged and had a nice butt. I flirted with him as he took my order. After what I'd said to Ethan the other day, I was feeling bold. I think the waiter might've been interested, although I wasn't sure. I wished I had a phone number to leave behind or something, but that was out since I didn't have a phone.

I enjoyed the pleasant atmosphere of the restaurant. It was fancier than the other places in town. It had a lot of plants hanging from the ceiling and dividing the tables. There was even a little fountain near the center of the restaurant. I had a nice little table off to the side, mostly screened from view by a huge tropical plant. I almost felt like I was eating in a jungle. It was all romantic looking in the dim light. It was too bad I was alone.

The waiter was soon back with my Chicken Alfredo. "Thanks, Armando," I said, straining to read his small name tag.

"If there's anything else I can get you, let me know," he said. He seemed to stress the "anything," but maybe I was just imagining it.

Yeah, there's somethin' you can get me, big boy, I thought as he left. I watched him as he walked away. He sure did have a nice butt. I liked his name. It was unusual, but it fit him. Armando was tall and slim with black, curly hair and dark eyes. He stirred up my hormones more than most guys. Granted, they weren't too hard to stir up, but there was something especially sexy about Armando.

The Chicken Alfredo was incredible and it came with breadsticks that were out of this world. I devoured them and Armando kept bringing me more. He kept my Coke filled up, too.

I openly checked him out every time he came to my table. He liked it. He was looking me over, too. When he brought me the check, I asked for his number and he gave it to me! My head was spinning. He had to be about twenty-one or so and he was giving me his number! The bold new me was pleased.

"When do you get off?" I asked.

Armando leaned in real close and said, "That depends on you." His voice was throaty and his hot breath made me want to grab him right then and there. "I'm off work at ten."

"Wanna meet me?" I asked. I put my hands under the table. They were trembling.

"Where?"

"The park, near the drinking fountain."

"I'll be there," he said and departed.

I sat at the table and sipped my Coke for a while. I couldn't get up and leave immediately. My shorts were tented and everyone in the restaurant would see if I stood up. Finally, I calmed down. I left Armando a big tip, then departed.

It was nine. I had a whole hour to kill. *Oh please, let it happen*, I said to the air. I'd been waiting so long to be with a guy and all my efforts had failed. I was so worked up I wanted to go somewhere private and whack off, but I forced myself to save it. With any luck, it wouldn't be my own hand getting me off. My heart raced with the very thought of Armando touching me.

I walked around town and the park. The warm night air held a promise of things to come. I listened to the insects in the trees and to the distant croaking of frogs. The world seemed peaceful and beautiful.

I sat down on the bench by the drinking fountain five minutes before ten. Butterflies fluttered in my stomach and my heart felt like it was beating too high in my chest. I trembled slightly. The yearning ache in my groin heightened to a fever pitch. I felt as if I might explode.

Fifteen minutes later, Armando still hadn't showed. My heart fell. *What if he wasn't coming? What if he'd just given me a fake phone number and lied to me about meeting? Wouldn't that just suck ass? It would be just my luck, too.* Just as these thoughts entered my head, I saw Armando walking toward me, wearing the same black slacks and crisp white shirt he had on in the restaurant. I stood, hoping I didn't appear too eager.

"Hey," he said.

"Hey."

We stood there in silence. I felt as if I couldn't speak. I grew angry with myself. No. I would NOT be timid. I stepped closer to Armando.

"Where do you wanna go?" I asked.

"How about my car?"

"Okay."

I followed him back the way he came. He led me to a recent model Camaro. It was red with a black interior.

"Bitchin' Camaro, dude," I said.

Armando smiled and we got in. He started her up and drove down Main Street.

"How old are you?" he asked.

"Sixteen."

"Good."

"How old are you?"

"Twenty-three."

I moved closer to him and put my hand on his knee. He didn't stop me, so I rubbed his leg, right up to his crotch. I groped him.

"You're an eager one," he said.

"You have no idea."

"I think I do. I used to be sixteen. Man, I just about went nuts!"

"I am going nuts."

I kept groping him, touching him in a place I'd dreamt about touching. The front of his slacks tightened.

"So have you been with a guy before?" he asked.

"Oh, yeah," I lied.

Armando peered at me as if he knew I was lying, but he didn't say anything.

"So what are you into?"

"I...um...I wanna give a blow job...and get one," I said quickly.

"Mmmm. Sounds good. Are you a top or bottom? Not that we'll be doing that tonight, but I'm curious."

"I...uh..." I had no idea what he meant. "I'm uh, a top I guess."

"So you haven't done it?"

"No." There was no use in lying about it. He'd know.

"I'm versatile. That means I like both."

Our talk was increasing my excitement. The fact that I didn't understand it at all meant nothing. In fact, it made it all the more mysterious. I'd never talked with another guy about such things before. I kept feeling Armando as he drove out of town and then pulled onto a dirt road leading into a field. He shut off the Camaro and killed the lights.

"There's more room in the back," he said, motioning with his head.

We crawled over the seat. As soon as we were in the back, Armando crawled on top of me, pressing my back into the seat. He kissed me, right on the lips! *Oh my God! It's happening!* I thought to myself.

I felt his tongue part my lips and then his hand rubbed my chest. He moved it slowly down over my belly until he grasped my hard manhood. I moaned, lost control, shuddered, and made a big wet spot on the front of my shorts.

"Did you just...?" asked Armando.

I didn't answer.

"You did!" Armando snickered. I could feel my face go red, even though there was no way he could see it.

"Shut up!" I said and tried to get up.

Armando pressed me back down. I fought against him, angry and embarrassed.

"Hey, kiddo, calm down. I'm sorry—I shouldn't have laughed. Don't be embarrassed. The same thing happens to most guys their first time."

"It does?" I asked, forgetting that I'd lied to him and said it wasn't my first time.

"Yeah, it happened to me."

"Really?"

"Yes. There was this way cute boy at school. After, like, forever, I got together with him, under the bleachers after a football game. He touched my crotch and I creamed my jeans right then and there."

"Were you embarrassed?"

"Yeah, until he admitted he'd already shot without me even touching him." Armando giggled.

"Whew," I said. "I thought you'd think...I dunno."

"Shhhh," said Armando, putting his finger to my lips. "It's okay. I'm sure there's plenty more where that came from."

He kissed me again and started pulling my clothes off. I pulled his off too and experienced the delight of feeling skin on skin for the first time in my life. That night was full of firsts. We did each other, more than once. An hour later my virginity was gone, at least by my definition. We didn't get to any of the bottom/top stuff; at least I don't think so. He was on top of me a lot and I was on top of him some too, but I don't think that's what top and bottom meant. It didn't matter; we were way too busy with other things. When Armando dropped me back off at the park, I felt like a new man.

"That was wonderful!" I told him, as I stood outside his car window. "I love you!"

"It was good, kid. Thanks."

He left—too quickly. At last, I was no longer a virgin, but somehow I felt kind of empty inside. I'd shared my first time with Armando and he just left me and drove off like it was nothing. I felt like we should celebrate or something, but he was gone.

Ethan

I waited up for Nathan. I'd been thinking about Dane's threat off and on ever since he'd made it. I had two choices. I could have sex with Dane like he wanted. If I did so, Dane would keep his mouth shut and Nathan would never know about it, but I'd be betraying him. Or, I could deny Dane what he wanted. I wouldn't be betraying Nathan then, but Dane would do his best to make him think I did. I didn't want to cheat on Nathan, but I didn't want to risk our relationship by having him think I had. What if he believed Dane? Or, what if Dane's story created some doubt in his mind? I'd never be able to prove that Dane was lying. It wasn't the easiest choice. I could either be guilty or be innocent and be suspected of being guilty.

I guess it all boiled down to how much Nathan trusted me. In the end, there was only one possible decision. I couldn't cheat on Nathan—not with Dane— not with anyone. If Dane somehow managed to break Nathan and me up, at least I'd know that I'd been faithful. It would be far better to be wrongly dumped, than to live with the knowledge that I'd betrayed Nathan. I just couldn't do that.

I took a few moments to consider what I'd think if our situations were reversed. If some boy came to me and swore he'd slept with Nathan, and Nathan denied it, who would I believe? The answer was obvious—I'd believe my boy. Would there be lingering doubts in my mind? No, there wouldn't be— I knew in my heart that I could trust Nathan. If our situations were reversed, I'd want him to tell me what was going on. I sure as hell wouldn't want him sleeping with some other guy because he was afraid of being blackmailed.

I'd made my decision, but still I was uneasy when Nathan entered our bedroom. I was sitting on the bed, wearing only my boxers.

"Hey, sexy," said Nathan.

"Hey, babe."

"What's wrong?" Nathan could tell something was bothering me just by looking. I didn't have to say a word.

"We've got to talk," I said.

I told him the whole story about Dane, from giving him a ride to his threat to blackmail me.

"So," I said after I filled him in, "I knew I couldn't cheat on you, even to avoid the risk of losing you. But, when Dane finds out I'm not sleeping with him, he'll make trouble. He's going to come to you and…I don't know. He's going to make up some story about how we had sex."

"So let him," said Nathan. "Words can't hurt us, Ethan."

"They can if you believe them."

"You're really worried about this, aren't you? Do you really think I'd believe you cheated on me? I think I know you better than that. Is that it?"

I nodded my head, near tears over the very thought of losing Nathan. I loved him so much. He took my chin in his hand and made me look in his eyes.

"I trust you, Ethan. I don't care how gorgeous or sexy this Dane is, I trust you! You silly ass."

I smiled.

"I should've known. I guess I did know, but…I feel so stupid."

"I understand, baby. You're afraid of losing me. I know, because I'm afraid of losing you, too. We're not going to let some little creep come between us, though. If Zac and Devon and that crowd couldn't force us apart, some guy we don't even know isn't going to do it. So what's this guy look like?"

"He's a little taller than you, with dirty blond hair, and ice blue eyes. He's slim—not all that good looking really. I mean, he's okay, but nothing all that special. He's definitely not gorgeous."

"Not like you, huh?"

"I'm not gorgeous. You are."

"No, you are!"

"Truce," I said. I knew that argument would never end.

"You said his name is Dane?"

"Yeah, why?"

"That's the name of the kid that tried to force himself on Casper! The one Brendan threatened to pound! I bet it's the same guy."

"Well, he is a busy boy, isn't he?"

"Sounds like a Devon in the making."

"No. Devon's a basher and maybe a closet case. Dane is definitely not in the closet. He's tried for both Casper and me."

"Sounds like he's a wanna-be slut," said Nathan.

"Just you watch out for him. He'll be wanting you next."

"Wanting isn't getting," said Nathan.

"I want you," I said.

"In your case, I'll make an exception."

Nathan pulled his shirt off, ripped down his jeans and pounced on me. He wrapped his arms around me and kissed me deeply. He kicked off his shoes and socks as we rubbed against each other. We tore each other's boxers off and wrestled naked on the bed. Who needed anyone else with a boyfriend like Nathan?

Casper

Casey came into *Ofarim's* by herself just as I was wiping off the last table. The place was dead and I had everything cleaned up, so I sat down in the booth across from Casey after I'd brought out her Diet Coke, grilled chicken sandwich, and fries.

"Um, Casey, there's something I'd like to ask you, but there's something I'm going to tell you first." I fidgeted in the seat, even though what I was about to reveal wasn't exactly earth shattering news. Even if Casey didn't already know, it wouldn't come as any big shock to her.

"Okay, shoot," she said.

"I'm gay," I said quickly, before I lost my nerve.

"Yeah, I kind of figured that. So is Brendan your boyfriend?"

"Yeah," I smiled.

"You go, boy! I had little doubt he was, but now that we're talking about it, how'd you land that hottie?"

My grin broadened. "It's a long story, but he saved me from some guys who were picking on me and then we got to know each other."

"How romantic," said Casey. "He's like your knight in shining armor."

"Yeah, he is." I could feel myself blush.

"You're lucky, Casper. Brendan seems really sweet and he's soooooo hot."

"I'm real lucky."

"Of course, and he's lucky, too. You're a total cutie and I don't know anyone that's nicer than you. That's worth a lot more than looks, not that I'm knocking looks." Casey laughed. I felt my face redden.

"You're very pretty," I said.

"Thanks. Now, what did you want to ask me?"

"It's kind of personal, so I won't feel bad at all if you tell me it's none of my business. I'm just really curious about somethin' and if what I suspect is true, then maybe we can be even closer friends. Although, we can be close even if it isn't, but…well, maybe I better just ask."

"Yeah," said Casey, giggling.

"Nathan said he and Ethan saw you parked out near the graveyard last fall. They weren't spying or anything, but they said they saw you with Erica Reynolds."

"Oh," said Casey, reddening a bit herself. "Did they tell you what they saw?"

"Nathan said you and Erica were making out. So what I'm wonderin' is, are you, like, gay or bi or what?"

Casey smiled at me. "I guess we weren't nearly careful enough if Ethan and Nathan saw us. I'm gay. You know, I'd be terrified if anyone but you or Ethan or Nathan were approaching me about this."

"Your secret's safe with me and them—and Brendan, of course."

"I know, that's why I'm not afraid, but I don't want people knowing. They can be so cruel. What they did to Mark and Taylor…it was just so horrible. I don't think I'd get beat up or anything if people found out, but I'd just as soon they didn't know. I'm especially worried about my parents discovering I'm not quite the daughter they think I am."

"I'm glad I asked. I can see there are lots of things we can talk about. Maybe I can even help you, not that I know much about bein' a lesbian." I giggled. Casey reached across the table and squeezed my nose.

"It will be nice to have someone to talk to. I even thought about coming out to Ethan or Nathan, but the time never seemed right."

"I'm sure they'd be happy to talk to you, but what about Erica?"

A wave of sadness passed over Casey's face. "That didn't last long. We messed around a couple of times, but things never went very far. Then, Erica told me she couldn't do that anymore. She said she'd just been experimenting and it wasn't for her."

"What did you say?"

"I was heartbroken. It wasn't just experimenting for me. I loved her. That's not what I told her, though. I lied. I said I understood because I was just exper-imenting, too. I've never tried anything with her since then, so I think she believes me."

"I'm sorry," I said, and I truly meant it. Casey had tears in her eyes. I pulled a paper napkin out of the holder and handed it to her. Casey cried a little and

I reached out and held her hand. "I know what it's like to be lonely. Before I met Brendan, I thought I'd never find anyone. When I realized he cared about me, it just blew me away. I never dreamed a guy like him could go for a little shrimp like me. I never thought *any* guy would want me."

"You're not a little shrimp, Casper, and you have plenty to offer."

"Well, I'm sure not big and strong. I know that it takes all kinds to make the world go around, but I guess I just never felt like I was worth loving."

"That's so sad, Casper."

"It's okay. I know better now. I just want to make sure you know better, too."

"Oh, I do, Casper. I know I'm worth loving. I know I have a lot to offer. It's just hard to find anyone when you're hiding in the closet. It gets pretty lonely in there." She smiled through her tears. "It's not all bad, though. I have friends, good friends. My life isn't complete, but it's no nightmare either. I'm happy most of the time."

"You have me a little confused. I mean, you dated Devon and you're dating Shawn. Are you really gay, or do you mean bi?"

"I just like girls. It's kind of funny. I love looking at hot guys, like you and your boyfriend, and that stud, Ethan, but I'm not interested in anything physical with them. That had always kind of confused me. It made it real hard for me to accept who I am, but I know it's true. It's kind of weird, though, huh?"

"Maybe, maybe not. I notice when girls are pretty, like you. I don't want to kiss them or anything, but I still know a hot babe when I see one. Like right now."

Casey laughed.

"Maybe I'm not as weird as I think."

"You're not weird," I said. "I'm wonderin', though, what about Devon, and Shawn? You didn't exactly say, but I thought you and Shawn were going out, as in boyfriend and girlfriend."

"That's what everyone is supposed to think. Can you keep a secret?"

"You know I can."

"I mean a *big* one. This one doesn't involve me. Well, it does in a way, but it's someone else's secret and it's extremely important that it be kept."

"I won't tell a soul," I said, crossing my heart.

"You've probably already guessed I date Shawn to hide that I'm gay, but there's more to it than that. It's a cover for both of us."

"You mean Shawn's gay, too?"

"Oh yeah, and more terrified than me about being found out. He's convinced his dad and brothers will hurt him and hurt him bad if they discover his secret. He's sure he'd be kicked out of the house at the very least. He's worried about how the guys at school would react, too, although not so much after Ethan came out and everything was cool for him. Mainly, he's worried about his family and he has cause to worry. I've been around them enough to know."

"Really?"

"Yeah. It's a long story, but I don't dare tell it here. I shouldn't even be talking to you about Shawn where someone might hear."

"Agnes wouldn't say anything, even if she overheard."

"I know, but someone could walk in. What time do you get off tonight?"

"Um, I'm not sure, probably around nine or ten."

"I'll tell you what. If you want, I'll come around near closing and then we can talk in my car or something."

"Okay," I said. "What about Devon? Why did you go out with him?"

"For the same reason I'm dating Shawn, except it was only a cover for me and not him. For all Devon knew, I was interested in him. He moved way too fast for my comfort, however, and he was a complete ass. Dating him seemed like a good idea at the time. I figured people would be less likely to suspect me if I was with him. Devon's about as anti-gay as anyone can get, so I figured that if I dated him, people would think I didn't like gays either. That way, they wouldn't suspect me at all."

"That's a good line of thinking."

"Yeah, but I couldn't stand being near him. Even before he tried to force himself on me, I was so sick of hearing him call Ethan and Nathan fags all the time—other guys, too. He did it over and over like he was obsessed with it. If any guy was the least bit sensitive, he'd start talking about how he figured the guy must be a queer. And the things he said about Mark and Taylor..." She shuddered. "I couldn't stand being near him. He's beyond horrible."

"Yeah, I can imagine. I've heard plenty about him from Ethan and Nathan."

"I'm sure he would've freaked out if he knew I was gay," said Casey.

"He might have used it as an excuse to force you. He might've said he was trying to change you."

"I hadn't thought of that, but I wouldn't put it past him."

We talked for a while longer. I felt good inside, like I had a sun blazing away in my chest. I knew Casey and I could be good friends and I had a feeling our conversations would help her. That's what really made me feel good. People like Brendan and Uncle Jack and Ethan and Nathan had done a lot to help me and now I could do the same for someone else. I kinda felt like maybe that's why I was here. Casey seemed happy when she left and she even gave me a hug. I found myself looking forward to when I could talk to her again after work.

***

Casey showed up a little before ten and Agnes let me go. I followed Casey outside.

"Whoa, nice car," I said.

"Thanks, Dad bought it for me."

"I love Mustangs. It's a '66 right?"

"Yes, you must know your cars."

"Nope, just Mustangs. If I could have my pick I'd get this model and this color. Red is the best for Mustangs."

"Definitely."

We climbed in and Casey started to pull away.

"Oh! Wait! I have to tell Nathan I'm going with you. We usually meet up after work and walk home together, or call and have Brendan or Ethan pick us up."

"I can drive you both home."

"That'll be great, but what about our talk?"

"I can say anything in front of Nathan that I'd say to you," she said.

"Okay, lemme see if he can leave yet."

I hopped out of the car and ran up the street to the *Paramount*. Nathan was just shutting down the main lobby lights.

"Hey, can you leave? I have us a ride."

"Um, yeah, sure. I was going to restock concessions, but I can come in a bit early tomorrow and do that. Who are we riding with?"

"Casey, and before you ask, I told her I'm gay, and dating Brendan. She told me she's gay, too and we're gonna talk."

"That sure explains a few things."

Nathan shut off the last of the lights and followed me out to Casey's car. He hopped in the back and I sat down in the passenger seat up front.

"Hi, Nathan."

"Hey, Casey. How's it going?"

"It's been an interesting night. Did Casper tell you?"

"About what you told him? Yes."

"Where to?" she asked.

"How about we go right to the farm?" I asked. "We can talk there and have some pie."

"Mmmm, you know the way to a girl's heart, Casper."

Casey pulled out. I ran my hand along the dashboard. "I can't believe I'm in a real Mustang."

"You can drive it sometime."

"Really?"

"Of course. We gays of Verona have to stick together." She giggled.

We didn't say more until we were all sitting around the table in the kitchen. I put the kettle on for tea while Nathan uncovered the pies sitting on the kitchen counter.

"It looks like we have apple and cherry," said Nathan.

"Mmm, apple for me," said Casey.

"Anyone else want biscuits?" I said. There was a plate full left over from that morning.

"Me," said both Nathan and Casey.

I pulled the blackberry, strawberry, and plum jams from the refrigerator and sat them on the table. By that time, the water was beginning to boil. I set out cups and tea bags for everyone and got out the sugar bowl and creamer as well. We all sat down to a late supper of sorts.

"So tell us about Shawn," I said.

Casey took a bite of pie and chewed slowly while thinking.

"It kind of started by accident. It was just a couple of weeks ago when I walked into the parking lot by the park to find Shawn's older brother, Tom, giving him a hard time. When I came within hearing range, I heard Tom saying something like, '*You're probably a queer, just like those two that offed themselves, aren't you?*' Shawn replied with something like, '*You're out of your fucking mind!*' Then Tom pulled him close and said, '*I've been wondering about you for a long time, little brother.*' There was pure spite in his voice. It was then that Shawn noticed me coming toward them. There was sheer terror in his eyes. He pushed his brother back and said, '*Shows what you know. I have a girl-friend and here she comes right now.*'"

"That took me by surprise because I didn't even know Shawn all that well. I could see he was in real trouble, however. Tom was menacing. Shawn pleaded with his eyes for me to save him, so, I walked right up to him, said '*Hi, baby*', and gave him the deepest kiss he's probably had in his entire life."

I couldn't help but laugh.

"Way to go, Casey!" said Nathan.

"Then, I looked over at Tom and said, '*So this is your older brother?*' Tom seemed confused, but I think he was too dumb to be suspicious. '*Yeah, this is the one who thinks I'm queer,*' said Shawn. I laughed so loud that Tom jumped. '*If you think he's queer, then you don't know anything about your little brother*', I said, devouring Shawn with my eyes as if he was the sexiest thing ever. I looked back at Shawn and said, '*Why didn't you call me last night?*' That kind of put Shawn off balance and he stammered, so I said. '*That better not happen again or you'll never get to third base.*' By then, Tom was buying the whole thing and looked as if he felt a little foolish. He left and I made sure to give Shawn another big kiss as he was going. Ever since then, Shawn and I have dated."

"So, I guess Shawn knows about you, right?" I said.

"Yes, he knows I like girls. I told him everything. It seemed safe enough, even though I didn't know he was gay for sure at first. We're dating for show. It's a perfect arrangement and great cover for us both. My dad was so happy that he just about wet himself when I told him I was dating Shawn. And no one suspects the football jock and his girl of being queers in disguise. We've become good friends, too, so our dates are real, except we don't have sex. When we're out, we hold hands, make out, and let our hands wander a bit. That keeps everyone thinking we're serious. When we're alone, he tells me what guys get him hot and I tell him about the girls I find attractive."

Nathan giggled. "Sometimes it seems like this whole town is gay."

"No," said Casey, "Verona has what, a couple thousand people? If 10% of them are gay, that's about 200 people. How many do you know?"

"Um, with you and Shawn, less than ten."

"See, you don't even know 5% of the gays around here."

"I guess not," said Nathan, "I never thought of it that way."

"I'm sure I don't have to say this, but what I tell you here must be kept secret, especially from Shawn's family. His dad and his brothers are dangerous."

"Everyone knows the Myer family is trouble," said Nathan.

"Worse than you know. Shawn's dad caught him and his little brother, Tim, skinny dipping once. He beat them both bad enough that they just about had to be taken to the hospital."

"Damn," I said.

"Shawn's dad told them if he ever found out one of his kids was gay, he'd kill him. Shawn is sure he means it."

"No wonder he's being so careful."

"So you guys can't even be friendly to Shawn if anyone is around. If his dad or brothers saw him with you, he'd get beaten badly. I'll let Shawn know that I told you about him, but don't expect him to be friendly. He can't risk it."

Ethan and Brendan came in just then, shirtless, dirty, sweaty, and exhausted from farm work. Brendan headed upstairs for a shower and Ethan grabbed a biscuit and devoured it as if he was starving.

"You want me to make you something?" asked Nathan.

"Thanks, but I'll just find something."

Ethan dug around in the refrigerator and came out with a plate of cold chicken. He sat down at the table while Nathan and I brought him up to speed on Casey and Shawn.

"You tell Shawn we'll keep our distance, but if something bad goes down he can come to us. We'll help him," said Ethan.

"Thanks," said Casey.

"The same goes for you, if you need help, although I'm guessing we don't have to stay away from you?"

"You can talk to me all you want, just don't expect Shawn to be friendly. It's just too dangerous for him."

"Understood. You tell him he can call me a "fag" or whatever for show when his brothers are around. I'll act pissed, but I won't hurt him."

"I'll tell him." Casey smiled. "I feel a little better now. I've been scared about Shawn. His family is so violent he could really get hurt, or maybe even killed, if they found out the truth about him."

"I'd advise him to be *very* careful," said Ethan. "Does he have a boyfriend?"

"No. He's too scared to even approach anyone. He's terrified of being outed."

"I had no idea his family was *that* bad," said Ethan. "I knew they were trouble, but we've never had any problems with them. They're jerks at times, but that's been about it."

"I think his brothers are a little afraid of you. In that family, it's survival of the fittest and they respect strength, if nothing else."

"Too bad we can't find him a boyfriend," I said, "but everyone I know is taken."

"I think it would be too dangerous for him anyway," said Casey.

"You're probably right," said Ethan. "In his case, I think he'd better keep a low profile until he's away from his family. You tell Shawn we're here for him if he needs us. We'll steer clear of him, but if he wants to talk, he can sneak out here or we can meet him someplace and we'll keep it all quiet."

Brendan came downstairs all squeaky clean just then and Ethan ran up for his turn in the shower. We all ate and talked and didn't say any more about Shawn. Brendan didn't know what was going on, but I planned to fill him in later. Hearing about Shawn's troubles just went to show that someone else always has it worse. My own past was worse than Shawn's, but the potential for trouble in his life was extreme. I hoped nothing bad would happen to him.

Brendan

I disliked Tom Myer even more after Casper related what Casey had said about him. Of course, I wasn't too fond of him before that. At tryouts, he'd been borderline hostile. He obviously saw me as a rival for quarterback and he didn't like the competition at all.

I headed straight for the gym when I got to school. Coach had promised to post who'd made the team first thing that morning, with only a select few being put on the varsity team. There was a small knot of guys around a paper taped near the entrance to the locker room. Some were walking away none too happy, while others were smiling. I walked up to the list and grinned—not only had I made the team, but Coach Jordan had already put me on varsity! He'd only assigned four guys to varsity and I was one of them! Yes!

Tom made varsity, too. I had to admit, he was good. If we were going to be on the same team, it was important we get along, or at least manage to play together. I didn't like him, but I guessed I could put that aside when we were on the field. I just wondered if he'd be able to do the same.

While we were dressing out for practice after school, Tom gave me his hostile glare. I would've thought his face was frozen like that, but I'd seen him smile at other guys. He was surrounded by a tight little knot of friends on the team and none of them were very friendly toward me either. Most of the guys were cool, though, and I was on the way to making some new friends.

Coach had everyone practicing together, since we weren't all divided up into varsity and junior-varsity yet. The JV coach was at practice too, of course, as were the assistants. We did a lot of running for our first real practice. I was surprised to find that it didn't seem as difficult as I was expecting. Normally, I got a little out of shape over the summer. I lifted weights, of course, but the running always killed me the first few practices. It was no walk in park this time, but it wasn't too bad either. I guessed that working on the farm had something to do with it. I worked so hard there that football practice paled in comparison.

Tom was a dick during practice. He shouldered me a few times when he got the chance. I think he was trying to intimidate me, but he found out real fast that that wasn't gonna fly. I wasn't afraid of him. He was a bad-ass, I'm sure, but I was bigger, stronger, and tougher. I think that's what really set him off. He couldn't stand it that he was no longer clearly top dog. He had competition and he didn't like it.

It was too bad he had to be such a dick. I was there to play football. I would become quarterback if I could manage it, but if I didn't, I'd be content to play just the same. Tom saw it all as some kind of contest. What a jerk.

He spoke to me for the very first time in the showers. He looked me up and down and then smirked, like he thought he was superior. I just looked at him flatly.

"I hope you don't think you're gonna get my spot away from me," he said.

"Your spot?"

"Quarterback. I waited all last year for it and now it's gonna be mine."

"It's not 'your spot'," I said. "If you make quarterback, that's fine, but if I get it, so much the better."

Tom didn't like that at all.

"You live out there with those queers, don't you?"

"You mean Ethan? I'd watch what I said about him if I was you. He can kick your ass with one hand tied behind his back I'm sure."

Tom didn't care for that at all. He spit on the floor. "Fuckin' queers!"

I thought about kicking his ass right then and there, but it would hardly make a good impression on the coach if I attacked another player in the showers. Perhaps that's what Tom wanted. Maybe he thought I'd do something stupid and get kicked off the team before I even got started.

"Everyone is entitled to their own stupid opinion," I said, then turned and rinsed off.

"You're not as good as me," said Tom, as I turned off my shower. I stood there, letting the water drip off me.

"Then you have nothing to worry about, do you, Tom?" I said, then walked out and grabbed a towel from the towel boy.

I think Tom and his buddies were disappointed. I think they were hoping I'd fight. I would've wiped the smirk off Tom's face real fast if I had fought.

He wasn't nearly as tough as he thought. Most of the guys in the showers just seemed kind of nervous over our confrontation—apparently Tom had a reputation.

I wasn't going to antagonize Tom, but I wasn't going to take any crap off him either. I'd keep things as civil as possible with him and make sure if there was a fight, that he took the first swing. If Tom's attitude was any indication, the first punch wouldn't be long in coming.

I dressed and then hurried home. There was a ton of farm work waiting on me and I had homework to do after that. I'd be lucky if I made it to bed before midnight. The late hours were worth it though—I'd have done just about anything to play football.

Dane

I tried Armando's number for the fourth time and received no answer. "Damn it!" I said as I hung up the payphone. Armando had given me my first taste of male-to-male sex and I wanted more—much more. I wanted to try it all.

I'd been looking for Armando all day without success and now it was evening. I'd eaten lunch at *The Park's Edge*, hoping to catch him, but he wasn't there. I'd wandered around town after that, but hadn't caught the slightest glimpse of him. I guess that should've come as no surprise. I'd never laid eyes on him until the night we met.

I smiled as I crossed the street to the park in the failing light. I was no longer a virgin. I'd kissed another guy—right on the lips. Armando had slipped his tongue in my mouth and I wasted no time in shoving mine between his lips. We'd gotten naked together and the sensation of bare skin on bare skin was more sexy and arousing than I'd dreamed. And then, when he'd taken me into his mouth at last…the mere memory of it made me throb. I closed my eyes and pictured myself as I tore at his boxers and wrapped my lips around him. I felt like I'd dreamed about that moment forever.

What I'd had was only the first taste. I wanted—no—I *needed* more. Sex was like a drug that addicted one to it with a single dose. I knew I could never get enough.

I was shaken from my memories by the sound of a truck pulling into the gravel parking lot nearby. I grinned as Ethan opened the door and stepped out. Maybe I didn't need Armando quite so badly after all. Ethan had come back and he was ten times hotter than Armando. Ethan spotted me and approached. He was wearing jeans and a tank top. He looked good enough to lick. I couldn't wait.

"So," I said, "you think about it?"

"I'll get right to the point," said Ethan. "I'm not doing anything with you. I don't like guys who try to force me into things and I have no use for anyone who tries to get me to cheat on my boyfriend."

My heart fell and the disappointment was bitter. I wanted him so bad I could taste him. *I thought I had him. Fuck.* The game wasn't over, though. I still had cards to play. "I guess I'll just have to talk to your boyfriend and tell him what a great time we've been having together."

"You do that, Dane. Go ahead. I've already explained everything to Nathan."

"Sure you have." He was bluffing. It's just what I would've done, if I had a boyfriend, that is.

"Listen. I have work to do. I'm not going to stand here and waste time on you. You're not worth it. Tell my boyfriend a bunch of lies or don't. I don't care. It doesn't matter to me. We trust each other and you can't force me to cheat on him."

"Are you telling me you've never thought of cheating on him? There's never been some guy who gets you so hot you haven't at least thought of it?"

Ethan didn't answer.

"Yeah, I thought so." I was getting under his skin. I just knew it.

"Listen, you little punk, I know what you're trying to do and it's not going to work. Take your sick little game somewhere else, because I'm not playing."

"Oh, I think you'll play. I'm calling your bluff. You leave here without giving me what I want and I'll go straight to your boyfriend."

"You just do that, Dane, and see what kind of reaction you get."

Damn, this isn't going at all according to plan, I thought to myself.

"And another thing," said Ethan. "I know what you tried to do to Casper. You keep your hands off him! If I find out you've tried to pull something like that with him again, I'll break you in half."

"How do you know Casper?"

"Never mind. I've wasted enough time on you. Just leave him alone and stay away from me. You'd better grow up, Dane, and stop playing games before someone hurts you."

With that he was gone. I sat down heavily on the park bench. All my plans seemed to end in failure. I wanted Casper, but he got away from me. I desperately wanted Ethan, but I couldn't make him do what I wanted. Then there was Armando. *Where was he?* He was as into our time together as I was, but he was nowhere to be found.

Have a little patience, Dane, I told myself. I guess I was rushing things. I could wait a little while before Armando and I tore each other's clothes off again. But, I didn't want to wait!

My failure with Ethan was hard to swallow. Fuck, I wanted him! He was my dream stud. At least I'd tried. The old Dane would've never had the balls to do something like that. I was quite proud of myself. Besides, there were other fish in the sea, although that was a pretty bad analogy. Fish is the last thing I wanted.

I had a late supper at *The Park's Edge,* but there was still no sign of Armando. Had I dreamed him? No, I wouldn't have dreamed about losing control and embarrassing myself in front of him. He was real. I ordered Pasta Carbonara, but its taste was wasted on me. I didn't want food. I wanted sex. I lingered for nearly two hours, having two desserts, in case Armando was coming in late, but there was no sign of him. It was one more disappointment in a pitiful day.

I left the restaurant and went next door to *The Paramount.* The movie was well underway, but that didn't matter. That's not why I was there. I'd done some checking around and it wasn't hard to find out about Ethan's boyfriend. He worked at the theatre. It was payback time for Ethan. He'd put up a brave front, but I still had a sneaking suspicion he was bluffing. He'd denied me what I wanted, so it was time for a bit of revenge and there was no use in waiting. With any luck at all, I could fuck up things between Ethan and his boy. That'd teach him. There was a price to pay for defying the new Dane.

"You Nathan?" I asked the blond boy behind the concession booth. He was the only guy in sight.

"Yeah."

"I'm Dane and I have something to tell you."

"So you're really dumb enough to try this, huh?" asked Nathan. "Ethan told me about you."

"Oh, did he?" I said, "That's a surprise." I was beginning to get worried. Maybe Ethan hadn't been bluffing. There was nothing to do but play it out, however.

"Yeah, he told me all about you, Dane, so save your breath."

"It figures Ethan would try to cover his ass," I said. "What did he tell you? Surely he didn't say anything about us getting it on."

"He told me you're a little blackmailer who's desperate to get into his pants."

"Nice story, but I've already been in Ethan's pants, a few times."

"Uh huh," said Nathan.

"Hey, if you wanna believe his lies, go ahead, but I just thought you'd want to know your boyfriend has been screwing around behind your back."

"You're very entertaining, Dane. I'd just love to stand here and listen to more of your story, but tell me this—if you've been sleeping with my boyfriend, why come and tell me about it and ruin it for yourself?"

I paused. *Shit.* Telling him wouldn't have been logical if I really was getting it on with Ethan.

"Because...because he pissed me off! He got mad at me last night over something stupid and he hit me! Nobody hits me and gets away with it." *Nice save*, I thought to myself.

"That's funny; Ethan's not the kind to strike without need. When did this happen anyway, what time?"

"About ten or so."

"That's funny, too; Ethan was working in the fields at ten."

"Well, it might've been later. How am I supposed to remember the exact time? It doesn't matter anyway. He hit me, so I'm telling you!"

"Dane, if you're going to lie, at least be smart about it. I'll tell you this much, though, so you won't have to kick yourself for being too stupid to think your lies out properly—I wouldn't believe you if your story was perfect down to the last detail. You see, I trust Ethan. I know him. He'd never cheat on me. If he did something he even remotely thought of as cheating, he'd come right to me and tell me all about it. You picked the wrong set of boyfriends to try your crap with, not that I think it would work with anyone else. I don't know what your problem is, Dane, but this isn't cool. And, what you did to Casper was far, far worse! Now, I'm tired of messing with you, so get your ass out!"

I could feel myself turning completely red, half from embarrassment and half from fury. How dare that little punk stand there and lecture me! I felt like hurtling over the counter and punching him right in the face, but he looked kinda strong. There was his boyfriend to consider, too—that boy was built. No, it was time to cut my losses and get the hell out.

"Fuck you!" I said, flipping him off as I departed.

"No thanks, Dane, but I appreciate the offer."

Oh, how I hated him!

I was steaming. I was pissed. I was also feeling rather foolish. What a mess I'd made of things. Hell, Nathan even knew Casper. I felt like I'd stirred up a nest of angry gay boys who were just waiting to descend on me and beat me senseless. This was *not* what I'd planned. Couldn't even *one* fucking thing go right? Well, there was Armando, but where the fuck was he?

I whiled away the next hour or so until it was time to meet Boothe in the park. He had another job for me. He was hitting the big graveyard at the edge of town. We were meeting at 10:00 PM—early—but we had to get to it because the grave we were hitting tonight was a recent one. We'd have to dig deep.

Boothe arrived slightly late. The sight of him did nothing to improve my mood. He was such an ass. I hated sitting next to him in his fancy truck, but at least it wasn't a long ride.

I climbed down out of the cab. The moon was bright and illuminated the cemetery in a bright, blue light. It was just as well for we couldn't risk using a light, at least not until we were down a few feet. I didn't scare all that easily, but the graveyard gave me the creeps. I wish the night was over and I had my $40 in my pocket.

"Shit! I forgot the crowbar," said Boothe when we'd walked several yards into the cemetery. You go on and get started and I'll catch up. It's that grave over there, just the other side of that big cedar," he said, pointing.

I didn't answer, but shouldered the shovels and walked on. I found the grave soon enough. It looked fairly fresh. Grass was growing only lightly over the disturbed earth. I read the stone in the moonlight, *Taylor Potter*. The name meant nothing to me, but it was interesting that he'd died when he was only sixteen years old. What was stranger was that the grave next to him bore the very same date of death—November 3, 1980. Weird, they'd been born the same day, too—August 21, 1964. What were the odds of that? Born and died on the same dates? I wondered who those two were—Mark Bailey and Taylor Potter. I guessed I'd get to see old Taylor soon enough, however. I pushed the shovel into the dirt of his grave and begun to dig.

"Not there, you dumb fuck," said Boothe, as he slapped me in the back of the head. "There!" He pointed to a grave one row over.

"But you said the grave just past the big cedar."

"Yeah, fuck-head, cedar. C-E-D-A-R. This is a pine!"

"Well, how I'm supposed to know the difference? They're both trees!"

Boothe gave me a look that plainly said he thought I was too stupid to live. How I hated him.

"Come on," he said, dragging me away to our work for the night.

Four hours later my back was breaking and my muscles screamed. I don't know how many feet we'd dug down, but I expected us to pop out in China any minute. My shovel hit something hard at last. I kept digging until I'd uncovered the top of a crypt.

"Get out," said Boothe.

I climbed up the rope ladder that hung on the side of the grave and Boothe went down, taking the crowbar with him.

"They seal these things pretty good," he said, "but if you just keep trying they…break loose." I heard what sounded like an enormous slab of stone sliding on top of another. "There. Now hold the light."

I lay looking down into the grave. I snapped on the flashlight, taking care to keep it pointed down so it wouldn't show above ground any more than was necessary. As Boothe pried the lid of the crypt up, I could see the casket inside. It looked new. It was bronze with silver handles. I'd looked at the tombstone and the guy we were digging up had been buried fifteen years go.

I stifled a cry when Boothe opened the lid. Mr. Baymont looked like he'd just been buried yesterday. In fact, he looked like he could sit up and climb out.

"You sure this is the right grave?" I asked. "He don't look like he was buried fifteen years ago."

"Of course, I'm sure, dumb-ass. These new crypts keep 'em fresh. No air gets in."

Booth busied himself removing rings from Mr. Baymont's fingers and gold cuff links from his shirt sleeves. "People are nearly always buried in their best," said Boothe, approvingly.

In less than five minutes, Boothe had looted the casket and closed it back up. He slid the lid of the crypt back into place and ordered me to start shoveling. While I worked, he examined his haul.

"Shit, most of this is just gold plated. I'll be lucky to get $100 for all this. They sure didn't bury him with much. I guess his relatives didn't think much of him."

"Well, I still get my $40. That's the deal."

"Shut up, bitch. You'll get your money. I don't squelch on deals, even if you do shovel like a girl."

I bit back the comment I wanted to make. As much as I hated it, I needed this crappy job. Working for minimum wage in some restaurant was looking better and better, however. I indulged in a fantasy of smacking Boothe upside the head with the shovel and burying him with Mr. Baymont. I giggled and Boothe gave me a strange look.

"You're a sick little fuck, aren't you?" he said.

Look who's talking, I thought to myself.

Just as I was about to drop from exhaustion, we finished. Boothe paid me and drove me back to Austin's place. I was hoping he'd be home for a change, but he was nowhere to be found. *Probably turning another trick,* I thought to myself. I was too tired to think about it. I lay down and went fast asleep.

Ethan

I stopped by Mrs. Pearson's after my confrontation with Dane. She'd called the evening before to say she needed a lift to the store. She was all smiles when she opened the front door.

"I'm here to escort you to the grocery," I said. "I'm sorry I couldn't make it before, but I had school, and then wrestling practice."

"That's quite all right, dear. I appreciate you taking me. Come in while I get my purse."

I sat on the couch in the living room while I waited on her. Mrs. Pearson didn't move very quickly. I had much to do on the farm, but I didn't begrudge the time. I only hoped I'd have someone around to take me to the grocery when I was old. Of course, I'd have Nathan, so we'd take care of each other.

Mrs. Pearson's living room was a throwback to the 1950's. All the furniture was out of date and even her TV looked ancient. There were tons of pictures hanging on the walls of all sorts of people. I stood and examined some of them. There was even a picture of me and Jack when I was about twelve. There were several photos of one man, some of them with a younger Mrs. Pearson and some without. The photos showed him at different ages, ranging, I supposed, from his thirties to his sixties. I guessed he was Mr. Pearson.

Mrs. Pearson came out of the bedroom with her giant wicker purse and I helped her to the door and into the truck. She seemed to enjoy getting out a great deal, but I guess I would've too if I almost never left the house. It was only a short drive to the grocery.

"You need any money?" I asked, as I helped her out of the truck.

"No, I'm fine, Ethan, but you're so sweet to ask."

"Well, if you do, you just let me know." I wasn't really in the position to be handing out money to anyone, but I wasn't going to let a nice old lady go without.

"How's that cute little boyfriend of yours?" asked Mrs. Pearson.

I was slightly shocked she came right out and mentioned my relationship with Nathan. Even most people who accepted it didn't mention it and the older generations seemed to be the most disapproving. Not Mrs. Pearson apparently. She was full of surprises.

"He's wonderful," I said.

"You two make such a cute couple."

I smiled.

I saw Dane as we were entering the grocery, but he turned quickly and acted as if he hadn't seen me. That was fine by me since I didn't want to have anything to do with him. He was a messed up guy. It was just too bad someone couldn't talk some sense into him.

It didn't take too long for Mrs. Pearson to finish her shopping. Her needs were few. I smiled when she bought me a Hershey bar and squeezed my cheek. It was kind of nice being treated like a little boy again, if only for a moment.

Once I had Mrs. Pearson safely home, I headed back to the farm. I needed to get to work. With school and wrestling practice, there wasn't enough time in the day.

***

I gazed at Brendan's bare chest gleaming in the moonlight and smiled inwardly. I'd been tempted by Brendan's smooth, muscular torso and other appealing features, but Dane's attempt to blackmail me into having sex with him had brought me to my senses. Some people say that everything happens for a reason. Maybe the reason behind Dane's actions was to remind me that the last thing I wanted to do was cheat on Nathan. The sight of Brendan's well-muscled body had stirred up sexual need and fantasy within me. I'd been edging closer and closer to making a serious mistake, but Dane jerked me back to reality. When he tried to force me to cheat on Nathan, it awakened a fierce protectiveness in me and opened my eyes to my own foolishness. I loved Nathan with all my heart. That was never in doubt, but somehow I'd let myself stray in thought, if not in action. True, Brendan was strong and beautiful, but as long as I loved Nathan, Brendan and I could be no more than close friends. I knew I'd love Nathan until my dying day, and beyond.

It astounded me that I could even be tempted by Brendan, especially when I'd traveled this road before. The world was not black and white, however; it was filled with shades of gray. If I was perfect, I'd have eyes only for Nathan and wouldn't notice if Brendan or any other guy danced before me naked. But I wasn't perfect—no one was. I was just glad I'd resisted the temptation. Maybe that even made my love for Nathan stronger. I'd been tested and I'd passed. I despised Dane for what he'd tried with me, but I felt I owed him in some way. He didn't try to blackmail his way into my pants to show me the error of my ways, but that was the end result. I didn't want to even go near Dane again, but I couldn't find it in my heart to be sorry for what'd happened. His actions had kept me from harming the one I loved. Likely I would've stopped myself in time, but who knows what I might've done in a moment of weakness? I looked at Brendan again. He was handsome and sexy, but I loved Nathan. Brendan was like a painting in a museum—beautiful, but not to be touched.

***

Brendan headed toward the farmhouse, but I lingered behind. I threw myself on the ground and lay on my back, looking up at the stars. My muscles ached and I felt like I could go to sleep right there.

My body cooled slightly in the night air since I was no longer working, but sweat still dripped off me. I felt like I was sweating twenty-four hours a day, except when I was in school where there was air conditioning. The cool air there was delicious, but I didn't mind the heat too much.

I breathed in deeply. The scent of honeysuckle was carried on the slight breeze. Frogs were croaking in the distance and insects were singing their songs all around me. I thanked God that I lived in such a beautiful place.

I'd been thinking about Mark and Taylor more than ever since their birthday and my thoughts turned to them once again as I lay there gazing at the stars. One of the things Nathan suggested we do with the money that Mark left me was put up a memorial plaque for them on the soccer field. I was beginning to give that some thought. It would be nice to have a bronze plaque, perhaps embedded in a huge granite boulder or something. I'd have to do some looking around to see just where I could get a plaque made. I thought I'd ask Coach. The school had plaques like that done sometimes. I already knew where I could get the boulder. We had one that was just perfect right on the farm. Big rocks weren't exactly a rarity in northern Indiana. The glaciers had pushed plenty of them into the area thousands of years ago and the farm had its share. They could be a pain in the butt, but at least one of 'em could be put to good use. It would take a backhoe or something to move it, but that could be done. I was thinking it was time to put my plan into action.

I was too tired to do anything about it for the moment. Then, like an angel out of my dreams, Nathan walked up from the house. He lay down beside me and took my hand. We didn't speak a word. We just lay there quietly, looking at the stars. Somehow I had the feeling that Mark and Tay had enjoyed doing the same thing. Sharing one of their joys just made me feel that much closer to them right now. I squeezed Nathan's hand, and he squeezed mine back.

I forced myself to sit up and we both stood. If we'd stayed on the ground, we would've surely fallen asleep right there. We stumbled toward the farmhouse. I had just enough energy to take a quick shower and then fall into bed, hugging Nathan. I was too tired to even eat.

Casper

Casey and Shawn came into *Ofarim's* for supper a couple days or so after she'd come to the farm and told us their story. Shawn was polite to me, just as before, but I didn't try to strike up a conversation with him. His eyes locked on mine for a moment and I knew Casey had told him everything. I nodded, but gave no other sign that I knew anything or that things had changed between us. That's the way it had to be for Shawn's protection.

There weren't many people around to see even if I'd hopped on Shawn's lap or something. There were only a couple of old ladies having pie and the U.P.S. guy taking a break after his rounds.

I stole a few looks at Shawn and Casey as they ate. They looked like any other couple. They talked and laughed and were oblivious to the world. If I didn't know better, I'd have assumed they were dating, without a doubt. I knew they were safe from discovery. No one would suspect that a football jock and a pretty girl were really a gay boy and a lesbian just pretending to be a couple. It still kinda blew me away.

Devon came in for ice cream just as Casey and Shawn were about to leave. He eyed Shawn angrily, but it had nothing to do with Shawn being gay. Devon didn't have a clue about that. He was obviously still ticked off that Casey had dumped him. I smiled when Shawn gave Casey a passionate kiss just before they went out the door. They did some serious tongue-wrestling and I knew it was for Devon's benefit. He was seething with such anger that I halfway expected smoke to come out his ears.

I wondered what Shawn thought about kissing a girl like that. Or, for that matter, what Casey thought about kissing a boy. I didn't think I'd like kissing a girl much. I guess it wouldn't be all that bad, but it just didn't appeal to me. I was happy I didn't have to play games like that. It felt wonderful to be open about who I was.

Dane just missed getting to see the show by about thirty seconds. He would've probably got off on watching Shawn make out, even if it was with a girl. If Dane wasn't such a total jerk, I might've thought about telling Shawn that Dane was gay. If he was looking for a casual hookup, I'm sure Dane would've been all for it. I wasn't about to do Dane any favors, however, after all the crap he'd pulled. Shawn needed a real boyfriend anyway, not just someone for casual sex.

I took Dane's order for a banana split and began making it. Dane barely made eye contact with me, but that was no surprise. It should've been out of shame, but I was sure it was out of fear. Brendan had come down on him hard and I'd learned that Ethan reamed him out, too.

I resisted the temptation to make Dane's banana split with a dill pickle instead of a banana. It would've been fun to see the look on his face. I couldn't do it, however. I had to be professional, even if Dane was a jerk. At least I had fun thinking about it.

I watched in amusement as Dane looked Devon over. I guess Devon looked pretty appealing to Dane. He was actually quite handsome, if you didn't know him. His ugly personality made him hideous to anyone familiar with him, but to a stranger such as Dane, he did present a nice package. I could see where he'd turn Dane's head, although I was beginning to believe anyone who had something swinging between his legs looked good to Dane.

Better watch yourself, I thought silently to Dane. He was checking Devon out a little too openly. That kind of thing could earn him a fist in the face from Devon, or far worse. I actually wouldn't have minded watching Devon pound Dane. I couldn't think of anyone who deserved it more, except for Devon himself. Maybe Dane would even get a few good hits in while Devon was kicking his butt. Like the pickle, it was fun to think about. Devon didn't take much notice of Dane, however, as he was lost in his own thoughts. He caught him looking, but I think he missed Dane's obvious interest. Devon left pretty soon and it was probably a good thing for Dane.

"Casper, could you sweep off the front walk?" asked Agnes.

"Sure thing."

I grabbed the broom and went out front. Agnes liked to keep the place neat and tidy and that included the sidewalk in front of the restaurant. Even though the sky was darkening fast, sweat formed on my brow almost before I got started. Soon, it was running into my eyes, stinging them. I thought northern Indiana was supposed to be cooler than down south, but I couldn't remember such a hot August even in Kentucky. It was far less humid, at least, but I felt like I'd stepped into an oven every time I left the air conditioning of *Ofarim's*. I didn't see how Brendan or Ethan could stand it out in the hot sun. Of course, I'd been tolerating it myself before I'd taken a job to bring in some money.

I missed working on the farm and especially my work in the garden. Nathan had done most of it before Grandma came along, but once she was there, I'd taken to it too. There was plenty of work for all of us, but now Grandma had to tend it mostly by herself. I did a little weeding or watering or whatever in the mornings before I left for school, but Grandma did the bulk of the work. I knew she didn't mind, but I still missed it. I enjoyed what little time I had to spend there. Sometimes, I even spent a little time tending the garden in the moonlight, when the moon was full enough to illuminate it. It helped put me at peace after a long day. I liked being in the garden at night. Instead of the bright colors evident in the day, the flowers and vegetables were cast in a hundred shades of blue. The daisies were such a light blue that they nearly appeared their true color of white, but other flowers and vegetables were of darker shades, some so dark they nearly appeared black. The garden was almost Elfin in the night.

I smiled thinking of Grandma. So many years had slipped by without her in my life, but she was back at last. Relationships didn't have to last for years to be important. I remembered a couple of boys I met in the park in Kentucky. They were the sons of some relative of someone in town and they were only there for a day, but we became friends in that short time. I was never outgoing or popular, but they took right up with me. We laughed and played hide-and-seek and tag all day long. We were the best of friends, if only for a few hours. I sometimes wondered where they were now and if we'd still be friends if we met again. Likely not. I think some friendships were meant to be short. I still thought of those boys as my friends, however, even though I knew them only for a few hours and hadn't seen them in years. My time with Grandma was kind of like that. We hadn't been together for long, but I loved her with all my heart and was happier because she was in my life now.

My shirt was plastered to my chest and back by the time I returned to the cool comfort of *Ofarim's*. I shivered in the sudden coolness, but it was refreshing. The place was empty for the moment; even Dane had departed, so I availed myself of one of the perks of my job. I made myself a free vanilla ice cream cone and even put sprinkles on top. I smiled as I sat at the counter and thought of Brendan. A wonderful boyfriend and free ice cream—life didn't get much better than that.

***

When I arrived home from work, there was a letter waiting on me. I smiled. It was probably from Stacey—she was about the only one who wrote me. That made sense, because she was my only real friend from Kentucky. When I looked at the letter, however, I knew it wasn't from her. I didn't recognize the handwriting. When I looked at the return address, I nearly dropped the envelope. At the very top it read, *The Cloverdale Center.* I looked again to make sure the letter was addressed to me. It was Brendan, and not I, who had been in that horrible, horrible place. I thought maybe someone he'd met in there had written him, but no, the letter was addressed to me.

I took it upstairs and opened it with trembling hands. I pulled out the letter, unfolded it and began to read.

From Hell

Dear Little Brother,

First off, if you answer me, DON'T write me at the center. Use the enclosed address instead. There's a guy who works here that's agreed to smuggle letters for me. You can get stuff like that done here if you want, for a price. I know you probably hate me. I'd hate me if I was you. You'll probably just tear this up without reading it, but I just had to write you anyway to say I'm sorry. I know that doesn't cover it. I don't expect you to forgive me for the stuff I did.

I'm not the same now, little bro. Things have changed me. People here have changed me. You would not believe the fucked up shit that goes on here, but then maybe you would if Brendan has told you about it. I won't go into that now, 'cause what I wanted to say is that I know how horrible I was to you when we were living at home. You see, the same stuff has been happening to me here. That'll probably make you happy—big bro getting it just like he gave it out. I can't sleep most of the time, cause I just lay here waiting on them to come and get me. Sometimes it's for a "treatment", what we here in hell call torture. Sometimes, it's one of the orderlies that's decided to have fun with me, or that I'll be his bitch for the night. When you're lying here, knowing what may happen at any moment, you can't sleep. They give you lots of drugs and those would probably help, but I've been keeping from taking them as much as I can. I've seen some of the guys in here and what the drugs have done to them. It fries their brains. Maybe that's not so bad, though. I may start taking what they give me, instead of tucking them under my tongue, or barfing them back up. I dunno. Sometimes, I just wanna die, 'cept I think I might go to the real hell for the stuff I've done, so maybe this place is a little better than what waits for me.

Write me, little bro. Even if it's just to tell me how much you hate me. I need to hear from someone on the outside. I'm goin' crazy in here. I can't stand it. I'm payin' for what I did to you, more than you can imagine. I'm sorry, Casper, please, please write me back.

Jason

Brendan

I came in from the fields a little after eleven. I was thankful I had almost no homework to do. All I really wanted to do was take a shower and slip into bed. Casper wasn't in our room when I arrived, so I stripped down, wrapped a towel around my waist, and headed for the shower.

I was sweaty, but I still used hot water. My tired muscles needed it. Football practice, followed by a few hours of farm work had just about exhausted me. My shoulders felt like they were in knots. The hot water pounding down upon me did the trick, however. I slowly relaxed. Of course, that made me sleepy and I couldn't go to bed just yet.

I dried off, returned to our room, and slipped into a pair of boxers. I sat at the desk and worked my way through a government assignment and a few other short pieces of homework. By the time I'd finished, it was a little after midnight. Casper still hadn't returned. I wondered if he was downstairs.

Just as I was getting ready to go and check, I saw him through the window, walking alone in the moonlight. I slipped on some shorts and a pair of shoes and went outside to join him.

"Casper," I said, as I neared him. I didn't want to frighten him.

"Hey, Brendan," he said.

"What are you doing out here?"

"Looking at the stars and thinking."

"Thinking about what?"

"Jason. I got a letter from him today."

"What?" I asked, too loudly. "Jason sent you a letter?" I asked more quietly. I didn't want to wake anyone inside the farmhouse. Jack and Ardelene were asleep and so was Dave. Ethan and Nathan likely were too, unless they had enough energy for making love. I wished I did.

"Yeah."

"He's not on the loose or something is he?" I asked. I feared he'd escaped or something. Jason was dangerous. The last time I'd seen him, he'd tried to kill Casper. I'm pretty sure he would've killed us all.

"No, he's still locked up in the *Cloverdale Center*."

I felt a wave of relief, but I was still fearful.

"Why did he write you?"

"He says he's sorry. He said some bad things are happening to him there and they've made him think about what he did to me."

"Do you believe him?" I asked.

"I'm not sure," said Casper quietly. He was staring up at the stars, looking away from me. I walked up behind him and took him in my arms. He leaned back against my chest as I wrapped my arms around him. We both gazed up at the vastness of space, neither of us speaking for several moments.

"Are you okay?" I asked. I knew Jason had hurt Casper. I knew he'd done horrible things to him. I wondered what was running through Casper's mind.

"It's just kind of weird," said Casper. "After everything he did to me, now he's writing and saying he's sorry."

"He may be lying."

"I know."

"Did he ask you for anything?"

"No. Well, yes. He asked me to write him back, but I don't think he expects me to."

"Are you going to?"

"I dunno. I've been trying to put Jason behind me and just forget about everything that happened, but now he's in that awful place and I can't help but feel sorry for him."

"He put himself there," I said. "He made his bed and now he's lying in it."

"I know. He deserves to be there, if anyone does. I can't help thinking of Jason *before*, you know? He was a good brother once. I loved him and I'm pretty sure he loved me. Something happened to him that changed him, made him different. I know that doesn't make the things he did okay, but I can't keep from thinking that things could've been different. Something happened to him to make him like he is—I dunno what, but he wasn't always the way he is now. His letter…he's changing again, at least I think so. Maybe he's gonna be more like he used to be—*before*. Or, maybe not. I'm not naïve, but it's some-thin' I gotta think on."

"I understand," I said, hugging him. "I just don't want you to get hurt. Just remember who you're dealing with. When he says he's sorry, it could be nothing more than another lie."

"I know. I'm gonna think about it. Maybe I'll write him back, maybe I won't."

Casper turned around and I hugged him again. I leaned down and kissed him. He squeezed me tightly as our tongues entwined and I leaned into him.

"You must be tired," said Casper.

"Exhausted."

"Then we'd better get you to bed."

"Yeah, baby!" I said.

"That's not what I meant!" said Casper, giggling.

"I know. I'd be too tired to do it anyway."

"I'll be happy just sleeping by you."

I kissed Casper again and we made our way back to the farmhouse and then to the soft comfort of our bed.

Dane

I slammed down the receiver of the payphone and kicked the door of the booth, Armando's words still ringing in my ears:"*It was just a one night thing, kid. Don't call me again.*" I trembled with anger at being called a kid. Who the fuck did he think he was anyway? Why did it have to be a one night thing? I wanted to do it with Armando again and again and again, but he had other ideas. He'd made that clear enough. I'd gone to *The Park's Edge* for an early supper and he was there—only he totally ignored me. I smiled at him and his expression didn't alter. I waved at him and he looked through me like I wasn't there. Just before leaving, I tugged on his sleeve and all he said was '*Don't bother me, kid, I have work to do.*'

I thought maybe he was just busy and in a bad mood, so I'd waited until a bit later and called. He was actually home. It rang forever, but he answered, finally, only to dump me. I wanted to kick his ass. How could he have sex with me and then tell me he didn't want to do it again? Was I lousy at it or somethin'? I thought back to the way Armando moaned when we were together. He sure seemed to think I was good then. So why didn't he want more? I sure did. I wanted more so bad I almost couldn't stand it.

I walked around town, kicking rocks and cans and anything else in my path. It was a poor substitute for kicking Armando's ass.

"What's the matter with you?"

I looked up. Austin was gazing at me as if I was some kind of freak show.

"I'm just bored outta my mind and Boothe is a jerk!" I wasn't about to tell him the real reason I was pissed off, although I'm not sure why. Austin was a rent boy, after all. He sold his body to guys, so why did I care what he thought? Why did I even think he'd somehow disapprove of me getting it on with one guy when he'd probably done it with a hundred? *You know why, Dane, just admit it. You're in love with him.* I silently told myself to shut up.

"Boothe does have a rather interesting personality, doesn't he?"

"He pisses me off. He's always callin' me *dumb-fuck* or some shit like that." I was beginning to warm to my new topic. It was better than letting my thoughts run where they wanted.

"Ah, don't let him get to you. He calls me *whore-boy* half the time."

"You should slug him in the mouth."

"Nah, I call him names, too, besides, it's true. I am a whore, although I prefer to be called a *rent-boy*—sounds more glamorous and professional, don't you think?"

"Don't say that."

"What? That I'm a rent-boy? Well, I am. I'm good at it, too. It's sure a hell of a lot better than working in some factory or flipping burgers or some shit like that. The hours are short and the pay is good. Sometimes, I even enjoy it. When I don't, I just remember the money."

I looked away for a moment. I didn't like it when Austin talked about being a prostitute. I didn't want him to be that. There was something I really, *really* liked about him. He was strong, confident, and brave. He was cocky, witty, and built. He wasn't particularly handsome, I guess, but I liked his looks. He was the "boy next door" type in a way, but with a twist. There was a wickedness and mischievousness lying just under the surface that made him appealing as hell. He was older and so much worldlier than me. I wanted a guy like him. I wanted *him*. Damn, I needed a good, swift kick in the butt. I had a crush on Austin like I was some kind of teenage girl.

"What did you do today?" I asked, trying to change the subject.

"I don't think you want to know."

"Tell me."

"I did Mr. Everson."

Eww, I guess he was right. I didn't want to know.

"How old is he, anyway?"

"I dunno, forty-somethin'. He's in pretty good shape. I don't mind being with him."

"You want to…like, go to the movie?" I asked, trying to forget about what he'd just told me.

"I might get some business."

"Give it a rest, Austin. You can take one night off."

"I take lots of nights off. That's the problem. You know how hard it is to get paying customers in a little one-horse town like this? Well, lemme tell you, it ain't easy! I have my regulars and they keep my head above water, but this place sucks! I just thank God I don't have any competition. I'm the only game in town."

I didn't want to hear anymore about that. Austin had mentioned leaving for a big city like Los Angeles or New York before and I didn't like it. I didn't want him going anywhere.

"So, if you probably won't be busy, let's catch the movie."

"Okay, okay, if it'll shut you up. I guess you aren't working tonight."

"Nope, we hit a grave last night. Boothe wasn't pleased with his haul."

"Well, that's good news for you. It means he'll be digging up someone else soon."

I laughed out loud.

"What?"

"I was just thinking. A few months ago, if someone had told me I'd be standing here talking to you about prostitutes and grave robbing, I'd have thought they were crazy."

"We do more than just talk about it, you know."

"Yeah, and that's even more amazing."

"You missing home?"

"Hell, no! Living with you is great. Even digging up dead people is sure a lot better than waiting for Stephen to come and beat the shit outta me or…" I looked away, feigning shame. On the inside, I was pleased with myself. I was quite the actor. I'd lied so much to Austin about having an older brother I was beginning to believe in him myself. At least my stories made me interesting.

"What?"

"I don't want to talk about what else he did to me. Being here is *way* better."

Austin eyed me curiously.

"The other stuff he did to you—the rape. He really did that?"

"Yeah, but I don't want to talk about it. Whatever you're imagining, what he did is ten times worse I'm sure. I should've killed him before I left."

Austin let the matter be. He pulled out a cigarette and lit it up.

"You smoke too much," I said.

Austin coughed, "Only a couple of packs a day."

"You're killing yourself."

"Do you think I care? Besides, what are you, a Boy Scout or something?"

"Shut up."

Austin laughed.

"I've seen you smoke a few yourself, so get off my ass."

"Give me a drag," I said.

Austin passed me his cigarette. I took a puff and handed it back.

"Hey, want to invite Boothe to the movie?" he asked.

"Hell, no!"

Austin laughed louder.

"Come on," he said, "let's go."

Austin and I walked toward *The Paramount*. The marquee was lit up with hundreds of lights. It was getting close to seven and wasn't near dark yet, but there was something almost magical about the old theatre. Maybe it was just because I was with Austin. I felt like we were on a real date.

I walked up to the concession stand and Nathan took my order for a couple bags of popcorn and two drinks. He was a dick, but he was cute. I wouldn't have minded jumping on him. If his boyfriend wasn't so strong, I might've tried. Why did all the cute boys in town have freaking body-guards?

"How's Casper, and how's your boyfriend?" I asked, just to piss him off.

The look Nathan gave me wasn't friendly at all. I was glad Austin had gone to the restroom. I didn't want him knowing about the whole situation with Casper and company. Just as that thought entered my mind, I looked over to see Austin coming back. I quickly paid for the popcorn and drinks.

"Stay away from him," said Nathan as he handed me my change.

I didn't know whether he meant Ethan or Casper, but I beat a hasty retreat from the concession stand.

"What was that about?" asked Austin. *Damn, he'd overheard.*

"Oh, um…a friend of his tried picking on me the other day and I kicked his ass. Now he's acting like it was all my fault!" I thought I did a good job of thinking on my feet, but I wasn't sure if Austin believed me or not.

We walked into the dimly lit theatre and picked out seats about halfway down, near the center. I handed Austin popcorn and a Coke. I was keenly aware of his presence as I sat beside him. I could hear his breath and smell his cologne. His golden chain glinted red on his chest in the light of the exit signs. I wanted to put my arm around him, or, better yet, I wanted him to put his arm around me, but neither happened.

Austin was what I wanted. I wanted to date him. I wanted him to buy me flowers and tell me how much he loved me. I wanted to have wild sex with him, but I also wanted to walk hand in hand with him in the moonlight. I wanted us to hold each other and kiss long and passionately. I wanted him to be my boyfriend.

I sat there and pretended he was my boyfriend during the movie. I pretended we'd be going out for a bite to eat after the show and then we'd be going back to his place where we'd make love all night long. In the morning, I'd wake up in his strong arms. I actually made myself believe it for a while, but when reality came back in and crushed my fantasy, it crushed me. I was glad Austin couldn't see the tear that ran down my cheek in the darkness.

Ethan

I faced Zac on the mat. Coach had assigned us to practice together, since we were two of the best. He didn't know about the shit Zac had pulled last season.

"So we battle again," said Zac.

"You've really got to stop reading the comic books, Zac. You're far too melodramatic."

I could tell Zac wanted to say something nasty, but he bit it back, no doubt remembering that I could've had him locked up.

"You got somethin' more this time, Zac? I sure hope so; it would be nice to have a little challenge."

Zac scowled. His muscles tensed and flexed. I was intentionally egging him on, precisely because I did love a challenge. I'd never admit it to Zac, but he was good. Pissed off as he was, I knew he'd put everything he had into our match.

"Let's go," I said.

Since it was just practice, and not a real match, Zac and I circled each other on the mat. There were a few onlookers, but most of the guys were wrestling each other, trying to hone their skills. Coach hadn't made the cuts yet, so some of the guys had something to prove. I already knew I was on varsity, so it was just practice for me.

Zac darted in and tried to get his shoulder under me so that he could lift me right off the mat. I sidestepped him and grabbed him around the middle. Before he could twist away, I got a firm hold on his abdomen. He tried to throw me off, but I just held onto him. While I was attempting to lift him so I could throw him down on his back, Zac made a swipe with his arm, trying to get me in a headlock. He failed, but it threw me off balance and I lost my grip. He escaped.

Zac was powerful. I could tell just by looking that he hadn't been idle during the summer. He'd obviously been working out. His chest was a bit thicker and it looked like he'd been working on his arms, too. He was definitely stronger than last season, but so was I. If he thought he was going to get the upper hand, he was sorely mistaken.

Zac was a good practice partner because he was a good wrestler, but he was a little frightened of me. He tried to hide it, but wasn't entirely successful. I didn't blame him for being scared. I'd held his life in my hands a few months ago. I could've killed him. I could've done anything I wanted to him. Zac knew it. If I'd been the same type as Zac or Devon, Zac wouldn't have been wrestling me now. He would have been dead. I wasn't that type, however, although I'd come to the edge. I often wondered what I would've done if Brandon hadn't been on the verge of cutting Devon's throat, the night Zac, Devon, and their buddies jumped Nathan and me. I'd been within a hair's breadth of killing Zac in my anger, but seeing Brandon about to commit murder brought me back to my senses.

I slammed Zac to the mat. I got him in a headlock. He fought like a tiger, but couldn't break free. His failure took the fight out of him. In a few moments I had him pinned. He walked away—pissed. I smiled. Beating Zac was my revenge on him. I intended for it to be the same every time we wrestled. I knew it would make me a better wrestler still. I had to keep ahead of Zac. I could never let him win.

I watched some of the other guys as I caught my breath. A few of them didn't seem to know what they were doing, but the guys who'd been on the team last year seemed even better than before. I guessed they'd kept in shape over the summer, too. I was in the best shape I'd ever been in. My wrestling skills were finely honed, too. Brendan might not be a wrestler, but he was strong as a bear and we'd wrestled many times over the summer. I'd likely improved not only because of Brendan's strength, but because he was an inexperienced wrestler. He threw some unusual moves my way—things someone on a team wouldn't be likely to do. He was unpredictable and I'd benefited from that. Hopefully, it would help me to make it to the championship again.

I looked at the wrestling banner hanging on the wall. There was my name, the most recent one added. If I had my way, my name would be on there twice. My eyes moved to the large soccer team photo next to the banner. There was Taylor, smiling and carefree, and Mark beside him, looking at Tay instead of the camera. Only a year ago they'd both been alive and well. It seemed like they'd been gone forever, but at the same time I still expected to see them walk into the gym.

I thought of myself at this time last year too. I had so many secrets then and such fear. I lived in dread of being outed and I'd been so alone. Had I known my friends would be so accepting, I could've avoided a lot of needless pain. I guess everything happened the way it was supposed to happen, though. I just wished Mark and Tay were still alive.

***

Nathan stepped behind me and massaged my shoulders as I sat at the kitchen table drinking iced tea.

"You're so tight," he said, "what's worrying you?"

My boyfriend knew me well.

"Money," I said. "I was going over the bills with Jack and we're barely making it. If we have some big, unexpected expense…it's all over. Even Dave's doctor bill and prescription just about put us under. I don't like living this close to the edge."

"Yeah, I know, babe."

"It just eats at me—not knowing if we're gonna have enough money to pay the bills."

"We're doing all we can," said Nathan, "there's no use in worrying about it."

"Yeah, I know. I've been telling myself that, but it's not easy."

"I know it's not. I'm worried too."

"I don't know what we'd do if you and Casper weren't bringing in money. You two are saving our butts right now."

"It's our turn to be the heroes," said Nathan. "You and Brendan get to do it all the time! Besides, I know it isn't bringing in anything right now, but all your work is what keeps the farm going. If you and Jack and Brendan weren't working the farm, we'd be done for already."

"I just hope we can scrape by somehow."

"We will, Ethan, don't you worry."

"You're quite the optimist."

"You're quite the pessimist!"

"Yeah, I'm sorry. I'm just a little down. Everything's piling up a bit too much right now. You're right. Everything will be okay. I need to stop worrying so much."

"There's my Ethan!" Nathan kissed me on the cheek. I stood, grabbed him, and kissed him passionately. Dave came in from the barn just then.

"I'm not lookin'!" he said as he entered, holding his hands over his eyes. That made us laugh.

"How's Henrietta?" I asked.

"She's asleep. Chickens go to bed early, you know."

"And how are you?"

"I'm fine. My fever's all gone."

Nathan kissed Dave's forehead and nodded. "I think you should get to bed anyway," he said.

"Ah, man."

"Go on, you've been sick and you don't want to push it. Besides, it's getting late. We're going to bed soon, too."

"Yeah, but you won't be sleeping!" giggled Dave.

"I'm gonna have to tickle you for that!"

"No, Nathan!"

"You'd better run!"

Dave tore out of the kitchen, with Nathan close on his heels. I smiled as I heard them running up the stairs. How could I not be happy living with Nathan and Dave and the others?

Brendan and Casper came in the back door just then. They'd been outside, walking in the moonlight. They were both smiling shyly. Brendan noticed the stack of bills that were still lying on the table.

"How are we doing?" he asked.

"It's going to be tight, but we're making it—thanks to our two totally cute boyfriends."

"I always knew Casper wasn't just another pretty face," said Brendan.

Casper reddened. "Stop it!" he said. Brendan laughed and mussed his hair.

Brendan and Casper went on up to bed, leaving me sitting alone in the kitchen. Jack and Ardelene had already turned in for the night. I took a sip of iced tea and tried to relax. Things could be worse—they could always be worse. I had a lot to be thankful for. I was healthy and had pretty much my whole life in front of me. Beyond all hope, I was on the wrestling team again and it looked to be a kick-ass season. I was tired from work, but it was work I loved. And, if all that wasn't enough, there was Nathan, Jack, Ardelene, Dave, Brendan, and Casper—not to mention Jon, Brandon, and my other friends. I knew in my heart that I'd rather be here with my extended family—money problems and all—than anyplace else. There were always problems. Everyone had them. If my worries were only about money, then I didn't really have anything to worry about. Somehow, I knew in my heart that everything was going to be okay, just like Nathan said. Maybe things would be tight for a while, but what did that matter when I was surrounded by those I loved? I couldn't think of a life I'd rather live.

I drained my glass, turned off the kitchen light, and climbed the stairs in search of Nathan. It was time to go to bed, but not to sleep. The best things in life are free and making love with Nathan was the most wonderful thing of all.

Casper

I walked up the trail on the far edge of the park. The evening shadows were growing dim, but I was still a bit too warm in my t-shirt and khaki shorts. A trickle of sweat ran down my back and another crept from my chest to the band of my boxers. Still, it was far more pleasant than the intense heat that beat down for the greater part of the day. I savored the evening hours when the heat began to lessen.

I wondered if Shawn would show. Casey said he wanted to talk to Brendan, Ethan, Nathan, or me if it could be arranged. Brendan and Ethan were far too busy with the farm to get away from it just now and Nathan worked at the movie house during the evening hours. I was the only one who could get away from work for a while in the evening and that's when Casey said Shawn needed to meet. His dad and brothers all worked evening shifts and it was the one time of the day he could be sure they wouldn't spot him talking to one of us. Still, he was taking no chances. Casey had set up a secret rendezvous for us on the trails by the park. No one would see us together there and we could hear anyone coming long before they saw us. It was sad to have to take such precautions, but Shawn was that deeply in the closet. He couldn't risk his family finding out or his very life might be in danger.

I saw a shadowy figure up ahead. My heart fluttered slightly with fear. I remembered the night Dane attacked me.

"Shawn?"

"Yeah. It's me."

I drew closer. Shawn stepped out of the shadows. He was dressed as if he were on a stealth mission—wearing a tight, black tank top and black football shorts.

"Hey, Agnes gave me an hour off, so we'll have some time to talk."

158

"Cool. I've wanted to talk to one of you guys, but I'm just so afraid Tom or Tim or Dad will find out."

"It really wouldn't hurt if they just saw us talking, would it? They wouldn't know what we were talking about."

Shawn shook his head. "No, man. I'm not *allowed* to talk to any of you guys. As far as Dad and my brothers are concerned, anyone who talks to queers *is* queer. They'd mess me up bad for it."

Shawn looked around as if he feared one of them might be lurking in the shadows. "I parked over by the high school and walked through the trails. That way no one will see us leaving together."

I nodded. Shawn seemed paranoid, but perhaps it was necessary. I had a little trouble understanding his fear, because Shawn had a powerful body. I'd lived in fear like him once, but I was puny and had trouble defending myself. Shawn was muscular—not as built as Brendan or Ethan, but very strong. He could probably kick ass in a fight, but maybe strength didn't matter. Perhaps there were some fights that couldn't be won. At the moment, Shawn seemed more like a frightened puppy than a football jock. I wanted to take him in my arms and hold him.

"I just wanted to talk to another gay guy," said Shawn. "I feel like I'm the only one in the whole world. I've seen a few guys at school I've kind of wondered about, but I can't take any chances. I just wish there was some way I could tell if a guy was gay by looking at him. It would be cool if there'd be some kind of green halo around his head or something."

"I used to think like that, except I never thought of the green halo."

"I guess green kind of stands for *go*, as in it's okay to try something. I want to do something with another guy so bad I can't stand it!"

"So you've never…"

"Nothing, man. Well, other than…" Shawn made an up and down motion with his hand. "But that hardly counts, as it's all by myself."

"Listen, I know what it's like. Before I met Brendan, I'd never done anything with another guy." That wasn't entirely true, but I didn't want to tell Shawn about Jason. It was too private. I'd certainly never done anything willingly before Brendan and I met.

"I'm about to go crazy!" said Shawn.

I smiled. "Yeah, I remember *that* feeling well. It was all the worse because I figured I'd never get to be with another guy."

"You sure ended up with one hot boyfriend. I'd give *anything* for a guy like that, or for any guy for that matter." Shawn laughed weakly.

"Well, I know it probably doesn't help now, but you'll find someone, Shawn."

"Yeah, it doesn't help, but I know what you're sayin'. You're probably right, but I just feel like I'll never be with a guy."

"You will be—you're handsome, you're built, and you're a real nice guy, according to Casey. A guy would have to be crazy not to go for you—a gay guy that is."

"I feel so trapped, dude," said Shawn. "My dad's crazy and my brothers are about as bad. If they even thought I was gay, I'd be in for it. I don't even dare keep workout magazines around for fear Dad will think it's queer. I don't even have the possibility of finding a guy now. I don't know if I could work up the courage, but even if I wanted, I wouldn't dare approach another guy. If Dad got wind of it he'd kill me, and I'm not exaggerating."

Tears welled up in my eyes. Shawn's situation was different from what I'd experienced before Brendan rescued me, but it was close enough.

"I'm so sorry. Listen, if there's any way we can help you, we will. If things get so bad you've got to run away, you come to the farm and we'll hide you. We'll help you get away. That's the message I brought from Ethan to you. He'll help you, Shawn."

"I'm too scared to run, Casper. I'm sixteen and Dad still owns me for another couple of years. If I run, he'll come after me and I don't even want to think about what would happen if he caught up to me."

The situation sounded familiar. "I think you ought to talk to Brendan sometime. He had to run from his parents. His reason for running wasn't the same, but he still had to get away and he did. Talking to him might help."

"Maybe I will, if we can arrange it sometime."

"I'm sure we can. Casey is a safe go-between."

"God, it just hurts so much," said Shawn. "I haven't even had anyone to talk to about it. I couldn't trust anyone."

"You can trust me," I said, "and Brendan, and Ethan, and Nathan. You're not alone anymore, Shawn."

Shawn began to cry. At first, he cried softly, but his sobs grew louder. I wrapped my arms around him and held him as he cried. I knew what it was like to need to be held. It didn't matter that I was smaller than Shawn. He just needed to feel cared for and I did care for him. I hated to see anyone in pain.

Shawn cried for a few minutes, before his tears quieted and he wiped his face with the back of his hand.

"I'm sorry," he said.

"Don't be sorry. There's nothin' to be sorry about."

"I feel so stupid—crying like a little baby."

"Dude, anyone would cry if they had to deal with the stuff you do. No one should have to live with that kind of fear."

"Sometimes, I just can't take it!" said Shawn loudly. "I feel like just killing myself."

"No, Shawn, you can't do that."

"Like anyone would care."

"I'd care. Casey would care. Maybe she's not your girlfriend, but she is your friend—a good one. What do you think she'd go through if you killed yourself? You can't do that, man."

"I know. It's just that I don't know what to do—I'm trapped. It's all so hopeless."

"What about when you turn eighteen? What are you going to do then?"

"I'm gonna leave. As soon as I'm free, I'm outta here. I'm going far away where my family can't find me and I'm going to start all over."

"There's hope then. You just have to hang on somehow until then. I'll help you and so will the guys. When the time comes, we'll help you get away. If you need us before that, we're here."

Shawn smiled. His tears were gone. "It helps so much to have someone to talk to about all this. I've been holding it all inside. Just having someone listen to me and understand helps."

We talked for a good long time there in the shadows. Shawn poured out his heart to me. I mostly just listened, but I was pleased I could offer him some advice and wisdom as well. I wanted to do anything I could to help him, just as others had helped me.

"I'm here anytime you need me, Shawn. Brendan, Nathan, and Ethan will be there for you, too. That's how we get through things—by helping each other." I looked at my watch. "Whoa, we've been talking almost an hour. I have to get back soon."

Shawn nodded.

"Have Casey tell me when you want to meet again. She can be our messenger."

Shawn hugged me. "Thanks, Casper." I hugged him back.

"It'll be okay, Shawn."

We each went our separate ways. I pitied Shawn. I hoped everything would be okay with him, but I knew his tough times weren't over. At least maybe I could help him in some way. At least now he knew he had somewhere to run. I wished I could do more, but I didn't know how. It was really true what they said, about thinking your problems are tough until you meet someone who has it worse.

Dane

I climbed down from the tree, grinned, and then laughed. Casper had escaped from me, Ethan had denied me, and Armando had left me, but at last I was going to have what I wanted. Shawn had a secret and chance had delivered it into my hands. I'd seen him coming as I sat perched in a huge oak above the trail. I remained quietly hidden above so I could check out his sculpted arms and muscular chest. I was delighted when he halted right beneath me. It was almost as good as my fantasy of having a secret two-way mirror in the locker room at school. Even though it'd grown too dark to see much, I was willing him to pull off his shirt when Casper arrived. I was pissed that the little jerk had come along, but that's when the fun began. That's when Shawn said things that made my head spin. He was a queer in hiding—the answer to my prayers. Shawn wouldn't slip out of my grasp like Ethan. He was going to be mine or I'd feed him to the wolves.

It was almost too dark to see under the trees as I walked along the path. My step was light as my mind raced with plans. I knew what I wanted from Shawn, the question was how to go about getting it. I'd blackmail him, of course, but I wanted to plan it so I could derive maximum pleasure from it. I was going to thoroughly enjoy controlling him. Jocks like Shawn had always lorded it over me. They thought they were so superior with their muscular bodies, popularity, and athletic prowess. Now I had one under my thumb and I was going to make him squirm. If he thought fearing his dad and brothers made his life hell, he was soon to learn what real suffering was all about.

Casper

After work, I arrived home to find another letter from Jason waiting on me. I'd written him back the day after I'd received his first, but I was still surprised to hear from him so quickly. I frowned as I held the letter in my hands. I wasn't so sure becoming involved with Jason again was a good idea, even if it was only letters. The last one had stirred up a lot of memories—mostly of Jason before he turned into someone I didn't even know. Before he began to change, I looked up to him. I was proud of my big brother. I even wanted to be like him. I remembered how he played Monopoly with me and how he tried to teach me how to catch. I smiled again as I thought of the Jason that had been, but sadness fell upon me when I remembered that the old Jason was no more. He was as good as dead. That's what Jason's first letter had done to me and I wasn't exactly eager to open up the second, to open up more memories of the past.

There was no use in putting it off, though. If I set the letter aside, I'd just think about it until I finally opened it. It was better to do it now and get it over with.

From Hell

Dear Casper,

Thank you for writing me back. I didn't think you would, but I'm glad you did. You have no idea how much even a friendly word can mean here. I'm glad you are doing fine. I really am. I understand that you don't feel you can trust me. I don't expect you to, not after everything I did. If you think about it, though, I've always been truthful with you. Okay, I did say I'd hurt Stacey when I hadn't and I told Brendan I'd hurt Brad when I hadn't done that either, but I was out of my head then. You know I was, you were there. Anyway, I've never lied to you about anything and I'm not now. Like I said, I don't expect you to trust me, but what I say is the truth. Maybe someday I can regain your trust, maybe not, but at least let me try.

I feel like sitting down and writing "I'm sorry for what I did to you, Casper" about a hundred thousand times, but I know that wouldn't undo the past. I feel like I've been sent to Hell, Casper. It's like I'm being tormented for all the bad stuff I did in life, only I'm not dead. That's the only hope I've got really—getting out of this place. Don't worry, though, little brother, if I do get out, I won't bother you. I'll sure never do anything bad to you again. I owe you a debt I can't repay and by that I mean that I need to make up for all the horrible stuff I did, but I don't think there's any way I can do that. So you won't have any trouble from me—not ever. I know I'm repeating myself, but I just wanna make sure you know.

Somethin' bad happened to me since I wrote you. Three of the other boys cornered me. The pulled me into a room and beat me up. I fought 'em, but it was three on one so I didn't have much of a chance. They took some drugs I had on me that I was gonna use to bribe an orderly. Brian, one of the orderlies, saw them grab me and beat me up, but he didn't do anything to stop them. He just watched through the window. It's like that here. If you step out of line, the staff is all over you, but if someone is getting beat up or something, the orderlies are just as likely to join in as not. I'm pretty tough, but there are guys bigger than me in here. I've been making friends with the biggest one I could find. His name is Ike. I've been giving him stuff and doing things for him. The orderly that mails my letters for me also gets me stuff I want. I pay him in drugs I don't take and sometimes in other ways. He's gonna get me switched to Ike's room, I'll be safer there. Ike is kinda off in the head, probably from the drugs, but he's a badass and even a lot of the staff is afraid of him. I've been trying to hang around him a lot. When I'm with him, I'm safe. Ike says he'll protect me when I become his roommate, if I...well, there's no pretty way to say this and you'll probably think it's my just punishment anyway, so here goes...Ike says he'll protect me if I'll be his bitch. I'm sure you know what that means. This place is a lot like prison.

Please write me back, Casper. Tell me about the farm. Tell me about anything outside. There's a little park-like place here at the center, but I'm not allowed to go there because of some of the trouble I've caused. I can't even remember what it's like to feel the sun on my face. I never thought I'd miss being outside so much. I miss a lot of things. Write me about anything you want, but please write me, I'm begging you.

Jason

Grandma came into the kitchen to make some lemonade just as I finished reading Jason's letter. I hadn't told her about the first one yet, although I'd been thinking about it. After all, she was Jason's grandmother.

"Are you okay, Casper?" asked Grandma as she pulled the old pink pitcher out of the cabinet.

"I got a letter from Jason," I said. I didn't mean to just blurt it out like that, but out it came. Grandma looked worried.

"How is he?" she asked. I knew then that her apprehension wasn't so much a fear of Jason returning, as it was a fear for Jason.

"He's...not good," I said. "I mean, he's not sick or anything, but the place where he's at—the *Cloverdale Center*—it's a bad place, Grandma."

She nodded, looking teary. Grandmother knew about the *Cloverdale Center*. Brendan and I had told her our entire story. We glossed over some of the more grisly details, but Grandma knew that Brendan still had nightmares about that place—it was that bad.

"What did he say?" she asked, sitting down by me.

I hesitated for a moment, and then handed her my letter. She brought her hand to her mouth as she read it and tears came to her eyes. I wondered if I'd made a mistake. Like me, Grandma no doubt had good memories of Jason. It was hard to think of *that* Jason in such a terrible place, even though my brother was no longer the kind brother he had been. Were his experiences in the *Cloverdale Center* changing him back again? Had he really learned his lesson, or was he just lying? I wondered if maybe I shouldn't just ignore his letters, but some little part of me didn't have the heart to completely turn my back on him.

"So," said Grandma, "you can write Jason?"

"Yes," I said. He sent me a letter just a couple of days or so ago and I wrote him. He already answered back with that one." I pointed to the letter in Grandma's hand.

Grandma folded the letter and handed it back to me.

"Would you like a glass of lemonade, Casper?"

"Sure," I said.

Grandma finished mixing up lemonade in the old pitcher, filled glasses with ice, and then sat down again.

"When you write him again," she said, "I'd like you to send a note along from me."

"Of course. Do you think he's changed, Grandma?"

"I don't know, Clint—I don't know. But, I want him to know I still care. If he hasn't changed, maybe that will help bring back the Jason I once knew, and if he has, I want him to know I love him."

I noticed that Grandma called me "Clint." That was my real name, but even Grandma didn't use it unless something serious was going on, or when I was in trouble. It was a sign that Jason had stirred up uncomfortable feelings for her. I wondered if I'd done the right thing in telling her about the letters, but she deserved to know the truth. I just hoped it wouldn't upset her too much.

I sat at the kitchen table and drank lemonade with Grandma while waiting for Brendan to come in from the fields. I smiled. Whenever I had troubles, I thought of Brendan and everything seemed better. I loved him with all my heart.

Brendan

I walked into the house to find Casper sitting with Ardelene at the kitchen table. Ardelene offered me some lemonade, but I was too tired. All I wanted to do was grab a shower, do some homework, and get into bed. Well, I didn't really want to do the homework, but I couldn't leave it for the next day—not unless I wanted to get up about 4:00 AM.

After my shower, Casper handed me a letter he'd received that day. It was another one from Jason. I didn't like that he was writing Casper. Jason was dangerous. It wasn't all that many months ago that he'd come close to killing both of us.

I finished reading the letter. I wanted to talk to Casper about it, but when I turned to him, he was already sound asleep. I stood, walked to the bed, gently raised his hair and gave him a kiss on the forehead. He looked so sweet and innocent. I couldn't bear to think of the things Jason had done to him. That night we'd run from our hometown in Kentucky was still etched firmly in my mind. My thoughts drifted to that night and I relived it inside my head:

I heard Casper scream from somewhere in the house. "Let me go! Get off me!"

Without thinking, I charged inside. I followed the sounds of a scuffle to what I guessed was Casper's room. I burst through the door. Casper was lying across the bed. His clothes were torn. His brother was holding him down.

I launched myself at Jason and knocked him to the floor. We came up swinging. I was going to kill that fucking bastard. He'd hurt Casper for the last time. I punched him in the face as hard as I could. I didn't care if I killed him. He deserved to die.

Jason was tough. He took the pummeling I gave him and came right back at me. He swung his fist full force at my stomach. I tightened my abdominal muscles, but it still hurt like hell. I flew at Jason, catching him around the waist, sending us both crashing to the floor. I managed a quick jab to the gut before he got me in the face. My head snapped back. I don't think I'd ever been hit that hard before. Jason slammed me down before I had a chance to recover and pressed his knees painfully into my chest. He slugged me in the face over and over until I managed to punch him in the throat and get him off.

I came up swinging. It was all a blur after that. We slugged each other as hard as we could manage, fighting through the pain. All I really wanted to do was drop to the floor and moan and writhe in agony, but as long as I could stand, I was determined to keep fighting. This wasn't just any fight. It wasn't about something stupid. I was fighting to protect Casper. I'd die for him.

I was out of shape from all that had been done to me in the hospital and I took quite a beating. I gave better than I took, however. I was enraged. Jason had hurt Casper. There was no forgiving that.

Jason was no pansy, but he couldn't take the beating I was giving him. He was doing a lot of damage, but I was fucking him up good. I landed a good, solid punch to his jaw that sent him sailing back into the closet. The door collapsed under his weight. For a moment, I thought I'd killed him.

Casper ran to me, running his hands all over my body, making sure I was all right. I wasn't really, but it wasn't like I was going to die, it wasn't like I had any broken bones or anything. I wasn't so sure about Jason, he was barely moving.

"I'm okay, Casper." I looked down at him and the worried expression on his face. I hugged him close to me. "I love you. It's going to be okay now."

I let my guard down. It was a mistake. I caught movement behind Casper. I jerked my head up. Jason was just getting to his feet, he was pointing a double-barreled shotgun right at Casper.

"I told you you'd pay, little brother," he snarled. I'd never seen anyone look so menacing before, not only menacing—insane. I stared at Jason in horror.

Almost without thinking, I shoved Casper behind me, although I didn't know how much good that would do. I hoped that Casper would bolt for the door when Jason shot me. At least then he'd have a chance to get away. I knew what I was going to do. Jason only had two shots. When he fired, I'd push myself forward and grab the gun if I could. Maybe Jason would use his second shell out of fear. He only had two shots before he had to reload. Maybe he'd even blast me with both barrels at once. At least Casper would have a fighting chance to escape.

I knew even as I thought it, however, that it was a plan doomed to failure. The first blast would probably blow me off my feet. There would be no surging forward. I'd be dead. There was nothing else for it, so I'd do whatever I could manage to do.

"Pretty brave for a faggot. Not that it'll help you much. Not so tough now are you? Those muscles aren't much good against this," he said, patting his gun. "This is gonna be a pleasure."

Casper tried to force his way in front of me. I knew what he was trying to do, but I couldn't allow it. I couldn't let him die for me. Even if I somehow managed to survive, I knew I could never live without him. I pushed him back. At the same moment a deafening shot assaulted my ears, sounding like a stick of dynamite had just gone off. I jerked my hands to my chest and looked down, but there was nothing to see. I looked up as quick as lightning and saw Jason falling to the floor, even as his shotgun blasted the air like a cannon. Jason hit the floor hard. Even as he did so, there was a loud thump in the doorway. I looked over to see an older man laying there, his stomach red with blood.

"Dad! Dad!" yelled Casper and ran to him.

I walked to Jason. There was a lot of blood. The sight of it made me sick. I expected him to be dead, but I could hear him breathing and see his chest rise and fall. He'd been hit in the shoulder.

Brad, Stacey, and Chad came running in.

"Oh my God!" said Stacey.

I took a shirt, wadded it up, and pushed against Jason's shoulder. I took the sheet from the bed and tied it around his shoulder to help stop the bleeding. I wasn't quite sure why I was helping him, but I couldn't just let him lay there and die, even if he did deserve it.

I turned to Casper. He was holding his dad's head in his lap, crying. His dad was speaking to him, so quietly I could barely hear.

"I was never a good dad," he croaked out. "I'm sorry...No time to...You were a good son. I love..." His head fell over in Casper's lap and he was gone.

Casper looked up at me, his eyes filled with tears. He gently let his father's head slip to the floor, then ran to me and clasped me about the waist, crying. I held him tight.

"We've got to go," said Brad desperately. I looked at Jason lying on the floor, then back at Brad. I nodded. I knew he was right.

I led Casper out of his old home. We got in the car, and sped away, only to stop after a couple of blocks. Stacey hopped out and called an ambulance for Jason, and then we took off again. We'd done as much for Casper's brother as we could. It was way more than he deserved.

I held Casper as he cried. I couldn't imagine what he was going through. He'd seen his own brother and father shoot each other before his eyes. He'd lost his dad. Maybe his father wasn't a very good one, but he was still his dad. Casper's thin body was racked with sobs.

Tears stung my eyes. The things Jason had done to Casper were unspeakable. His own father had shot him to keep him from killing Casper and me. Jason had thought nothing of turning on his father and killing him on the spot. Jason was a monster.

I looked down at Casper sleeping peacefully. It was all behind us, or so I'd thought. Now, letters were arriving from Jason. I wondered where they'd lead. Still, they were only letters. Jason couldn't hurt Casper. He'd never get the chance again.

***

Devon glared at me as he passed in the hall. That was a sure sign that the word was out. It came as no surprise. I'd kissed Casper right on the lips between first and second periods. There weren't many people around, but we'd shocked a small knot of girls who were passing by my locker. I smiled when I heard one of them say, "Damn, all the hot ones really are gay," as she walked on down the hall with her friends.

There was a time when the very thought of being outed terrified me right down to my toes. Those days had passed. I expected it to happen at V.H.S. It was inevitable. After all, Casper and I were best buddies with Ethan and Nathan, the only openly gay boys in the whole school (as far as I knew). Casper and I didn't try to keep our relationship a secret either. If someone would've asked us, we would've told them. In the morning, the desire to kiss Casper came upon me as we were talking between classes, so I did it. It was as simple as that. Now word was out. I was actually kind of excited to see what would happen. I did intend to put Ethan, Nathan, Brandon, and Jon on alert so they'd join me in keeping watch on Casper. I didn't want anyone giving him any crap.

Devon had never been fond of me, but I was sure he hated me now. That was no loss. Even if I didn't know about the terrible things he'd done in the recent past, I'd have disliked him just because he was a jerk. He was conceited, rude, mean-spirited, condescending, and an all around fucker. Most of that wasn't directed at me, probably because Devon knew I could and would kick his ass for it. I'd observed him interacting with others long enough, however, to know that Devon was an evolutionary error. One of Devon's biggest problems, other than being a homophobe, was that he desperately wanted to be a badass, but he just didn't quite have what it takes. Ethan had filled me in on him. Devon acted when he had other guys to back him up. He was nothing on his own. He stirred up trouble and acted the bully, but he needed someone standing behind him to get anywhere. What a loser. I turned my mind from Devon. I'd thought more than long enough about him.

I paid attention as others passed me in the halls. A couple of my team-mates were looking at me oddly, but didn't seem belligerent. A lot of girls were looking me over. They seemed to be going out of their way to get a look at the queer football jock. It amused me that my sexual orientation came as such a shock. People really were blinded by stereotypes. If you didn't bend your wrist and speak with a feminine tone, most people just assumed you weren't gay. I wondered how many guys who did have the wrist and feminine voice thing going were really straight. Stereotypes were such crap.

During the next break between classes, the inevitable happened. Some of the girls had been watching me during class and one of them stopped me just outside the room.

"Is it true?" she asked. "Are you really gay? Were you really kissing that boy in the hall?"

"Yes, yes, and yes," I said.

"Whoa," she said, looking astounded. "I mean, that's cool and everything. It's just…wow."

I smiled. "I've got to get going," I said.

"Okay, well, see you later, Brendan." She turned to her friends and began talking excitedly. I guess the time had come for my fifteen minutes of fame.

No one said anything to me in the locker room before football practice. I undressed and then suited up as always. I made no special attempt to keep my eyes from roving. A lot of my teammates were attractive, and a few were downright hot, but I loved Casper. I had no need to check out other guys when I had the best boyfriend in the world at home. Sure, I did do a little looking, but I was always careful not to look in such a way as to make anyone uncomfortable. That was especially important now, but it's something I'd done from day one at V.H.S.

I grinned when I thought about my situation. A gay boy in the guy's locker room was a lot like a straight boy in the girl's locker room. I was sure I had way more control than any of those around me. I could just imagine my team-mates gawking if there were naked girls around. Of course, not all the guys were into girls. There was Shawn and most likely others. It wouldn't have surprised me one bit to find out there were a couple of other gay boys on the team and probably a bi one or two as well.

The unpleasantness Tom had shown during the tryouts and earlier practices was even more pronounced. If he was simmering before, he was boiling now. He was the only one on the team that muttered "faggot" under his breath during the first practice after I'd been outed. I wasn't even quite sure he'd said it. It could've been my imagination, but if anyone was going to say it, I was sure it was him.

Coach Jordan had picked out the varsity squad. Shawn was out of the running for quarterback, although he was still on the varsity team. It was down to just Tom and me. Even if Tom hadn't had a thing against gays, we still wouldn't have gotten along. He was obsessed with being quarterback and I was definitely in his way. I think what pissed Tom off the most is that I was clearly superior to him. He was a good quarterback, but I was better and we both knew it. I'm sure Tom would've died before admitting it, but there was no doubt. I just hoped Coach thought the same.

I showered after practice and walked into the locker room wearing only a towel. As I was getting dressed, I heard Tom mutter "faggot" under his breath as he looked at me. There was no doubt about it. I heard him clearly this time, as did most of our team-mates who were still in the room.

"If you have something to say, say it to my face," I said, turning to Tom.

Tom had his jeans on, but was still shirtless. He crossed his arms over his chest and said, "Okay. You're a faggot."

I just stood there looking at him.

"You don't hear him denying it, do you boys?" he said, looking around.

"Why would I deny it?" I asked, calmly. "It's true, although the proper term is gay."

"Whatever you call it, it's sick. We don't need a queer ogling us while we're naked."

"First off," I said, "I've never ogled anyone. Second, Tom, you aren't that hot, so why in the fuck would I be checking you out? Third, I have a boyfriend. I don't know how loyal you are to your girl, but I'm completely loyal to Casper. I'm not interested in anyone else. Yeah, I'm gay. I'm attracted to guys. So what? Is there anyone in here who thinks I've been checking them out? Is there?" I looked around the room. A lot of the guys looked uncomfortable, but not one of them spoke up.

"This team doesn't need a queer quarterback," said Tom.

"Is your problem with me because I'm gay," I said, closing the distance between us, "or is it because you're afraid I'm better than you at football."

Tom looked ready to pounce. Shawn was looking on in fear, as if he believed Tom would jump me at any second. I knew there was a good chance of that and I was ready. If he made the first swing, I was gonna pound him into the ground. Tom controlled himself, however.

"Yeah, right! You better than me? I don't think so!"

"I do," I said.

"If Coach picks you, then he don't know shit and I'm walking off the team. Who's with me?"

Tom looked around the room, but no one joined him. He glared at his brother and Shawn said, "I am," after a significant pause. I knew his support of Tom meant nothing. It wasn't real.

Tom grabbed his shirt and shouldered past me. Just as he did so he muttered "faggot" once more. I grabbed his shoulder and swung him around.

"If you *ever* call me that again, you'll be picking your teeth up off the floor," I said, menacingly. I'd have bet anything Tom would take a swing at me, but instead he jerked away and stomped out of the locker room.

Shawn was only a few steps behind him. He glared at me as he passed and spat "faggot." I slammed him up against the lockers, going for a good show instead of actually trying to hurt him. "The same goes for you, Shawn," I said, "I'd better never hear you call me that again." Shawn looked angry. He was a good actor. He pushed my hands away and stomped out like this brother. I smiled inwardly. Shawn's actions would no doubt get back to his brother and help him avoid detection.

No one else gave me any crap. In fact, a couple of guys came up and said they hoped I'd make quarterback. I was pleased to find that the team had only one resident homophobe. The rest didn't seem to have much of a problem with my sexual orientation.

Dane

I was so pleased with what I'd discovered about the football jock, Shawn, that I didn't even dread my next night of employment with Boothe. I'd seen Shawn in *Ofarim's* a couple times and thought he was yummy. Even through his shirt, I could tell he had the kind of body I liked—hard and muscular. He had a nice ass too. He was always with that girl, however, so I assumed he was straight. He wasn't, though—he was as bent as bent could be.

I wasn't so happy the next night when I found out my job involved a little something extra—something ghoulish and disturbing. Grave robbing was already ghoulish and disturbing, but Boothe took those terms to new heights. The digging was just the same—backbreaking, sweaty, and dirty, but the difference came when we got down to the coffin. Boothe pried open the crypt with the crowbar and slid the lid out of the way. He stepped down into it and opened the casket lid. Inside was a young man who'd probably died in his late twenties. The tombstone indicated that he'd been buried some fourteen months before. As Boothe shined the light on him, I noted he was well preserved, except he looked kind of—purple. Boothe rummaged around in the casket and came up with a couple of rings and a pocket knife. I'd noted in my short time working for Boothe that rings were the most often found items in caskets. I guess that made sense—there wasn't a lot of room in a coffin, so it was small things that got buried with people. It's not like there was space for a TV or somethin'. Besides, I guess things like rings were more personal.

I was surprised that Boothe didn't start cussing at the meager haul, but that's when I learned that he was taking his grave robbing a step further. He actually gripped the corpse by the shoulders and lifted him to a sitting position.

"Throw me the rope," he said. "There's one in my pack."

I did as he said, curious as to what he wanted with rope and repulsed that he was actually handling a dead guy. I'd seen him rifle through the pockets of the deceased and even take necklaces from around their necks, but I'd never seen him wrestle one around before.

Boothe secured the rope under the arms of the corpse and climbed up the rope ladder.

"No way!" I said when it became clear he intended to take the body out of the casket.

"Shut up and pull," he said.

I did as I was told, but I wasn't happy about it. The dead dude weighed a ton, even though he looked to be of normal size. I thought we'd never get him to the top. Boothe got him under the arms and pulled him out onto the grass.

"Help me carry him to the truck."

I just stood there gaping. I was in shock.

"Help me carry him, dumb-fuck."

"Fuck no!" I said. "I'm not touching no dead dude. That's not my job. You pay me to dig and that's it! No fucking way!"

Boothe grabbed me by the front of the shirt and snarled at me, "Grab his feet, now!" I feared Boothe was going to clobber me if I didn't do as he said. I grabbed the gloves I wore while digging and put them on, and then gripped the corpse by the ankles. Feeling the corpse, even through the gloves made me woozy and nauseated.

"I thought they were supposed to be all stiff after they died," I said.

"That's right after they die, stupid. They limber up later and then get all squishy."

My skin crawled. It was bad enough to dig up a grave and watch Boothe steal from the dead, but to actually touch a rotting corpse…it was just…ewww. If one of the corpse's arms or something pulled off I was gonna puke and freak out right then and there.

I couldn't see the body well in the dim light, but I didn't know if that was good or bad. I had the feeling my imagination was worse than reality. My whole body trembled slightly. I had an irrational fear that the dead guy was going to wake up and then eat our brains or something. *Stop it, Dane. Just stop it.* I was scaring myself. I put the corpse out of my mind as much as possible and concentrated on hating Boothe instead. It wasn't difficult. Even if Boothe wasn't a total asshole, I'd have been pissed at anyone who made me carry a dead guy.

After what seemed like an hour, but was probably only about five minutes, we reached the truck. We lay the corpse on the tailgate, and then Boothe dragged it into the bed of the truck. He pushed it to a sitting position, then put his hand behind its head and said, "Hey, you, come here. I'm dying to meet you," like it was some kind of ventriloquist dummy.

"That's not funny!" I said, edging toward tears.

"Don't be such a pussy. It's not like he cares. Isn't that right, Ryan?"

"You *knew* this guy?" I asked, horrified.

"Yep, we used to hang out, didn't we old buddy? This is just like old times."

"You're sick," I said.

"Shut up, you little shit."

I glared at him, but he couldn't see my expression in the darkness.

"Ryan used to be a customer of Austin's."

"You're making that up!"

"Not at all. Ryan here was a major fag and deep in the closet. Even I didn't know he was queer until Austin told me after Ryan died."

"I don't wanna hear any more," I said.

Boothe moved the corpse's head again and said, "Bye, dumb-fuck, nice to meet you." Boothe laughed. He thought he was so funny. I thought he was a sick bastard. He was freaking me out. I gazed at Boothe with pure hatred, not caring if he could see me or not. Booth laid the corpse out flat and covered it with a tarp.

"Come on, we still have to fill in the grave."

I followed Boothe back to the open grave, wondering what would happen if someone lifted the cover in the back of his truck. If there was trouble, I was going to run and leave Boothe to himself. It was his truck, after all, and no one knew I was helping him, except for Austin and he'd never squeal.

"What are you going to do with the body, anyway?" I asked as we were shoveling dirt back into the empty grave. "You going to sell it to some medical college or somethin'?" I'd read about grave robbers doing that, but that was way, way back and in London.

"Something like that," said Boothe and that's all I got out of him.

Boothe handed me $40 as we climbed back into the truck after we'd finished our task.

"I should get more for helping you carry that dead dude. That's not my job."

"Your job is what I say it is, bitch," said Boothe.

"Don't call me bitch, fucker!" I yelled. I'd had quite enough of Boothe.

Boothe clobbered me in the jaw, hard. "Don't talk back to me, *bitch!*"

I glared at him, but bit back the words I wanted to hurl at him. My jaw ached and I was scared. Boothe was bigger than me and I knew I couldn't take him. I'd get a few good punches in if we fought, but he'd kick my ass good. It wasn't worth it.

"Yeah, that's right, *bitch!*" he said. I wanted to kill him.

Boothe let me out of the truck and took off with his corpse. Who knew what he was really going to do with it. I never did find out. Mostly, I just didn't want to think about it. I rubbed my sore jaw and walked toward home, turning my thoughts from Boothe to Shawn and all the fun I would soon be having with him.

Ethan

After yet another wrestling practice, I changed clothes and then hurried to the barn. I found Dave there, taking care of his chickens. I remembered the day I gave him Henrietta; it seemed ages ago. Now he cared for all the chickens.

I made sure there was plenty of water in the trough, and then walked outside and looked at the perfectly clear sky. The evening sun beat upon my face. I kicked a dirt-clod with my shoe and it exploded into a little cloud of dust. If it didn't rain soon, there'd be no crops at all. We had under a hundred dollars in the bank and we owed more than we should. The rain still refused to come. I wasn't worried, though. Somehow, I knew things would work out. I didn't know how, but everything would be okay. I just had to trust in that and keep going.

A cow ambled around the side of the barn. I crossed my arms over my chest and gazed at her sternly. "And just what do you think you're doing, miss?" I asked. She didn't answer, of course, but looked at me with her big brown eyes. "Go on. Your great escape has been foiled this time." I shooed her back the way she'd come.

I followed her and she led me to the fence that the cattle had pushed over, again. I surveyed the situation and decided I'd need to set a new post or we'd just have to keep repairing it over and over. I walked back to the barn, grabbed a posthole digger, a spare post, and other tools I'd need. I had to make two trips.

Less than two minutes of digging had sweat running off my bare chest and back in streams. I never minded sweating, so it didn't bother me, but it was just another reminder of how infernally hot it was.

I grinned as I pulled dirt out of the new posthole, remembering when Nathan and I had put in the line of fence. It was only a few months before, but in some ways it seemed like years and years ago. I wondered if time could pass like that. Could it be that years had really passed, even though we only aged a few months? I sometimes felt that an hour lasted for days, or that days lasted but an hour. I had a sneaking suspicion that time was not constant, but I guess I could never prove it. I suppose it didn't really matter. I even had a theory that time didn't go in a straight line at all. I knew I was no Albert Einstein, but I had the sneaking suspicion that everything that had happened, was happening, or would happen was really happening all the time. There was no past, present, and future. Everything was going on all at once and forever. If that was true, then each moment was eternity. I kind of liked the idea of that, for it meant that I was still working with Nathan on the fence, I was still laughing with Mark and Taylor, and I was still eating chocolate chip cookies while I talked with my Mom. I guess I'd never know for sure, until maybe after I died.

I considered asking Nathan to help me with the posthole for old times' sake, but then I remembered he was at work. I missed seeing him working in the garden and around the farm. Nathan had only a few precious hours for farm work. Sometimes he made it home from his job in town by ten, but sometimes he came in much later. By the time he did homework and got some sleep, it was time to get up and go to school. My own schedule was little better, although all my work was right on the farm. I still felt guilty that I was wrestling, but I was happy to be on the team too. This was my last chance to wrestle. This time would never come again. I hoped that all time really was going on forever, because that way I'd always be wrestling.

I had to make a trip back to the barn for wire-cutters. I saw Ardelene working quietly in the garden, watering the thirsty plants. I wondered what it was about the garden that made it so soothing. Everyone seemed drawn to it. Casper's grandma spent a good deal of time in it, carefully tending the flowers and vegetables. Casper himself seemed to find it a place of peace, too. Sometimes I saw him just standing in the garden alone at night, gazing at the plants or the stars above. Sometimes, I saw Nathan out there just before we left for school, doing just a bit of gardening before he started his day. Maybe Ardelene, Nathan, and Casper found the same contentment in the garden that I felt on the whole farm. There was just something about making things grow, riding a tractor, or even repairing a broken fence that gave me peace. I knew I was lucky. I was exactly where I belonged. I had problems to be sure, but I rarely failed to find pleasure in my life on the farm.

I had to stop and rest before I finished the job of repairing the fence. I was breathing heavily and my heart pounded in my chest. The heat made everything more difficult. I'd always liked it hot, but I knew enough to use some common sense. After a short break, I got back to it and before long I had the fence repaired. The cattle would have to find another exit if they wanted out of the pasture.

Brendan came home just as I was putting up the tools. Uncle Jack found us in the barn and suggested we haul in some of the hay he'd baled during the day. There was next to no chance of rain, but it was a task that needed to be performed nonetheless.

I hopped on the tractor, started it up and drove it around the side of the barn where the flatbed wagon was sitting. Brendan helped me hook it up, and then we were on our way. The shadows were beginning to deepen and the lights of the tractor cast a golden glow upon the earth as I drove toward the field where Jack had spent his day. Brendan and Jack rode on the wagon— Brendan laying out full length as if napping.

I stopped the tractor and Brendan hopped off the back. We started grabbing up bales and tossing them onto the wagon while Jack stacked them. When we got too far ahead of Jack, one or the other of us would jump up onto the wagon and help him catch up. That wasn't too often, however, as Jack was a tough old guy. I had to stop lifting bales now and then to move the tractor up a few feet.

We were getting quite a workout and that was fine by me. I didn't have time to lift weights like I wanted. I was even skipping out on some of the team lifting sessions to put in more time on the farm. But tossing bales onto a wagon was just as good as pumping iron. My aching muscles spelled that out for me in no uncertain terms.

The stars came out overhead and the moon was a brilliant white-blue. I could hear the frogs croaking and the insects singing their nightly songs. Night was a good time to gather the hay. I'd done it in the blistering sun in summers past and it wasn't the most pleasant experience. I was sweating profusely and was hot as could be, but at least the sun wasn't beating down on me.

I felt dehydrated when we stopped for the night, even though I'd drunk nearly a gallon of water. I was glad to call it quits. I was exhausted and my body ached.

As I ambled toward the farmhouse, I saw Nathan in the garden. He was busily watering plants in the bright moonlight. I left Jack and Brendan to go on by themselves and joined Nathan in his place of peace.

"I'd hug you, but I'm all sweaty," I said. I was still breathing hard as if I'd been running.

Nathan put down his watering can and hugged me tight. "It's okay, I'm a little sweaty myself."

Tired as I was, I grabbed another watering can and helped him for a few minutes. It seemed like I never had enough time with Nathan these days. We didn't get to make love nearly as much as I wanted and there was never enough time to just sit down and talk. That was okay, however, for I slept by his side each night and saw him every single day, even if only for a while. And then, there were our late-night love making sessions. When we'd both gone without for far too long, we reached for each other in the darkness and made wild, passionate love in the wee hours of the morning. I wish we had some time for that just now. I craved Nathan. I wanted to feel myself inside him.

I pulled Nathan to me and hugged him again. I kissed him passionately, slipping my tongue into his mouth. I pressed my hardness against him and he pushed himself against me.

"I want you so bad," said Nathan.

"You can have me," I said.

"Right here?"

"Why not? Everyone is inside asleep, or soon will be. The darkness will hide us."

Nathan smiled wickedly and sank to his knees in the tilled earth. My jeans and boxers slid down to my ankles and I felt Nathan engulf me. I ran my fingers through his hair, moaning my appreciation.

My lack of control was a sure sign of how sex-deprived I'd been. I could usually hold out about as long as I wanted, but three minutes was the extent of my control on that night. I threw back my head and moaned, then relaxed completely. Nathan stood and kissed me, and then I sank to my knees before him.

There was something innately exciting about unfastening his belt and unzipping his jeans. No matter how many times I did it, my fingers trembled with anticipation. When Nathan's jeans and boxers were around his ankles, I leaned in and slowly swallowed him, savoring the sound of his voice as he moaned, "Oh, yes, Ethan."

Nathan didn't last long either, but that didn't matter. We stood and necked in the garden for a few minutes, hugging each other close. Every time with him was like the first time—filled with excitement and pure, wild, sexual energy. I could never get enough.

I kissed him once more, and then drew back. "I've got to get some homework done, and then I plan to pass out."

Nathan kissed me again, "I'll been in soon, babe. I'm going to finish here and then grab a shower. I'll be waiting for you in bed.

I smiled as I walked to the house. It was wonderful to be in love.

Casper

"Oh, man, that kills my chest," I said as I got off the weight-machine. It was early Saturday morning and Brendan, Ethan, Nathan, and I were all taking some time to workout. Ethan said everyone needed a bit of a break from our usual routine.

"It wouldn't if you did it more," said Ethan. "You ought to start working out regularly."

"I would if I could find the time."

"You can make the time. Even if you just get in half an hour every other day, it would make you feel great."

Brendan and Ethan worked out whenever they could and so did Nathan a lot of the time, but I hadn't gotten into it as much as I would've liked. I was going to change that, however, starting today. The benefits of working out were obvious. All I had to do was watch Brendan bench-pressing to see that.

My eyes were glued to Brendan's bare chest as he benched over 200 pounds. The way his pecs surged and flexed turned me on like crazy. I wished I had muscles like that. Of course, having a built boyfriend was probably even better. Having muscles would be awesome, but getting to explore them on my boyfriend was…well, shall we say, more stimulating? Just looking at Brendan's chest made me drool. He was beautiful, like one of those Greek statues that are in museums. It was almost unbelievable that anyone could look that good.

It was funny, though, as much as I was attracted to Brendan's body, the things I really loved about him had nothing to do with looks. Brendan was sweet, kind, and loving. He made me feel good about myself. He was funny and fun and I loved just talking to him. It was those things and not his muscles that made me love him. I could've been in lust with Brendan's body without those things, but I could never have been in love with him if there was no more to him than looks.

It was Nathan's turn next. He didn't have near the build of Brendan or Ethan, but he looked fine lifting weights. His muscles were slim, but he was bigger than me. I guess he was kind of a preview of what I could become if I was more dedicated to lifting. I liked what I saw, and I'd be happy if I could achieve a body like his. If he could do it, I decided, I could do it too.

We went through bench presses, butterflies, lateral pull-downs, rows, curls, ab crunches, and a few other exercises. By the time we were done my body felt tight and ached just a little. I liked the tight feeling. It made me feel healthy and in shape. I also felt strangely energized, instead of tired. I wished I could do workouts between school and working at *Ofarim's*, but it wouldn't make much sense to come home and then go back into town, even if I had the time or the means, which I didn't.

I sure liked looking at Brendan after he'd worked out. He was all toned and buffed up. He always looked hot, but after he'd finished his workout he looked especially fit and sexy.

"I need a shower," said Brendan.

I smiled wickedly and followed him. Neither Ethan nor Nathan said a word, but they didn't miss the look on my face. I was sure they knew that Brendan wouldn't be alone in the shower. Grandma and Jack were in town, so we were safe from getting caught by them. They both knew that Brendan was my boyfriend, but I'd have died from embarrassment if they caught us together in the shower.

Brendan didn't realize I'd followed him. I waited outside the bathroom door until he'd slipped out of his clothes and stepped into the shower. I slipped inside the bathroom as the steam began to waft over the shower curtain. I pulled off my shoes and socks, then my shorts and boxers. I was so aroused already that I just about couldn't get my boxers off. I'm sure you know what I mean.

Brendan was slightly startled as I pulled the shower curtain open. He was soaping up his hard chest as I climbed in with him.

"Let me do that for you," I said.

I took the washcloth and ran it over Brendan's smooth skin. I always marveled that his skin felt so silky and smooth when the muscle underneath was so hard. I lathered his chest and then his tight abdomen, tracing his muscles with the soapy washcloth. The hot water pounding down upon us and the steam that rose from our bodies made everything that much sexier. When I ran the washcloth lower and grazed Brendan's manhood, it was already standing straight out from his body. I grinned. It made me feel good that I could arouse him—me, *Casper the Friendly Runt*.

I ran the washcloth over his length, back and forth, just a few times before running it lower and then down his legs. I wanted to get him all worked up, but I didn't want to do anything sexual just yet.

When I'd worked my way down to Brendan's ankles, he grasped my shoulders and pulled me to my feet. He pressed his lips to mine and kissed me as the hot, steamy water flowed over us.

Brendan took the washcloth from me and ran it all over my body as I had his. It made me tremble with passion. Brendan turned me so that I was facing away from him and ran the soapy washcloth over my back and buttocks. The washcloth fell into the tub and Brendan held me tightly against him. I leaned my head back and kissed him as I felt him enter me.

We'd never made love like that in the shower before. The hot water, the steam, Brendan's arms wrapped around me, and Brendan deep inside me all combined for exquisite pleasure that I'd never dreamed possible. As Brendan thrust, his hand closed around my hardness. His fingers were warm and soapy and I moaned with the pleasure he was giving me.

I'm sure we could be heard outside the bathroom, but we didn't care. Ethan and Nathan wouldn't mind. We heard sounds coming from their bedroom at night that left no doubt as to what they were doing. There was nothing wrong with making love.

Our breathing quickened to panting and our moans grew louder until we both found release. I lay back in Brendan's arms. He held me and then turned me around so he could hug me and kiss me and say, "I love you." Nothing was more special than hearing those words.

"I love you, too, Brendan." I smiled and nuzzled my nose against his.

We rinsed off and climbed out of the shower. We dried each other off, then wrapped towels around our waists and went to our room. Ethan met us in the hall and his smile made it obvious he had a good idea of what had been going on in the bathroom. I had a feeling he'd be disappearing with Nathan soon enough. We all had to make good use of the little time we had together. Sometimes it seemed like we were all so busy working that we barely got to see each other.

In our room, we dropped our towels and fell onto the bed in each other's arms. We hugged and kissed and rubbed against each other, enjoying the closeness and intimacy. Our sexual needs satisfied for the moment, we were content to cuddle and kiss. Our time was brief, but I lay there naked in Brendan's arms as we discussed our hopes and dreams. I was completely content. I could not see into the future, but I knew that wherever it took me, Brendan and I would go there together.

***

Agnes didn't need me at *Ofarim's* until about three, so I spent the rest of the morning helping the guys load hay. Jack had returned with Grandma and he was out inspecting the soy beans, seeing if there would be any need to even try to harvest. Brendan, Ethan, Nathan, and I were picking up bales and loading them onto a big wagon. Nathan drove the tractor through the field, while Brendan and Ethan tossed bales onto the wagon and I stacked them as neatly as I could. Brendan said the work went loads faster with Nathan and me helping.

Nathan had the easiest job. All he had to do was sit on the tractor and slowly drive, or stop for a bit when the guys got behind. My job wasn't too tough, however. The stack on the wagon grew higher, but Brendan and Ethan were always able to throw the bales to the top. I took over from there. The bales were heavy, but I mainly just had to pick them up and move them a short distance. Even that was almost too much for me after our morning workout. My biceps, shoulders, and back were screaming for a break. We all drank gallons of water—literally. I felt like I sweat it out as fast as I could drink it.

We stopped for lunch a little after noon. My poor muscles were sure glad of the chance to rest. Grandma had a nice lunch waiting for us—fried pork chops with green beans, peas, and mashed potatoes that'd all come from our own garden. There were also fresh yeast-rolls that Grandma had baked and warm apple pie. Yum! The pork chops were kind of a treat. Money was real tight, so Grandma was sparing with the meat in the freezer. It had to last for who knew how long. Most everything else came from the farm, even the apples for the pie.

After we'd all stuffed ourselves, I ran out to the mailbox to check the mail. I was kind of expecting another letter from Jason. He'd sent two so far and it only took a couple of days for them to reach me after I'd written him. That seemed pretty fast, but then Kentucky wasn't *that* far away. It wasn't like he was writin' from California or somethin'.

There was another letter from Jason in the mailbox, along with the usual junk mail, bills (ouch), and the paper. I walked back inside, dumped the other stuff on the kitchen counter, and took my letter upstairs to read while the other guys were heading back to the fields. I'd join them as soon as I could, but I wanted to read my letter first.

From Hell

Dear Lil' Bro,

Thanks for telling me all about Grandma's garden. You probably won't believe this, but I read your last letter at least twice a day. I read it and close my eyes and pretend I'm there in the garden with you and Grandma. I can just about see the flowers and the tomato plants. I wish things had worked out different. I wish I could take everything back and be there with you and Grandma. I guess if I did, then you'd probably be back home with me and Dad, though, instead of where you are with Brendan. I've been thinkin' about Dad a lot. My lawyer told me not to say anything about him or the night he died, so I won't, but I just wish he was still alive.

Things are getting worse here. Those three boys that I told you about, the ones who beat me up, they got me again, only this time it was worse. It was that fucker, Brian, the orderly from Hell that made it happen. He made me go in the basement with him and they were all waitin' on me in a room down there. I won't go into details cause it's too horrible, but they raped me—gang-banged me, and Brian joined in. I wish he was dead. I didn't know, Casper, I didn't know how horrible the things I did to you were until I got put in here. I'm sorry, Casper. I know I can't make up for it, so all I can do is say I'm sorry over and over again.

Tell Grandma I got her note and that I love her, too. I'm surprised she wrote and said she loved me. How could she after all that I did? I believe her, though, and it makes me feel good inside, like maybe there's still hope for me. I dunno, though, I don't think there is much hope in this place.

I'm rooming with Ike now, just starting today. I feel safer. Even Brian is afraid of Ike, so I won't have to worry about him getting me at night or anything. I'm going to stick with Ike most of the time, but I can't always because…well, I can't say in case the wrong person reads this letter. I don't think that will happen, but I gotta be careful just in case. That's the same reason I never tell you the name of the orderly who sends my letters and gives yours to me. It's part of the deal. If it was found out that he's helping me, he'd be gone and I'd be up shit creek.

I know I already said this, but I just wanna promise you again that I'll never bother you. I'll probably be locked up in prison if I ever get out of here, so I wouldn't have the chance if I wanted. But, even if I was free, I'd never bother you, little brother. Never again.

Love,
Jason

I put Jason's letter with the others, and then went back downstairs. I filled a couple of gallon jugs with cold water and headed back to the field where the guys were busy loading hay. Grandma was in the kitchen, but I decided to tell her about the letter later as I needed to get back to work. The boys needed me.

Brendan

Casper was unusually thoughtful as he joined the rest of us in the field. He tugged off his shirt, climbed onto the wagon, and began lugging bales of hay into place. He didn't speak to anyone after greeting us and his eyes were distant. I knew why—he'd received another letter from Jason.

The letters made me edgy. Part of me didn't want Casper even reading them. Jason was just this side of Jack the Ripper as far as I was concerned. Hell, he was even worse because he'd hurt my boyfriend. The letters were Casper's, though, to read or not read as he decided. It wasn't my business. Maybe I was worried for nothing. After all, Jason was locked up in the *Cloverdale Center* and unless the jury at his trial let him off, he'd be going from there to prison. There was no way a jury would find him innocent. There were too many witnesses...

My mind traveled back to the day Jason had come to the farm to kill Casper. Ethan and I walked into the barn and there he was. I could see it in my mind's eye as if it were all happening again:

"Miss me stud?"

I just stood there gaping. Jason had his arm around Casper's throat, slightly choking him. Nathan was standing just in front of him and a bit to the side.

"You seem surprised," he said. It was an understatement. Jason was the one person I never expected to see again. I'd never given him a moment's consideration after the night he'd tried to kill me and Casper. He wasn't a part of my life after that. I couldn't believe he was here. I had no idea how he'd been able to track us down.

"You and your butt buddy get over there," said Jason, pointing the pistol he was holding to a spot in the middle of the barn. "You too," he said to Nathan as he shoved him roughly from behind.

I started to step toward him, but he whipped the pistol around and pointed it to Casper's head.

"I wouldn't try that Brendan, or things could get messy."

I stood there glaring at him, my muscles bulging. I wanted to tear him apart. Ethan was standing next to me. He looked like he was itching to get at Jason too. I saw Nathan looking around. I could tell he was thinking of what he could do. There was nothing any of us could do, however. Jason had the gun, and Casper.

"We've got a score to settle, little brother," he said. "Your friends caused me a lot of trouble; almost got me put in jail. Luckily, I was able to convince the judge that I was only looking out for my poor, baby brother." His voice was dripping with sarcasm and menace.

"Casper saved you," I said. "We could have just let you lay there and die, but he called an ambulance for you." That wasn't entirely true, Stacey had called the ambulance, but Jason didn't know that.

"So he's stupid, as well as a little queer," said Jason. His features were filled with hatred. He looked at Casper. He grabbed him by the front of the shirt and made him face him, mere inches away. He pointed the barrel of the pistol right between his eyes.

"Show your friends how you can beg, Casper. Beg me not to blow your brains out."

It was all I could do to keep from pouncing on Jason, but I knew Casper would die if I did. Jason would pull the trigger. I'd be just as guilty of Casper's death as if I'd shot him myself. I hoped that Ethan and Nathan wouldn't try anything stupid.

"No," said Casper. I knew he was scared, he had to be, but Casper stood right there and defied his brother. I couldn't believe his courage. It infuriated Jason.

"You'll beg me, you little fucker!"

He forced Casper down onto his knees and put the barrel of the pistol right in his mouth. I wanted to close my eyes. It was too horrible to watch. I was crying. I wanted to jump Jason. I'd have done anything to stop him, but I was powerless.

Casper looked up at his brother and shook his head "no." I thought that was going to be the end. Jason screamed in rage and smashed Casper in the face with the pistol. I leapt forward, so did Ethan, but Jason whipped the pistol around and leveled it on us in an instant.

"If you won't beg for yourself, then maybe you'll beg for your friends. I was going to let them live, Casper, but now I'm not so sure. Which one should it be first, little brother?" he asked.

Casper was still on his knees, he was trembling and the side of his face was turning purple where Jason had hit him.

"Maybe this one," he said, pointing the gun at Nathan. "He looks kind of like you, Casper. Shooting him will almost be like shooting you. Want to watch him die before I kill you, little brother?"

Casper didn't answer.

"Or maybe this one," said Jason, pointing the gun toward Ethan. "Damn, he's got even more muscles than your boyfriend. I bet you and him are real close, aren't you, Casper? You like 'em built, don't you, little brother?"

"No," said Jason, pointing the gun at me, "I think it's got to be Brendan. I think killing him will pay you back more than anything else I could do to you. I might spare him if you beg me, Casper. Do a good enough job and you'll be the only one that dies today." He turned and looked at Casper, smiling.

"Oh," he said, "I almost forgot. I already did a little paying back, just before I came here. Remember your little friend Stacey? Do you Casper? I paid her back good." Casper's heart broke and he bawled.

"I hate you," he said between sobs.

"And Brad," said Jason, turning to me, "He begged. He squealed like a girl begging me not to kill him. Too bad he didn't beg quite hard enough."

I trembled. I didn't know whether to believe him or not. I feared the worst, however. Jason was a sick bastard. Something in his eyes made me believe it was true. I slowly shook my head "no" as tears flooded my eyes. My best friend, Brad, who had stood by me when I'd needed him the most, gone, killed by that evil bastard. It was more than I could take.

Jason pointed the gun square at my face. He turned to Casper. Beg me not to kill him, little brother. Beg me not to turn his pretty face into goo. Beg me!"

Before I knew what had happened, Casper launched himself at Jason. He didn't punch. Instead he bit Jason right in the nuts, clamping down with his teeth full force. Jason screamed. He whipped the gun around toward Casper. I flung myself at him. Ethan and Nathan launched themselves at him, too. All three of us smashed into him at practically the same time. I feared the sound of the pistol. I feared it would fire and at least one of us would fall dead. It flew from Jason's grasp, however, and landed harmlessly on the hay.

I slugged Jason hard in the face. I threw him onto his back and just kept slugging him. I would've beaten him to a bloody pulp, but Ethan pulled me off him. Ethan tied Jason securely and I ran to Casper to make sure he was safe. He was crying, so was I. He was unharmed, except for the bruise already forming on the side of his face.

"Brendan, are you okay?"

I didn't realize I'd been standing there, just staring out into the distance as I relived those terrible events yet again. I was trembling. Everyone was looking at me.

"Yeah, I'm fine. I'm sorry, I was just thinking about something."

I grabbed another bale and hoisted it onto the wagon. Jason couldn't be trusted. Someone who did what he'd done couldn't change overnight—no matter what he'd gone through.

We worked a couple of hours more before Casper had to leave for *Ofarim's*. Ethan called for a break and I walked with Casper back up the hill. It was my chance to talk to Casper about Jason's letters.

"Listen, Casper…I've been thinking about Jason and…well, it's your business, but just be careful, okay?"

"All his letters start out *From Hell*, Brendan. That's where he is really, in Hell. You know what it's like in that horrible place."

I nodded. No one knew better than I what horrors went on in that "hospital." Some nights, I still woke up shaking from nightmares that I was still back in the *Cloverdale Center*.

"He's in a horrible fix, Brendan. We think we have troubles because money is so tight, but our problems are nothin' compared to his."

"Jason made his own trouble, Casper, you know that."

"Yes, of course, I do. It's just that…I don't like thinkin' of him in there. I remember when he was younger, before he turned bad. I just can't stand to think of him going through all that."

"You have a good heart, Casper. You care even about those who've put you through Hell. I guess I pity him in a way, but I can't find it in my heart to be too sorry for him."

"Yeah, I know. He's just so pitiful now, Brendan, and he says he's changed."

"Do you believe that?"

"I dunno. Maybe it doesn't even matter. I mean, all he wants is for me to write him. He already knows where I am, so it's not like I'm givin' anything away. If he escaped and came after me again, well, he could do that just as easy if I wasn't writing him. Maybe the letters will make it even more unlikely."

"I hadn't thought of that," I said. "I just want you to be careful, Casper. I worry about you."

Casper turned to me and hugged me around the middle. I hugged him back and covered his face with kisses. I loved him so much that sometimes it hurt.

***

Our first football game was against the *Wildcats*. Tom smirked at me in the locker room as we were suiting up, because Coach was putting him in as quarterback for the first quarter and maybe for the entire game. Tom had been a real dick since I'd been outed, although he was a pretty big jerk even before that. I'd found some disgusting drawings stuffed into my locker and some nasty notes, too. I had little doubt they were from Tom. The drawings and notes neither angered nor frightened me. If anything, they made me pity Tom a bit for being so childish. He acted like he was ten. Then again, Dave was ten and was much more mature than Tom.

The *Wildcats* were tough, which was somewhat of a surprise because all the guys said they weren't that much of a threat. Coach Jordan was the only one who seemed to think they'd be a problem and he was right. I didn't know anything about them, of course. That was one disadvantage of playing for a new school. Back in Kentucky, I knew all about every team we'd ever played. When a game was coming up, I had a fairly keen insight into our opponent's strengths and weaknesses. Such was not the case in Verona. I didn't have a clue.

Tom scored an early touchdown and he was insufferable. You'd have thought he was a one man team. It was a good play to be sure and Tom handled it well, but without the linemen covering his sorry butt he'd have been toast. He was able to run to the end zone only because the team had made it possible.

For some reason, Tom seemed to think he'd scored on me instead of the other team. He seemed surprised when I cheered with the other guys after his touchdown. I even told Tom himself he'd done a good job. I don't think he could comprehend my attitude and more's the pity.

Tom didn't do so well after his first touchdown. He hesitated way too long when passing the ball. A good quarterback has to wait until he's got a man open, but I witnessed plenty of times when there was a man open and Tom still didn't throw the ball. Twice, that open man was me and Tom *intentionally* didn't throw to me. I was so pissed the second time he refused to pass that I stalked over to him, ready to knock some sense into him.

"Get your head out of your ass, Myer," I yelled. "I was in the clear! There wasn't another player within a mile of me! If you would've passed me the ball instead of being a dip-shit, I could've scored!"

Tom jumped to his feet from the ground, where the *Wildcats* had shoved him.

"Bull shit, Brewer! You weren't in the clear. No one was in the clear. Why do you think I held the ball?"

"You held the ball because you're a fuck-up! You're so determined not to pass to me that you'd rather get sacked than let me make a goal!"

Tom took a swing at me. Instead of clobbering him, like I should've done, I jerked his jersey up, tangling his arms in it. That threw him into a fit and Coach Jordan had to come over and yell some sense into him. I thought Coach should've pulled him, but he let him keep going. Tom gave me a superior glare as he took the field once more.

By half-time, we were down 12-6. Part of the reason we were trailing was that the *Wildcats* had an aggressive offense and a tight defense that was difficult to penetrate. The biggest reason the *Wildcats* were in the lead was Tom—he was making some foolish mistakes and displaying poor judgment. I tried to give him some advice, but he angrily told that me that *he* was quarterback and he could handle it. He obviously couldn't.

Tom did something during half-time that infuriated me. He went over and talked to the other team for a bit. I didn't know what he'd done until the second half started. It was then that the other team started in on me—calling me *fag, pillow-biter,* and a string of other names. They made plenty of rude comments, too. Tom gave me a smirk. If I'd had any doubt about what he'd done, it would've been erased by the look on his face. I couldn't believe he'd actually gone to the other team and told them I was gay.

Tom got sacked, *again,* not far into the third quarter. Not long after that, he screwed up a pass so badly that the other team got possession of the ball. That was enough for Coach. He finally pulled Tom out and put me in.

It was the moment I'd been waiting for. I'd been dying to get back on a football field as quarterback. In a way, I felt like that's what I was made for. Tom was being a real ass in the huddle—giving me so much crap I was having difficulty setting up the play. It was a mistake. Coach Jordan overheard him, grabbed him by the collar, and jerked him right out of the huddle. He replaced Tom and sat him on the bench. I didn't even bother to observe Tom's reaction, as I had no doubt he was sitting there steaming.

With Tom gone, I set up a series of short passes. Our guys were having a hell of a time breaking into the clear, so I thought we'd better go for some short yardage. Short was better than nothing, which is mainly what we'd been getting. The short passes worked and we started to inch down the field.

The *Wildcat* quarterback was sharp. He knew what I was doing, and so did his coach. They adjusted to my tactic, so I figured it was time to go to the long pass. I set up the play and crossed my fingers.

I held the ball, pretending to look for an opening near at hand, while I prayed my receiver would make it into the open. The *Wildcats* had tightened up their defense, adjusting it so that there was a nearly solid wall of players immediately before me. That's what I was hoping. Perry shot into the clear and

I passed. Perry snatched the ball out of the air and ran like hell. Seconds later, he'd scored and we tied up the game.

Scoring on the *Wildcats* was tough. I kept mixing things up and that seemed to confuse them. After several passes, I took a chance and ran wide with the ball. I didn't make it, but I made several yards before they took me down. Later, as I was looking to make another long pass, an opening presented itself and I tore through the defense. I broke away and sprinted nearly three-quarters of the way down the field to score. It was such a rush!

The *Wildcats* only scored on us one more time. Their quarterback made a sweet pass that dropped right into the hands of his receiver. Our defense nearly nabbed him, but he escaped by the skin of his teeth. When the game ended, we won 25-18 and I knew we were lucky to pull it off.

Tom was pissed, of course, because I'd done well while he'd screwed up. If looks could kill, then I'd have been dead on the locker room floor. Tom tried to be a dick, but the rest of us were celebrating and no one paid him any attention. That angered him even further and he left in a huff. I wondered how a guy could be like that. He couldn't even be happy about our victory because things hadn't gone his way. I just hoped trouble wouldn't come of it; the glare he gave me when he departed was filled with menace.

Dane

I followed Shawn and a girl into the theatre and sat behind them. I had to say one thing for him; he put on a good act. He kept his arm around her almost the entire time and even kissed her once or twice. About halfway through the show, he got up and went to the lobby. I followed a few moments later.

I saw no sign of him in the lobby. Nathan threw me a disapproving glare, but I ignored him and went into the men's room. Shawn was just finishing up at the urinal. We were alone. It was the chance I'd been waiting for.

"Hey, fag," I said.

"Excuse me? What did you call me?" Shawn zipped up and came toward me. He had the intimidating jock act down real well. I nearly took a step back from his threatening glare and stance, but kept in mind who was really in control. I knew he could tear me to pieces—one look at his biceps threatening to rip through his sleeves or his chest as it pressed against his shirt made that clear. The boy was obviously built and powerful, but that wouldn't save him. He was soon to be mine.

He bore down on me, but I stopped him with four words, "I know your secret."

A look of fear passed over his handsome features. "Secret?" he said, now playing the dumb jock.

"Yeah, the secret you'll do anything to keep your dad from uncovering. The secret that you pray every night Tom won't discover."

Shawn turned deathly pale.

"You really should make sure you're alone when you discuss things with Casper," I said, grinning. This was just too good.

"Who *are* you?"

"I'm the guy who holds your life in his hands. You wanna know who *you* are now, Shawn?"

"Who?" he said fearfully.

"My bitch."

Shawn swallowed hard. "What do you want?" he said, shaking with fear.

"I'm glad you're smart enough not to try and deny the truth. That would've just wasted our time and pissed me off. But, to answer your question, I want a lot."

"Dude, I don't have much money. I'm…"

"I don't want your money. I want something a lot more…personal." I smiled. Just fucking with that jock was satisfying and arousing. He was scared, terrified. I had him right where I wanted him.

"What sport do you play?"

"Huh?"

"You're a jock, right? You're built and you dress like you think you're hot shit. So what sport do you play?"

"Um, football."

"Excellent—I've always had a thing for football players. You remind me of our quarterback at home. He was such an asshole. Anyway, I know you need to be getting back to your *girl*, so I'll wrap this up. I want you to come to the trails in the park, where you talked to Casper, tomorrow at 6:00 PM."

"I can't make it at six."

"I can show up at your house instead," I said, pointedly.

"Okay! Okay! I'll be there at six."

"Wear your football jersey and those shorts you had on when you talked to Casper."

"Why?"

"Just do it, bitch!"

"Okay," said Shawn meekly. Damn, jocks were fun when you had 'em by the balls.

"Now get lost," I said.

He hurried out and I smiled. I couldn't wait until the next evening.

***

I arrived fifteen minutes before our meeting time, wondering why I hadn't ordered Shawn to appear earlier. The anticipation was stimulating in its way, but it was also a torment. At last I was on the verge of gaining my heart's desire. Shawn couldn't get away from me like Casper. He couldn't defy me like Ethan or dump me like Armando. He was mine, to do with as I pleased for as long as I pleased. I knew blackmailing him put me in some danger, but I'd taken steps to protect myself.

Shawn showed up just before six in his football jersey and shorts, just as ordered. He looked good enough to eat.

"I'm here," he said, stating the obvious, his voice quivering.

"It's a good thing," I said, trying to put as much menace into my tone as possible.

"So now what?" he asked, looking around. He was pathetic. It was so obvious he lived in constant fear of being discovered that it placed him entirely in my power. It was almost too easy.

"Take off you shorts."

Shawn pushed his shorts down, reluctantly.

"Now the boxers."

"Dude, please."

"Now!"

My slave-jock did as he was told. He was naked from the waist down and he was excited.

"Hmm, this is interesting," I said. "Does being my bitch get you hot, huh?"

Shawn remained silent.

"Answer me!"

"Yes! No! I don't know. Why are you doing this to me?"

"Because I can, Shawn—because I can. Oh yes, before I forget. Just in case you get any ideas, I've written down everything I know about you. I also added a few stories of my own. I made copies and sealed them up, addressed to your dad and older brother. If anything bad should happen to me, like, if I was to disappear or get beat up, a friend of mine will mail them. Do we understand each other?"

Shawn nodded.

"Now take off the shirt."

Shawn pulled off the football jersey. He was completely naked now, except for his shoes and socks. He was muscular and beautiful.

"Get on your knees."

"Please, dude," said Shawn. "Don't. Please. Please, man. Don't do this to me. Oh God…"

He started bawling, not just crying, bawling. I'd never heard anything sound so pitiful and heart wrenching in my entire life. It was like Shawn somehow reached inside me and pulled out emotions that I didn't want to release.

"Shit," I said softly, and then I yelled, "Damn it! Fucking hell!"

I was aroused beyond belief. I had a gorgeous jock kneeling in front of me. I had complete control over him. I could do anything I wanted to him. I could make him do anything. He was my slave, but he was crying so pitifully that it tore at my heart. It wasn't supposed to be like this.

"Damn it!" I yelled again. "Damn it to hell!"

I couldn't do it. When it came right down to it, I couldn't make Shawn blow me. I couldn't make him do any of the things I had planned. It was maddening. I'd planned so very much—wild, intense, kinky sex, more and more until I'd made up for my long, tortured virginity. But I couldn't do it. I couldn't force him. Something within me wouldn't allow it. I cursed myself, but I couldn't go through with it.

"Stand up," I said. Shawn kept blubbering. "Get up!"

He stood, shaky and weeping.

"Just…just put on your clothes! Just put 'em on and get the fuck outta here before I change my mind."

Shawn jerked his chin up and looked me in the eyes. He hastily pulled up his boxers and shorts, hiding his nakedness.

"Thank you," he said and beat a hasty retreat, not even bothering to put his shirt on before he ran away.

You're such a loser, Dane, such a loser. You had him and you let him go. You are a dumb-fuck.

I was disgusted with myself. I'd just let go of my wildest fantasy because of pity. I remembered how good Shawn looked naked. "Fuck!" I yelled and kicked the nearest tree. I cried out in pain.

I stood right where I was for a few minutes, and then began to walk up the trails, away from the park this time. What was wrong with me? There was absolutely nothing stopping me this time, but still I hadn't gone through with it. I felt like some kind of failure. I couldn't even manage to score when I had a guy completely under my control. I was stupid for letting Shawn get to me. I should've just taken what I wanted from him. He deserved it just for being a jock, if for no other reason. Jocks thought they ruled the world and they needed to be taken down. So why hadn't I made use of such a golden opportunity?

I had plenty of questions, but the answers weren't coming. It was time to turn my thoughts in another direction. Maybe I hadn't gone through with my plans for Shawn because Austin was on my mind so much. I wanted something from him, too, but something quite different from what I'd wanted from Shawn. Well, part of it was the same. I wanted sex—lots of sex, but I desired more than that. I craved his love. I wanted walks in the moonlight, hugs and kisses and cuddling in the darkness. I wanted Austin to be my boyfriend.

I was feeling like a girl with a crush again. I had to admit it to myself—I did have a crush on him. Whenever he was near, or even when I just thought about him, I got this tingly feeling all over. No, that wasn't quite it, but there were no words to describe how I felt. It was as if something was welling up inside my chest, but that didn't quite pin it down either. No matter—I knew how he made me feel.

I wanted a lot of boys I'd seen in Verona and I'd tried for a few. I'd failed, with the exception of Armando, even though that felt like a failure, too. They were all weak replacements for Austin, however. I guess I'd just been too afraid to approach him. Yeah, he was giving me a place to live, but it wasn't the fear of losing that which held me back; it was the fear of rejection.

Where was the new Dane I'd promised myself to be? Wasn't I making the same mistakes all over again? How many times had I been too afraid to approach guys I found attractive? Not once in my entire life had I had the balls to ask a guy out. Yeah, I'd tried to get into Casper's pants because I thought he was an easy mark. I'd tried to blackmail Ethan and Shawn. I had been more outgoing with Armando, but only after it was obvious he wanted me. I'd never taken a real chance. Perhaps it was time.

I felt butterflies in my stomach. I turned in my tracks and headed first to *Ofarim's*, where I sat down and nervously ate a cheeseburger and fries. The sight of Casper made me more determined than ever to tell Austin how I felt about him. I wanted something like Casper had—a real relationship with sex and companionship and all the rest. Casper was lucky. He even had a boyfriend who'd protect him when he needed it. I smiled, thinking of Austin threatening to pound anyone who gave me trouble.

After my supper, I walked home to Austin. He was actually there for once. Perhaps it was a sign. He was sitting outside on the step, shirtless, facing the huge old mansion, no doubt trying to cool off in the slight breeze. The failing light gave him a golden glow, tinged with red. The sight of his firm, sinewy body stirred up my lust. With any luck at all, I'd be able to explore his sexy chest and all the rest of him soon enough. I wanted more than just that, however. I took a deep breath. This was it. This was the moment when the new Dane truly was born.

"Austin," I said, "I've been…" My words trailed off. There were perhaps a thousand ways to say what I wanted, but all of them had fled from my mind. "I appreciate you letting me stay here with you."

"It's no problem, dude, I hardly know you're here."

That wasn't exactly what I wanted to hear. I struggled on. "I don't know if you've noticed, but I, uh…I kinda like you."

Austin looked at me with an odd expression I couldn't read, but said nothing.

"Well, more than kinda. I *really* like you."

"Dude," he said, "you're not a fag, are you?"

His words hit me like a slap in the face. I didn't even have to answer. He knew just by looking at my expression.

"Fuck," said Austin, "is the whole fucking world queer? Dude, just stay away from me. I'm not into that shit."

"But, I love you!" I said. I hated the pleading tone in my voice; it was as if I were begging him.

"Dude, that's sick. I don't want to hear it."

"But, I…I thought we were…I mean, we're friends and you do it with guys all the time. I thought that we…that…"

"First of all," said Austin, sternly, "I don't do it with guys all the time. There isn't enough business in this crappy little town for me to do it *all* the time. Second, that's business. I'm a rent boy. I do it for the money and only for the money. You got that? You think I like fucking old ladies? You think I like old dudes blowing me? Sometimes I get an attractive, younger woman and yeah, I'm into it then, but mostly I have to do things I don't wanna do. If I wasn't getting cash, and plenty of it, I wouldn't touch another dude. I'm not a fucking queer like you. I do it for the money! If you want me, you've gotta pay like all the rest!"

Austin might as well have had me on the ground, pounding my face with each word. That's what it felt like—like he was hitting me over and over, harder and harder. Tears came to my eyes and I angrily wiped them away.

"Yeah, right. You do it for the money. Bullshit! You're just afraid to admit you feel something for me. Someone's done something bad to you in the past or something, but you don't have to be afraid. I love you, damn it!"

Austin rolled his eyes. "Well, I don't love you! I don't even care about you! Plenty of people have fucked me over, but that has nothing to do with this. I'm not afraid of anything and I'm sure not afraid of you. You're just some boy I let stay with me for a while, that's all. I was just helping you out because it's a hard, cruel world and no one else is gonna help you. So why don't you go back to Mommy and Daddy and quit playing games."

"I told you why I can't go back! I told you about my brother!"

"Yeah, let's talk about your brother. I had a little talk with my cousin. He goes to your school. Yeah, that's right; I know you lied about coming from Chicago. I asked him about you and your brother and you know what? You don't even have a brother! You just fed me some bullshit story so I'd feel sorry for you. How dare *you* accuse *me* of lying! All you've done is lie. I bet none of the shit you told me about your parents is true. All the shit you told me about 'Stephen' abusing and molesting you sure the fuck isn't. I dunno, maybe you're so fucked up you even think he's real, or maybe you just wish you had someone to molest you, you sick little faggot!"

I flew at Austin in a rage. I aimed for his face, but only managed to hit him in the chest. He slammed his fist into my jaw and I went down, tasting blood. Austin stood over me, fists ready. I stayed down.

"Fuck, I'm sick of this place!" yelled Austin. "You know, this is it! I'm getting out of this fucked up town!"

He turned and went inside. I just lay there for a bit, rubbing my jaw and spitting out blood. I wasn't hurt too bad, but I wasn't feeling too good either. I wasn't used to getting hit in the face, or anywhere for that matter. I heard Austin inside, shoving and tossing things around. After a couple of minutes, I worked up the courage to go in.

Austin was shoving his meager belongings into a duffle bag.

"You're really leaving?"

"Yes."

"Where you going?"

"I'm not sure. I'll decide that when I get to the bus station—New York most likely, but maybe Los Angeles. I can make a shit-load of money there; maybe even get into adult films. I hear it pays big."

I shook my head in disgust.

"You're sure one to judge me, you fag," he spat at me. Tears welled up in my eyes again, but I fought them off. I would *not* cry. It was a struggle to hold the tears back. The boy who was supposed to be my boyfriend had called me a fag and slugged me in the face. Maybe I *was* sick. I still felt for him and yet I hated him, too. I want to hurt him. I wanted to beat him senseless. But, I knew I couldn't take him.

"Well, the place is all yours, queer boy. Say 'bye' to Boothe for me or maybe I'll see him before I go."

"Goodbye," I said, as I followed him to the door and watched as he walked away. I wanted to say more. There was so much to say, but I couldn't find the words. I felt so alone just then—and afraid. Suddenly, the old mansion that stood so near seemed more threatening than ever. The shadows were coming on. It would be night soon. I pulled the door shut and fastened the hook. I lit the oil lamp and closed the old, tattered drapes. I tossed myself onto the pallet on the floor and bawled my eyes out. I felt as if I no longer had any reason to live.

Ethan

I looked up at the huge wrestling banner that hung on the gymnasium wall. There was my name in big, bold letters. I'd worked like crazy to come out on top, but what I'd gotten out of it far exceeded my goal. When I was working out, practicing, or wrestling, my thoughts were on the banner and on the chance to be the best, just once. I'd achieved my goal, but along the way something more important than wrestling took center stage. Zac was determined to come out on top too, and he was more than willing to out me to get what he wanted. He blackmailed me. I'd always lived in fear of others finding out I was gay. It came down to a choice—give up what I wanted the most of all or face my greatest fear. That was the toughest wrestling match of my entire life, because I was forced to struggle with my own fears and insecurities. In the end, the real victory wasn't having my name up on the banner, or even etched in the huge trophy that sat in the trophy case at the entrance to the school. My real conquest wasn't over Zac, or any other opponent—it was over myself. Now, I could stand before the banner without fear of being outed, without fear that others would hate me if they knew the truth. The truth was already out there. Everyone knew I was gay and most of them didn't care. I didn't have to live in hiding anymore; I could live my life as my true self. That was my real victory and it would last as long as I lived and maybe even beyond.

Wrestling season had just started, but it was going well. We'd had our first meet and I'd won with ease. Most of the others did well too, including Zac, my arch enemy. I almost laughed when I thought of him like that. It made me feel like I was in a comic book. *Hmm, maybe I could be Batman and that would make Zac…The Joker.* I did laugh at that thought.

It was time for our second meet and I was expecting some tougher competition. We were up against the *Vikings* and they were supposed to have some hotshot transfer student from Germany who kicked ass. He was in my weight-class and Coach said I'd most likely be wrestling him. That didn't bother me. I loved a challenge. The only problem was that a loss could knock me out of the competition to be the best. I didn't care so much about getting my name up on the banner again, since I'd already done it once, but I sure as hell didn't want to be outdone by Zac. That jerk deserved nothing.

I walked into the locker room and stripped down to my socks. I put on my jock and then pulled on my blue and white singlet. I always felt nearly naked in my singlet. Those things were skimpy and thin and put your goods on display for all to see. I didn't really mind, but I occasionally felt like I was walking out in front of the crowd in my underwear or something. Nathan liked me in my singlet, but that's another story.

Once I'd dressed and Coach had given us his little speech, I took my place on the bleachers beside my teammates. The lower weight classes were up first, so I just leaned back on my elbows and watched, or, more often, leaned forward shouting advice.

The wrestling meets were only sparsely attended. Wrestling didn't pull in the crowds like football or basketball. Of course, at our school, soccer was the big thing. Jon said they had a pretty good team this year, all things considered. They'd already won their first couple of games. I was sure they were nothing compared to what they could've been if Mark and Tay were still around. Those boys were unstoppable. I had little doubt that they came down from Heaven to watch their teammates play. Sometimes, I felt like they were watching me.

I felt just a touch lonely. Nathan wasn't there to watch me. It was about six so he was already at the theatre. Casper was working too, and of course Brendan and Jack were hard at it on the farm, unless Brendan was still at football practice. I'd join them whenever I finished. I knew they'd be waiting to hear how I'd done.

I saw a familiar face not far away in the crowd. It was Dane, the little jerk who had tried to blackmail his way into my pants. That boy had a problem. I felt like smacking him around and telling him to start thinking with his head instead of his dick. He was intently staring at the wrestlers, probably undressing them with his eyes. I bet he just loved how the singlets showed off each wrestler's stuff. He was sure a horny little bastard.

Coach told me I would indeed be wrestling the German dude. I got a good look at him and knew I had my work cut out for me. He looked like he had a few pounds on me in size. We were both in the same class, but my weight was near the bottom of the range and I bet his was right at the top. He was muscular and extremely well defined. He had short, straight, blond hair and brown eyes. I guess he was kinda cute in his way too, but that didn't matter. I was gonna wrestle him, not date him. I thought too much about looks sometimes. They didn't really matter all that much. I knew that if something messed up Nathan's looks that I'd stick right to him just the same. I loved him and most of what I loved about him was on the inside. His appearance truly didn't matter. That was easy to say since he was cute, but I meant it nonetheless.

I wished I had a chance to watch my opponent wrestle before our match. That way I'd know what to expect. I was the first on our team to ever wrestle him, however, so I wouldn't have that opportunity. I'd have to figure him out on the fly. I smiled. I loved wrestling precisely because anything could happen. Most people thought it was all about strength, but it was even more about wits and strategy—that's why little guys could sometimes take out big guys.

Finally, I was up. I took my place on the mat and the blond German shook my hand. He didn't smile; he just nodded. He was all business. The whistle blew and we circled one another. Close up, my opponent was rather intimidating. He had a powerful looking chest and arms that rippled with muscle. I was glad I worked out on a regular basis. I was strong, but there was always someone with even greater strength.

Blondie dove for me and clamped himself around my midsection. Damn he was strong! He lifted me up off the mat, but it threw him off balance and I hooked his leg. I took him down and dropped on him. The crowd went crazy, but I knew I wasn't going to get a pin that easy. I was right; my opponent grabbed my arm and twisted out from beneath me. I didn't let him escape. I pinned one of his arms to his torso, but now he was face down on the mat. I strained to force him onto his back, but it was like wrestling a tiger. I wished I could practice with this guy. I was sure I'd be a far better wrestler if I had to combat him on a regular basis. Our team didn't have anyone like him.

The first period ended without me getting Blondie on his back again. I did score a takedown, so I was ahead on points. I knew that didn't mean much. There were still two periods of two minutes each left to go. That might not seem like much time, but it can be an eternity when you're wrestling a tough opponent. Both Blondie and I were breathing hard when we stepped out of the circle.

I started the second period in the defensive position. I waited on my hands and knees as Blondie encircled my abdomen with one arm and positioned himself with one knee to the mat. I knew he was going to bring his power to bear and flip me right over on my back. I considered my moves and decided to try and use his strength against him. That's often a good move. Even a smaller guy can take a larger one if he uses his opponent's strength against him properly. I was pretty evenly matched in strength with the young German, so I could work it even more to my advantage.

The referee blew his whistle and I felt powerful arms forcing me onto my back. I added my own muscle to the effort, but it failed to yield the intended result. Blondie was ready for me. He controlled his momentum and flipped me right on my back. It wasn't too difficult for him since I was basically helping him. That's the problem with that particular move; if your opponent is expecting it, you're screwed.

He dropped on me, pressing his whole body down upon me. I struggled against him, but my shoulders kept going closer to the mat. It reminded me a bit of the championship match against Zac. He had me in the same position and I lifted him off. I didn't think that was going to work this time, so I focused my energy into twisting beneath my opponent. He used his powerful arms to halt my movement, but I managed to squirm around under him until my face was on the mat. It wasn't the best of positions to find myself in, but it was far better than being on my back about to be pinned.

Blondie furiously worked to get me on my back again. He grew frustrated—I knew as much from his grunts and groans. To a wrestler, they are a language all their own. My opponent put all his power into turning me over, but I resisted him. That's when the break came—Blondie slipped—his hand slid from my lats and his own momentum threw him back. I snapped into action and pushed myself up and over. I grabbed the well-muscled German by the shoulders and whipped him around onto his back. He was now in the position I'd been in such a short time before. He fought against me furiously, but I dropped on him, and then forced my full weight and strength against his shoulders. He inched down, even though he was using everything he had to lift himself off the mat. My combined weight and strength were too much for him, however. His shoulders touched and moments later, the referee pounded the mat then declared me the victor.

I jumped to my feet, elated. My win against the transfer student was quite an accomplishment. I learned later on that he'd never been defeated before and he was never defeated again that season. Before we walked off the mat, he shook my hand and said with a halting German accent, "You are a damn good wrestler."

"You're the toughest opponent I've ever had," I told him and it was the truth. He smiled. I could tell he loved wrestling as much as I did.

"So you beat the Nazi," said Zac with a sneer as I sat on the bench.

"He's not a Nazi, dumb-ass. He's German. It's not the same thing. The war's over. He's also a hell of a lot better at wrestling than you."

Zac didn't like that, but I didn't care. He was such a jerk. I watched the rest of the meet while I recuperated from my match. I felt like I'd been through a tough workout and then several hours of farming. I was gonna be dead on my feet before I got to bed.

***

"Hey, Brandon," I said, as he looked over the fence. I hadn't heard him drive up. I was struggling with a stubborn sheep, doctoring a small cut it'd managed to get on its leg. It wasn't easy since I was trying to do it with only the moon and a flashlight for illumination.

"Here, let me hold the light," said Brandon.

"Thanks."

"I thought the wrestling meet was over," said Brandon, watching me struggle with the sheep.

I laughed, finished my task, and stood.

"I caught your match," said Brandon. "I was impressed."

"I think I was lucky."

"Ah, don't sell yourself short, Ethan. You're a killer wrestler."

I smiled. "I'm not *that* good."

"Hell, I bet you could be in the Olympics or somethin'."

"That'll never happen. How you doin', man? I haven't seen much of you for a few days."

"I'm...okay."

I noticed then, for the first time, that he almost looked as if he were about to cry.

"You don't look okay," I said.

"I'm not really. I had one of my dreams last night."

I didn't have to ask what the dream was about. Sometimes, Brandon dreamed about the night we found Taylor dead. It'd happened less than a year ago, in the early days of November. Brandon was Mark's best friend and he'd been close to Taylor, too. I'd been friends with them and their deaths messed me up, but Brandon was even closer and sometimes I didn't know if he was going to make it. Their suicides had nearly driven him to his own.

"I'm sorry," I said.

"I just wish…" There was no need for him to continue. We'd discussed it over and over. Brandon wished the same thing that I did—that we could've somehow stopped the events of that horrible night. We'd done all we could to get to Taylor in time. I remembered only too well the frantic search of the old Graymoor Mansion, then racing to the soccer fields, only to find that we were too late. The image of Taylor sitting there leaned up against the soccer goal, dead, would forever be etched in my mind.

Mark's death tormented Brandon, too. That was part of his dream as well— Mark shooting himself in the head on the very spot where his boyfriend had died only a few hours before. I could almost predict what Brandon would say next.

"I should've stayed with Mark. I should've known! I did know!" said Brandon.

"Brandon, you couldn't have stopped him. Think of how hurt you were by Taylor's death. Think of the pain. It was a hundred times worse for Mark. Maybe you could've prevented him from taking his own life when he did, but the grief would've driven him mad. Look what it's done to you and me. If you had managed to stop him, it would've only postponed the inevitable."

"Maybe you're right. I don't know. It's just…none of it should've happened!"

"I know, I know."

I put my hand on Brandon's shoulder and guided him to the grassy road that ran down between the fields. It was time for us to stroll around the farm and talk, as we had many times before. Usually Brandon came to me when he was in pain, like now, but sometimes I called upon him when I was the one suffering. We shared a common pain and talking about it helped.

"It's weird, you know?" said Brandon, as we walked in the moonlight. "Sometimes, I drive by Mark's house and I just can't believe he's gone. I even…I've even picked up the phone and started to call him." He shook his head. "I just feel like I'm trapped in some weird reality that shouldn't exist, or in some screwed up dream that I can't escape. It shouldn't be like this. They shouldn't have died."

"Remember that day we went to *Halloween World*?" I asked, trying to turn Brandon's mind to more pleasant times.

"Yeah, that was a blast."

"Yeah, like when you dared Mark into riding *The Poltergeist* and you ended up blowing chunks!" I laughed.

"Don't remind me. That was *so* embarrassing."

"Did you suspect them then? I mean, did you suspect that Mark and Tay might be more than friends?"

"Well, yes and no. I just couldn't believe Mark could be gay, you know? I didn't know any gay guys then. Well, I did, but I didn't *know* they were gay. Hell, Mark, Tay, and you were all gay and I had no idea! Anyway, all I knew was stuff I'd heard and Mark didn't fit any of that. I knew there was something between them. You could just tell, you know? It was more than them hanging out with each other all the time. It was…I dunno…there was just somethin' there."

"It was in their eyes," I said. "I wasn't sure, but I suspected them. Of course, I know more about such things than you."

"Yeah, you do."

"Maybe it takes one to know one. I don't know, but I could kind of tell."

"Why did it have to be that way?" asked Brandon.

"Huh?"

"I'm not sorry they were gay, but I keep thinking if they weren't, they'd probably still be alive."

"It wasn't being gay that killed them, Brandon, it was the way everyone treated them."

"I know. It's just…I don't want them to be dead. I keep thinking all these thoughts, like what if I'd done this or they'd done that or whatever."

"I've done some of that myself, Brandon, but thinking about the 'if only's' doesn't help. Even if we could go back in time, we might not be able to stop what happened. Maybe nothing could stop it. Maybe it was even *supposed* to happen. I sure wish it hadn't, but you know what I mean."

"Yeah, I understand. I'd just about sell my soul to bring them back. I'd definitely give up my own life in exchange for theirs, but I guess you're right. I guess thinking about this stuff doesn't help."

"I'll tell you something," I said. "I don't think they would've changed things much if they could've. I know they wouldn't have given up each other and that means they wouldn't have given up being gay—not that becoming straight was even a possibility for them. I know how they felt about each other, because that's how I feel about Nathan. If I knew that loving him would bring about my death, I'd do it anyway. If I knew, for sure, that I was going to die because of our relationship, I still wouldn't let go of it. I'd just treasure the time I had with him. If someone came along right now and killed me, I'd consider mine a happy life because of Nathan. I wish Mark and Taylor were still alive too, but I know in my heart that they wouldn't have given each other up even if they'd known how it was all going to end. I just know that they treasured every minute together. What happened to them was horrible, but a lot of their life was wonderful, too. I take some comfort from knowing what a special relationship they had with each other. When you love someone like that, you're truly blessed."

I was sometimes amazed that I could say such things to Brandon. I don't think I could've talked to anyone else like that, except for Nathan, of course.

Brandon nodded. "I'm sure you're right. It doesn't stop me from missing them, though."

"Me, either," I said. "Maybe we should just try to focus on the good times and not the bad."

"Yeah, but it's hard, you know?"

"I know. I'm not even sure I can follow my own advice. I have all these regrets. Mainly, I wish I'd stood up for Mark and Taylor more. I could've helped them out a lot more than I did, but I was too worried about my own problems."

"You were there for them, man. They appreciated it, too."

"I know I was there for them some, but I could've done way more. I should've been following Mark around as a bodyguard or something. Maybe I could have kept Devon and his creeps from jumping Mark, maybe I..."

"You're getting into the 'if only's' again," pointed out Brandon.

"Yeah, I know. I've told you all this before, too."

"It's okay. It's not like this is the first time I've cried on your shoulder about all this either. It helps to talk, though. I don't feel so alone with it when I talk to you. I discuss it with Jon some too, but in this you and I are closer, you know?"

"Yeah."

I suddenly smiled.

"What?"

"I was just remembering Mark and Tay wrestling me at the water park. They were hilarious. Taylor was stronger than he looked, too."

"I wonder what it would be like to look like Taylor," said Brandon. "I mean, I've never seen a guy that good looking before. I'm not saying I want to look like him. I wouldn't want to be that pretty, kinda girl pretty, you know? I'm not putting him down. I don't mean it like that, but Taylor was so pretty he could've been a knockout as a girl. But anyway, I just wonder—Tay looked like a model or something. I bet he could've been one if he'd wanted."

"Well, I can't help you out on this one. I don't know what it's like to be that good looking either."

"Ah, come on, Ethan, you're very handsome and you've got the best body I've ever seen on a guy. Hell, I'm straight and you almost make me hard."

I laughed so hard I just about fell down on the ground. Brandon laughed, too.

"I think you're just so sex crazed that anything that moves turns you on!" I said.

"Well, you could be right about that, but don't tell Jennifer!"

"How's it going with her?"

"Awesome, man! I really think I'm in love with her. Before I only thought of girls as sex objects, but Jen...she's somethin' else man. She's more than a girl-friend. We're friends, too. You know?"

"Yeah, it's like that between Nathan and me. We're intimate on a lot of levels."

"Exactly! And the sex, damn dude, she is so incredible at...um, you probably don't want to hear a bunch of heterosexual details."

"It's okay, Brandon, I won't hold being a hetero against you!"

Brandon laughed.

"Well, I'll spare you the details, but she gives incredible head, man, and when we fuck, mmm, we go at it for hours."

I nodded my head. "I'm happy for you, Brandon."

"Anyway, as I was saying, you're very good looking, Ethan."

"So are you, Brandon. Don't take this the wrong way; because you know I love Nathan and am totally devoted to him, but you're hot. You're handsome and you have a hard, sexy body. You're not pretty like Taylor, but like you said, you don't want to be that kind of pretty; it's just not your style. I'd say you're about as good looking as you could be without getting pretty. I hope me say-ing that doesn't freak you out."

"Relax, Ethan, why should it freak me out? We're friends and, like you said, you're totally stuck on Nathan; anyone can tell that just by watching you two. Even if you were single, I wouldn't mind you saying that. You know I'm not gay. I know you wouldn't put the moves on me even if there was no Nathan. I take what you said as a compliment. I mean, a gay guy ought to know as well as a girl what guys are hot!"

"We sure do," I said, "and you are hot, so you should know something about what it's like to be extremely good looking."

"So should you, even more than me. You've got a way better body and my butt's too big."

I laughed. "You're starting to sound like a girl, Brandon. I think Jennifer's affecting you."

"Considering what she does for me, she can affect me all she wants."

"New topic!" I laughed. "I fear some hetero details are coming up!"

We walked and talked for quite a while longer and spent some time just listening to the frogs and insects. I could hear the sound of the tractor in the distance. Jack was working late again. I needed to put in some more time working, too, but I was so exhausted I didn't know if I had the energy to walk back to the house.

By the time Brandon left, he was in much better spirits. And, considering that he was going straight to Jennifer's, I had no doubt his high spirits would continue. I was feeling happier, too. It felt good to spend time with a straight boy who had no reservations about hanging out with gay boys, even when they were telling him he was hot. A lot of straight guys would've totally freaked out over that, but not Brandon—he had the kind of accepting attitude that I wished the whole world could share. Brandon gave me hope that someday all would be well with the world.

Casper

Casey slid a sealed note across the table to me. "This is from Shawn, to Ethan. You can read it if you like. He sealed it for safety, not to keep you from knowing what's in it."

"I'll just wait until Ethan reads it, then he can tell me if it's something he thinks I should know," I said, slipping the note into my pocket. "How's Shawn doing?"

"I don't know. He seems frightened, more than usual, but he won't talk to me about it. Sometimes he really worries me. I care about him a lot. I kind of wish he'd just run away, even though it would mean I wouldn't get to see him again. I'd miss him, but I'm afraid his dad or his brothers will end up doing something really bad to him. Sometimes I'm afraid that Shawn will…no, I shouldn't say it. It's just an irrational fear of mine anyway."

"You can tell me, Casey. I mean, if you don't want to that's fine. I won't pry, but if you think it would help to talk about it, I'm here."

Casey reached across the table and squeezed my hand. We were sitting in a booth at *Ofarim's*. It was well after the supper rush and the place was empty.

"I'm afraid Shawn will get so upset and scared that he'll do something horrible. I'm afraid he'll just crack and end up killing his family or something. I've heard about things like that happening and he's so scared, so trapped that he might feel it's his only way out."

"I sure hope that doesn't happen," I said. "Whoa, this is kind of over my head. I wish he'd talk to Ethan about stuff. He's wise. It's like he's a lot older in his head than he is in his body, you know?"

"Yes. He is very mature for his age."

"I bet he could help."

217

"I hope so. I don't know what's in that note, but I know he wants to talk with Ethan."

"I'll make sure Ethan makes time for it. He's real busy with the farm and everything, but this is too important to put off."

Casey smiled and squeezed my hand harder. I liked her a lot. She reminded me a great deal of my friend Stacey from Kentucky. I missed her.

"How about you, Casey, have you found anyone you're interested in?"

"I have a couple girls I like, but I don't know if they're interested in me. Lesbians seem to be few and far between around here, although Verona seems to be loaded with gay guys."

I smiled. "That's just because you know most of us personally!"

"Probably, but I'm still lonely. Shawn's a big help. He's like a girlfriend in a way. Maybe he wouldn't appreciate me saying that, but I can talk to him about things, share my hopes and dreams with him. Sometimes, I almost wish Shawn and I were both straight. He's made such a sweet boyfriend and he's hot, too. It's a shame guys don't turn me on."

"Well, it would likely be worse if they did, because then you'd want Shawn and he'd still be hot for guys."

"True. I guess I should just be happy with what I've got. I don't know what I'd do without him. I'm scared, Casper."

"Hey, it'll be okay. You'll see." I hoped I wasn't lying to her. Shawn's case seemed pretty desperate to me. "I'll tell you what I'll do. I'll keep my eyes open and talk to girls and maybe I can find out if one's gay. Since I'm gay, they'll probably tell me if they are. You never know, one might even come up and just start talking to me. I mean, you're in hiding and you talk to me, so maybe other girls will, too."

I turned my head. Agnes had been emptying the change out of the jukebox, but now she was approaching our table.

"Mind if I join you?" she asked.

"It's your restaurant," said Casey nervously. I wondered if Casey feared what I did—that we'd been talking too loud and Agnes had overheard.

"I didn't mean to eavesdrop, but I heard part of what you were saying." Casey turned white. "Now, don't be afraid—your secret is safe with me. We girls have to stick together." She patted Casey's hand. "I know what it's like for you."

"You *know*?" asked Casey. Agnes nodded.

"We can talk about that some other time, but I have a grand-niece that you might be interested in meeting. She's your age, very pretty, and lives not far away. She's very lonely and only has me to talk to about certain things. Her parents don't know about her, but she's very open with me, for obvious reasons. I can talk to her if you'd like. You seem like a very nice girl. I've seen you in here several times and have heard more than I meant to. I think Sandy would be very interested in meeting you. At least you could be friends and who knows?"

Casey seemed very nervous to be talking about such things so openly, but she seemed excited, too. A couple of high school boys entered just then, but Casey leaned over and whispered, "I'd very much like to meet her, if she's willing."

"I'm sure she will be, dear," said Agnes, as she walked to the counter to take orders.

"See! I told you things would get better!"

Casey smiled. "Did you know about…?" she nodded in Agnes direction.

"Not a clue."

"I'm so excited!" said Casey.

"And I'm so happy you have this chance. Even if it doesn't work out, it just goes to show that there's always hope."

"Yes," said Casey, "there's always that."

Brendan

I heard a growl behind me. It sounded almost like an animal, but I was showering after practice, so it had to be one of the other guys. I rinsed the shampoo out of my eyes and turned around. Tom was glaring at me. We were alone. All the other guys were already in the locker room dressing or on their way home. Tom looked as if he were trying to bore a hole into me with his eyes.

"Let's have this out, Brewer. You and me. Here and now."

"Let's have what out?"

"It's time to decide who's gonna be quarterback."

"That's the coach's decision, not ours," I said.

"It's ours if the winner takes all."

"Huh?"

Tom was acting more than a bit bizarre. He seemed to live in his own little world. I had no idea why he'd chosen to call me out in the showers. Hell, we were both naked and soaking wet! It hardly seemed the place for a homophobe to initiate a fight.

"You and me, Brewer—right here. We fight it out. The winner becomes quarterback, the loser quits the team."

"Dude, that's just stupid. I'm not fighting you."

"You a coward, Brewer?"

"If you think I'm afraid of you, you're dreaming," I said. "If we fight, I'll kick your ass, but this is pointless."

"Yeah, you're chicken—just like I thought."

Tom stepped toward me. He reached out with both hands and pushed hard against my chest. I took a step back.

"Come on, Brewer. Bring it on!"

"I'm not throwin' the first punch. This is insane."

"Okay, coward, then I will."

Tom aimed his fist for my face, but I blocked. He slipped on the slick floor, but came up swinging. He punched me in the gut and I grunted. I shoved him away, but he came right back at me. He swung wildly with one fist, and then the other. One of his punches contacted with my jaw and my head snapped back. I lost my temper and dove for him, grabbed him around the waist, and took him to the floor. He punched me hard in the chest and I slugged him in the face. Tom lurched up and I slid off him. We were both soapy and wet so it was hard to keep a good hold. It was also hard to keep from falling. I just about went down on my ass more than once.

Tom grabbed my shoulders and tried to head-butt me, but his fingers slipped and his forehead rammed against my shoulder. I pushed him back and punched him in the face. He staggered backward and I jabbed him hard in the abs. He grunted and doubled over.

"You had enough yet?" I asked, stepping back.

In answer, he charged me and took us both to the floor. We wrestled around, punching at each other while we slid and slipped. I heard someone run into the shower room. I punched Tom in the face again to get him off me, but he just wouldn't stop. He was getting the crap beat out of him, but he didn't seem to care. He just kept coming back for more.

"Alright, you two! That's enough!" It was Coach Jordan.

I got up and so did Tom, but he lunged for me. I shoved him back, but he came at me again while Coach was yelling at him to stop. A couple of guys from the team had to run in, grab him, and hold him.

"You," said Coach, pointing a finger at Tom, "settle down now!" That seemed to pierce his thick skull. "Now, go get dressed and go to my office."

Coach turned to face me. "All right, Brendan, what's this all about?"

I told Coach Jordan the whole story of what'd happened. There was a small knot of players standing around me.

"Tom's been on his ass for days, Coach," said Perry, when I'd told Coach everything. "He's always trying to start something up with Brendan."

Some of the guys nodded their agreement. Shawn was there, but he didn't say anything.

"Okay, Brewer, I believe you. I know you're not a troublemaker. Now, go get dressed. If Tom's still in there, you stay away from him."

"We'll make sure nothing happens," said Perry.

I rinsed off and was followed into the locker room by the guys, but Tom was already sitting in Coach's office. I dried off and dressed. Why did Tom have to be such a jerk?

I waited around to talk to Coach. I could hear yelling coming from the office. It was Tom. He was screaming obscenities at Coach. He really was an idiot. I heard what sounded like some furniture being pushed around and moments later Coach Jordan came out, twisting Tom's arm behind his back.

"I'll kill you, fucker! I'll kill you!"

Tom had obviously lost it. Maybe he wasn't an idiot, maybe he was just plain crazy. Coach took Tom toward the office, still screaming and fighting. I stood there stunned for a few moments, but then I thought I'd better follow along in case Tom broke loose and attacked Coach or somethin'. I followed the yells up to the office, where I saw Coach slam Tom down into a chair and tell him not to move. The principal was there and was calling someone on the phone. Less than five minutes later, I knew who he'd called because the town cops showed up. They cuffed Tom and took him away.

Coach had me walk with him back to his office, where we talked about Tom some more. After a good long while, Coach said, "I'm making you quarter-back, Brendan." I just sat there, but didn't say anything.

"Isn't that what you wanted, Brendan?"

"Yeah, Coach, but I didn't want it like this."

"This," said Coach, indicating recent events with a sweep of his hand, "doesn't have anything to do with it. I'd already decided to go with you. I was just waiting for the right moment to give you the good news."

I smiled.

"What about Tom, Coach?"

"He's off the team. I won't have a loose cannon like that running around. He'll be suspended. Would you like to press charges against him?"

"Charges?"

"Assault."

"Nah, I don't want to press charges. He didn't even hurt me that much."

"Okay, Brendan, it's your choice. I'll need a statement from you later, though, for school records."

"Sure Coach, anything you want."

Coach Jordan stood up and I gathered that our talk was at an end.

"Congratulations, Brendan. I'm sure you'll make a fine quarterback."

"Thanks, Coach."

***

Casper was delighted that I'd been made quarterback. He seemed more cheerful than he had been in a long time. I think he was happier about it than me, and that was saying something. Once the shock of Tom's attack and being made quarterback wore off, I was able to realize what'd happened. It just didn't seem real at first, but once it soaked in that I was the permanent varsity quarterback, I was elated.

Of course, it didn't solve all our problems. The farm was still in serious trouble, which meant Casper and I could lose our home. Casper had worries, too. He was cheerful for the moment, but I knew he'd been worrying a lot over his brother. Those letters had stirred up a lot of emotions inside him. I wished Jason had never written him, but I couldn't change that. Casper didn't mention any letters, so I guessed he hadn't received another yet. I wished he'd never receive one again.

***

Jon was helping me load hay bales when Brandon arrived to lend a hand.

"I thought you said you had a report to finish tonight," said Jon, as Brandon approached.

"I do, but I had to get out of the house. Dad's being unreasonable yet again."

"He think you're gay again?"

"Yep."

I nearly laughed. From what I'd seen and what Ethan had told me, Brandon was about as straight as they come. He was girl crazy, a raging heterosexual. Brandon looked pissed, though, so it wasn't the time to joke around.

"How could he think you're gay?" I asked.

"It's his reoccurring nightmare," said Brandon. "It started last year when Mark and Tay were outed. Dad found out I was standing up for them, so he naturally assumed I was gay too. We had this big argument about it which ended up with him shouting that he'd kick me out of the house if he found out I was queer and with me yelling that I'd fuck a girl right in front of him to prove I was straight if it meant that much to him. We just about came to blows."

"Shit," I said.

"He's not like that all the time. It's just that sometimes he gets this idea in his head that I might not be a hundred percent straight and he freaks out. He makes such a big deal of it I'm beginning to think he has issues," said Brandon.

"Methinks he doth protest too much?" asked Jon.

"Exactly. I came so close to saying just that to him a few minutes ago, but I figured he'd go ballistic."

"Probably," said Jon.

"What set him off this time?" I asked, curious.

"You mainly, and Ethan."

"Me?"

"Yeah. Everyone knows Ethan's gay and everyone knows we're friends. Now word is all over the place that you're queer and Dad knows I'm friends with you, so naturally he assumes I've gotta be gay, too—the moron."

"This is almost funny," I said.

"Yeah, I'd think that too if I didn't have to live with him. Maybe I should invite Jen over and let him 'catch' us doing it. Maybe he'd shut up then."

"He could still accuse you of being bi," pointed out Jon.

"He probably would at that."

"I didn't know you had to take crap from your dad because you hang around Ethan and me," I said.

"Don't sweat it. It's Dad's problem, not yours. Unfortunately, he makes it my problem. He's tried to force me to end my friendship with Ethan before, but I'm more stubborn than he is. If he keeps pissing me off maybe I'll just freak him out by kissing a boy in front of him. You know any single gay boys, Brendan?"

"Well...I don't think that's a good idea, Brandon, and I don't think you'd enjoy it."

"I know it's not a good idea, but could you imagine? Dad would probably drop dead of a heart attack right then and there."

"Yeah," said Jon, "but if he didn't, you'd have to come and live with me."

"And then Dad would accuse us of being lovers."

Jon laughed. "No way! If I go gay, I want Ethan or Brendan."

"What's wrong? I'm not hot enough for you?" asked Brandon.

"I can't believe you guys are arguing about this," I said. "Besides, you can't go gay."

They both smiled. "Yeah, we know," said Brandon, "but Jon could do a lot worse than me if he *was* queer."

Jon rolled his eyes.

"You guys are better than TV," I said.

We continued stacking hay on the wagon and the talk turned to football. Brandon and Jon seemed almost as psyched as I was that I'd been made quarterback.

"Maybe we'll actually win a few games this year," said Brandon.

I smiled. I had every intention of winning more than a few games for V.H.S.

Dane

The darkness was nearly complete. Even the moon seemed to cast no light. The night matched the darkness of my heart. Could my life possibly get any worse? The summer was supposed to be about a whole new me, about finding sex and more, but it had been one big disappointment after another. None of my plans had worked out. Now Austin was gone too, and with the words he hurled at me, he might as well have plunged a knife into my heart as he left.

Stupid, Stupid, Stupid! Maybe Boothe was right—maybe I was a dumb-fuck. I'd sure destroyed things with Austin. Not only did I not get to have sex with him or land him as a boyfriend, I'd driven him right out of town. He was gone and wasn't coming back. I'd screwed up every single encounter I'd had with another guy, except for Armando—that was his doing. Then again, maybe I'd somehow driven him away, too.

Why the fuck did I let Shawn go? That was the most ignorant thing I'd done of all. It was also the one thing I could undo. Nothing had really changed. I could still put him under my thumb any time I wanted. Maybe that time had come. Hell, there was no maybe about it. What was I thinking? Was I really gonna let him off like that? I could do anything I wanted with him. Anything! He was my toy.

I'd been stupid to let him go. So what if he got all upset? What did I care? He was a jock, one of those guys who thought he was so damned hot—conceited bastards. Everyone hated jocks, except for other jocks. Shawn deserved anything bad that came his way. I decided right then and there that I'd track him down as soon as I could—then the real fun would begin.

Thoughts of just what I'd make Shawn do, and do to him, entertained me as I walked to the park to meet up with Boothe for yet another job. I'd pick up right where I'd left off with Shawn, only this time I wouldn't let him get to me. In just a few short hours he'd be mine.

I had no time to plan more. Boothe was already waiting for me and he was in a surly mood, even for him. He cussed me for being late, even though I wasn't and continued to be a complete dick all the way to the cemetery. Once there, he bitched at me for digging too slowly and called me "dumb-fuck" more times than I could count. I wanted more than ever to knock him down and pound him senseless. If I wasn't depending on him for money and if he wasn't way bigger than me, I might've done it.

My muscles ached as I dug deeper and deeper into the grave. There had to be a better way to make money. I wondered if maybe I should consider taking up Austin's old job. It almost had to be better than this, but no; sexy high school and college boys wouldn't be paying me for sex; it would be nasty old men and women. Gross! I was willing to do it with about any young and reasonably good looking guy, but not someone I found repulsive.

I bet Austin had done it with guys who would make me sick. Maybe they even had diseases. Maybe I shouldn't have been so hot to get into Austin's pants. Who knew where he'd been or what he had? I couldn't believe I'd ever had a crush on him. I was almost glad now that his stinging words had destroyed it. Austin was nothing more than a filthy whore.

"Ohhhh!" I said when my shovel hit something solid. "What's that smell?" I wrinkled my nose. Rotten, putrid air filled the grave. It made me gag.

"What do you think it is, dumb-fuck? It's a rotting body. Now clear off the lid!"

I tried not to breathe as I shoveled the dirt off the wooden lid of the coffin. The wood was weak and I lived in fear that I'd break through and fall into whatever disgusting thing lay hidden there. I finished quickly and crawled up the rope ladder, gasping for a breath of fresh air. None of the graves we'd robbed had smelled like this.

"Pussy!" said Boothe as he climbed down the ladder and opened the lid of the coffin.

The stench was even more powerful once he'd taken off the lid. I ventured a look into the coffin. "Ohhhh yuck!" I said. It was disgusting, but I couldn't take my eyes away—it was like looking at a car wreck. The corpse was rotting and the flesh had turned a dark brown-black. The eyes were gone and the rotting lips revealed a macabre grin. The corpse was male, but I had no idea of his age at death. He could've been eighteen or eighty. His hair was brown and fallen off his skull. I could see worms wriggling where his stomach should've been. I didn't know how Boothe could stand it down in the grave. It was all I could do to keep from retching, even though I was up in the fresher air. I was starting to get sick. I looked away.

"Shit, there's zilch! Not a single ring, cuff-link, or chain!" said Boothe, clearly pissed that all our work was for nothing. There was a long pause in which both of us were silent. Boothe rummaged around in the coffin, trying to find something of value, but his search was fruitless. Boothe slammed down the lid of the coffin.

"Austin left," I said, trying to get the revolting image of the corpse out of my mind.

"Did he?" asked Boothe, as if he couldn't have cared less.

"Yeah, he said to tell you *bye* in case he didn't see you before he took off."

"I guess he got tired of you following him around like a little love-sick puppy," said Boothe, looking up at me from the grave.

"What's that supposed to mean?"

"You know what it means, fag."

"Don't call me that!"

"I'll call you what I want, fag. You are one after all."

"You're crazy."

"Oh yeah? You think I didn't notice you checking out Austin *all* the time? Hell, you can't even pass a guy without staring."

"Shut up!" I yelled.

"Don't tell me to shut up, you little fucker. Just for that, you're not getting paid tonight!"

"The hell I'm not!"

Boothe came climbing up the ladder just then. "You'd better get one thing straight—I'm the boss and what I say goes."

"Fuck you."

"No, fuck you. Now start filling up the grave."

"No."

"Don't *ever* say no to me, boy!" said Boothe as he slapped my face hard.

I snapped. I'd had more than enough of Boothe. I flew into him. I landed a quick punch to his gut that made him grunt and double over. That was the only punch I got in, though. He nailed me in the face and I went down.

"It's time to teach you what's what," said Boothe. "It's time to show you that you're my little bitch."

He was scaring me. I was still lying on the ground. I scrambled backwards on hands and feet as he came towards me. I twisted to turn and run, but he was on top of me before I got off the ground. He forced me onto my back, straddling me. His hands painfully squeezed my wrists.

"You're hurting me!"

"I'm going to hurt you a lot more before we're done tonight, queer boy."

He sat on my chest and glared at me for a few moments. Then, to my horror, he unfastened his belt and pulled down his pants, while holding me down with one hand pressed against my chest. I tried to scream, but he slugged me and told me to shut up. I did as he said. I was afraid he'd hit me again if I didn't.

I was shaking and terrified. "Boothe, please dude, lemme go, okay? I won't tell anyone, I swear. I'm sorry, all right? You're the boss, like you said. You don't have to pay me tonight, it's okay man—just lemme go."

"You've sure changed your tune, haven't ya? Aren't you the same boy who was being such a fucker just a few minutes ago? You shouldn't play with the big boys fag, you'll get hurt."

He pawed at me then. His hands were all over me. I feebly resisted, but I was just too plain scared to fight him. He ripped my shirt in his impatience to get at me. He jerked down my jeans and boxers, tearing them in the process. He groped me while he leaned over me. He shoved his lips against mine and kissed me, forcing his tongue into my mouth. I was crying in sheer terror.

"I can make you do anything I want," Booth said to me when he pulled his lips from mine. "I can do anything to you I want." His words were so similar to my thoughts about Shawn that I felt almost as if a recording of them were being played back to torment me. Boothe was going to use me, just as I'd planned to use Shawn.

Boothe grabbed my hand and forced it onto his crotch. "You like this, huh, do you?"

"Please, Boothe, please let me go."

"You're not going anywhere until we're done," he said. I was bawling. I wished I'd never left home. I wanted my mom and dad.

Boothe forced me onto my stomach and used his knee to pry my legs apart.

"No, Boothe! Please, for God's sake NO!"

I knew what he was going to do to me. I pleaded, begged, and cried, but he had no mercy. I screamed as I felt blinding pain that only grew worse. Each moment was an eternity of pain and humiliation.

Suddenly, Boothe was jerked away. "Get off him!" I heard the sounds of a scuffle. I rolled over and saw two dim figures struggling. I saw Boothe take a hard punch to the gut and go down. The other figure landed another punch that snapped Boothe's head back, and then Boothe lay still.

"Hey, hey man, are you okay?"

I looked up in wonder. It was Shawn. I couldn't answer. All I could do is bawl.

"Shawn?" a voice called from a distance.

"Yeah, Ethan! Over here! Hurry!"

I felt quick footsteps thudding on the ground, and then heard "Shit! What happened?"

"I dunno. I walked up and he was on top of him."

I recognized the other voice. It was Ethan, the built boy I'd tried to black-mail into having sex with me. "You go get some help," he said. "I'll take care of things here."

"Okay, man," said Shawn, then took off running.

Ethan picked up the flashlight that was still on and shined it so he could see me better.

"Dane? Shit! Are you okay?"

I shook my head and cried, "No!" I lost it and bawled.

"It's going to be okay, Dane. You're safe. Shawn's gone to get help."

Ethan leaned over and pulled my boxers and jeans up, covering my naked-ness, and then stood and went to Boothe. I leaned up on one elbow and watched as he used Boothe's belt to tie his arms behind his back. I began to shiver, wondering how it'd gotten cold so fast. Ethan returned to me. He rolled up Boothe's pants and put them behind my head for a pillow.

"I feel cold," I said. I was all shaky and felt kind of sick.

"I think you're going into shock," said Ethan, "but you'll be okay. We'll take care of you." He pulled his shirt off and put it over me like a blanket, then took my hand and held it between his own. I couldn't stop crying—I didn't think I'd ever be able to stop crying.

The next hour or more was all a blur. I saw flashing lights, then felt myself being lifted by strong arms and carried. Images of doctors and nurses swam in and out of my head. Through it all, I could hear Ethan and Shawn telling me I was going to be okay. Then, I was being carried again. I didn't remember any-thing more until I woke up the next morning in a bed in a strange room.

"It's about time you opened your eyes, sleepyhead."

I sat up slowly. I felt pretty good, except for where Boothe had slugged me and for the pain in my ass. It was sore beyond belief. I had trouble focusing my eyes and was a bit groggy, as if I'd been drugged.

"Nathan?" I said, growing fearful. *Am I dreaming?* I wondered. "Where am I?"

"You're at the Selby farm. Ethan and Shawn brought you last night."

"Selby farm?" The name didn't mean anything to me. I was disoriented.

"Yeah, Ethan's farm."

I swallowed hard, still confused. I felt panicky.

"What's going on? Why am I here? I want to leave!" I scrambled backwards on the bed, away from Nathan, just as I had last night when trying to escape from Boothe. Now as then, there was nowhere to go.

"It's all right. Calm down. You're safe here, Dane. No one's going to hurt you."

I just looked at him for a moment. Nathan's voice was calm and meant to be reassuring. It quieted my fear a bit, but a part of me was terrified that they'd brought me here for revenge. I'd done some pretty nasty to things to the boys who lived here and now I was at their mercy. I was away from Boothe, but...what's that old saying *Out of the frying pan and into the fire?* Ethan was strong. He could make me do anything. But, he'd saved me from Boothe, him and Shawn. I was so confused, frightened, and upset that I began to cry. I wanted to escape, but I knew I wasn't strong enough to get away.

"Dane," said Nathan soothingly, reaching out to push the hair back from my forehead. "You're okay. No one's going to hurt you; you're safe here."

He spoke the same words as before, but this time they calmed me. My mind focused enough to make some sense of the situation. Surely, Ethan wouldn't have saved me from Boothe so he could take revenge on me. He could've just let Boothe go on. He could've even joined him.

"You hungry?"

I looked at Nathan and nodded my head. I wiped the tears from my face. Nathan held out his hand. I hesitantly took it and he helped me to my feet. I got up slowly. It was more painful than I thought it would be. I winced.

"Ethan said to tell you not to worry. The doctor said there was no permanent damage, but it'll hurt for a while."

I nodded. Damn, did everyone know what had happened to me? I was so embarrassed, but I was becoming less afraid. Nathan sure didn't act like someone who wanted to hurt me.

I pulled on my jeans, which hung over the end of the bed, and followed Nathan out of the room and down the stairs. We were in a big, old farmhouse. Nathan guided me to a chair at the kitchen table. There was an old lady stirring something in a big, heavy bowl on the counter. She looked like somebody's grandmother. She smiled at me as I sat down. Her presence put me a bit more at ease. I was kind of freaked out to find myself in Ethan's home, but the old lady sure didn't look like someone who would be a part of a kidnapping.

"Just a sec," said Nathan, and then opened the door. He stuck his head out and yelled, "Dave! He's up! Get Ethan!"

My heart lurched. I was jumpy and fearful.

"How would you like some bacon, scrambled eggs and biscuits?" asked the old lady.

"Anything's fine. I'm so hungry."

"Hot tea?"

"Yes, please."

My head was clearing and one thought was foremost on my mind—*why is everyone being so nice to me?*

The old lady handed me a cup of steaming tea a couple of minutes later.

"Thanks," I said, "I'm Dane."

"I'm Ardelene."

I was beginning to relax and feel safe. They wouldn't have been giving me breakfast if they were going to hurt me. Ethan came in, fixed himself a cup of tea, then he and Nathan sat across from me.

"How are you feeling?"

"I'm kind of scared and confused and my...backside kind of hurts," I said, looking at Ardelene to see if she was paying attention. She acted as if she didn't hear as she prepared breakfast. I was sure she could, but I appreciated her acting like she couldn't. I was embarrassed about what'd happened. I felt all shaky.

"You don't have to be scared, Dane, no one will hurt you here. Boothe is behind bars right now and we'll protect you."

I nodded. I believed him when he said no one would hurt me. I'd had my doubts before, but everyone was being so kind it quieted my fears.

"What happened last night?" I asked. It was beginning to come back to me. I struggled to summon up the memories. "I remember you covering me with your shirt...and flashing lights and being carried, but...then it's all fuzzy."

"I carried you out to the road and put you in the ambulance. I went with you to the emergency room. The doctor treated you for shock and took care of your other injuries. We didn't know how to reach your parents, since no one knew your last name, so the Sheriff let me bring you home with me. He'll be coming back today to ask you questions about last night."

I nodded. "I feel groggy," I said.

"That's probably the pain-killers," said Ethan. "They put you on some last night. They gave you sedatives also, to help you calm down."

Ethan wasn't going to hurt me—I knew that now. As my memories became clearer, I could see in my mind the look of concern on his face when he saw me lying on the ground. No, he wouldn't hurt me. He and Shawn had *saved* me.

I didn't want it to happen, but tears flooded my eyes and I began to sob like a baby. Ethan got up, came to my side of the table, and put his hand on my shoulder. I turned and wrapped my arms around his stomach and held him tight. Ethan petted my hair and reassured me that everything was going to be okay. Finally, I calmed down and sat back once more.

"I'm sorry," I said, blowing my nose with a tissue Ethan handed me. "I'm acting like a baby."

"No, you're not," said Nathan. "You've been through something very traumatic. What you're feeling is natural. It's okay."

Ardelene sat a big plate of scrambled eggs, bacon, biscuits, and gravy in front of me. "Enough talk for now. You need to eat."

"Thank you," I said. I almost felt like crying again, because she was being so kind to me.

Ethan and Nathan had themselves some breakfast too. We sat at the table in silence for a while, concentrating on eating. I was so hungry I had to keep myself from wolfing everything down. The food was delicious.

Ardelene took my plate away when I'd finished and gave me more tea. She went outside and left me with Ethan and Nathan. I felt a whole lot better, but still unsafe. I no longer had any suspicion that Ethan might hurt me, but after what Boothe had done to me, I just didn't know if I'd ever feel safe again.

"Do you want to talk about it?" asked Ethan quietly.

I nodded, but didn't say anything for a long time. Finally, I found the courage to begin.

"It was so horrible," I said quietly. "Boothe has always been a dick, but last night he was worse. He hit me and then he started touching me. He got me on the ground. I tried to get away, but he was too strong. I begged him to stop, but he wouldn't. I just felt so helpless. He made me do things I…I can't even talk about…and then he…raped me."

I didn't really want to say the words. It was humiliating.

"God, it hurt worse than anything. I cried and struggled and begged him to stop, but he didn't care. He had no mercy. He just kept doing it. If Shawn hadn't come along…Oh, God!"

I began to cry again. Ethan reached over and placed his reassuring hand on my shoulder once more. When I had myself under control, I raised my eyes to see Ethan and Nathan watching me with pity. They really cared.

"Why are you guys helping me?" I asked. "After the things I did and the stuff I tried to do, you should hate me. And Shawn…I…but he saved me. He should've just left me there," I said bitterly, thinking of what a monster I'd become.

"We're helping you because you need help," said Ethan. "It's as simple as that."

"But why? After the stuff I did, why do you care?"

"We've all been in tight spots," said Ethan. "We've survived by being there for each other. You need help right now and we're the ones here, so maybe we're meant to help you."

"But I did such horrible, horrible things."

"You did some bad things, Dane, especially what you tried with Casper, but that doesn't mean we're going to let someone like Boothe abuse *you*. I wouldn't wish rape on my worst enemy."

"It's horrible," I said, shuddering at the very memory. "I didn't know what he was going to do to me. I felt so powerless. Just before Shawn came, I was thinking, *this is it. When he's done, he's going to beat me, and then kill me and dump me in that grave.* It hurt so bad I just wanted to die, to get away from the pain and the humiliation."

I looked down at my lap. I didn't want them looking at me. I was dirty and nasty. Ethan and Nathan knew exactly what Boothe had done to me. Ethan had seen me lying there naked. I was ashamed.

"What happened wasn't your fault," said Nathan.

"Maybe it wasn't my fault, but I can't think of anyone who deserved it more," I said.

"No one deserves that," said Ethan.

I nodded, but I wasn't so sure.

Ethan showed me around the farm after breakfast. I knew he was doing it to calm me and to help me get my mind off what'd happened. I appreciated it. The sheep came when Ethan called them and I petted one through the fence. I liked the barn. It smelled like hay. The chickens were really cool. I petted one of them too.

Ethan was wearing a shirt, but he looked so strong. He was strong in other ways besides physical too. I'd felt that at the kitchen table when he was assuring me I was safe. There was something about him—something I can't put into words, but he had a strength that had nothing to do with his muscles. His muscles…boy was he gorgeous, but I felt guilty for thinking of him like that. There was way more to Ethan than his incredible body. I'd treated him like an object before, like something to lust after. I'd been wrong. He was a person, not a thing. I was beginning to think I'd been wrong about lots of things.

Later on, the Sheriff came and asked me lots of questions. I was embarrassed to have to explain what happened in detail. He said he'd have to contact my parents, but if I promised not to run, I could stay where I was until they arrived, which would probably be that very night. I had no intention of running. I wanted to go home.

Ethan

I pitied Dane. He'd been badly used by Boothe. I hoped he'd be able to get over it someday, but I knew that kind of thing took a long time. Physical wounds healed quickly, but emotional ones often did not. Nathan was still dealing with the pain of his past and sometimes it was hard for him, even though he was surrounded by those who loved him.

I felt as if Shawn and I had been guided, so we would be in the graveyard to save Dane. I'd come in answer to Shawn's note, asking me to meet him in the cemetery at 2 a.m. If we hadn't been there…I shuddered to think about it. I had the feeling Dane was right. Boothe would probably have killed him when he was finished, so that he could never talk. It would've been pretty easy to dump his body in that open grave and cover him up. He was a runaway and I seriously doubt if anyone would've noticed he was gone.

I listened to Dane talk to the Sheriff, although I left the room when it came down to the details of the rape. I didn't want to embarrass Dane by forcing him to talk about it in front of me. I learned that Boothe and Dane were robbing a grave just before it happened and that they'd violated graves before. According to Dane, Boothe was a full-time grave-robber. I couldn't imagine doing that—digging up the dead and stealing from them. The idea that he might've dug into Mark or Taylor's grave upset me so much that I left after the Sheriff did and drove to the cemetery to make sure all was well. I checked carefully, and there was an indication that one of the graves had been disturbed. There was an area where someone had recently turned over a couple of shovels full of earth on Taylor's grave, but that was all, thank goodness. If they had started digging here, they must have been interrupted. It was a good thing Boothe was in jail, and wouldn't be able to return to disturb those two graves any more.

If either Mark or Tay's grave had been disturbed, it would've been hard not to pound Boothe into the ground. I think that's what's so horrible about grave-robbing. It doesn't seem like such a big deal when you just think about it in general. It's bad, sure, but it doesn't seem that much worse than any other kind of theft. But when you fear that the grave of someone close to you has been disturbed, it's a whole different story. It becomes unthinkable. If he'd dug up Mark or Taylor...I shuddered. I couldn't bear the thought of either of them being disturbed. It was just...I didn't want to think about it.

Ardelene looked after Dane while I was gone and even after I came back. It was a Saturday, but there was still tons of work to do. We all had to keep working, or we could lose the farm.

I was getting better at not worrying about our lack of money so much. I could worry myself sick over it or I could just put it out of my mind and do the best I could to help make ends meet. Worrying about it didn't help, it only made life unpleasant. Seeing what had happened to Dane, I realized I had far too good a life to let it be ruined. I had the best boyfriend in all the world and I had good friends besides. I had Jack and Ardelene, too. On top of all that, I got to spend my life working on the farm. I was exactly where I wanted to be, doing precisely what I wanted to do. How many people had that?

Dane stayed with Ardelene in the farmhouse most of the day. He'd taken to her—everyone did. I think she helped him feel safe and that's just what he needed. In the late afternoon, Casper went to the house to fetch water and brought Dane back with him. Casper had been working outside with us since he'd returned from *Ofarim's* mid-morning. He didn't usually work the morning shift, but Agnes had asked him to come in. He was working the evening shift too, but he helped us in between.

Dane seemed a bit ill at ease around us, but made an effort to be friendly. We were once again loading bales of hay and Dane even pitched in. I smiled to myself as I watched Dane out of the corner of my eye. He was forever stealing glances of our shirtless torsos and then looking guiltily away. Sometimes, he just stopped and stared at Brendan, watching his muscles tense and flex as he worked. Then Dane would remember himself and get back to the hay. He checked me out a good deal too, but I didn't catch him at it as much, probably because he pulled his eyes from me when I looked in his direction. I felt sorry for him. I remembered what it was like, being overpowered by the desires nature put inside me, feeling as if they'd never be satisfied. It was like being hungry, only more intense.

I was surprised that Casper and Dane got on as well as they did. I knew what had passed between them and I knew that Casper had both feared and hated Dane for what'd happened. I'd seen them talking as they slowly walked to the field where we were working, so maybe they'd talked things out.

Dane was especially fearful of Brendan, no doubt because Brendan had recently threatened to beat him senseless if he ever bothered Casper again. Brendan was friendly to him, though, and Dane was dumbfounded that Brendan and the rest of us were nice to him. He just couldn't get over it. I could understand that, at least partially. I had the feeling Dane had been hanging around the wrong kind of people for far too long.

When it came time for Casper to head back to *Ofarim's*, Brendan gave him a hug and a passionate kiss. Dane hungrily watched them together. I couldn't tell if he was merely aroused, or if there was something more to his gaze. He seemed especially taken as he watched Brendan lovingly kiss Casper on the forehead as he bid him goodbye.

Later, when it was time for Nathan to go to work and we put gathering hay aside for the day, I took Dane with me as I performed chores around the barn. I wanted some time alone with him, to speak with him about things that would've been uncomfortable for him if I discussed them around others. Dane seemed like a very misguided boy and I hoped I could help him in the short time we had. I engaged him in small talk for a while and then moved on to more important matters.

"Have you ever been in love, Dane?"

"No. Well, kinda, but not really. He didn't want me anyway."

"Love's what it's all about. I know when you're just beginning to explore such things that sex is what's on your mind, but as you get a little older you find out that love is what's important. I'm not saying sex isn't great, but it only reaches its full potential when it's combined with love. It's the love that really matters. I think you've been getting a little confused—you've been looking real hard for sex, when you should've been looking for love."

I knew I was throwing a lot at him all at once, but this was my only shot to help him. I didn't have weeks or even days to explain it, so I jumped right in and gave Dane my improvised, five-minute course on the true nature of happiness. I hoped he could get a little something out of it.

Dane turned red. "I'm sorry I tried to make you have sex with me. It's just that…I'm so horny all the time! I want it so bad, but there's no way to get it! I was wrong, though, I know. I should've never tried that with you. I should've never tried to force myself on Casper and I should've never blackmailed Shawn either."

I didn't know about Dane's situation with Shawn, but it didn't matter; I didn't ask for details.

"Those things were wrong," I said, "but that's not what I'm talking about. Instead of trying to get into a guy's pants, you should be trying to get to know him. Become friends first and then see what happens. I know you're impatient for sex, but if you start out with that, then that's all there is. It's empty."

"I guess maybe you're right. I dunno. I've just had dick on my mind so long it's hard to think of anything else. You have a boyfriend. You get all the sex you want. It's different when you're not getting it. I only had it once with a guy I met in town."

"I know. It's hard when you're trying to find your way. I used to think mainly about sex, too. I guess I was lucky. I became friends with Nathan and started caring about him before I really even thought about sex with him. We developed a relationship almost by accident, and then later, we fell in love and then the sex just happened."

"It's difficult," said Dane. "Back home, I see all these boys I like, but I have no idea if they're gay or not. I'm afraid to even hint around. If I do that with the wrong guy, I could get my ass kicked. I'd get labeled as a 'fag', too and that's like a death sentence where I come from."

"I understand your fears," I said. "Believe me, I know. I'm out now, but I wasn't until several months ago. For a long time, I lived in terror of being found out. It all worked out really well for me, but I don't know what things are like where you're from so it's hard to give advice. There are lots of gay boys out there, however. Most guys aren't gay, obviously, but I lot of 'em are—more than you'd think. Maybe you should just try to make friends with some of the guys you like and see what happens. As you get to know them, you'll get a better feel for whether it's safe or not to open up to them. You might end up with a boyfriend, but even if you don't, you're likely to make some friends and that's a good thing too. Maybe you'll find someone you can share your feelings with, even if he isn't gay. We have straight friends who we hang out with all the time." I thought of Jon and Brandon. I was lucky to have such friends.

"You may be right, but that doesn't exactly solve my problem," said Dane. "I really feel like I'm going to just die or something if I don't get sex soon. I've had it once, but I want it more. Except, I don't want it like I got it last night. That was a nightmare."

"That wasn't sex, Dane. That was violence. The acts may have been sexual, but it wasn't sex. Even sex with someone you don't love is about feeling good and making the other guy feel good. Boothe wasn't trying to make you feel good. He was only thinking of himself."

Dane's lower lip started to tremble. "I'm so horrible," he whispered hoarsely.

"You're not."

"But I am! I'm just like Boothe. I would've forced Casper if I could've. If he hadn't fought me off, I'd have done him just like Boothe did me. And Shawn, you know what I had planned for him? Today, I was going to track him down and use what I know to force him into sex with me. I was going to do the most horrible things to him. I was going to use him just like Boothe did me and yet Shawn saved me! The very guy I was going to use saved me from being used! I'm so ashamed."

I pulled Dane to me and hugged him as he sobbed. I held him tight.

"Dane, listen; I'm not saying you haven't done wrong, because you certainly have, but you shouldn't punish yourself for things you *thought* about doing. We all think about doing bad things. What matters is whether or not we do them."

Dane bit his lower lip and nodded. I think that maybe he understood.

Casper

I wasn't quite so sure I wanted to see Dane when I went up to the house to get water. I almost didn't go because he was there. It seemed better just to keep gathering hay bales than to set eyes on *him*. I'd briefly seen Dane when Ethan brought him home the night before, but he was so out of it then he hadn't noticed me. Agnes had asked me to come in and work during the morning, so I was out of the house before Dane awakened. When I returned, I went straight to the fields because I didn't feel comfortable at all about being around the boy who'd tried to take advantage of me. Ethan told me what'd happened to him and I pitied him, despite everything he'd done. I knew what it was like to be abused. Still, I didn't feel comfortable with the idea of being around Dane.

I eyed Dane uncertainly as I entered the kitchen. He turned his head in my direction when he heard me come in. He was sitting at the table having some milk and cookies while Grandma busied herself about the kitchen. Dane swallowed hard and looked about in discomfort, unable to look me in the eyes. My first instinct was to lash out at him in anger. He'd attacked me and now he had the nerve to be sitting in *my* home, talking to *my* grandmother. I noted that he'd been crying, however—his eyes were puffy and tears still rolled down his cheeks. He looked frightened, vulnerable, and ashamed. I was accustomed to seeing none of these emotions on his usually arrogant and cocky face.

"Dane's been keeping me company," said Grandma, patting his shoulder.

For a moment I felt anger, as if he was stealing her, but I noted the look of concern in Grandma's eyes and the misery in Dane's.

I nodded. I didn't quite know what to say.

"I have to go to work in a while," I said, stepping to the sink. I filled a gallon jug I'd carried from the fields, screwed on the lid, and then carried it to the refrigerator. I put it inside and grabbed a gallon that was good and cold. There was nothing better than chilled water on such a hot day. It was even better than water from the old pump.

I tried to pretend Dane wasn't there. It was an awkward situation. I just didn't know how to interact with him. As I moved past, Dane reached out and gently grabbed my arm. My eyes met his.

"Can we talk? Please?" he asked. His voice was so humble and gentle that I felt myself softening toward him. Something had changed him.

"Okay," I said, "I can give you a few minutes." I looked up at Grandma. "I'll take Dane down to where we're working." She nodded.

We stepped out the back door, the screen door slamming shut behind us. The heat hit us in a wave. Dane spoke as we walked slowly across the yard.

"I'm sorry for what I did to you and for what I tried to do. I don't have an excuse, because there isn't any—there can't be. I was just plain wrong."

"You've got that much right," I said as I wiped newly formed sweat from my brow.

"I knew it was wrong when I did it," said Dane, "but I didn't realize until last night just how horrible it was. When Boothe got on top of me and started ripping my clothes…" A sob escaped from Dane's lips and I felt my heart going out to him. "When he made me…I can't even say it. I had no idea what a horrible, horrible thing it was that I tried to do to you, until Boothe did it to me. If it hadn't been for Shawn, I think Boothe would've killed me when he was done with me."

Dane was crying again. I found myself reaching out to hold him. He wrapped his arms around me and hugged me tight. "I'm so, *so* sorry, Casper. I'm so sorry."

I held Dane and tried to quiet him as he apologized over and over for what he'd done to me. I felt the anger in my heart for him melt away. I knew what it was like to be a victim. That's the very reason I'd fought when Dane attempted to force himself on me. I knew the pain, the humiliation, and the fear. Whatever Dane had been, he was just a scared boy right now and I couldn't find it in my heart to do anything other than pity him.

"It's okay, Dane. You're forgiven. I almost can't believe I'm saying it, but you're forgiven. You seem to understand now what a terrible thing you tried to do."

"I'm such a horrible person. I wanted to…if I could've, I would have forced you. I…"

"What you tried to do was horrible, but that doesn't mean you are. You don't seem so bad now."

"Oh, I'm bad," said Dane. "I tried to force you and Ethan and Shawn. I didn't care that Ethan was taken, I tried my best to force my way into his pants anyway. I took advantage of Shawn. I learned his secret and thought only of how I could use it to my own advantage, when I should've sought to help him. I feel like everything I've done has been wrong, like I've made all the wrong decisions, and gone down all the wrong paths. I've screwed up everything!"

Dane had learned Shawn's secret? How did that happen? I guessed that wasn't important now.

"Maybe you have screwed up everything, but maybe not. I think you should be asking yourself if you'd make the same choices all over again."

"Never!" said Dane. "There's no way! I don't want to be like that anymore. I want what Ethan and Nathan have and what you've got with Brendan. I want someone to love me enough he'd threaten to beat anyone who messed with me, like Brendan threatened me after what I tried with you!"

"Maybe you're no longer that boy who tried to force me. Maybe you're no longer the same person at all. Maybe you should forgive yourself. Remember your mistakes so you won't repeat them, but forgive yourself so you can start all over again."

If anyone had told me even a few minutes before that I'd be speaking such words of comfort to Dane, I would've been positive they were insane. I'd despised Dane. He was the very worst sort, but now tragedy had befallen him and laid him low. He'd changed from perpetrator to victim and seemed as much changed as Scrooge in *A Christmas Carol*, after he'd been visited by the ghosts.

"I don't deserve what all of you are doing for me," said Dane. "I was such an ass and yet you're all helping me like I was your best friend or something." Dane seemed truly astounded that any of us cared.

"Everyone makes mistakes. They shouldn't be punished for them forever."

Dane pulled off his shirt. It was already soaked. Damn! When would the heat let up?

"I feel scared, like I'll never be safe again," said Dane.

"That feeling will go away, little by little, although it may never completely disappear. It will get better, Dane—I can promise you that."

"How do you know?"

"Because it got better for me."

I explained my experiences with my brother, how he'd sexually abused me, until Brendan rescued me. Dane listened attentively, sometimes in horror at what Jason had done to me. The mere memory of it was painful for me, but I was safe now with Brendan, Ethan, and Nathan. I told Dane the short version of my story, so he'd know that there was life after such a traumatic event.

When it was happening to me, I thought I was the only boy in the world who was being abused, but I was fast learning that such things happened all too frequently. Nathan, me, and now Dane had all gone through something similar. The details were different, but the abuse was just as real. I felt as if the whole world was screwed up somehow, but then it wasn't like that for everyone.

"I feel even worse now about what I did to you," said Dane, after I'd finished telling him my story, "I'm so ashamed."

"Then maybe you'll be okay," I said.

Brendan

Casper got home from *Ofarim's* earlier than usual. It was only about eight when he came walking across the field towards me. Ethan was off working elsewhere with Dane, and Nathan was at the *Paramount* handling the evening show. I grinned when I saw Casper and gave him a big hug, despite the sheen of sweat that covered my body. He didn't seem to mind.

"Another letter?" I asked as my eyes wandered to the envelope he held in his hand.

"Yeah, wanna read it?"

"I guess so," I said. I didn't really like having anything to do with Jason, but I wanted to know what he was writing to Casper. I didn't trust Jason—not at all. Casper handed me the envelope. I wiped my hands on my pants and took out the letter.

From Hell

Dear Lil' Bro,

I can't tell you how much I hate it here. It is Hell. There's nothin' good here. Ike's protecting me now, but even that comes at a high price. I sure never thought I'd be in the spot I'm in now, but that may be changing soon. I don't dare talk about it, but this may be my last letter to you from here. Remember what I wrote before, little brother. I'll never hurt you again, so you don't have to fear me. I know you might not believe me, but maybe somehow you can. It's the truth.

Thanks for the pictures you sent me of Grandma's garden, the barn, and the fields. I just stare at those photos and pretend I'm there. You said you've all been working hard. I wish I was with you. I never thought I'd want to work in the hot sun, but I'd do it willingly for the rest of my life if I got the chance. Anything would be better than being here.

Listen, I got somethin' I'm gonna do and I don't know if I'll be around after I do it. So, I have somethin' I want to tell you. I love you, Casper. I really do. I wish things would've been different, but they weren't. You'll probably always hate me, but I'll always love you. You probably don't believe any of this, but that's okay, because I know it's true. I'm gonna try and make up for what I've done. That's why I think maybe God will help me. I bet you never thought you'd hear me talk about God, did you little bro? Anyway, I've already said more than I should.

Love,
Jason

I looked up. Casper's eyes were a little watery.

"Do you think he's changed, Brendan?"

"I don't know, babe. I just don't know. I don't really trust him, but who can say?"

"I think he's changed, I really do. Now, don't get worried," said Casper, putting his hand on my shoulder. "If he showed up all of a sudden, I'd take off running. I'll still be careful, but when I read his letters, they just *feel* like he's different somehow. He's more like the old Jason."

"Well, let's just hope he's changed, but, even so, he's likely to be sentenced to a long time behind bars for what he's done."

"I know," said Casper. "I was thinkin'. When he does go to prison, maybe I could go and visit him sometime, and I can write him. Grandma can send him cookies or something if it's allowed."

"I think that would be nice," I said. "When the time comes, I'll take you."

"Thanks, Brendan," said Casper, giving me a hug. "Thanks for understanding."

"Hey, he's your brother and it's all up to you. I just don't want you getting hurt."

"I'll be careful, Brendan. I'll be careful."

I leaned down and kissed my boyfriend. I wished I could freeze time. It was moments like these that life was all about.

Dane

Something really struck me as odd during my day at the farm. Ethan, Nathan, Brendan, and Casper all seemed…happy. They were all gay boys, but there was no day to day struggle with self-doubt, no terror about being exposed, and no fear of being hurt. Maybe I wasn't seeing the whole picture, but there was no denying that they enjoyed their lives. I began to hope that—just maybe—I could enjoy mine too.

I still had a long way to go, however. I spent a good part of the day with Ethan, Brendan, and Nathan as they worked. They were shirtless and sweaty. I think I spent the entire day with a hard-on. I even had to go off by myself for a while and whack it in the barn because the sight of those hunky boys was giving me a bad case of blue-balls.

I had all these ideas of love and relationships running around in my head, but it was business as usual as far as my body was concerned. I was determined to learn to think with my brain and not my dick, but I knew it wasn't going to be easy. I tried to not be too down on myself for getting turned on by Ethan and Brendan. What was important is what I did with those feelings. I could just think of dick or I could consider the whole guy. I didn't know if I'd be very good at that, but I sure didn't want to continue being the Dane I'd been since coming to Verona.

Shawn came to the farm long after it was dark. I was sitting on the sofa in the living room when he walked in. He was so sexy and handsome. My first instinct was to devour him with my eyes and bring up the naked images of him I'd stored in my head. I wanted to just jump on him. It was those thoughts that had led me down the wrong path, however, so I forced myself to look into his eyes and see Shawn and not his body.

Shawn was a very good looking guy, but beyond that he seemed sweet and just plain nice. In another life, he could've been my boyfriend, if I could've gotten him interested that is. He was out of my league with those muscles and…*Stop, Dane. Just stop.*

I got up and walked to him. Ethan, Brendan, and Casper were there and so was Nathan's little brother, Dave. Nathan himself had just come home from work. I felt a little awkward and nervous speaking in front of everyone, but I knew I was among friends.

"Thank you," I said, "thank you for saving my life."

Shawn smiled. "You're welcome, but I wouldn't go so far as to say I saved your life."

"I would. Boothe would've killed me; I'm pretty sure about that. Even if he didn't, every second with him on me was pure hell and you stopped him. I won't *ever* forget that. I don't know what help I can offer you, but I'll do anything I can for you—anytime."

I surprised myself by grasping his hand and kissing it. I didn't even worry that Shawn or anyone else might think I was some kind of freak for doing it. My heart was so filled with gratitude I didn't know how to express it. I felt like getting down and kissing his feet.

Shawn smiled at me, but said nothing. I hoped I could be like him someday—and like all the others. My whole trip to Verona had been one big, fucked up mess, but I wasn't sure I was sorry. Even with what Boothe had done to me, it just might've been worth it. I ran away to become a whole new me and I had the feeling I'd done that, just not the way I'd pictured. I'd had the chance to get to know some real gay boys, too. I just wished it would've been under other, better circumstances. I wished we could have met as friends. I wished I could take back everything and start all over again.

My parents arrived about an hour after Shawn. I was afraid they'd be mad and just start in yelling, but instead they ran to me and hugged me, crying.

"I'm sorry," I said. "I'm so sorry." It seemed I spoke those words all the time now.

After several minutes of Mom and Dad expressing their gratitude to Shawn and Ethan, we climbed into the old, familiar family car and headed for home. When I'd left my parents behind, I was thrilled to be away from them, but now I wanted nothing more than to be with them. I didn't care how mad they were at me. I didn't care if they grounded me forever and never let me watch TV again. It just felt good to be safe and to know that I had someone to love and protect me.

Ethan

After Dane and his parents departed, Shawn, Brendan, Nathan, Casper, and I sat down and had a long overdue talk. Jack came in from the fields, but he disappeared upstairs with Ardelene. I think they knew we wanted some time alone.

I think just being able to talk to other gay boys helped Shawn a great deal. I pitied him; no one should have to live in fear like he did.

"I'm just going to try and ride it out," said Shawn after we'd been talking awhile. "I've made it this far. In another couple of years I can graduate and get away."

"Two years can be a long time," I said.

"You've got to get out of there now," said Brendan.

"I can't and besides, it's not that bad. As long as Dad doesn't find out about me, I'll be okay."

"But how long will you be able to keep your secret, Shawn?" asked Brendan.

"I dunno, but I'll keep it as long as I can. If Dad or Tom finds out about me, I'll just run for it. I wish things were different. I wish I could be open about who I am and have a boyfriend like you guys, but it's not like that for me."

Brendan looked at me desperately. I wished I had an easy answer, but I couldn't see one. Shawn's dad was kinda psycho and who knew what he'd do? He might even kill Shawn if he got wind of his being gay. Still, there was only so much we could do. Unless Shawn was willing to run away or something, there wasn't much we could do for him.

"I bet Mr. Sawyer and Judge Wheeler could help," I said at last, as the idea occurred to me.

"How?" asked Shawn, showing the first sign of hope I'd ever seen on his features.

"Your dad, you said he's hit you, right?"

"More than once—he's beat us all at one time or another."

"That's child abuse," said Brendan.

"And Tom, he's beat you up?"

"Yeah, it's one of his hobbies."

"We can get a restraining order or something on your family," I said. "We can find you somewhere to live. Hell, you can even live here. I'm sure Jack would be okay with it. We could run it past him anyway. In any case, you can stay here until we check things out and…"

"No," said Shawn, shaking his head.

"Why not?" asked Brendan, before I got the chance.

"I can't do all that. It's too much. It's too difficult. And what if it didn't work out? What would happen then? I'm sorry. I appreciate you guys trying to help, but I can't. I just can't!" Shawn got up and headed for the door. Brendan tried to stop him, but I held him back.

"We can't help him if he won't let us, Brendan. Give him some time."

Brendan didn't look happy, but he didn't go after Shawn. I think he realized I was right.

"Shit!" said Brendan, hitting the table. "I really wanted to do something for him."

"Me too, but this isn't a novel where everything can be wrapped up all nice and neat at the end. Not every problem can be easily solved. We're just going to have to bide our time on this one. With any luck, we'll be able to help Shawn. When and if the time is right for him, Shawn will let us help him."

"God, I hope so," said Brendan.

"Me too, Brendan. Me too."

***

I lay in bed beside Nathan that night, holding him in my arms as we talked about Shawn. Nathan's presence calmed me. As always, I felt as if nothing could harm me when I was in his arms.

"Why are people like that?" I asked, although I didn't expect an answer. "Your mom, Casper's brother, and Shawn's dad and brother—it just doesn't seem like it should even be possible."

"I don't know," said Nathan. "Mom was always kind of…I dunno…there was always something a bit odd about her. She didn't seem like other moms. Like in kindergarten, all the other moms would bring in cupcakes or cookies when their kid had a birthday, or for Halloween or whatever. My mom never did anything like that. It might not seem like a big deal, but it showed she didn't care. You know she never hugged me, even when I was little?"

"No, I didn't know that." I knew almost nothing about Nathan's mom. This was the first time he'd ever done more than mention her in passing and even that was rare.

"She never kissed me, except when…well, you know. She never kissed Dave either. She never even told either of us she loved us. I don't think she did. We were just there—an inconvenience and an unwanted expense. I don't know what made her like that. For a long time, I thought it was me. I thought something was wrong with me to make her like that. I know it's her, though. It still hurts, but that's just the way it is."

"Yeah, but it's still not fair. You should've had parents who loved you."

"Life isn't fair, Ethan. It's just not like that. What you've got to do is enjoy whatever you can in life. When bad stuff comes, you endure it and make it through as best you can. Even when things were at their worst at home, I just tried to deal with it and forget it. When Mom came into my room and…when she abused me, I just got through it as best I could. The moment she left me, I'd start reading, or close my eyes and imagine I was in some beautiful place, or I'd look out the window at the stars. I'd act like nothing had happened and try to make the best out of things. I think that's what Shawn is doing."

"I just wish everyone could be happy. I wish my parents hadn't been killed. I wish your mom loved you like she should have, instead of doing what she did. I wish…"

"You know, if those wishes came true, we wouldn't even know each other," said Nathan. "If your parents hadn't died in that car wreck all those years ago, you wouldn't be living here. You might've visited your uncle some, but the chances of us meeting would've been slim. We wouldn't have each other."

"I never thought of it that way."

"I'm not glad your parents are dead or that my mom never cared about me, but at least those things brought us together and I *am* happy about that. Maybe things have to be the way they are, even the bad stuff, to get us where we belong and to make stuff happen that's supposed to happen."

"I've always wondered why bad things happen," I said. "I mean, if God is supposed to love us and he's supposed to be all-powerful, then why isn't everything perfect? Why is there sickness, sadness, pain, loneliness, or any of that? Why does anyone even have to die? Why can't everyone just be cool to everyone else and live forever?"

"You're expecting *me* to answer that question?" asked Nathan. "It sounds like you're describing Heaven. I don't know why bad stuff happens, but I figure there's got to be a reason for it all."

"Do you believe in God, Nathan?"

"Yeah, and I know what you mean about not getting why bad things happen if He loves us and can do anything. It doesn't make any sense, so that's why I think the bad stuff has to happen. Maybe it's even that way to make us enjoy the good things. Think about it like this: when it's really cold out, doesn't it make you feel all warm and comfy to come inside and have a hot cup of tea or cocoa? Or when it's really hot, like it's been lately, doesn't it feel so good to jump in the lake and feel all the cool water?"

"Yeah, I get what you're saying."

"That's probably not really the answer," said Nathan, "but I think it might be part of it. I don't think we'll ever know, not in this lifetime anyway. I think when we die that we all go to Heaven, so even if things are bad for us, it's still okay because everything will be so good then. Maybe our whole lives are like bein' out in the cold and Heaven is like coming inside for hot cocoa."

I smiled. Nathan's life had been ten times as tough as mine, but his attitude and outlook was so much better that there wasn't any comparison.

"I like thinking that Mark and Taylor are in Heaven," I said. "It kinda takes away the sting of their deaths, you know? I wish they were still alive, but since I can't do anything about that, I like thinking that they're happy."

"Yeah," said Nathan. "And even if we're wrong and everyone just disappears when they die, at least it's an end to pain. If we just, like, wink out of existence, it's not like we'll be sorry or lonely or whatever. We just won't exist. I don't think that's how things are, but if it is like that then it's not so bad either. I just don't like to think about Mark and Tay and everyone not existing at all, though. I want them to still be alive somewhere."

"Yeah." I paused for several moments before I spoke again. "I guess we'll just have to wait and see about Shawn," I said. "I wish he'd let us help him."

"Give him some time, Ethan, like you told Brendan. What you're asking is hard for him. To get restraining orders and stuff he'd have to tell a lot of people he's gay and all that. It won't be easy for him."

"He needs to get out of there now."

"Yeah, but he may not be able to. He's got to get himself to the point where he can accept help."

"You know way more about this kind of thing than me, so I guess we'll just wait."

"I love you," said Nathan.

"I love you, too."

I kissed Nathan and then we lay there quietly until we both fell asleep.

Casper

Agnes had given me the night off so I could watch Brendan's game. I sat in the stands, watching as Brendan ran to the end zone and scored a goal. Everyone around me cheered, but I yelled the loudest of all. He looked up in the stands and waved to me. God, he was fantastic. No—he was magnificent! The sight of him in his football uniform sent a chill down my spine. Sometimes, I still couldn't believe he was my boyfriend.

If it wasn't for our money troubles, then I think life would've been about perfect. It was kinda like we'd gained back everything we'd lost when we had to flee from Kentucky. Yeah—we'd gained back everything, and then some. Brendan was the quarterback of the varsity squad once more. I'd made some great friends and had a wonderful family. True, I'd lost Dad and nothing would ever bring him back, but I had Grandma now and she loved me a lot more than Dad ever had. Well, he loved me, I guessed, but he sure hadn't shown it much in the last years of his life. He had given up his life to protect me in the end, however, so I guess he did love me. That made me feel pretty good.

I wrote Jason again, but I hadn't received a letter from him yet. I was kinda worried. His last letter hinted at something dangerous and I wondered what was up. I hoped he wouldn't get himself hurt. There was a time I wouldn't have cared, but he seemed different now. I had hopes that he'd eventually change, if he hadn't already.

After the game, I was walking toward Brendan and the team, when Tom yelled at him from the stands. "You suck Brewer!" Tom was drunk. I was afraid there might be trouble, but I think Tom was too out of it to start anything up. He threw a beer bottle at Brendan, but missed by a mile. The coach went up into the stands and grabbed Tom. As I walked away with Brendan, I heard the coach saying something about violating suspension. It sounded like Tom was in even bigger trouble than before.

I waited quietly in the locker room while Brendan showered and changed. Everyone knew Brendan was my boyfriend, but no one gave me any trouble about it. It made me feel real good. Here I was, sitting in the locker room, while all these guys who knew I was gay were changing and they didn't seem to care. I kept my eyes averted from anyone who was nude, but I kinda think they wouldn't have even cared if I looked at them. I'd sure never have dreamed things would be like this when I was living back in Kentucky. I figured I'd get beat senseless if other guys knew about me and I thought jocks would've been the worst. I hoped that the world was changing. Maybe someday, sexual orientation wouldn't matter at all. I saw no reason why it should.

I noticed no one was leaving the locker room. Everyone was hanging around. Brendan came out of the showers, dried off, and dressed. We were just getting ready to leave when the coach came out of his office and said, "You can't go yet."

There was a sense of expectancy in the room. Brendan looked around confused.

"The guys have an announcement," said the coach.

One of the players, his name was Perry, I think, awkwardly approached Brendan.

"We've all discussed and voted," he said, "and we've decide that you should be team captain."

Brendan grinned and all the guys cheered. I was so happy I just about cried. We really had gained back everything we'd lost.

I knew what being team captain meant to Brendan. He was already the quarterback, so he pretty much ran things on the field, but being made captain meant all the guys accepted him. They didn't care if he was gay or not. They accepted him as he was and that was the most important thing of all.

Brendan grabbed me in a bear hug that about squeezed the life out of me and then kissed me on the lips. The guys just kept congratulating him and slapping him on the back, even while he was kissing me. It just might've been the best day ever.

Brendan

My back was getting sore. So many guys from the team had slapped it that I nearly winced when one approached. Five of them came up to me before I even made it through the doors of the school. I was still soaring over being made team captain. I knew some people would think I was just plain silly if they knew how elated I was over it, but it was a big deal to me. The guys had chosen me—guys who knew I was gay—guys who ran around naked in front me every day and didn't think anything of it. It was the acceptance, even more than the honor that meant so much to me. I remembered only too well how I'd actually contemplated suicide when I thought I was about to be outed back in Kentucky. My best friend Brad had stopped me. If he hadn't, I would've thrown my life away out of fear. In my case, it was a fear of something that didn't even exist. I had it easy coming out; I knew a lot of boys weren't so lucky and that made the acceptance of my teammates all the more important.

I'd no more than pulled my books out of my locker for first period when Ethan came charging toward me.

"Come on," he said, jerking me by the arm so hard he nearly pulled me over. There was such a great sense of urgency about him that I followed him at a run toward the rear entrance of the school.

"What's this all about?" I asked.

"We've got to get you out of here—*now.*"

"But, why?"

"Tom's coming in the front of the building any minute, and he's got a gun."

"What?" I asked, incredulously.

"Shawn just told me. He found me just before I came after you."

"We've got to tell someone!"

"Shawn's already telling the office. They've probably already called the cops by now."

"Casper!" I said, jerking to a halt. "We've got to get Casper!"

"No, we don't. Tom isn't coming after Casper. He's not coming to shoot up the school. He's coming for *you*."

I swallowed hard and let Ethan pull me out the back doors. We ran to the truck, jumped in, and Ethan tore out of the parking lot. Only then did I speak once more.

"He's coming for me?" I asked.

"Yeah, Shawn told me. He's pissed about you beating him out for quarterback—beyond pissed. He got wind of you being made team captain, too. I think that's what pushed him over the edge. Shawn found out this morning. He saw Tom in his room cleaning the gun. He asked Tom what he was doing and he told him. He said he was going to…to shoot you in the stomach and make you beg to die."

I was scared. Tom was more of a psycho than I thought.

"Shawn went out and let the air out of Tom's tires to slow him up, and then ran like hell for the school. He was gasping when he told me what was going down. I couldn't even understand him at first."

"Shit!"

"Shawn told me that Tom said, '*I'm gonna kill the faggot. Let's see him play football after he's dead*.'"

"Ethan, what if he goes for Casper? We have to go back."

"No. I was with Nathan when Shawn told me. Nathan went for Casper, just in case. He's gonna run him up into the paths by the soccer fields."

I noticed that Ethan was driving just out of town, circling around to the road that cut near the woods behind the school. He pulled the truck over moments later and we ran into the forest. We made our way through the trees, trying to avoid the limbs slapping us in the face. Ethan already had a welt on his cheek from a sassafras that had smacked him as he ran through its branches. We ran on until a trail crossed our path. We stopped. Ethan turned his head this way and that, listening. We heard heavy footsteps coming from the direction of the school. Ethan and I ran to meet them.

In a few moments more, we saw Casper and Nathan running toward us. I smiled—Casper was safe. We ran right into each other's arms like they do in the movies and I hugged and kissed him. Ethan was hugging and kissing Nathan, too. We turned and walked back down the trail, until we reached the point where we'd cut through the woods. We walked back through the trees, more carefully this time, and all piled into the truck.

Ethan drove us to the police station, since he wasn't sure it was safe to return to school. We weren't that sure of Tom's timing. There was a flurry of activity when we arrived. We found out soon enough that Tom had been apprehended. The police got to the school just as Tom was going up the steps. They drew on him and he was smart enough to throw down his gun.

I was relieved no one was hurt. Tom was apparently coming just for me, but who knows what he might've done when someone tried to stop him. Tom was obviously unstable. A guy like that with a gun was capable of just about anything. I sat there in the station with my head in my hands. I was shaking on the inside. When were people gonna stop trying to kill me? First Jason, now Tom—that was two more attempts than most guys my age had to survive. Sometimes, I just wished my life would be dull and boring.

Because I was the target, the police wanted to talk to me. I knew I was probably looking at hours of questions. Casper said he'd stay at the station with me. Ethan and Nathan offered to stay as well, but there was no need. They left for home in the truck. School was cancelled and everyone sent home because of what had happened, or almost happened. Just before I went in a back room to start answering questions, Casper gave me a hug. I could feel his love flowing through me and I knew everything was going to be okay.

Dane

I wasn't in nearly as much trouble as I'd imagined. Mom and Dad told me on the ride home that they weren't going to ground me or anything like that. I think my parents had been so worried that they'd never see me again and were so relieved that I was okay, that they were willing to forgive me. Mom was crying most of the way home and kept telling me how she and Dad had been so distraught they couldn't eat or sleep. When I realized the hell I'd put them through, I felt worse than I ever had in my entire life. The new Dane I'd tried to become was a monster in more ways than one.

As we pulled up our drive, I looked out the window. There it was, the only home I'd ever known. It was the same white house with blue shutters, but it looked better somehow. My tire swing was hanging from the tall maple in the front yard and I could just make out the edge of my old tree house in the limbs of a huge oak out back.

I climbed out of the car and glanced across the overgrown field to the west. I could see the home of our closest neighbors, the Masons, looking almost like a model in the distance. In all other directions, only trees were visible. I'd once thought I lived in the most boring place in the universe, but now it looked like paradise.

I had a lot of explaining to do, and I do mean *a lot*. It was late when we got home, so Mom and Dad put me to bed and said we'd talk in the morning. I dreaded it. I was relieved and so glad to be home that I slept like a baby, despite my apprehension. I didn't remember my bed feeling so comfy before.

In the morning, Mom made breakfast, Dad stayed home from work, and we all sat around the kitchen table. My stomach was quivering with thoughts of what I had to tell Mom and Dad, but I couldn't help but be happy. It felt good to be back home.

So much had happened to me and there was so much of it I *didn't* want to share with my parents. I wasn't going to tell them everything, that was for sure. I didn't want them to know what a little deviant their son had become. That was behind me, anyway. I'd learned a few things. I was no angel to be sure, but I also wasn't going to repeat the mistakes I'd so recently made.

The hardest thing to tell them was the reason behind it all—I was gay. It was a long time before I could tell them. I sat there while silent tears flowed down my cheeks. The silence was replaced by sobs and then Mom held me while Dad said I could tell them anything and they'd still love me. I sure hoped that was true, but I wasn't sure. I was afraid they'd hate me when they found out what I was. I was afraid they'd make me leave for good. I knew what it was like trying to make it on my own, and I didn't want to do that ever again. Well, at least not until I was grown. I'd thought I was all grown up when I ran away, but I knew I'd been wrong.

After the longest time, the words came out: "I'm gay, Mom." There was more to say, but I lost it and bawled.

"Dane," said Mom, stroking my hair, "Honey, it's okay. It's all right. We love you."

My sobs quieted and I looked at my dad out of the corner of my eye, fearing his reaction. Mom was holding me, but I was afraid Dad might hit me or something when he found out I was a queer. He stood up and walked toward me. I involuntarily flinched, but he held out his arms to me. I ran to him and he hugged me. I cried into his chest. "It's okay, Dane, it's all okay." Mom joined us in our hug. I cried some more, with relief.

"I thought you wouldn't love me anymore," I said, between sobs.

"We'll always love you, Dane."

"It's okay that I'm gay?"

"It's okay, Dane," said Dad. "It doesn't make any difference in the way we feel about you."

After that, the rest was easier. We sat back down at the table after a bit and I talked with Mom and Dad about a lot of stuff I never thought I'd be discussing with them. I didn't tell them about what I'd done to Casper, or what I'd tried with Ethan and Shawn. I was too ashamed of myself. We did talk about what Boothe had done to me. Mom and Dad already knew what had happened because they'd talked to the police in Verona. I would have to go back to answer more questions pretty soon, but this time, my parents would be with me. It was *real* hard talking about what Boothe had done to me. I knew it wasn't my fault, but I still felt ashamed, humiliated, and dirty. Talking helped, though, and Mom and Dad helped me deal with it. They said I could see a psychiatrist if I wanted.

Mom and Dad insisted that I go to the hospital later that day to be checked out. The doctors in Verona had said there was no permanent damage, but my parents wanted to make sure. The examination was humiliating, even though it was just me and this real nice doctor. I didn't like getting naked in front of him and having him examine me *there*. He kept talking to me about stuff, though. He told me about his dogs and was kinda funny, so it wasn't as bad as it could've been. I was still relieved when it was over and I was allowed to dress. I was sure glad I hadn't violated Casper or Shawn like Boothe had me. I don't know if I could've lived with knowing I'd done something like that. The examination itself was an ordeal. I don't think anyone who hasn't been raped realizes just how bad it is. What Boothe did to me was horrible, but the examinations and all the questions afterward were almost as bad. Having my parents know what'd happened wasn't fun either. They were understanding and kind, but I still felt kinda ashamed. I knew what happened was Boothe's fault and not mine, but it was still hard to shake the shame and guilt.

***

I walked down the old blacktop, my sneakers sticking to the hot tar. It felt good to be home. I wondered how Ethan, Brendan, Shawn and all the others were doing. I wondered where Austin had ended up and if he was still prowling the streets. It all seemed like a dream now, but if only a dream it had still taught me something. I hadn't become the new Dane I'd planned, but I was glad of that. I did intend to become a new Dane, but I'd base the new me on what Ethan had told me.

I walked on toward where Billy Holmes lived. I'd mooned over him for more than a year. He had the sweetest smile, the kindest face, and the coolest hair, not to mention a nice little butt. The old Dane wouldn't have had the courage to approach him. The Verona Dane would've thought only about what was in his pants. But, the new Dane—the real Dane—was going to take Ethan's advice: I'd seek his friendship and see what happened. Maybe I'd end up with a boyfriend or maybe I'd just end up with a good friend. Either way, there was nothing to lose and everything to gain.

I walked across Billy's yard and there he was shooting hoops in the drive. He was more beautiful than I remembered. When he looked up and saw me, he smiled.

"You wanna play?" he asked.

"Yeah," I said, "I sure would." I knew I'd just made a new beginning.

Ethan

It was Saturday morning. All of us were sitting around the kitchen table having breakfast. There was a knock at the front door. I left my bacon, eggs, and toast and walked through the living room to answer. I was shocked to see Mrs. Pearson standing there. I opened it quickly.

"Come in. Come in," I said.

"I can only stay a minute," she said.

"How did you get here?" I asked. I knew Mrs. Pearson didn't drive and we usually did all her running around for her.

"I walked," she said, then laughed. "Mrs. Took, my neighbor, was kind enough to bring me by."

"You could've called and we would have come to get you," I said.

"I know, I know, but this is meant to be a surprise."

I ushered Mrs. Pearson into the kitchen where everyone was delighted to see her. Uncle Jack pulled up a chair for her. Ardelene offered her breakfast, but she said she'd already eaten. I gazed at Mrs. Pearson. She seemed livelier than I'd seen her in a long time.

"I've brought something for you," she said, digging into her oversized wicker purse. "I know you've been having troubles with money."

I smiled, but I didn't know where this was going. Mrs. Pearson pulled out a check and handed it to Uncle Jack. There was a flicker of surprise in his eyes for a moment and then he looked back at Mrs. Pearson.

"We can't take this," he said. "I appreciate the…"

"Nonsense! You *are* taking it Jack Selby and that's that. I knew your mother and if she were here, she'd knock some sense into your head. Besides, it's not gentlemanly to refuse an old lady."

I nearly laughed at the sight of Uncle Jack being dressed down. For a moment, he looked like a guilty little boy. I wondered what he'd been like when he was young.

"Whoa!" said Nathan, when he got a look at the check.

"But how?" asked Jack. "Why?"

Mrs. Pearson laughed.

"My sister in California passed away a few weeks ago. I've come into an inheritance."

"I'm sorry about your sister," said Ardelene.

"Don't be, it was her time. She was bad off." A wave of sadness came over Mrs. Pearson's features, but quickly passed and she smiled again. "Sadie left me everything she had. The house just recently sold so I've come into money. That's for you," she said, indicating the check.

"This is far too much!" said Jack. "You can't give us this."

"Haven't we already been through this?" said Mrs. Pearson. She smiled. "For years, I've barely been able to pay the bills. Sometimes I couldn't and you were always there to help me out. When I was out of food, you bought me groceries. When I couldn't pay the gas bill, you did. You shoveled my walk for me in the winter and took me to the store anytime I needed to go. You took me to the library or anywhere I wanted. These boys have been taking care of me, too. I'm sure part of your money problems come from being too generous to people in need like me. You've kept helping me, even though you didn't have the time. You've bought me groceries, even though you didn't have money to spare. I appreciate it. Now, I'm finally able to pay back some of your kindness."

"But you need this," said Jack, waving the check.

"No, I don't. Don't worry about me. I've kept as much as I've given you. I split it, fifty/fifty. I have enough in the bank now to last me the rest of my life. Now, I need to be going. Mrs. Took is waiting."

"Thank you," said Jack, still dumbfounded.

"No, thank you." Mrs. Pearson smiled and made her way slowly to the door, and I showed her out.

We all gathered around Jack after she'd gone. We just stared at the check— it was for $40,000.

I broke the silence by laughing. I felt as if a tremendous weight had been lifted from all our shoulders. Everyone began to laugh and talk at once. It was a few minutes before we settled down again.

"With this, we can pay off everything," said Jack. "I can even pay you back, Brendan, and there will still be a lot left over to go into the bank."

I grinned. I felt better than I had in a long, long time.

Casper

After Mrs. Pearson gave us all that money, I didn't have to work at *Ofarim's* anymore. I'd grown to like it, however, and I especially liked Agnes, so I stayed on—only I worked fewer hours. Nathan kept his job at *The Paramount* until Mr. Barr could find a replacement. He liked working there, but his true love was the farm. It was mine, too, but I was glad I could keep working at *Ofarim's*, at least for the present. I'd even be able to keep all the money I made, since we now had plenty. I felt rich.

Two weeks after Mrs. Pearson had come with her check, Casey came into *Ofarim's* with Shawn and a really pretty girl. Casey and Shawn were still "dating" and they both looked pretty happy. As I was taking their order, Agnes came out and hugged the pretty girl.

"Hi, Sandy."

"Hi, Agnes."

Sandy kissed Agnes on the cheek. I looked at Casey and she smiled. I knew then that she had a girlfriend. I smiled back. I was so happy for her.

Agnes went back behind the counter to work on their order and I stayed and talked, after I'd got their drinks. Casey and Sandy sat close together on one side of the booth. Casey seemed happier than I'd ever seen her.

The place was empty, so Shawn could talk. I thanked him for what he'd done for Brendan. Who knows what would've happened if he hadn't slowed Tom down and warned Ethan that Brendan's life was in danger. Shawn just might've saved a whole lot of lives by being so brave. Who knew? He sure saved Brendan and for that I'd be forever grateful.

"How are things at home now?" I asked him.

"A lot better. Tom's locked up in the county jail. They're going to try him as an adult since he brought a deadly weapon onto school grounds with the intent to kill. The lawyer Dad got him says he doesn't have much of a case, especially with me as a witness against him."

"That sounds dangerous," I said.

"Yeah, well, I'm gonna be a witness for the prosecution. Tom went way too far this time."

"Just remember," I said, "if you need us to help you disappear, we're here for you."

"I appreciate that, but I don't think I'll have to take you up on it unless maybe Tom gets off. The lawyer says he'll likely get a minimum of four years and I'll be long gone before he gets out."

"How about your dad? Isn't he upset that you're gonna testify against Tom?"

"No. Tom is costing him a fortune. He's beyond pissed at him. Tom's lucky he's locked up—otherwise Dad would beat the crap outta him. Dad's kinda calmed down with all the cops that've been around. I'm still not taking any chances, but things are better than they were."

I was sure glad to hear that. Maybe Shawn would be okay after all.

***

The moon cast its blue light over the garden and a whippoorwill called to me from the distance. I filled the watering can and carried it to the nearest tomato plant. The poor things wilted in the sun if they weren't watered regularly and it was best to water them at night. Grandma took good care of the garden, but I'd missed working in it. It helped set my mind at ease.

I wiped the sweat from my brow. It was going on past ten o'clock at night, but it was still plenty hot. I kinda felt like we were all in a big oven, being slowly baked alive. It seemed like the rain would never come. Ethan said if it didn't very, very soon, then that would be it for the crops this year. A lot of 'em were already dead. We couldn't water the corn, wheat, and soybean fields the way I could the vegetables and flowers. If the fields didn't get a drink soon, it would all be over. Thank God Mrs. Pearson gave us that money. If she hadn't, and the crops failed, we would've probably lost the farm.

I waved to Brendan as he drove the tractor into the barn. My heart swelled with happiness just looking at him. Brendan, Jack, and Ethan had an easier time of it now, with Nathan working on the farm full-time and me putting in more hours. I was glad, especially since that gave Brendan more energy for other things—things we did in bed. Mmmmm. I was definitely gonna attack him when he came to bed tonight. We'd been going at it pretty steadily, but we had tons of lost time to make up. I got hotter just thinking about it.

I watered the garden a bit more, then put up my watering can and joined Grandma and Nathan in the kitchen where they were frying chicken and fixing mashed potatoes. I pitched in by setting out the plates and silverware and getting out the butter and salt & pepper for a late supper.

When Grandma pulled freshly baked yeast rolls out of the oven the smell was heavenly. My stomach rumbled with hunger. There was no food as good as that prepared on the Selby Farm.

Brendan came in and then Ethan, soon followed by Jack. They washed up and we all sat down to supper. Dave was a bit late because he was in the barn seeing to his chickens. I had a feeling that boy would end up owning a chicken farm someday.

I looked around the table as we ate and talked and laughed. It was just supper, but it felt like Thanksgiving or something. All of us were sitting around the table, enjoying each other's company. Brendan stopped devouring chicken and corn long enough to give me a kiss on the cheek and I grinned. Grandma smiled at us. It sure felt good to be loved. Ethan and Nathan smiled at each other and Dave talked and talked, not caring whether or not anyone was listening. Even Jack seemed to be enjoying himself. I was content. This was my family and we were all together. I hoped we'd be together forever.

Just as we started in on the apple pie I heard a rumble. I knew Nathan heard it too because he looked confused, as if something were quite out of place and he didn't understand it. In a few seconds more there came another rumble, then the window panes rattled and there was a flash of light from outside. Brendan got up and looked out the window.

"Rain," he said. "It's raining!"

The wind blew raindrops up against the glass, at first only a few, but then more and more. We all got up from the table and ran out the back door as if there was something to see outside that we'd never seen before. For the first time in weeks, I felt raindrops on my face. I licked them from my lips as the rainfall became a downpour. The heavens just opened up and rain came pouring down so hard and fast I couldn't see trees that stood only a few feet away. Ethan was whooping and hollering, holding hands with Nathan and pulling him around in a circle. Brendan grabbed me and did the same while Dave stomped newly formed puddles, sending water flying in all directions. Grandma and Jack watched from the porch. We were all drenched, but no one cared; the rain had come at last.

Brendan pulled me to him and we kissed—deeply and passionately. I melted in his arms. I was completely happy and content. At that moment, I felt as if I knew all the secrets of the universe. I knew what it felt like to be truly happy.

"I love you," said Brendan.

"I love you, too," I said.

I rested my head on Brendan's chest, listening to his heartbeat. I didn't know what the future had in store for us, but I knew that no matter what, we'd be together and I'd always love him with all my heart.

Brendan

Casper never did get another letter from his brother. I was relieved. The mere thought of Jason made me nervous and not without reason. Casper told me he'd written Jason a couple more times, but then he stopped because he never received an answer. Casper seemed a little sad about that.

We found out why there were no more letters from Jason soon enough. It was Jack who spotted the article in the paper. When I came in from the fields for supper, he handed me The South Bend *Standard* and there it was right on the third page:

CLOVERDALE CENTER DESTROYED BY FIRE
—ARSON SUSPECTED

I eagerly read the article. The *Cloverdale Center* had burned to the ground. It was completely destroyed. There was only one death, an orderly named Brian. I knew that name all too well. Even Jason had mentioned him. I didn't like wishing death on anyone, but Brian deserved it if anyone did. Besides, I didn't have to wish it on him. He was already dead.

The article said most of the patients had not only escaped from the fire, but had since disappeared completely. That right there should've told anyone with any sense what a horrible place it'd been; when they got out, the patients just kept running. Jason was listed with the names of those who were missing. It sent a chill up my spine. What if he came for Casper?

I read on. The patients that could be rounded up were taken to other hospitals, real hospitals and they were talking. The *Cloverdale Center* patients were examined and questions were raised. I smiled when I read that charges were forthcoming against the owners and the doctors who ran the place—malpractice, abuse, sexual misconduct, and more. The day I'd prayed for had arrived at last. The damned place had finally burned down and it looked like it would never rise again.

Casper came home soon and I showed him the paper. He was as shocked as I. "We'd better be on guard," I said. "Jason knows where you are."

"He's not coming," said Casper, confidently. "I believe what he wrote me. He changed, Brendan, I really think he did."

I wasn't so sure, but Casper's confidence helped put me at ease.

"You remember what Jason wrote me, in his final letter?" asked Casper. "He said it would probably be his last later, because he wouldn't be around much longer. He also said there was something he was going to do, but he didn't dare talk about it. Brendan, I think my brother burned down the *Cloverdale Center*."

I stood there shocked. All the pieces did fit. There was no proof, of course, but what Jason had written did fit in nicely with the fate of the *Cloverdale Center* and Jason hated it enough to burn it down. He was just the kind that would do it, too. Could it be? Had he really done it? I doubted we would ever know, but if he was responsible, I was silently thankful.

"I'm gonna burn all his letters, just in case," said Casper. "If he did do it, then it's the one thing he doesn't deserve to be punished for."

I couldn't have agreed more.

***

The next day was a Saturday. We were all getting ready to leave for a dedication ceremony when Casper came running back from the mailbox with a letter. There was no return address. Casper ripped it open.

"It's from Jason," he said.

Casper read the letter out loud. It was a short one.

Dear Casper,

In case you're wondering, yes—I did it. I burned it down. It's the one illegal thing I've done I don't regret. I'm on the run and I'm gonna keep on running. Ike's with me and he says he can help me start over with a new identity, even a new social security number and all. He's got connections that I didn't know about. I don't think he even knew it when he was all drugged up in that place. Anyway, I don't expect you'll ever see me again. The cops'll be thinking I'm coming your way, so I can't come near. I kinda wish I could, just so I could give you a hug. Have Grandma give you one for me. Don't worry about me. I'm gonna be just fine. I love you, little brother, please believe me. I'm sorry for what I did and I learned my lesson. I'm gonna start a new life now. I'm thinkin' that there are other places out there like the *Cloverdale Center* and somebody needs to take 'em out— somebody who isn't afraid to break a few laws. I guess I haven't changed completely, have I? Goodbye, little brother. I hope you have a long life filled with happiness.

Love,
Jason

No one spoke—I think the letter said it all. Finally, Jack broke the silence. "We'd better get going if we don't want to be late."

Jack and Ardelene climbed in the front of the truck with Dave, and the rest of us sat in the bed. Jack drove us to the high school where we all got out and followed Ethan to the soccer fields. There were several people there, mostly guys our age, but older people and girls, too. They were gathered around a huge shape sitting on the grass, covered with a big piece of cloth.

The whole soccer team was there in their blue and white V.H.S. soccer uniforms, minus Devon and his buddies of course. They'd shown up as a sign of respect for their old team-mates. Tears were running down Brandon's face and Jon's eyes were watery.

Ethan nervously stepped forward. "I want to thank everyone for coming and I want to thank the school for letting us place this memorial here. I'm not much good at speaking, so I'll let the memorial speak for itself."

Ethan reached down, picked up a corner of the cloth, and pulled it off the huge boulder. There, gleaming in the sunlight was a large, bronze plaque that read:

THIS FIELD IS DEDICATED TO THE MEMORY OF MARK BAILEY AND TAYLOR POTTER. THEY DIED HERE ALL TOO EARLY BECAUSE OF HATRED AND INTOLERANCE. MAY THE FUTURE LEARN FROM WHAT HAPPENED AND NOT LET IT HAPPEN AGAIN.

There were a lot of tears from those who knew those boys. Brandon and Jon were crying openly after reading the inscription. I found myself wishing that I'd been lucky enough to know Mark and Taylor, too. We'd never met, but we were brothers nonetheless. My hopes were those of the memorial itself—that the mistakes of the past would not be repeated. Life was far too short to allow prejudice and hatred to exist.

Ethan was crying. He hugged Nathan close and let his tears flow. No one said anything about one boy hugging another. Everyone knew that Ethan and Nathan were boyfriends, but not one person uttered an unkind word or gave them an unkind glance. Perhaps it was because we were surrounded by those who knew and missed Mark and Taylor, or perhaps it was because things were beginning to change. Maybe everyone was beginning to realize that love was love and that's all that matters.

I hugged Casper and felt his comforting embrace. We'd both been through a lot, but it was worth it all if we could live our lives with each other. I didn't know what the future held for us, but I knew that I'd be happy as long as Casper was by my side.

The End

About the Author

Mark A. Roeder is the creator of the *Gay Youth Chronicles*, a continuing series followed not only by gay youth, but by readers of all ages—gay, bi, and straight. Since the age of fifteen, Roeder has been turning out articles, columns, and novels and for the last several years has dedicated his life to writing heart-warming stories about gay youth. He currently resides in southern Indiana. Information on his current and upcoming books can be found at markroeder.com.

Other Books by Mark A. Roeder

Listed in Suggested Reading Order

Gay Youth Chronicles:

Ancient Prejudice Break to New Mutiny

Mark is a boy who wants what we all want: to love and be loved. His dreams are realized when he meets Taylor, the boy of his dreams. The boys struggle to keep their love hidden from a world that cannot understand, but ultimately, no secret is safe in a small Mid-western town.

Ancient Prejudice is a story of love, friendship, understanding, and an age-old prejudice that still has the power to kill. It is a story for young and old, gay and straight. It reminds us all that everyone should be treated with dignity and respect and that there is nothing greater than the power of love.

The Soccer Field Is Empty

The Soccer Field Is Empty is a revised and much expanded edition of *Ancient Prejudice*. It is more than 50% longer and views events from the point of view of Taylor, as well as Mark. There is so much new in the revised edition that it is being published as a separate novel. *Soccer Field* delves more deeply into the events of Mark and Taylor's lives and reveals previously hidden aspects of Taylor's personality.

Authors note: I suggest readers new to my books start with *Soccer Field* instead of *Ancient Prejudice* as it gives a more complete picture of the lives of Mark and Taylor. For those who wish to read the original version, *Ancient Prejudice* will remain available for at least the time being.

Someone Is Watching

It's hard hiding a secret. It's even harder keeping that secret when someone else knows.

Someone Is Watching is the story of Ethan, a young high school wrestler who must come to terms with being gay. He struggles first with himself, then with an unknown classmate that hounds his every step. While struggling to discover the identity of his tormentor, Ethan must discover his own identity and learn to live his life as his true self. He must choose whether to give up what he wants the most, or face his greatest fear of all.

A Better Place

High school football, a hospital of horrors, a long journey, and an unlikely love await Brendan and Casper as they search for a better place...

Casper is the poorest boy in school. Brendan is the captain of the football team. Casper has nothing. Brendan has it all: looks, money, popularity, but he lacks the deepest desire of his heart. The boys come from different worlds, but have one thing in common that no one would guess.

Casper goes through life as the "invisible boy"; invisible to the boys that pick on him in school, invisible to his abusive father, and invisible most of all to his older brother, who makes his life a living hell. He can't believe his good luck when Brendan, the most popular boy in school, takes an interest in him and becomes his friend. That friendship soon travels in a direction that Casper would never have guessed.

A Better Place is the story of an unlikely pair, who struggle through friendship and betrayal, hardships and heartbreaks, to find the desire of their hearts, to find a better place.

Someone Is Killing The Gay Boys of Verona

Someone is killing the gay boys of Verona, Indiana, and only one gay youth stands in the way. He finds himself pitted against powerful foes, but finds allies in places he did not expect.

A brutal murder. Gay ghosts. A Haunted Victorian-Mansion. A cult of hate. A hundred year old ax murder. All this, and more, await sixteen-year-old Sean as he delves into the supernatural and races to discover the murderer before he strikes again.

Someone is Killing the Gay Boys of Verona is a supernatural murder mystery that goes where no gay novel has set foot before. It is a tale of love, hate, friend-ship, and revenge.

Keeper of Secrets

Sixteen-year-old Avery is in trouble, yet again, but this time he's in over his head. On the run, Avery is faced with hardships and fear. He must become what he's always hated, just to survive. He discovers new reasons to hate, until fate brings him to Graymoor Mansion and he discovers a disturbing connec-tion to the past. Through the eyes of a boy, murdered more than a century before, Avery discovers that all is not as he thought. Avery is soon forced to face the greatest challenge of all; looking into his own heart.

Sean is head over heels in love with his new boyfriend, Nick. There is trouble in paradise, however. Could a boy so beautiful really love plain, ordinary Sean? Sean cannot believe it and desperately tries to transform himself into the ideal young hunk, only to learn that it's what's inside that matters.

Keeper of Secrets is the story of two boys, one a gay youth, the other an adoles-cent gay basher. Fate and the pages of a hundred year old journal bring them together and their lives are forever changed.

Do You Know That I Love You

The lead singer of the most popular boy band in the world has a secret. A tabloid willing to tell all turns his world upside down.

In *Do You Know That I Love You*, Ralph, a young gay teen living on a farm in Indiana, has an aching crush on a rock star and wants nothing more than to see his idol in concert. Meanwhile, Jordan, the rock star, is lonely and sometimes confused with his success, because all he wants is someone to love him and feels he will never find the love he craves. *Do You Know* is the story of two teenage boys, their lives, desires, loves, and a shared destiny that allows them both to find peace.

This Time Around

What happens when a TV evangelist struggles to crush gay rights? Who better to halt his evil plans than the most famous rock star in the world?

This Time Around follows Jordan and Ralph as they become involved in a struggle with Reverend Wellerson, a TV evangelist, over the fate of gay youth centers. Wellerson is willing to stop at nothing to crush gay rights and who better to halt his evil plans than the most famous rock star in the entire world? While battling Wellerson, Jordan seeks to come to terms with his own past and learn more about the father he never knew. The excitement builds when an assassin is hired and death becomes a real possibility for Jordan and those around him. Jordan is forced to face his own fears and doubts and the battle within becomes more dangerous than the battle without. Will Jordan be able to turn from the path of destruction, or is he doomed to follow in the footsteps of his father? This time around, things will be different.

The Summer of My Discontent

The Summer of My Discontent is a tapestry of tales delving into life as a gay teen in a small Midwestern town.

Dane is a sixteen-year-old runaway determined to start a new life of daring, love, and sex—no matter the cost to himself, or others. His actions bring him to the brink of disaster and only those he sought to prey upon can save him. Among Dane's new found "friends" are a young male prostitute and the local grave robber who becomes his despised employer.

The boys of *A Better Place* are back—Ethan, Nathan, Brendan, and Casper are once again dealing with trouble in Verona, Indiana. Drought and circumstance threaten their existence and they struggle together to save themselves from blackmail, financial collapse, and temptation.

Brendan must cope with anonymity after being one of the most popular boys in school. Casper must face his own past—the loss of his father and the fate of his abusive brother, who is locked away in the very hospital of horrors from which Brendan escaped. Letters from his brother force Casper to question his feelings—is Jason truly a monster or can he change?

Dark, foreboding, and sexy—*The Summer of My Discontent* is the tale of gay teens seeking to find themselves, each other, and a better place.

0-595-29806-0

Printed in the United States
71252LV00005B/49